OUT OF RANGE

In the Shadow Book 2, a Christian romantic suspense

JL CROSSWHITE

Other books by JL Crosswhite

Hometown Heroes series

Promise Me, prequel novella

Protective Custody, book 1

Flash Point, book 2

Special Assignment, book 3

In the Shadow series

Off the Map, book 1

Out of Range, book 2

Over Her Head, book 3 (Summer 2021)

The Route Home series, writing as Jennifer Crosswhite

Be Mine, prequel novella

Coming Home, book 1

The Road Home, book 2

Finally Home, book 3

Contemporary romance, writing as Jennifer Crosswhite

The Inn at Cherry Blossom Lane

Eat the Elephant: How to Write (and Finish!) Your Book One Bite at a Time, writing as Jen Crosswhite

Devotional, writing as Jennifer Crosswhite

Worthy to Write: Blank pages tying your stomach in knots? 30 prayers to tackle that fear!

Published by Tandem Services Press

Post Office Box 220

Yucaipa, California

www.TandemServicesInk.com

Ebook ISBN 978-1-7341590-9-7

Print ISBN 978-1-954986-00-8

Library of Congress Control Number: 2021906860

This book is a work of fiction. Names, characters, places, and incidents are either products of the author's imagination or used fictitiously. Any similarity to actual people, organizations, and/ or events is purely coincidental.

Cover design credit: Alexander von Ness of Nessgraphica

To my writing students.
Your diligence and fresh enthusiasm inspires me.

I can do all this through him who gives me strength.

Philippians 4:13

Chapter One

It was old school, but Kim Taylor searched for a flash of genius at the end of a precisely sharpened drawing pencil. She tapped it on the paper in front of her in their open workspace at House of Elan. She needed inspiration. Plus, her hands ached from being at the computer so much. Design Review was coming up, and it was her chance to get her work in front of the big names at the studio. Junior designers presented a portfolio of their top styles to the head designers who would then choose the winner to work with them for the next year. It would be a huge jump for her career.

She had sewn up several of her designs into actual outfits, one of which she was wearing. A few others had become computer designs, and she was creating her portfolio to present. But which were the best ones to choose? She'd gone over the trend reports until her eyes were bleary. Her trip through the Southwest had given her a ton of ideas. But it had also left her with nightmares, thanks to being grabbed by Willie Dumas. Thankfully, he couldn't ever hurt her again.

Her mentor, Lynnae MacKenzie, owned a boutique in Newport where Kim had worked in high school and college. She learned much of what she knew about the business from Lynnae, who'd always encouraged her to pursue design. She would show-case Kim's clothing and often sent clients to her for custom work, especially if they were hard to fit. Kim was bringing her designs to her tonight for her summer wear fashion show next month.

"Searching for brilliance?"

Henry's voice behind her made her jump then flip over her sketchbook. A quick glance at her computer showed that it was on screensaver.

Henry Smythe was her biggest competition. With his spiky black hair and retro New Wave fashion sense, his designs had a lot of flair, but were more appropriate for clubbing than women looking for something to wear to work or out with friends. Still, he'd managed to get some face time with the senior designers. He had connections in the industry. And he never failed to let her know it.

She gave him a sweet smile. "Just letting my creativity wander, now that I've got my presentation all locked up." It wasn't a complete lie. She'd picked her portfolio items; she just hadn't decided if they were final. She hoped to get Lynnae's input tonight when they met.

His gaze scanned her head to toe. It wasn't a come on; he was evaluating her outfit. He swirled his finger in front of her. "Is that one of yours?"

He knew it was. This outfit, and ones she was bringing to Lynnae, she'd sewn up at home. It wasn't like she didn't trust leaving them at work. But she wanted to try them on herself. She specialized in clothes for every woman, but with those unique touches that made the outfit look one-of-a-kind.

And she *didn't* trust leaving them at work. Design Review was too important. Not that she thought anything would happen. She didn't. But better to be safe than sorry. Besides, seeing her clothes on the dress form at home or even wearing them had often given her an idea for a change or alteration.

She didn't bother to answer him. "Did you need something?"

"Just wondering how your portfolio was coming along. Only two weeks left, so if you need to get a design made up, you'd better get it to the seamstresses today."

"Got it covered. Thanks."

He gave her another appraising look then turned on his heel.

She'd learned early on not to give Henry any fuel for his rumors. Or even his innuendo. She turned back to her drawing. She seriously doubted he came by to give her a friendly reminder. More like he wanted to see what she was working on. This business could be cutthroat, but she'd been fortunate enough to work with really great people. Henry was the exception rather than the rule.

Her phone buzzed, and she snatched it up.

But it was Matthew.

I'm in town. Want to catch dinner?

She dropped the phone on her desk and rubbed her hands over her face. Matthew. She hadn't seen him in nearly two months. They'd gotten close on the Great American Road Trip—he'd even kissed her, twice—but after she'd been grabbed by Willie Dumas, she'd been shaken. And she realized that Matthew couldn't handle her breadth of emotions. He was a fun guy to hang out with, but expecting anything more from him was a recipe for heartache. And she had too much on her plate as it was.

But she knew this day was coming. They'd texted, and he'd told her he got the job with DataCorp and was relocating to Orange County, but she'd pushed it out of her mind, not wanting to think about what it'd be like to be in the same geographical region, with the same friends, as he was. But it looked like that was coming to an end. She did have a reprieve for tonight: an appointment with Lynnae.

But she couldn't put off meeting him forever. What was she going to do about him?

She texted his sister Allie. And after a moment's thought, added in Jessica.

<hr>

Matthew Ellis tried to keep his attention on what the HR person was saying. He hated all these forms and video training on how not to be an offensive coworker as well as learning about company values. His flight this morning had been early, and he was struggling. Until DataCorp finalized the lease on their own building, they were meeting in the conference rooms at the hotel where they were all staying. His sister Allie was the relocation specialist coordinating all the details for the company.

He had an appointment with the Chief Operating Officer, Edward Jacobsen, and the Chief Marketing Officer, Anne Radcliff—the woman who'd hired him—about the timeline for opening the Orange County, California, branch of DataCorp. He knew it was necessary; he just wanted to get on with it and get to the good part.

Which he hoped would include dinner with Kim. But she hadn't answered his text yet. He knew she was busy preparing for Design Review. And her brother was getting married next month. She had texted with him a bit over the past two months since their Great American Road Trip. They'd gotten close on the adventure, but he'd screwed it up. Now it was his chance to prove to her that he could do better.

But it was hard to do that if she wouldn't see him.

He signed the papers the HR person pushed across to him and smiled and thanked her. Then he headed over to the next room. He'd just grabbed the coffee carafe to pour himself a cup —he'd need the caffeine to stay awake—when his phone buzzed. He set the cup down and looked at his message.

Sorry, I can't.

From Kim. His mood soured. This was going to be harder

than he thought. Just being in the same town as her wasn't going to be enough. He picked up his coffee and took a sip. He knew someone who would have dinner with him.

And he still had another plan up his sleeve.

It had been two months, but she had never left his mind. Or heart, if he was honest. So all he wanted to do was to get through these meetings and have dinner with her. Maybe tomorrow. He let his mind wander about where they could go, what they would talk about, how she would look—

"Matthew?" The director of sales, Chris Sandoval, called his name. He and the chief marketing officer, Anne Radcliff, had been discussing something about the Seattle headquarters. Nothing that had to do with him. Or so he thought.

"Sorry, could you repeat that?" Matthew scrambled to figure out what he'd missed.

"I think you should join us, get the pulse of the team." Chris frowned. Even though Anne had hired Matthew, Chris would be his boss. It wouldn't do to get on his bad side. "About a third will be relocating down here. You can give us some input on what holes we'll have in our team, and who we should be looking to add."

"Sure, I can do that." Getting to know new people would be a lot better than hanging around in these boring meetings.

"Great." Anne looked at her phone. "Our flight leaves in two hours. Why don't you go grab what you need from your room and meet us in the lobby in twenty minutes? I'll have our admin send you your boarding pass via email."

He nodded. "Sounds great." But inside he was a little panicked. What had he just agreed to? He didn't want to admit he had spaced out. Usually if he played along, it would become clear. Apparently he'd agreed to get on a flight somewhere.

They stood and headed out of the room toward the elevators together. Chris turned to him. "I like your perspective on things. You have your feet on the ground and are closer to knowing what our clients want and need, what will make them say yes and close the deal. We need a few more like you. Maybe you can help us find them."

"Sure, I'd like that."

The elevator doors opened, and Anne stepped inside first. As the doors closed, she said, "Edward's not completely convinced that the OC branch needs its own sales department. He thinks they can travel down from Seattle just as easily, since so much work is remote these days."

Chris scoffed. Matthew didn't say anything, but inside he was screaming *no, no, no, no, no!* He had relocated his whole life to Southern California. For this job and to be with Kim. Long distance wasn't going to cut it for either of those things. He needed to help convince Edward that an OC sales department was in the company's best interest.

He didn't know how he was going to do that. He wasn't even sure where they were flying to. Seattle, maybe?

Only one thing was clear. Kim wasn't on the agenda for today, but maybe the job he had barely started was.

Caught off guard by how quickly the time had flown, Kim slipped her sketchbook in her bag, double-checking that it nestled securely inside. She didn't want it falling out and getting lost like it had a month ago. Luckily someone had found it and returned it to her desk, because it was waiting for her there the following morning. She'd never felt so relieved to see it. She'd about turned her place upside down the previous night looking for it when she realized it hadn't made it home with her.

She plopped into her baby-blue VW Bug, starting it and blasting the air. It was already getting warm for the end of May. She was eager to meet Allie and Jessica for lunch. She was really hoping for some intel on Matthew, on how long she could avoid seeing him since Allie was his sister. Or maybe she just needed to treat it like a bandage and rip it off. The first meeting was always going to be awkward, so the sooner they got past it, the better. She couldn't avoid it forever. But she hoped Allie would give her an idea of when that might be.

She and Jessica had been friends growing up, as she was Scott's little sister, and the two of them often tagged after their older brothers. She had missed that Jessica. Last November, Jessica had made a fool of herself showing up drunk to a barbecue at Kyle's. Jessica had been in recovery for the past six months, and Kim had wanted to support her friend, so she invited her whenever she could.

Besides, she needed the distraction of Jessica's friendship. Kim's life felt like it was zooming along full-speed ahead with Design Review, Kyle and Heather's wedding, and of course, Matthew. It all allowed her to duck her memories—mostly—of being grabbed by Willard Dumas in March. Until her nightmares reminded her. Still, she hadn't had a knife to her throat like Melissa had, so she really should be over it by now. There was plenty to look forward to.

Shoving her confusing thoughts away, she pulled into the parking lot at Mimi's Cafe. She needed one of their big salads. Allie met her inside. Jessica came in just after her, and they were immediately shown a booth. Once they had iced teas in front of them and had placed their orders, Allie leaned forward. "Have you talked to Matthew?"

"He texted me that he was in town. I didn't realize it would be so soon."

"DataCorp's plans are moving along. They're hosting everyone in a hotel until they can move into their property. So he's here for good."

Oh. "He wanted to have dinner tonight, but I'm meeting with my former mentor, showing her some of my designs for her boutique."

"Ah. That explains it." Allie took a sip of her iced tea.

"What does that mean?"

Allie shrugged and glanced at Jessica. "Nothing. Just that we

—Collins, Melissa, and me—are having dinner with him and Austin tonight, and I wondered why."

Kim giggled. "You are his sister."

"True. But he would have rather been with you than anyone else."

"Who's Austin?" Jessica asked.

"Matthew's future roommate. They worked together in Phoenix, and Matthew convinced him to come out here and join DataCorp. They were thrilled to be getting one of the best in the business. He's a brilliant programmer and a nice guy, if a little quiet."

Kim waited for the server to set the salads in front of them, make sure they didn't need anything else, and leave. She took a bite of the chicken-and-quinoa Mediterranean salad, flavors cascading over her tongue among the crisp leaves of romaine and kale.

They chatted over their salads about Allie's work with Data-Corp—a client acquisition that had saved her company—Kim's Design Review, and Jessica's cosmetology school, which she was on a break from for the month.

"The bridal shower should be fun Saturday. How has it been working with Heather's sister Kellie? Have you met her yet?"

Kim shrugged. "We've talked over FaceTime but haven't met in person. With her two hours away, she's left a lot of it to me, just giving input on what she thinks Heather will like." Kellie was Heather's maid of honor, but Heather had asked Kim to help. She'd been doing a lot more than helping, but every time that thought irritated her, she reminded herself that she was doing it for Heather.

"That's a lot with Design Review coming up."

"It is, but I think I've got both of them handled. I've got all the games figured out and prizes bought. Kellie is supposed to call the restaurant to give them a final headcount and the deposit. And you've got a lot on your plate with DataCorp, so even if I needed help, I wouldn't ask you. Jessica, I may ask you."

Kim laughed. "How is it going with DataCorp getting their new branch set up?"

Allie sighed. "It's the biggest job I've ever done. And I'm so glad I fired Rachel when we got back from our trip. My new admin from the agency is fantastic. When her ninety days are up, she's going to be a permanent hire. Makes me wonder why I didn't do it sooner."

Kim laughed. "I'm not Melissa, so I won't say I told you so."

"Thanks. Anyhow, DataCorp is keeping me busy. Their COO, Edward Jacobsen, is an interesting guy. Very hands on and detailed."

"So a control freak."

Allie tilted her head. "In some ways. He's college buddies with the CEO, so there's talk that he got the job because of that. I think he's concerned about this branch pulling its weight. The decision was made before he was hired, so I'm not sure he's entirely in favor of it."

"Do you think he'll try to close it or keep it from getting off the ground? They've put so much time and money into it already." The idea of Matthew coming to OC had taken some time to get used to. But how would she feel if he left again? Her own feelings were too confusing, even for her.

"I know. And I'm not sure. I just know he wants it to turn a profit fast."

"If anyone can get people to buy things, it's Matthew."

"True statement."

"Have you had time to pick out places for him and Austin?"

Allie handed over her phone. "Swipe through these."

Kim did as she shared the phone with Jessica. "There are some real possibilities here." They talked through a few of them, eliminated some.

"I need to meet with both of them to set up some showings, but it's hard getting on Matthew's schedule. They have him busy."

Kim's phone buzzed. She had an Instagram message. Swiping

it open, she gave a snort and deleted it. That was the downside to trying to make a presence on social media. It attracted creepers. She put her phone back in her purse, determined to ignore it.

"Jessica, you're coming to Heather's bachelorette weekend, right? It's next Saturday."

"I am. I've got the time off work, but I do have to work Friday during the day."

"So how many does that make?" Allie held up her fingers. "Us three, Heather of course, Kellie, Sarah, and Melissa? Seven of us?"

"Yep. It works out perfectly. Having Collins in your life is awful handy." Kim grinned at her. "His connections from his time up at Holcomb Springs netted us a really great cabin. With the bunk room, there is plenty of space for us."

Allie smiled. "He's good for a few other things as well."

They finished their lunches, paid the bill, and left. Outside the restaurant, they exchanged hugs.

"I'll see you both at the shower Saturday." Allie waved and walked off.

"Can't wait." Kim headed to her car, but Jessica trotted alongside her.

"I meant what I said about offering to help. Please let me know. Keeping busy is a good distraction." Jessica gave a soft smile. "Actually, I'm not sure how you do it all. You've always been so focused on going after what you want. I remember playing paper dolls with you and the designs you created for them. I wish I could figure out what I wanted to do."

Kim reached out a hand and squeezed Jessica's. "I will call if I need anything. And you'll figure it out. It might just take some time."

Jessica gave her another hug and waved as she walked off.

Kim climbed into her car, the silence allowing her thoughts to surface. It was a good thing Matthew was gone. She had a lot on her plate and should spend the evening reviewing her checklists. Maybe there was something Jessica could do. She had Heather's shower to look forward to, then the bachelorette weekend, Design Review, and the wedding. Enough activities to keep her mind off things. Or off someone.

Though she couldn't help but wonder what it would be like when she saw Matthew in person again. It was like a bandage that she kept picking at. She just wanted to rip it off and be done with it. But life wasn't cooperating.

She turned the key and her car took its own sweet time starting. One more thing to add to her plate.

Chapter Two

Dragging his carry-on behind him, Matthew strode down the airport concourse after leaving security, the first private moment he'd had since he'd met Chris and Anne in the lobby of the hotel. He swiped up Kim's number. If he couldn't have dinner with her, he could at least hear her voice. Maybe make her laugh. But her phone went to voice mail. Dang, he'd missed her. He didn't want to leave a message; he wanted to talk to her. He really wanted to see her in person, but no way was that going to happen, short of some sort of teleport device.

"Hey, Kim, it's Matthew. I was hoping to catch you. I've been asked to go along on an emergency trip up to Seattle for DataCorp. I'm at the airport now. Not sure when we're getting back, but I'll let you know." He paused, not wanting to let the connection, however tenuous, go. "Allie's sent me a bunch of rentals that I'll be looking over on the flight. But I'll want your opinion on them, since you know which ones will have good light and atmosphere and all that." He chuckled, picturing her rolling her eyes at him when she got this message. "Anyhow, wish I could have talked to you." His voice softened, and he swallowed. "Give me a call when you can. Maybe we can talk tonight." He wanted to say more, but he wasn't sure what. Plus he had arrived at his gate where Chris and Anne were waiting for him. He hung up.

He sent Austin a quick text that he'd be gone. Austin seemed content to spend his evening alone in his hotel room, so Matthew didn't think he'd be disappointed. Maybe Austin would keep the dinner plans with Allie, Collins, and Melissa. Probably not. He didn't know them, and he wasn't the outgoing type. But since Matthew had recruited Austin from their old company to join DataCorp, he felt obligated to make sure the guy settled in and was comfortable here.

After boarding and taking off, Matthew contorted himself in his plane seat to get his laptop out of his backpack under the seat in front of him. He settled back and popped the computer open. Chris was next to him. Anne was in another row. But they might as well get some work done on the flight. Then tomorrow night he would be free to focus on Kim.

Chris sighed. "This is the third 'emergency' meeting I've been to since Jacobsen became COO. You know he and the CEO were frat buddies, right?"

Matthew nodded. He had heard the rumors. He didn't know if that was necessarily true; gossip got started all the time. But they did go to college together. Didn't matter to Matthew as long as the guy could do the job. But Chris had worked in nearly every branch and department of DataCorp, chasing the next opportunity. He knew the players in this game.

"When you require everyone to drop everything and get back to the home office, it's not an efficient use of resources, in my opinion. Not that anyone is asking." His gaze moved to the second row in front of them where Anne sat. "Anne's a smart woman, but she knows the politics of this business as well as anyone. If we can convince her that the OC branch needs its own sales force, she'll make sure the CEO knows too. At least someone who has his ear is on our side. I'm letting you in on this because you are about to upend your life, but the way things are going, the whole OC branch is in question."

That wasn't something Matthew wanted to contemplate. He didn't like the idea of being based anywhere but in OC, but theoretically, if it was part of his territory, he could make a case for living down there and working out of that office. But if the whole branch was gone… It didn't bear thinking about.

God had made this opportunity for Matthew, hadn't he? This is what Matthew had been preparing for his whole professional life. Surely, this was just a small obstacle they'd forget about once the branch office opened.

Because Matthew had nothing to go back to in Phoenix. His old boss had thought it was disloyal of Matthew to leave, and especially to take Austin with him. So there had been some hard feelings there, which had been disappointing to Matthew. He didn't like to leave on bad terms with anyone.

He turned his laptop so he and Chris could review reports together.

Chris gave him the rundown on each of the team members. "Everyone has strengths and weaknesses. My philosophy is to maximize someone's strengths and minimize their weaknesses. They have to be willing to get on board with it, though."

Chris looked at him. "You, for example. You're personable; you set people at ease. My guess would be you like a good time and hate paperwork."

Matthew tilted his head in acknowledgement.

"That's gotten you this far in your career. But if you want to go farther, you have to deepen your people skills. Be willing to go deep with them. You won't believe the personal issues people will bring to work, and thus, to you. The question is, can you do it?" Chris's gaze bored into him.

Matthew's first instinct was to say "Of course" and reassure Chris that he was the man for the job. But he considered the words. Yeah, bad news made him uncomfortable. He was never sure how to really comfort someone. Kim had been a case in point. But he was learning. He wanted to learn.

"It's an area I want to grow in. I recognize that."

Chris held his gaze a moment longer then nodded and moved on to the next person on the list.

They would make this work. They had to.

Kim slung the garment bag over her shoulder as she left her Bug and headed into Lynnae's boutique. But it pulled on her sore wrist, so she draped it over her arm. It was after hours, but the door was unlocked, and Lynnae waved her in.

"Kim! It's so good to see you!" The statuesque blonde old enough to be her mom wrapped her in a hug.

"It's been too long."

"I followed your road trip on Instagram. Sounds like an amazing time."

Kim sighed. "Yeah, that was the stage version."

Lynnae locked the door. "Come on back to my office. You can tell me all about it while I look at your new creations. I'm sure Instagram doesn't tell the whole story, about the trip or your designs."

Kim's troubles slipped off her shoulders like a cape in Lynnae's office. It was everything Kim wanted. A cozy seating area, a brightly lit workstation with a drafting table and a wall lined with whiteboards and cork, and a serious desk.

Kim hung the garment bag on a clothes rack and pulled the outfits out.

Lynnae handed her a blood-orange Pellegrino. "Still your favorite?"

Kim took the cold bottle gratefully. "Yes." Unscrewing the top, she took a long sip, letting the tangy bubbles carry away the day. She sank into the raspberry-velvet settee.

Lynnae tugged each clothing item out to the side, her experienced eye taking in every detail. If it were anyone else, Kim would feel apprehensive. But she trusted Lynnae and her judgment.

"These are good. Really good. As in, I think that trip inspired some of your best work. I can't wait to get them on Giselle and get some photos. There are a few places with southwest-inspired buildings." She went around her desk and made a note. "I'll call Zander Jakes again for the shoot. He really liked working with you back in February. And then I'll give you the photos to use in your Design Review portfolio."

It had been the first time she'd been on a photo shoot. Just watching, but still, it was great to be part of the process. And Zander had gone out of his way to talk to her and compliment her designs.

Lynnae grabbed another bottle out of her small fridge and joined Kim. "So tell me about your trip. I can't believe I haven't seen you in over two months."

Kim gave her the highlights, but also talked about Matthew and Willie Dumas.

Lynnae grabbed her hand. "I'm so sorry you went through all that. I'm glad he's no longer a threat. Does it still bother you?"

Kim shrugged. "Probably more than I'd like to admit. I have nightmares sometimes. But then I remember that Melissa went through worse. He had a knife to her throat. But I guess she's just a stronger person than me. She's certainly been through more."

"Don't compare your experience to others. Have you talked to her? Do you know how she's processed it?"

"Not really. I mean, we check in via text, but she's got a lot on her plate, so I don't want to make things worse by bringing it up."

Lynnae sipped her water. "It's possible that you don't really know what's going on with her. It's hard to share those details over text. Look, you didn't even tell me. And even if she was handling it perfectly, so what? What does that have to do with you? You are your own person."

Kim nodded. "That's true. I'm just used to always comparing myself to other people." Why did she do that? It never worked in her favor.

"In this line of work that's expected, even if it isn't healthy. But in your personal life? You be you. No one else can do that." She smiled. "And besides, something fantastic came out of that trip. These designs show a maturity I haven't seen in your work before. A confidence. It's like you felt secure enough to express your true thoughts. What's behind that?"

She knew the answer. Matthew. She'd felt comfortable enough around him to sketch, to let her mind wander. He had encouraged and supported her.

Lynnae gave her a knowing smile. "Could it be your young man?"

Kim snorted. "He's not my anything. We did get close on the trip. And yeah, okay, my heart got tangled up. But he's a good-time guy. He's funny and fun to be around. But he doesn't do sad emotions or anything deep. I don't think he can handle all of me."

Lynnae gave her a steady look, one that would make her squirm if it were anyone else. Then she studied the clothing Kim had brought. "I think these say something different. But only you can determine that. Now, show me what you've got for Design Review. I know Zander will do a great job and get us some good pictures."

They spent the rest of the evening ordering in Chinese food and discussing Kim's portfolio choices. She left feeling more encouraged than ever.

On the drive home, her thoughts wandered to what Lynnae had said about Matthew. The truth was Kim didn't quite trust herself around him. They had gotten close, and he'd wormed his way into her heart, like a bit of embroidery that was impossible to remove without leaving holes and picks in the fabric.

He was going to be in the same town as her. They had the same friends. She was going to have to figure out how to be with him.

What could dinner hurt? The first time meeting him in person since she'd left him in Phoenix would go a lot better if it was on her terms.

She sent him a text as soon as she got home.

Raincheck for tomorrow night?

Her phone buzzed. Maybe Matthew had decided to call her. It was getting late though. She needed to get to bed. Picking it up, she saw she had a text message from an unknown number. Weird. It looked an awful lot like the one she had gotten on Instagram earlier when she was having lunch with Allie and Jessica. She had deleted it, so she couldn't compare them.

In and of themselves, there was nothing creepy about them, just "I like your work." But how would someone get her phone number? And why would they go to the trouble?

Was it Nick? Her old high school boyfriend had gotten a little too familiar on social media after her road trip through the Southwest, and she'd had to block him. He'd probably just set up another account. But it was an odd message, even for him.

The only other person she could think of was Henry. Perhaps he was trying to shake her up before Design Review. Seemed a weird way to do it. Then again, she couldn't possibly explain how Henry's brain worked.

She deleted the message. It wasn't like it was a threat. It was just weird. And there was plenty of weird in the world. She pushed it out of her mind.

Chapter Three

Today was the first of the big events on Kim's calendar. She'd cringed when she realized Kyle and Heather's wedding came a week after Design Review. But since Kellie was the maid of honor, she should handle most of the details. Except Heather had asked Kim to help. And she would do anything for Heather. So with prayer and careful planning, she pitched in to make the two big events in her life happen almost simultaneously.

She did a last-minute check through the wedding box and made sure she had everything. Checklists weren't exciting, but they ensured everything got done. She wasn't going to let Heather down by winging it. Yes, with a quick stop to pick up some balloons, she was on her way. She might even pull this off.

Because no one had a house big enough to host the shower —except Kyle, and that just seemed weird—they were having it at a local Mexican restaurant that had a back room where they could set up a taco bar.

The weight slid off her shoulders as she reviewed the plans.

After piling everything in her baby-blue Bug, she stuck the key in the ignition, and turned it. Nothing happened. It had been acting weird the past two days, almost refusing to start. She had meant to do something about it, but she had forgotten with everything else going on.

She tried again. *Click-click. Click-click.* What on earth? She knew nothing about cars other than how to drive them. Kyle was always getting on her to get the oil changed and fluid levels checked.

Now what?

She banged her head on the steering wheel. Her dad and Kyle were right. She couldn't be trusted to pull off anything that required planning. Heather's shower would be ruined, she'd be a failure at Design Review, and it would be all her fault. Why hadn't she taken her car in for a check?

She ran through her options. None of them were good.

Goose bumps ran up her neck, and she swiveled around to see a black Honda crawl through the parking lot. The windows were tinted so she couldn't see anything. It was probably nothing. But with the weird texts and social media messages she'd been getting lately, she was more aware. Most likely they were all coming from her old boyfriend Nick. It couldn't be him in the car, though. He thought she still lived with her brother. And he wouldn't dare go near that house.

She picked up her phone and swiped a name.

MATTHEW PUSHED THE PAINT-FILLED ROLLER ACROSS Collins's family room wall. Collins was his sister Allie's boyfriend, and he had just bought this house a couple of months ago. Allie was helping him choose the paint and decor.

She was kneeling by the baseboards cutting in with a brush. He didn't mind painting, and it sure beat sitting around the hotel room all weekend. Especially after a week of being in meeting after meeting. He'd only gotten to see Seattle at night when they went out to dinner Thursday, and they'd flown home late Friday. Too late to have dinner with Kim, but it had been encouraging to him that she'd offered the raincheck. He was thinking of a way he could see her this weekend.

Since Collins would likely end up as his brother-in-law, Matthew was already pondering ways he could leverage this painting to his benefit.

Allie's phone rang. She reached for a rag to wipe her hands on before answering. "Hey, Kim."

Matthew stopped rolling and unabashedly listened to his sister's side of the conversation.

"Oh no. What do you think is wrong?… I don't know either… Yeah, I agree. Well, I'm currently in the middle of painting Collins's family room, so I can't come get you. I'll be rushed as it is to get home and showered and ready in time to get there. Did you try Jessica?…We need another solution." Allie looked up and grinned at Matthew. "I have the perfect one for you. He's on his way." She hung up.

"Kim's car won't start, and she needs to get to Heather's shower. She could call Triple A for a jump, but then it might not start again at the restaurant, and she still needs to stop and pick up the balloons. So, why don't you go get her?"

He didn't have to be asked twice. He put the roller in the pan and wiped his hands on a rag. He wrapped his sister in a hug. "Thanks for offering my services. Kim will be appreciative of my help, and we'll get time together." He gave her a final squeeze then grabbed the rental car keys and his wallet off the kitchen counter. "I'm off to rescue a damsel in distress."

Allie shook her head then called upstairs to where Collins was working to take over from Matthew so the paint wouldn't dry funny.

This had been the break he was looking for. He hopped into his rental car and headed to Kim's.

KIM ROLLED DOWN THE WINDOWS OF HER CAR, TRYING TO catch a breeze. It was already getting warm—hot for June—and she didn't want to trek up the stairs just to come back down again. Who had Allie meant by "he'll be right there"? Probably Collins. Who not only was Allie's boyfriend, he was Kyle's partner at the police department. So her brother would likely hear about this fiasco and be quick with his, "I told you so." Totally not what she wanted to hear. But she'd called Jessica first, who hadn't answered. She didn't have time to wait.

She hated being dependent on anyone. Well, she should have taken better care of her car. This was all on her. She just hoped it didn't impact Heather's shower.

She flipped through her social media, stopping at one profile. This was so odd. Over the past several weeks, the profile images of different accounts were reminiscent of a couple of her Southwest-inspired designs she'd posted. Not the whole image but like someone had zoomed in and chosen a section. Were people so inspired by her designs that they were using pieces of them as their profile pic? Seemed weird to her.

To wipe away those thoughts, she flipped to the site of one of her favorite designers, Maurice Worthington. Someday she wanted to work for someone like that.

She wasn't completely happy where she was, with very little opportunity for creativity. And Henry's constant taunting. Which was why she'd been working so hard on her own line. Maybe, just maybe, she'd go out on her own someday. She had played with the idea, and Lynnae was certainly supportive. It was a lot of work, which she wasn't afraid of. But there were certainly aspects of the business she didn't know that well.

Maurice Worthington had a good reputation for letting his designers have a lot more creative control. He was known as a fabulous mentor in the business. Maybe someday she'd be good enough to catch his eye.

In the meantime, between the wedding and the Design Review, she had no time to even dream about anything else. She stretched her wrists out and rolled her neck and shoulders. The tension was getting to her. Maybe she needed to book a massage. If she could find the time.

She glanced up as an unfamiliar car pulled into the parking lot. Not a black Honda. She went back to her scrolling. But it pulled into the spot next to her. She took another look.

A grinning Matthew Ellis stepped out. The last person she expected to see. Her heart rate picked up, the traitor.

"Hey, Kim. I've come to rescue you."

He was who Allie had sent? She couldn't believe it. Though at least Kyle wouldn't hear about this. She hopped out of her car. She hadn't seen him in nearly two months, and this was not how she had planned it. She wasn't sure what to do. Part of her wanted to throw her arms around his neck for rescuing her.

Then the other part of her—the logical part—remembered that he was a good-time boy who couldn't handle the rough things in life. Couldn't handle her emotions. She settled on friends. "Thanks. Did Allie tell you I'm headed to Heather's bridal shower and we need to stop and get balloons first?" She grabbed the box out of the car so she didn't have to look at him.

"She mentioned the shower but not the balloons. But I can take you wherever you need to go. I was just helping her and Collins paint, so anything that keeps me away from that…" He gave her his devastating grin.

Her heart flipped, but she shoved the box into his arms. "Great. We have to hurry. I need to be there early." She clicked the fob to lock her car, but it made a sick whine. She strode back and manually locked the doors. She'd deal with it when she got back.

She climbed into his rental car and buckled up, his clean and spicy scent surrounding her. She gave him quick directions to the party place, keeping her tone friendly and businesslike.

Even if he did just rescue her.

Seeing Kim in person after two months just about took Matthew's breath away. He concentrated on watching the road instead of her, but traffic was light this Saturday morning. She didn't seem as thrilled as he'd hoped she'd be at his rescue. Seemed like he was still in the friend zone.

But he wasn't going to give up hope. She had a rough morning with a lot on her mind. They just needed some time together without his work or hers or this wedding distracting them. The wedding would be over in a few weeks. His job… well, that had become more time consuming than he had expected. Not that it was a bad thing. He was actually excited about it and what he might be able to accomplish. He had been looking for a change in location and a chance to get geographically closer to Kim. But this job had surprised him with some challenges that could make his career leap ahead if he played it right. And he could still make time for Kim. Yeah, it was totally doable.

They got to the gift shop quickly. He went inside with her, and they were the only customers. The store clerk got the balloons blown up, ribbons attached, and cute weights in the shape of wedding bells kept them from taking off. He took the whole bunch and crammed it into the car, batting several out of his face so he could see.

Kim giggled.

Good sign. He couldn't see out the back window now, but that's what side mirrors were for. They headed for the Mexican restaurant. He checked his mirrors more often since he couldn't see out the back.

Conversation between them was nonexistent, and he tried to think of things to say. It had never been this hard, even when they'd been stuck in his truck and they'd barely known each other. "So, are you looking forward to the shower?"

A car sat on his tail. What was up with that? The traffic was light, so why didn't they just go around? He was in no hurry to speed up his time with Kim.

"Yeah, it'll be fun. My mom and Heather's mom and sisters will be there, as well as a lot of her friends. I hope she has a good time."

He switched lanes, but the car followed.

He glanced at Kim. She was studying the mirror on her side, gnawing her lip with her teeth.

"Are you worried about the shower?" He had no idea what all was involved with those things, but it was just a party, wasn't it? Weren't they supposed to be fun?

She let out a sigh. "I've thought through everything. I think it should go okay." At the stoplight, she studied the mirrors. Did she recognize the car behind them? It was hard to see from this angle, but it was a small car, dark in color.

"Do you know that person behind us?"

She shook her head. "No, I just thought I saw a similar car in my condo parking lot earlier. Probably just my imagination running away with me." She gave him what was clearly a forced smile.

He couldn't tell what kind of car it was. But she was definitely worried about something. And she didn't trust him enough to tell him what it was. He was at a loss. *God, some help here, please? How do I help her? How do I be what she needs?*

His first instinct was to tell her a funny story to take her mind off things. But that didn't work too well between them last time. He decided to go with straightforward. "Is there anything I can do? You look worried."

She looked at him for a moment. Then her shoulders visibly lowered, and she smiled at him. A genuine smile.

Ooh, he'd done something right.

"I'm fine. It's just one of those crazy times. Heather and Kyle's wedding and everything that goes along with that. Design Review at work, which I think I told you about. It's a big deal. But the timing stinks. Anyhow, today I need to focus on Heather and her shower. Thanks for picking me up."

"Kim, I'll do anything I can to lighten your load."

"I appreciate that." She paused a minute. "How was Seattle?"

"I hardly saw it. I was inside most of the two days we were there." He chuckled.

"They must think you're important if they flew you up last minute." She turned to look at him.

"I don't know. I think I was in the right place at the right time and got invited along. It was better than sitting in meetings all day, though. I got to meet some of the sales and support staff that will be relocating to OC. I think we'll have some good people on our team."

"That's something to look forward to. Allie showed Jessica and me some potential places for you and Austin. She's got some good ones picked out."

"I think so too. Which ones did you like?"

They talked through them for a few moments, and then the conversation lagged again.

"How's your prep for Design Review going?"

She told him about her meeting with Lynnae. "I feel like I've done everything I can. I just have one sample outfit with a seamstress. But part of me wonders if I'm missing something."

"You'll do a great job. I know you will. I have every confidence in you."

They slowed and turned into the parking lot for the restaurant. Kim's head swiveled as she turned to look at the car that was following them.

It sped past, and he couldn't see the driver.

But it was a black Honda.

Chapter Four

A chill washed over Kim as they sat in front of the restaurant. "Did you see the driver?"

Matthew shook his head. "Nope. Tinted windows. Plus, I had to concentrate on driving." He gave her a quick grin.

She didn't return it. "I wish I'd been able to see who it was. Then maybe I could tell if it was just a coincidence or someone I knew." She shouldn't even bring it up.

"Like an old boyfriend?" He frowned.

She shrugged. "Something like that. Too long to get into right now. Do you mind helping me bring the balloons in? I can grab the box." She needed to switch gears and focus on Heather's shower.

"Not a problem."

She got out and opened the back door, grabbing the box off the seat, while ducking balloons and making sure none escaped. Scanning the parking lot and seeing no one around, she hurried inside.

The hostess greeted her, eyeing the box in her arms. "Just one?" Then her eyes flicked to Matthew entering with the group of balloons. "Or two?" She reached for another menu.

"Oh, no. I'm here for the wedding shower. I thought I'd

come early to set up a bit. We're supposed to have the back room."

The girl's highly stylized eyebrows drew together. "I don't know anything about that. Let me get the manager."

Kim refused to panic. She glanced at Matthew. "She probably just doesn't know about it." That's all it was.

He nodded, making quite the picture with paint-splattered jeans and holding a bouquet of bridal balloons. But as with everything, he pulled it off with nonchalance.

But still, shouldn't they have the room set up already? Perhaps they did it last night.

The manager appeared. "You're Kellie? I called you two days ago to confirm, and I didn't get a call back with the final headcount or the deposit. So I assumed you had cancelled. I'm sorry. We're not set up for you. But we have to have this information from every party."

"I'm Kim, but Kellie didn't call you?"

He shook his head. "No one called. And we don't have a deposit."

Kim wanted to cry. What was she going to do? It was too late. Everyone would be showing up here soon. She should have doubled checked, even though Kellie had said she'd handle it. Why hadn't she double checked? Heather's shower would be ruined. She couldn't let that happen. "She was supposed to call you. Everyone will be here in about twenty-five minutes. Can we still pull something off?"

The man looked up, likely thinking how much money he'd lose if this party went somewhere else. "How many?"

"Seventeen."

"I only have one server. I called off the other one when I didn't hear from you. I'll call her and see if she can come in."

"What about the taco bar?"

He shook his head. "We don't have time to prep it. It's usually done the night before. Everyone will just have to order their own meals. It'll be a long wait for such a big party, but we can do it."

It would have to do. "Can we get started with bowls of chips, salsa, guacamole, and some quesadilla appetizers? Oh, and you can bring out pitchers of iced tea and water. That should give them something to munch on and drink. Then we can do the shower activities after they all order, so they have something to do while waiting for their food."

He nodded. "Good plan. I'm sorry. If you'd only called…"

"It's not your fault. I'll have to find out why Kellie didn't call you. Thanks for making this work."

He turned to the hostess. "Show her the back room and start setting it up to seat seventeen." He hurried to the back.

Kim followed the hostess, and Matthew followed them, the balloons trailing behind. She set her wedding box on the floor. Matthew tucked the balloons in the corner, and they helped the hostess push the tables together.

Matthew helped her with the balloons, untangling and handing them to her as she plopped them along the tables and tied the silver-and-white mylar BRIDE one to the back of the chair at the head of the table.

Matthew scanned the room. "Looks good. Do you need my help for anything else?"

"No, thank you so much for everything. I really appreciate it." This time her smile was genuine.

"You've done a great job. You'll pull it off, and Heather will love it."

His little bit of sincere cheerleading buoyed her spirits. "Thanks."

"When do you want me to pick you up?"

"Oh." She hadn't thought that far. "Um, I'm sure I can get a ride with someone."

He looked like he wanted to protest, but he didn't. "Okay. But I can come get you if you need me to. It'll get me out of more painting." He grinned and touched her shoulder. "But you'll still need to do something about your car. Text me when you're home, and I'll come look at it."

She nodded—having forgotten about her car—and he left the room, leaving a warm spot on her arm where he'd touched her. She watched him disappear and then studied the room. What was next? She considered texting Kellie to find out what happened, but there was no point. She was with Heather, and Kim wanted to keep this from her as much as possible.

She added party favors to the table and the sheets with the game instructions. The gift bags she kept by her chair, at the opposite end of the table so she could connect with the waitstaff without disturbing anyone. Luckily, she had managed those herself. All Kellie had to do was confirm the arrangement with the restaurant. No point in dwelling on it now.

With a final exhale, she examined the table and room. It looked good. Almost the way she had envisioned. Other than the food hiccup, it wouldn't be too bad.

"Oh, it looks so pretty!" Heather's voice came from behind her, and Kim turned. "You did such a great job. Thank you!" She wrapped Kim in a hug.

"I just want you to have a good time."

"I will." She moved to her seat and hung her purse over the back of the chair.

Kellie's golden blonde hair was paler than Heather's, but they had a similar face shape. They were clearly sisters. It was the first time she'd met her in person, though they'd FaceTimed. Kim motioned with her head to step to the side. They walked a few steps toward the main dining room. "Did you call to confirm the headcount and give the deposit?"

Kellie's eyes went wide. "No! I forgot. I remembered at one point, but we were having such a good time that I thought I'd do it later. I must have forgotten." She glanced around. "It looks like it turned out okay, though."

Kim worked to keep her voice level. This was Heather's day. "They had cancelled us because they didn't get a call. We won't have a taco bar, and the food will take awhile. I've got chips and appetizers coming while we wait."

"Then it's all taken care of." Kellie smiled brightly and flounced off toward Heather.

Heather's mom, Stephanie, and Heather's older sister, a very pregnant Aimee, came in next. They must not have hit much traffic on the drive down from the Valley north of LA. Saturday mornings usually weren't too bad.

Then Kim's mom, Karen, came in. Heather's soon-to-be mother-in-law. Kim stiffened a bit and studied the setup. Would Mom think she'd done a good job?

She gave Kim a side hug. "Hey, sweetie. It looks cute. Mexican was a great idea."

"Thanks. Is Grandma with you?"

"No, she wasn't feeling well, so I picked up her gift for Heather."

Kim nodded. "Go ahead and sit down by Heather. You all get the seats of honor." She smiled and let out a breath as her mom moved off.

Other girls started filtering in. Her friends Sarah and Cait, as well as Sharon and Linda from choir, and Laurie from Bible study. Kyle's coworkers—Hilary, Stacey, and Lisa—had been part of Heather's protection team after she had witnessed a gang initiation gone wrong. Finally, Allie, Melissa, and Jessica came in. They sat near Kim's end of the table.

Kim greeted everyone and directed them toward Heather. The owner came out with pitchers and chips, the hostess following him with bowls of salsa and guacamole.

Once all the women had arrived and were seated, a harried looking server came around to take their orders. When she got to Kim, Kim gave her order and whispered, "Thanks for coming in." The woman gave her an understanding smile.

Allie sat to her right, and Melissa and Jessica on the other side of her.

Jessica turned to her. "Sorry I didn't get your text sooner. My phone was recharging, and the sound was off. I didn't see your text until I grabbed it to leave. But it looks like you got a ride."

"Yeah, Matthew brought me."

Jessica's eyebrows raised.

Allie leaned in. "You did a great job. Is Matthew coming back to get you?"

She let out a breath. "He was a big help. But I told him I could find a ride home."

"I'll give you a lift." Jessica snagged a triangle of quesadilla.

"Thanks. You don't mind staying late?"

"My day is open."

Kim started the games while they were waiting for their food. She wasn't sure if the games were too silly, but even the moms seemed to be having fun.

However, it was going too fast. They got through the games, and had gone through all the appetizers, and their food still wasn't there yet. She caught Allie looking at her watch. The other girls were visiting and didn't seem to mind. Heather was doing a good job of including everyone in conversation.

The server brought out another round of chips and salsa.

Kim caught her attention. "Do you know how much longer for the food?"

"I'll check."

She leaned over to Allie. "When do you have to leave?"

"I can wait another half hour, but that's pushing it. We're finalizing the details for occupying the office space."

"On a Saturday?"

Melissa joined the conversation. "Yeah, some people in the corporate world have no sense of boundaries. They don't have a life, so they don't think you do either." She popped a chip in her mouth.

"Normally, I wouldn't agree to it, but not only is DataCorp my biggest client, they're on a time crunch to get into the building. So I'm doing it as a favor."

"Let's hope the food gets here soon, then." She stood and

headed toward Heather at the opposite end of the table. "How about you begin opening gifts? Kellie, can you write down what she gets so she can send out thank you cards?"

"Sure. Do you have a pen and paper?"

Kim rummaged through the wedding box for the items and handed them to her. Then she searched until she found the gift bag Allie had come in with. If Allie had to leave, then she could at least see Heather open it.

Kim passed Heather the gifts and took the opened ones and stacked them to the side, keeping an eye out for the server. If they ran out of presents before the food got here, what would she do? She tried to think of something while she managed the packages.

Finally, when there were only two presents left, the server and manager came in bearing large trays of food. Allie caught Kim's eye and pointed to her watch. She wasn't going to be able to eat.

While everyone was occupied with their food, Kim scooted back to the servers' station and grabbed a to-go box for Allie. At least she could eat it later. She gave Allie the box and a hug. Allie packed up her food, gave Heather a quick hug, and then left.

Kim pasted on a smile and began eating her enchiladas, barely noticing the combo of spicy sauce mixed with creamy cheese that she usually loved.

Most people were still working on their food when the server came around with the dessert tray offering honey-dipped and powered-sugar-dusted sopapillas—little puffed pastries of deliciousness—chocolate-drizzled deep-fried ice cream, or custardy flan. The dessert was supposed to come while they were opening gifts, but since that had all been done, there wasn't anything left to do. She hoped no one else was bothered by the off timing.

She hadn't gotten a cake, which would have been the traditional dessert for a shower, because Heather liked the Mexican theme. But they could have served the cake whenever. Too late now.

Still, most people took the dessert.

Kim had deep-fried ice cream. The hot, crispy shell broke away to reveal the creamy ice cream inside. The contrast was to die for. And it was a nice reward for how hectic the day had been.

After dessert, the guests started leaving. After all, the shower had been much longer than Kim had expected.

Heather hugged the last of her guests goodbye. She was spending the rest of the day with her mom and sisters before they made the drive back home.

Mom came over and gave Kim a hug. "Good job, sweetie. Other than it taking a long time for the food, it was a good shower. I think Heather enjoyed herself, and she got some nice gifts."

"Thanks." So Mom had noticed about the food. Figured. Sigh.

Kim paid the bill, putting an extra tip on for the server. Kellie was supposed to split the cost with her. Kim hoped she would actually follow through or her budget would be tight for the next couple of months paying this off. She packed up the wedding box and gathered all the balloons into one bouquet for Heather to take home.

Heather came over. "Kim, you did a fabulous job. Thank you so much. It was lovely."

Kim forced a smile. "I'm glad you liked it and that everyone could make it."

Kellie took Heather's arm and grinned at Kim. "See? It all turned out just fine."

They had different definitions of fine, but she wasn't going to mention the missing taco bar or the delayed food if Heather didn't. "Don't forget your balloons."

Heather laughed. "Snowflake should love these."

"Good thing we came in my SUV instead of your Miata. They'd never fit. And maybe if your cat chases the balloon strings she'll stop sleeping in my suitcase."

"I warned you not to leave it open. She likes piles of clothes."

Between them—with Jessica, Stephanie, and Aimee's help—they managed to get the balloons and gifts to Kellie's SUV in one trip. Aimee and Stephanie climbed into their car and followed Kellie out of the parking lot.

As Kim waved goodbye to them, she and Jessica headed back inside. "I'm going to run to the ladies' room," Jessica said. "Do you need help with anything?"

"No, I can get it. I'll meet you outside." Kim grabbed the wedding box. In it was the pen and notepad with Heather's gifts listed. Ugh. Kellie couldn't even get that right. It wouldn't help Heather with her thank you notes if she didn't have the list. Well, she'd take it over to her tomorrow. They'd likely go to lunch after church, unless Kellie was still in town. Then, who knew?

Box tucked under her arm, she thanked the manager and the server. In the foyer, she peered out the doors and searched the parking lot. No black Honda.

Hearing footsteps behind her, she turned.

Jessica. "Want to tell me why you're scanning the parking lot?"

Kim shrugged. "I'll tell you on the way."

They climbed into Jessica's Nissan, and she pulled out of the parking lot and onto the street. "Thanks for doing that for Heather. She and Kyle deserve some happiness after what they've been through."

"Yeah, they do."

"So what's going on? Aside from Kellie leaving you in the lurch."

"How did you know?"

"She's the maid of honor, but she came waltzing in after you'd already been there. Plus, I heard you talking to the server."

"Do you think anyone else noticed?"

"Nah. But something else is bothering you."

Kim told her about the texts and the black Honda.

Jessica didn't say anything for a long moment. "It could be nothing. Or it could be something. But I'm not a fan of coincidences, and by the time we figure out what's really going on, it could be too late." At a stoplight, she held Kim's gaze. "Tell your brother. He loves you and doesn't want to see you in danger. Besides, you know either of our brothers would kill us if they found out something was going on and we didn't tell them. Remember Bobby Willcox in fourth grade?"

The kid that had taunted them as they walked home from school. Until ninth graders Scott and Kyle had found out and put the fear of God into him. He walked home another way after that.

"You're right. I just don't want him to think that there's always drama in my life."

Jessica raised her eyebrows. "He can handle a bit of drama." She pulled into the condo parking lot and slotted her car next to Kim's then leaned over and gave her a hug.

"Thanks for coming. And the advice." Kim grabbed her box and climbed out. "Let's try for lunch again this week."

"Good idea." Jessica waved and backed out.

Kim climbed the stairs. The idea of heading into her quiet condo should be a relief after the chaos of the shower. But it wasn't. At the top of the stairs she turned. Jessica was still watching her. Kim waved and unlocked her door and stepped inside. Jessica pulled away as Kim closed the door.

Chapter Five

Matthew hustled up the stairs to Kim's condo. He'd waited awhile for her to text him, but when Allie had come back to Collins's dressed in painting clothes, he was sure the shower had been long over. Helping Collins paint was better than hanging out in a hotel room, but being with Kim would be even better.

So he had texted her to see if she was home, and when she said she was, he said he'd head over to see what was wrong with her car.

A balloon bobbed to the side of her door. He knocked then picked it up. Was it one from the shower that she hadn't brought in? No, this said THINKING OF YOU. Odd.

She opened the door in a T-shirt and shorts, her feet bare.

"How was the shower? Did everything work out?" He handed her the balloon. "This was on your porch."

She stepped back to let him in. "It did. Heather seemed to enjoy it. I think the only person it was a problem for was Allie. She had to take her food to-go to get to her conference call."

He shut the door behind him as she looked at the balloon. She frowned. "Who's this from?" She examined the string. There was a note attached next to the weight: To Kim Taylor, From a secret admirer.

Matthew raised his eyebrows. "You have a secret admirer. Anything you haven't told me?" He kept his tone light, but he wondered what had happened in his absence. Had she found someone else? Someone else had certainly found her.

She shook her head. "I have no idea what this is about. If my name wasn't on it, I'd think it was a wrong delivery." She bit her lip then went into the kitchen. "I bet it's Henry messing with me, trying to distract me." She grabbed scissors out of the drawer, punctured the balloon, and shoved the whole mess into the trash can. "He's got a lot of nerve."

She plopped onto the couch. "Today when I couldn't start my car, the Honda that I thought might be following us came through the parking lot, slower than most people do. It wasn't a familiar car, but the person could have been looking for an address. It's silly though. I was already edgy from the messages —" She clamped her lips shut.

What didn't she want to tell him? "What messages?"

She gave a half-hearted shrug. "I've been getting stalkerish messages on social media. Which is not a surprise, but I think some of them are from my old high school boyfriend, Nick Parker. I blocked him, but I think he's following me under different accounts. I suppose the balloon could be from him. Doesn't really seem like his style, though."

She stared across the living room before turning her gaze to him. "Sorry, none of this is your problem. You've been nice enough to give me a ride and help me out with my car when you probably don't have much down time."

He wanted to tell her that he'd do all that and more for her. But he didn't think she was ready to hear it. Instead, he glanced around her condo. "Cute place. It looks like you."

"Huh. Yeah, I guess you've never been here. Which seems weird, considering how much time we spent together on the road trip. Just seems like you'd know what my place looked like."

They'd dropped him off in Arizona, where he lived. And now he was staying in a hotel while Allie looked for a place for him and Austin.

The walls were painted with vibrant colors, and wood covered the floors. She didn't have much in the way of furniture. "I wouldn't have expected the minimalist look from you."

She shrugged. "Normally it wouldn't be. But I find it refreshing after dealing with the chaos of creativity at work. So I haven't bothered with more furniture. And it's not like I have people over. That's what Kyle's house is for."

"Let me go check your car, and then we'll decide what to do next. Keys?"

She pointed to the small table next to the door.

He headed back outside and tried to start her car. Sure enough, it sounded like a dead battery. He popped the hood and looked inside. He could swap the battery himself, but he didn't have any tools with him.

Closing the hood, he headed upstairs. Maybe his plan would work. If it backfired, Kim might not speak to him.

Work was going to keep him busy this week. He might have time to see her in the evenings, but probably not. He'd have a lot of prep to do each night. The challenge of getting a new branch office up and running was exciting. Not to mention the stakes were higher than he had originally thought. He just wished the timing had been better. Still, he had a plan that would give them some time together.

He walked inside. "It's definitely your battery. I can swap it out, but I don't have any tools. However, I bet Kyle does."

She nodded. "And he doesn't live too far away. I just wish I could handle this on my own without involving him."

"Kim, people who love you want to help. We help each other. Look how much you're helping him and Heather with their wedding. It's not because you think they're incompetent. It's because you love them."

She nodded, and her eyelashes dampened.

He wanted nothing more than to take her in his arms and make everything better, but being in her condo was progress. He didn't want to push it. "Is Heather at Kyle's?"

"No, she's hanging out with her mom and sisters for the rest of the day." She ran her hands up her arms. "But I'll go with you."

Good. The balloon and the Honda were weird. Maybe nothing. But if she came along, hopefully she'd tell her brother.

She picked up her phone and asked Kyle if they could borrow some tools. She briefly explained about the car battery and then hung up. "You were right. Kyle was more concerned than scolding."

He winked at her. "Of course I was."

"But I don't want to tell him about the balloon. It's silly."

He started to argue, but she grabbed her purse and shoved her phone inside. They headed downstairs and into his rental.

He scanned the parking lot for a black Honda and kept his eyes peeled for one on the way to Kyle's. It was a common car, but still, he'd rather be safe than sorry. And if Kyle went with him to get the battery, Matthew might talk to him about what had happened today.

And since Matthew couldn't keep an eye on her, he wanted Kyle in the loop as to what was going on. Maybe Kyle could do some background research on this Nick guy and see what kind of car he drove.

As long as it didn't get back to Kim.

Kim thought about what Jessica said as they pulled up to Kyle's house. He was working in the yard. Even though Jessica was probably right, Kim really didn't want to bring Kyle into this. The balloon coming on the heels of the messages, texts, and creepy car had freaked her out more than she wanted to admit to Matthew. Still, there was nothing illegal done, and she didn't even know who did it. She would just pay closer attention to what was going on around her.

With Design Review and the wedding, she didn't need one more distraction on her plate. She definitely didn't want Kyle hovering.

Matthew looked even better in person than in her dreams, where he stubbornly kept showing up. Nothing had changed, though. He was a fun guy and a good friend. But he just wasn't capable of handling her emotions. Life wasn't always fun and games the way he liked to think it was. There were deep valleys of sorrow, and bad things happened. No, if she let him back in, she'd just get her heart broken again.

This day had had enough twists and turns. When she'd woken this morning, she hadn't expected the dead battery, the problems with the restaurant, the black Honda, or the balloon. Let alone Matthew. But now all of those things were a part of her life. The question was, what was she going to do about any of it?

Kyle strode up to the car and opened Kim's door. She gave him a hug. "Hey Kyle, this is Matthew. Matthew, this is my brother Kyle."

Matthew came around the car and shook Kyle's hand. "Good to finally meet you in person."

"You too. So it's the battery then?"

Matthew nodded. "Looks like it. Do you mind if I borrow some tools to swap it out?"

Kyle gave him a steady look.

She'd seen that one before, where he was evaluating the person as his cop mind whirled to life. It always irritated her. Why couldn't he just take her friends at face value because they were her friends?

She let out a sigh. "I'm heading inside for a Diet Coke. You two can talk cars." She entered through the garage and into the kitchen, popping open the fridge and swiping the soda he kept there for Heather before plopping on the leather couch. Soon this would be Heather's house, too, and Kim wouldn't want to just pop in at any time. Things would definitely be different.

The front door opened, and Kyle and Matthew came in. Kyle didn't give her any overly concerned looks, so Matthew must have passed his scrutiny. And it didn't seem like Matthew had told him about the balloon. Good. Perhaps there was hope for them yet.

"We're going to head to the auto store to get you a new battery." Kyle turned to Matthew. "Want anything to drink before we go?"

"I'm good."

They turned and went back out the door, letting it shut behind them.

Huh. She wasn't sure what she thought about Matthew and her brother being alone. She should have thought this through better. But it was too late now. She could only hope she didn't regret this.

They were in Kyle's truck on their way to the auto parts store when Matthew weighed his words, for just a moment, before glancing at Kyle. He hadn't expected Kyle to go with him, but it was an opportunity he wasn't going to pass up.

"What do you know about Nick Parker?"

Kyle frowned. "Kim's old boyfriend? What brought him up?"

Matthew carefully chose his words. "Kim seems to think he's been texting her, checking up on her."

"You don't need to worry about him. She's been over him awhile. They went to prom together in high school, and he was part of her bad-boy phase. But I haven't heard her bring him up in a long time." He shot a look at Matthew. "Not that she tells me much about her love life."

Matthew was silent for a moment, pondering how to proceed.

They pulled into the auto parts store parking lot, and Kyle turned to Matthew. "What's going on? Nick Parker doesn't just come out of nowhere."

"Remember how I said she *thought* he sent her a text today? Well I guess he'd been creeping her out on social media so she blocked him. And she also blocked his texts. The number it came from wasn't familiar to her, but the text itself had a familiar tone. Almost like he wanted her to know that he could get around any attempt to block him."

Kyle was silent for a moment. "Is that all he's done?"

Matthew told him about the black Honda and the balloon delivery and note.

Kyle didn't say anything, just got out of the truck. They bought the battery and returned home.

"Don't say anything to Kim. She doesn't want you to know."

Kyle considered him a minute. "Why did you tell me?"

Matthew lifted his shoulder. "I care about her. A lot." That was an understatement, but he wasn't going to talk to Kyle about his feelings for Kyle's sister. "She might be mad that I told you. She might never speak to me again. I'd hate that, but if it meant she was safe, then—" He shrugged again. He couldn't quite put it into words. He just knew he had to keep Kim safe. No matter what.

Kyle nodded. "She'd speak to you again. Eventually, she'll come around. Her emotions tend to run away with her, but after a while things settle down and she comes to her senses." He gave Matthew a wry grin. "It could be Nick. In that case, I can have a talk with him."

"And if it isn't?"

"Then I'll have to blow your cover and tell Kim what I know. It's entirely possible it's part of her overactive imagination. I'll give you that. Though the balloon is strange. But if there's something else going on, I'll need her help to figure this out and to keep her safe." He held Matthew's gaze a moment. "Here's my advice when it comes to my sister. Listen and don't try to fix things. She just wants to be heard. And whatever you do, don't make light of it or try to get her to lighten up. That makes things worse."

"Yeah. I learned that the hard way."

Kyle popped him on the shoulder. "Go get my sister and get that battery in her car. And if you can, get her to be careful and pay attention to her surroundings until I have a talk with Nick."

Matthew's world skidded a few degrees off its typical center as he sat in Kyle's truck. Kyle was an anomaly in Matthew's world, where his advice usually came from his older sisters. He hadn't had a lot of men to seek advice from in his life. As he glanced around Kyle's well-kept house with its sense of roots and permanence, he wondered if his future might actually look like this, with stability and wise friends.

He just couldn't blow it with Kim.

Chapter Six

Sunday afternoon, Kim slid into her chair at the restaurant surrounded by most of her brother's group of friends. She supposed they'd become her friends as well. Matthew slipped in next to her. Even though he'd gotten the new battery installed yesterday and made sure her car started, he offered to pick her up for church. She was surprised to see Austin Montgomery, his future roommate, with him. Between his combed-back, jet-black hair and the shark's tooth on a leather string, it made her think he had Hawaiian ancestry.

It was the first time either Matthew or Austin had been to their church, but considering Matthew's sisters also attended, they'd likely make this their home church once they settled in Laguna Vista.

And since Kyle had shown no signs of knowing about her creeper, Matthew seemed to be keeping his word. Perhaps they could find a way to be friends. It would make things less awkward. So when Kyle and Heather invited them to lunch after church, she agreed to go, telling herself that it would be good for Matthew and Austin to get to know everyone. It would help them settle in.

Allie and Collins seated themselves across the table, and the rest of their friends found seats as well. Melissa had brought Jessica with her, and they sat across the table.

Matthew stuck out his hand. "I'm Matthew. You must be Jessica."

"I am. Nice to meet you."

"This is Austin."

Austin stared like a deer in the headlights for a long moment before taking Jessica's hand. "Austin. Montgomery. Roommate. Uh, of Matthew's."

Kim hid a grin. So Austin seemed a little star struck by Jessica. With her curly blonde hair that fell below her shoulders, a hot pink streak carved through the side, and her darkly made-up bright blue eyes the same color as her brother's, she was stunning.

Jessica smiled. "Hi. I'm Scott's sister."

Austin shrugged. "Which one is Scott? It's my first time meeting everyone."

Melissa leaned forward. "He's not here. He's stationed at NAS Whidbey Island in Washington state as a naval aviator trainer. But he, Kyle, and Joe grew up together." She pointed to Joe. "And that's Joe's fiancée, Sarah."

Jessica nudged Melissa's shoulder. "You left out an important fact about Scott: He's your boyfriend."

Melissa's cheeks pinked. "I'm sure we're confusing you with all of this. But you'll get to know everyone soon enough."

"Yeah, I think—" Austin started, but Matthew nudged him. When Austin raised his eyebrows, Matthew gave a small shake of his head.

What was that all about? Who knew?

The server brought out baskets of bread and took drink orders. Collins helped himself to a slice. "So, Matthew, what's it been like for you working with your sister and getting a new branch off the ground?"

"It's been great. Allie's going to find us a great place to live. The powers that be at DataCorp love the work she's done getting them situated in the new building and all the folks relocated out here. I've not been so thrilled with all the meetings. I spent two days last week in Seattle, but this week we're in town. We have a big team-building exercise going on Thursday, so I should meet most of the other staff then." His face revealed what he thought of the team-building exercise.

Kim wrinkled her nose. "That sounds like a bad corporate idea. Can you imagine a bunch of designers doing that? Um, no."

Allie laughed. "Edward wants the core team to be united and on the same page. He hopes this will help them get to know each other."

"Or hate each other." Kim slathered butter on a piece of bread. She was starving.

"It could go either way," Matthew said. "Depends on what he has in mind. I'm a bit afraid. But whatever it is, it has to be better than sitting in a conference room."

Allie nodded at Kim. "You've got your plate full at work too. How's the prep for Design Review going?"

She tilted her head. "Okay. I think I've settled on my portfolio. I'll get some great photos from the shoot. And Monique is working on sewing up my last outfit. Should be done when we get back from the girls' weekend away."

"I'm looking forward to enjoying the weekend away for Heather's bachelorette party. I've cleared my schedule of Data-Corp stuff. Do you need any help with that?" Allie took a sip of her tea.

"I don't think so. I'll run to the store Thursday night and make up some breakfast dishes to bring that we can reheat. I've got a list on my phone. I think everything is covered." She wasn't going to risk a repeat of relying on Kellie for anything.

"I can help too," Jessica added.

When they finished lunch and said goodbye to everyone, Kim pulled Jessica to the side. "Everything okay? You were quieter than usual today."

She shrugged. "I'm fine. It's just—" she glanced around— "I know I can be a bit much, and Austin seems the quieter type. I didn't want to put him off. I hope he feels comfortable with us as friends. It's got to be hard moving to a place and knowing only one person."

"I'm glad you're okay. And that's thoughtful of you. I'm sure we'll see more of Austin." She gave Jessica a hug then caught up with Matthew and Austin who took her home.

At the front of her condo, Matthew turned to her. "It's going to be a crazy week. I'll keep in touch as much as I'm able. Will you please let your brother know if you get any more weird gifts or texts?"

She sighed. "Okay. I will. I promise."

"Good." He walked to the base of her stairs and wrapped her in a warm hug. His familiar scent enveloped her, and she breathed deeply. But he let her go before she was ready, and she snatched her arms back.

He waited at the stairs until she got inside.

The rest of the evening, the day played through her mind. Matthew had been very friend-like the whole time. He hadn't even tried to kiss her, not even on the cheek. Was that because Austin was around? That hadn't stopped him before.

She didn't know how she felt about that. Was it possible he had decided that they should just be friends? It wasn't something she had considered.

But it was what she wanted. Wasn't it?

Chapter Seven

It was the middle of the week when Ashley Jacovich, their admin, stepped into Kim's workstation carrying a large vase of red roses. Ashley was working part-time here while attending the Fashion Institute of Design and Merchandising, the same Orange County campus Kim had gone to. It had allowed her to stay with Kyle and save money, which enabled her to take the study tours to Paris and Italy. They had been amazing experiences and had convinced her that fashion design was where her heart was. And she was happy to see Ashley following a similar path.

"These came for you." Ashley grinned as she set them on Kim's desk.

Wow. They were gorgeous. Who could have sent them? Matthew popped into her head. It was the kind of over-the-top gesture he'd make. But given how they'd left things Sunday, it seemed far more romantic than she thought their relationship warranted. She reached for the card.

Ashley hovered.

She slid the card out of its envelope, turning it so Ashley couldn't read it over her shoulder. Good luck with Design Review. I know you'll knock them out with your

DESIGNS. Sweet, though it wasn't quite what she would have expected Matthew to say. Then again, she wasn't expecting flowers either. Maybe these weren't for her.

"Who are they from?" Ashley leaned in, clearly wanting a peek at the card.

Kim examined it again. "There's no name. Are you sure they're for me?"

"Yes, the delivery person said they were for Kim Taylor. A mysterious admirer. How romantic. Don't you think?" Ashley's eyes were wide. Perhaps this was the most excitement she'd had in a while.

"It's very sweet. But I should get back to work."

Ashley gave a final glance. "I hope someone sends me roses at work someday."

Kim smiled. "I'm sure someone will."

Ashley moved off, and Kim studied the card again. Why wasn't Matthew's name on it? Maybe just an oversight by the florist? It was all very strange. As weird as it felt, she had to ask Matthew. If they were from him—and who else would send her flowers?—then she needed to thank him. She picked up her phone and texted him a photo of the bouquet.

These came today but there's no name on the card. From you?

His response came back quickly.

No, but I should have thought of that.

Then a moment later.

If I didn't send them, who did?

That's what she wanted to know. She thought of the balloon at her condo. Now flowers. Were they all from the same person? And if so, what was he telling her?

And also, Matthew wished he'd thought to send her flowers? Huh. This whole thing was getting stranger by the moment.

I'll see if I can find out.

Matthew replied with something she hadn't thought of.

Make sure you tell Kyle.

She called the florist on the card and explained about the mysterious delivery. But they wouldn't tell her anything, though the person she talked to had a response similar to Ashley's: Enjoy the attention of a secret admirer.

Frankly, she found it creepy. And since they weren't from Matthew, she didn't want them at her desk. She carried them to the common area where they often had food to share. That way everyone could enjoy them, and she wouldn't have to look at them.

Ashley's gaze followed Kim's actions. Now Ashley could enjoy the flowers too.

She'd text Kyle later.

Matthew tapped his pen on the conference table, rereading Kim's texts. He wished he'd thought of the flowers. The idea of someone else sending her roses turned his stomach. And it was an expensive bouquet. He'd never had a relationship serious enough to send a bouquet like that, though Kim was certainly worth it. But if he had sent them, wouldn't it have scared her off? Too much too soon?

So then who felt like they had a close enough relationship with her to send her those kind of flowers? The same person who sent the balloon? It all pointed to Nick.

Kyle hadn't gotten back to Matthew, so he didn't know if he'd talked to Nick yet or not. Or maybe Kyle had talked to Nick and didn't see fit to tell Matthew. Fair enough. As much as Matthew wanted one, Kyle didn't owe him an explanation.

None of it sat well with him, but there was zero he could do about it. He couldn't even try to see her tonight. They had a group dinner since everyone was coming in for the team-building exercise tomorrow. Not that seeing her would do anything other than reassure him, but still. Their hug Sunday wasn't enough, not by a long shot, but he wanted things to move forward at her pace, as hard as that was for him.

So not only did he have Kim's own reticence working against him, this mysterious admirer was potentially competition too. Or was he? Kim mostly seemed creeped out by it. But what if it was Nick in a misguided attempt to win her back? Was Kyle right, or was it wishful thinking on his part that Kim wouldn't get back with Nick simply because Kyle didn't like him? He didn't know Kyle well enough to make that call.

He rubbed his hands over his eyes. He needed to stop thinking about this and concentrate on work. There was nothing he could do other than hope Kim told Kyle and he took her seriously.

And pray Kim's secret admirer only had good intentions for her.

<hr>

Kim gathered her things and shut down her computer. She passed by the flowers, again wondering at the sender. The rest of the day had yielded no further clues.

Ashley smiled brightly as Kim passed her desk. "It sure was nice of you to share your roses with all of us."

"I thought we could all enjoy them. Brighten things up."

"Did you ever figure out who sent them?" Ashley leaned over her desk and lowered her voice.

"Nope. It's a mystery. See you tomorrow."

Once in her car, she thought about what Matthew said. Yeah, she should tell Kyle. It sounded silly, but he should probably know. Which meant she'd have to tell him about the balloon too. She could only hope he wouldn't go overboard on being protective.

She headed for home and called him via Bluetooth. He answered quickly, and she gave him the whole story.

He listened without saying much. But finally he said, "I know you've got an overactive imagination."

Anger pushed to the surface, but he continued, cutting off her retort. "Don't get upset. I think it's what makes you good at your work. But it could work against you here, making you see connections that aren't there and blinding you to the ones that are. What's the simplest explanation?"

She wasn't sure if she should be irritated with him or happy that he thought she was good at her work. But pushing her feelings aside—since they wouldn't get her anywhere with Kyle—she thought about his questions. "I don't know. I thought the flowers were a misdelivery, but when I called the florist they said they were for me, though they wouldn't tell me who sent them. I thought the same thing about the balloon, but it had my name on it. The only thing I can think of is Nick is somehow trying to get back with me. He's the only person I've blocked. If it was any other guy I've dated, I would think they would just call or text."

The line was quiet for a moment. "What about Matthew?" Kyle's tone had no inflection one way or another. "He was the one who found the balloon. I'm assuming you've spent more time with him lately than any other guy. He's interested in you and wants you back."

Shock raced through Kim. "No, he's not like that. I texted and asked him about the flowers, since that was my first thought, and he said no but he wished he'd thought of it. He's been nothing but concerned about me. He insisted that I tell you what happened, even though I didn't want to."

"But to be honest, you haven't known him that long. You went on a road trip together, which can give you a false sense of intimacy. You don't know him as well as you think you do."

Kyle's words were correct, but he was wrong. She just knew it, but trying to prove it to her suspicious brother was a wasted time. "Ask Collins. He was there."

"I have."

"And?"

A long sigh came through the phone. "You've dated some odd guys in the past. I don't think it's Matthew either, but I want you to keep your wits about you and not let your emotions cloud your thinking. Just because you like a guy doesn't make him a good guy."

Kyle sounded so much like their dad when he started to lecture her.

"Yes, Kyle, I know."

"Okay. I just want you safe, Kim."

"I know." He did mean well. But sometimes it felt smothering. Anyhow, she'd done her duty and told Kyle like Matthew wanted her to. Which just proved he couldn't be behind the balloon and roses.

Chapter Eight

Matthew sipped on his coffee in the to-go cup while the core members of the OC branch of DataCorp stood around at a local obstacle course early in the morning on Thursday. It was starting out with a little chill in the air, a light breeze picking up the scent of wet grass, but the sun promised a quickly warming day. He actually knew some of their names now after the meet-and-greet last night. But the appetizers had left him hungry, and he couldn't help but wish he was having dinner with Kim instead.

They'd texted and sent funny GIFs throughout the week. He was careful to keep everything friendly. He didn't want to spook her. And so far as he knew, Kyle had kept his secret. He wasn't sure if he wanted Nick to be her creepy secret admirer or not. Regardless, he planned on this weekend giving them time together.

She just didn't know that yet.

Edward Jacobsen was running today's event, decked out in some designer sweat suit with brand new tennis shoes. Matthew would have bet that the whole outfit came straight from some upscale store and had never been worn before today. He must have gotten this team-building idea out of a book, because he'd sure never broken a sweat, let alone tackled an obstacle course before.

Matthew wasn't opposed to the idea. He swung his arms around, loosening up. Anything beat another stuffy meeting. But an obstacle course run by someone without a sense of humor was going to feel a lot more like boot camp and a lot less like a team-building exercise. And he had doubts that this particular activity with this particular group of people was going to get much in the way of desired results. The team had showed up in a variety of athletic dress, from cutoff T-shirts and shorts to designer Juicy Couture workout outfits.

Edward lifted a megaphone to his lips, and Matthew groaned inwardly. "Okay, everybody. Listen up. This is going to be a team-building exercise, which means that for every obstacle on this course, you have to work as a team."

Matthew planted his hands on his hips and listened, suppressing a grin. This was like a bad high school football drill. Edward droned on, confirming what Matthew thought about getting this out of some corporate playbook. After a bunch more blathering, nearly everyone's eyes glazed over, except for Edward's, who apparently loved the sound of his own voice through a bullhorn.

Finally released, they headed for the first obstacle: a chin-up bar. Matthew and Chris Sandoval had no problem doing ten chin-ups. Austin aced it, surprising Matthew a bit. He didn't think Austin was particularly athletic. But no one else could until Matthew and Chris held their legs.

Jacqueline, their controller, couldn't even do that. Matthew doubted she'd done any more physical activity than flagging down a cab since she'd graduated from high school.

When they hoisted her up—she couldn't jump high enough to reach the bar—she couldn't keep her grip. The moment her weight hung on the bar, she yelped and let go. Matthew and Chris luckily still had a hold on her and eased her to the ground.

"What happened?" Matthew kept his voice upbeat.

"My ring. It must have pinched against the bar. Look." She showed him the red mark at the base of her finger. She nursed it for a minute while the rest stood and watched. They couldn't go on to the next station until everyone had finished.

"Just take your ring off," Chris suggested.

Jacqueline's pale face went even paler, if that were possible. "No! I couldn't do that. It hasn't been off my finger since my wedding day. That would be, well, I don't know, but something sacrilegious. I'm not doing it." She tightened her hand around her finger and stared at Edward.

"Team, figure something out." Edward used the megaphone though he was only several yards away. "Problem solve."

Matthew and Chris looked at each other. Austin stood to the side, studying the situation. The others had moved off, either talking among themselves or staring off in the distance, clearly not contributing to this team-building exercise. So it was going to be a Matthew-and-Chris building exercise. It was giving Matthew a good look at the kind of man his boss was. And he liked what he saw. Which might be the best outcome from today's events.

His first thought was to fling her over the bar like a rag doll. The image of her flopped over up there tugged up the corners of his mouth. He didn't think that would go over too well.

Chris stood under the bar and looked up. "Think we can lift her high enough so she doesn't have to put any weight on her hands?"

Matthew looked between Jacqueline and the bar. "Might be too high, but we can try. Austin, come give us a hand."

Austin moved next to them and nodded. "Between the three of us, we've got enough strength to do this."

They manhandled Jacqueline high enough where she was able to place her hands on the bar and bend her elbows without putting any actual weight on her hands.

Then for some reason, she flung up her arms and twisted around, screaming. "A bug!"

She threw the men off balance. Matthew took a step back to regain his footing. Chris lunged the opposite way, and Austin bounced off the support pole. And Jacqueline, panicking, decided to leap for Matthew, knocking him further off kilter.

He was toppling over, scrambling for purchase. But Jacqueline was wrapped around him like an octopus. He managed to get one arm free moments before they hit the ground.

And he heard his wrist pop loudly.

Another obstacle, God?

Kim dropped a takeout bag on her counter, along with several bags of groceries. Living on the second floor meant she had gotten good at getting as many things in one trip as possible. Considering the prep she was doing tonight for Heather's bachelorette weekend tomorrow, takeout had been the best dinner idea.

Her condo looked more like she was going on a vacation than its usual designer vibe. Clothes from the wash waiting to be packed, an ice chest, and bags of groceries dotted the area. Despite the chaos, she was looking forward to spending the weekend with these girls, even though most of this should have been Kellie's responsibility. But if it meant Heather had a good time and Jessica was able to feel like she belonged, then it would be a win in Kim's book.

She munched on a burger while she sorted through her groceries. Her phone buzzed, and her heart rate notched up. A glance told her it was a text from Jessica. She deflated a bit then scolded herself for anticipating a text from Matthew. *Just friends, remember?*

Have to work until 5 tmrw so I'll be late. Sry.

She hoped Jessica wouldn't use that as an excuse not to show up. Kim had originally planned on taking Jessica with her. She hated for her to drive alone; it gave her an excuse to back out.

Wait. Allie was driving up by herself because she was afraid she might have to work late.

Kim shot her a quick text.

How late are you working tomorrow? Can you pick up Jessica? She's working til 5.

Sure. It'll be good to have the company. I'll text her now.

Excellent. One problem solved. Now if only the rest of the weekend would go as smoothly.

She hadn't heard from Matthew today. Not that she really expected to. But she did wonder how his team-building event went and what they did. They had probably all gone to dinner as well. She shouldn't expect to hear from him until next week.

Her gaze strayed to her phone all evening as she prepped the food for the weekend. A couple of times she picked it up to text him, and then put it back down. No, they were only friends. She didn't want to encourage him. He'd clearly gotten her message.

But for some reason, that thought wasn't comforting.

Chapter Nine

It was Friday. Kim mentally reviewed her checklist as she sat at her workstation. All the food had been prepped last night. She'd leave work at lunch to throw together a carry-on and get everything in her car. Then she could arrive at the cabin before everyone else and get it all set up. Allie would bring Jessica. Kellie would bring the other girls. Everything was arranged.

Back to work. She'd gotten the photos from Lynnae. Zander Jakes turned things around fast and these were just proofs—but she needed to check with Monique on the final design she was sewing up. She slipped off her chair to head to the workroom when Henry came by.

"Just to let you know, Juan is holding a roundtable tonight for all of us who are competing in Design Review. He'll give us feedback on our ideas while we still have time to make changes." His gaze flicked up and down her. "You should come."

"Hmm. Thanks for letting me know."

He lifted one shoulder and spun on his heel.

Dang. She'd love to get Juan's feedback on her ideas. Of course if Henry was going to be there, she wasn't too hot on letting him see them. Plus, she hadn't decided which of her

Southwest designs to include. Zander Jakes had given her some gorgeous photos to choose from, but she had to go with what best showcased her abilities and her potential.

The roundtable was a moot point. She couldn't make it. She had to leave at lunch. This weekend was important to Heather. And Kim. She needed to pull it off without a hitch. Design Review was next week's problem.

She hesitated. Should she say something to Juan? She wouldn't want him to think she didn't take Design Review seriously enough to not show up. On the other hand, over explaining seemed unprofessional, like she wasn't confident in her designs. Ugh, what to do?

It was a good thing Heather was already like a sister to her or Kim would have bailed and let Heather's real little sister, Kellie, run the weekend. She plopped back in her chair and picked up a pencil, doodling around on her sketchpad as if the solution would come forth from the scribbles.

It was no use. She dropped the pencil and stood. Between Henry's words—which had his desired effect of rattling her—and worrying over all the last-minute things that needed to be done for this weekend, her mind was shot. She headed to the workroom.

Monique smiled when she saw her. "Come see what I've done." She led Kim to a dress form where one of her designs was draped. "What do you think?"

There was something magical about seeing her creations come to life, especially when someone else sewed them. This one was only basted, but the final form was evident.

She ran her hands down the bodice, checking for the lay of the fabric and the fit. She and Monique discussed a few options. She trusted Monique's opinion and experience and nearly always took her suggestions. With a plan in place for the alterations, Monique would sew the final design, and Kim would see it Monday when she returned.

At her workstation, she pulled open the email with the

photos Lynnae had sent her. She flicked through them, chills of excitement racing up her arms. There was just something about seeing her work come to life on models. Zander Jakes had found a great location, a small restaurant with a Southwest flair in its arched porticos, stuccoed walls, and handcrafted tiles. Her clothing looked made for the space.

"Ooh, are those Zander Jakes photos?"

Kim spun around. Ashley was peering over her shoulder.

"Yes, you know his work?"

"Of course. Doesn't everybody? He's one of the best in the fashion industry. How did you get him to shoot your designs?"

"A friend of mine owns a boutique. These are for her show next month."

Ashley frowned. "So they're not yours?"

"Oh, they're mine. She often shows my designs, and I take custom orders for her clients."

"Wow." Ashley stepped back, chewing on her lip, eyes fixed on the screen. "So these aren't for your Design Review portfolio?"

"Not all of them. I haven't completely decided."

"Huh." Her fingers twisted around themselves.

What had her upset? "Was there something you wanted my help with?"

Ashley dragged her gaze from the monitor. "Um, oh. You had said you were leaving at lunch. I just came to see if you needed anything from me while you were gone."

Kim's gaze darted to the time on her computer. She couldn't believe how much time had passed. It was later than she had thought. She shut down her computer.

"I don't think so, but it's sweet of you to offer. I've got to run. Have a great weekend." She grabbed her sketchbook and purse, and making sure everything was shut off, she headed out.

This weekend had better be worth it.

Kim lugged her carry-on and purse, with her pillow tucked under her arm, down the stairs from her condo to her car. She surveyed the area around her condo parking lot, even though this was her fourth trip. If anyone was lurking, surely they'd have shown themselves by now. But she hadn't seen the black Honda or received any more secret admirer gifts. They were probably tired of the game and had given up.

She clicked the key fob and unlocked the car. The ice chest and bags of food were already stashed inside. She tossed her baggage next to that and pulled up her checklist on her phone.

This was going to be the best bachelorette weekend. She'd rented a beautiful cabin in Holcomb Springs in the San Bernardino Mountains near the day spa, thanks to Collins's connections up there. And they'd even do a little kayaking on the lake and maybe a hike, an easy trail through the forest. It was the perfect, relaxing getaway two weeks before Heather's wedding to Kyle.

Kim wanted everything to be perfect for her. Going early meant she could get everything arranged so when Kellie brought the other girls up, it would all be ready to go.

This needed to be the perfect weekend to prove to Kyle and Dad that she could plan an event and pull it off, even while juggling the demands of work. Even if it was really Kellie's responsibility. They still thought of her as a flaky, head-in-the-clouds artist who couldn't really be relied on. Kyle had even set aside the rent she paid him when she lived with him so she'd have a down payment for her condo. He didn't trust her to save up.

But Heather trusted her. More than she trusted her own sister. And Kim would do everything in her power to ensure that trust was justified.

She scrolled through her phone to her list for this weekend, her mind occasionally wandering to Juan's roundtable. Had she made the right choice? Why was she torturing herself? It was too late to do anything about it now.

The food was in her car. Her stuff was in there too. She'd made dinner reservations and confirmed the cabin rental. Everything was set to go. She gave a little shimmy. She'd actually pulled this thing off. Heather would have a great weekend. And she'd forget about Design Review for a few days. She'd come back to the finished design from Monique, finalize her portfolio choices, and be done early.

She headed upstairs to do a final check and lock up her condo when her phone rang. Heather. Her heart clenched a bit, hoping nothing was wrong.

"What's up?"

"I totally forgot to get the ribbon swatches back to the florist. Kellie was going to run by and grab them from you before she came to my loft last night, but she forgot. We're down in Fashion Island, so there's no way we'll make it to your place and then the florist's because she closes early on Fridays. You still have them, don't you?"

Kim rummaged through the box where she kept all the wedding items. "Yep, they're right here. I was just getting ready to head out, so I'll swing by the florist's before I head up the mountain. I'll see you guys tonight."

"Thank you. You're the best!"

As long as Heather kept thinking that. Kim checked the time. It would be close, but she'd still have time to get everything set up before the others got there. A flare of irritation sparked, but she tamped it back down.

Kellie was supposed to be helping Kim throw the bachelorette getaway weekend. But Kellie hadn't been much help. And after the shower fiasco, Kim wasn't sure she could trust her with anything. At least not anything important.

Originally, Kellie had planned to go up early with Kim to set things up. But then she volunteered to drive the rest of the girls up in the SUV she rented: herself, Heather, Melissa, and Sarah.

While Heather's other sister, Aimee, had managed to make it to the shower, the idea of a car ride up mountain roads and the high altitude at eight-months pregnant didn't sound like a fun time to her. So she'd passed.

Kim made sure she had the correct ribbon samples then headed out the door, locking it behind her, and heading downstairs to her car. One final look at her list and she was good to go.

She had this.

Matthew sat on the leather couch in his sister Allie's office with Austin, a splint around his left wrist. After a trip to urgent care yesterday for the sprain, he and Austin had grabbed lunch and headed back to their hotel. The team-building exercise had been a bust, but luckily he'd been the only one hurt, if you didn't count Jacqueline's pinched finger. And it wasn't too bad as long as he remembered not to use it, took ibuprofen, and kept ice on it. At least today he had no work obligations and was free to find a place to live and get ready for the weekend.

After giving Allie the whole story, he and Austin went to work on telling her what they were looking for and which of the properties she had already sent them would be good fits. Today they were going to narrow down which ones they wanted to see next week. Apparently, he and Austin weren't always on the same page, so she wanted them both in the same room when they made the final decisions.

He was confident Allie would find them the perfect place. She was helping all of DataCorp's relocating employees. It was fun to watch his sister work. And they should have time to look at places next week, as long as Edward didn't try to reschedule the team-building exercise.

Allie looked at her Apple Watch. "If you were a normal DataCorp employee, I would say take all the time you need. But since you're my little brother I'm going to tell you to hurry it up.

I've got several more things to do before I can leave to get ready for the girls' weekend."

Yeah, that was the other part of his plan. He didn't think the sprained wrist would slow him down too much. He gave her his aw-shucks grin so she wouldn't be mad at him. "About that. Um, there's a good chance we'll see you up there."

"What?"

"Well, when I heard what you were planning, it sounded like a great idea. I told Scott that Kyle could use a guys' weekend away since Heather wouldn't be home. And I might have grabbed the cabin next to yours."

"Matthew! That defeats the purpose of a getaway."

"We probably won't even cross paths." Okay, so now he was venturing into lying territory. He didn't want to do that. "Well, wouldn't it be fun to do a hike together? Or have dinner?"

Matthew nudged Austin's shoulder. "So those super soakers and water balloons I got should make for an epic guys-versus-girls battle. It's been so hot lately everyone will enjoy a way to cool off. I'm thinking tomorrow afternoon. What do you think, Allie?" They'd had massive water fights as kids, involving strategy and ambushes. They were some of his favorite memories, executing a plan and having fun together. He'd want Kim on his team, so maybe not guys versus girls. The idea of planning something fun with her held a lot of appeal for him.

Allie scowled and snapped her laptop shut. "This is how you're trying to get Kim back?" She shook her head. "This is a bad idea. What if you just make her mad? This weekend is so important to her. And she's got Design Review coming up at work that's stressing her out. Don't add to her problems."

"What if I don't?" He sat forward on the couch, arms draped across his knees. "Allie, I don't have anything to lose here. If I spend time with her, I can show her that I can be what she needs. I'm so far in the friend zone that I have to do something drastic. I've been giving her the space she wants. Not hard to do, the way this job is going. But I may have competition." He told her about the balloons and flowers. "This is my chance to spend some time with her."

Allie sat back. "Just make sure everything you're doing is lightening her load, not adding to it. And I think you'd better leave the weekend plans to Kim if you want to stay on her good side."

"That was my intent." And he prayed Kim would see it that way. And that his sprained wrist wouldn't add to the problems.

"Did you two finally agree on places you want to see next week?"

Matthew scanned the sales flyers she had laid out on the table in front of them and pointed to two of them. "What do you think, Austin?"

He slowly nodded. "Let's add this one as well. I like its proximity to work. I could conceivably ride my bike there."

"Good enough. Set 'em up, sis. See you up the hill in a few. Oh, and do you know what time she was leaving to head up the mountain?"

Allie rolled her eyes. "She was trying to leave by two."

"Then we'd better get going." He pushed to his feet, and Austin joined him.

She was shaking her head and laughing—a common response from his sisters—when he pulled her office door closed behind them and headed down the tiled hall. With a wave to the older lady who was the receptionist, Matthew strode into the sunshine. It fit his mood perfectly.

They climbed in the rental, and Austin glanced over. "I don't know if I should go, man. I'm not the outgoing, life-of-the-party type like you are. Maybe I should just stay back. I've got plenty to keep me busy at the hotel."

Matthew was shaking his head before Austin even finished. "Nope. You're going. These people are going to be your friends. What better way to get to know them?"

Austin shrugged. Matthew didn't think he was convinced, but he didn't argue and that was good enough for him. He loved it when a plan came together. And this was working out even better than he thought.

Kim's phone buzzed as she reached the bottom of the stairs. A weather alert. Red-flag warnings started tonight, along with a notice about the power companies potentially shutting off power in fire-prone areas. Great. Just what they needed. A power outage. She trudged back upstairs to grab flashlights and candles. Just in case. And double checked she had her inhaler. With the winds picking up, she occasionally had a flare-up of her mild asthma.

Back downstairs, she added the new items to her bags.

A minivan entered the parking lot. With Matthew grinning at her from behind the wheel.

What was this all about? Why was he here?

He hopped out. "Hey, your ride has arrived." He gestured to the minivan.

"Why are you here?"

"We're giving you a ride. They gave me this at the car rental place when I turned the other car in—long story about that. I thought it was a mistake at the time, but now it's perfect. Austin and I will get everything loaded from your car into the minivan, and we'll be on our way." He reached inside and produced a double-shot iced caramel macchiato with whipped cream and handed it to her. "Your favorite, right?"

Right. She took the drink and sipped off some of the whipped cream. Then she spotted the splint on his left wrist. "What happened to your arm?" She heard the squeak in her voice and hoped he didn't.

He turned a grin on her that could make the cover of GQ. "I think they call it a training accident. But don't worry, it's not going to slow me down."

"A what?" He was saying words, but they weren't making sense to her.

Matthew grinned. He still hadn't answered her question.

Austin appeared around the van.

"Hi, Austin." She gave a small wave.

He lifted his chin. "Hey."

Matthew slid open the minivan door and then opened her car door. He and Austin started moving things over. He didn't seem to be letting the wrist injury slow him down much, though Austin did grab the ice chest.

She took another sip. The icy sweet caffeine helped her mood. "So you're just going to drive me up to the mountains out of the kindness of your heart? It's four hours there and back." She grabbed her backpack and headed around the minivan. A glance in the window showed there were already duffle bags, an ice chest, and a bag with big squirt guns sticking out. Classic Matthew. Did Austin know what he was getting into with Matthew as a roommate? She shook her head. "Are you going somewhere this weekend?"

Matthew loaded the last of her stuff in the minivan and closed the door to her car. He was awfully quiet.

He still hadn't answered her question. She stared at him.

A sheepish grin crossed his face. A sure sign she wasn't going to like what he had to say. "Uh, Austin and I are headed up to the mountains for the weekend too."

Oh. OH! Of all the— She couldn't even find the words. "You can't crash our bachelorette weekend. If this is some misguided attempt to get me back, you are sorely mistaken. I don't care if you are injured."

He held his hand out. "It's not. I mean, the guys liked the idea of a weekend trip in the mountains."

"You've got to be kidding me." She wanted to chuck her drink at him, but decided it wasn't worth wasting it. She took a long, slurpy sip, considering her next move. Having the two guys to haul everything into the cabin wasn't the worst idea. And she didn't mind not driving the mountain roads or spending the money on gas. But they'd better not mess up her plans.

She yanked open the door and climbed in. She was going to make the most of it. "We've got a stop to make before we head up the mountains, so get a move on."

He grinned as he climbed in and shut the door behind him.

Austin had grabbed one of the captain's chairs in the second row, and Air Pods filled his ears.

Just as well. Because she had some words for Matthew.

Chapter Ten

Matthew glanced over at Kim as they headed to the florist's. Her beauty was only enhanced by her creativity. Her clothes looked as if they were made for her, with the touches that were pure Kim. She was mad, but he just needed to get back on her good side. She'd see how great his plan was.

She tilted her head toward his arm. "Now, how did that really happen?"

"Ah, you don't believe the training accident?"

She shook her head. "Not in white collar jobs. Unless it's a wicked paper cut."

"It was that team-building exercise. Except Edward was going out of some book, doing it on a local fitness course. Needless to say, it didn't work out too well. Chris Sandoval, my boss, and Austin and I basically had to get everyone through, particularly the controller, who is the most unathletic person ever. We were lifting her up on the chin-up bar when she starts flailing, knocks all of us off balance, and I fall, spraining my wrist. She survived without a scratch. I, however, was the company's first training casualty."

Kim broke out in giggles. "I'm sorry. It must be painful. But oh what a story."

He laughed with her, just relieved that she'd gotten over being mad at him. "You look great. Is that one of your designs that came out of our Great American Road Trip?"

She gave him the side eye, but a smile crept around the corners of her mouth. She smoothed down the full skirt. The sleeveless top accentuated her tanned arms, and there was a tie and some fancy embroidery around the neckline.

She touched the silver-and-turquoise necklace. "Yes, it is. One of a kind. I like to sew up my designs to make sure they work with the real world. I sent most of the ones I had made up over to my friend who owns a boutique. But I kept this one to wear. The jewelry is custom made by one of my classmates from the Fashion Institute of Design and Merchandising." She lifted up a leather-sandal-clad foot with pink toenail polish. "I didn't make the shoes." She grinned.

He laughed. Okay, he'd gotten her to smile. Talking about her work always helped. And it wasn't a gimmick. He liked hearing about her creativity, even if he didn't understand a thing about women's clothes.

Her smile faded. "Matthew, don't ruin this weekend for me, okay? I've worked really hard to give Heather a great weekend away leading up to a great wedding." She blinked rapidly. "I just can't have this screwed up."

He reached over and touched her arm. "I won't. I promise. If Heather wants us to stay out of the way, we will." He gave her a quick grin. "But if she wants a massive water fight, we can accommodate."

Kim laughed and looked out the window.

Yes! He'd made her laugh again. That was something, right? He had the whole weekend to win her over. And he would. Because the alternative didn't bear thinking about. She wouldn't want to hear how lonely he'd been for her voice the past two months, how empty life had been without her. How he refreshed his Instagram feed all the time to see if she'd posted anything new. Spending time with her last weekend had just whet his appetite for her. Not seeing her this whole week had made her absence all the sharper. She would lose all respect for him if she knew what a sap he was.

He pulled up in front of the florist's, and she ran in and back out in a flash. They hit the freeway early enough to avoid the heading-out-of-town Friday traffic. Plus, with three of them, they could use the carpool lane.

He settled back against the driver's seat. "So who all is coming?"

"Heather and her sister Kellie, Sarah and Melissa, me and Allie. Oh and Jessica, Scott's sister. I think you met everyone but Kellie Sunday at lunch."

He raised his eyebrows. "Speaking of Scott, he's coming."

Kim swiveled in her seat. "Really? How did you work that? Melissa will be thrilled. He hasn't been able to come down at all since the movie night after the road trip."

"I know." He winked. "He was saving his leave for this weekend. I convinced him that he had to support Kyle's bachelor weekend."

She nodded but chewed her lip. His heart dropped for a moment. He knew what she was thinking. Melissa would want to be with Scott, which meant the girls and the guys would do things together. Which was what he had counted on.

What he hadn't counted on was how distressed it would make Kim to have her plans hijacked. He didn't want to upset her, he just wanted to spend time with her. For once, he wondered if his plans had gone too far.

"So who else?" Her voice was tight. He could see the wheels spinning in her head.

"Kyle, Scott, Joe, Collins, me, and Austin." He wasn't sure where she was going with this.

"You should have brought along another guy so we'd have even numbers."

"I didn't know about Jessica."

"Scott didn't mention it to you when you guys cooked up this scheme to surprise Melissa? Because he's the one who asked me to include her."

He shrugged. "Probably didn't think it would matter to me." He tried to read her expression while still keeping his eyes on Southern California traffic.

"No, he probably didn't." She turned and looked out the window, away from him. "How long have you been planning this?"

She wasn't going to like his answer. "About as long as you have."

Somehow he'd messed this up. And he wasn't quite sure how it got sideways. He unlocked his phone and handed it to her. "I have our playlist on here from the road trip. Want to sync it to the minivan?"

She met his gaze for a second, their hands brushing as she took the phone from him. Her touch made him melt like butter in a hot skillet as always.

He could only hope he had the same effect on her.

KIM'S EYES TOOK IN THE CABIN AS THEY PULLED UP TO IT. It looked even better than the pictures with a big wrap-around deck and lots of windows. She hopped out of the minivan and punched in the code the owner had given her for the front door. She swung it open and looked around. The big stone fireplace, beam-vaulted ceilings, and chef's kitchen were perfect. This was going to work out, Matthew's shenanigans not withstanding.

Austin came in carrying an ice chest. "Where do you want this?"

"In the kitchen."

The one good thing about having guys around was that she wouldn't have to tote that heavy ice chest again. And she had to admit it was enjoyable watching Matthew work. Only Matthew could hijack her plans and make her laugh at the same time.

It was impossible to stay angry with him. She'd spent the trip up the mountain thinking of how to alter her plans to accommodate the guys. She didn't think they'd want to join the girls for a spa trip tomorrow morning, but other than that, everything else was doable. Maybe Heather would enjoy this even more.

But even if they had a great weekend, she was not going to let him take her heart again. There was no way they would ever work out. It was great to have a friend who was funny and made you laugh. But a boyfriend needed to be able to handle her serious side. And he just couldn't. She had to remind herself of that.

She began putting away the groceries she bought. It was sweet, though, that he'd noticed her outfit. He was right that it had been inspired by the desert of their road trip. She liked how it all came together, and it pleased her that he'd noticed. No one else had. No one but Allie had even asked about how the trip had influenced her designs.

But Matthew had asked about it in his weekly texts. If she was going by word count alone, he was the most supportive person in her life of her work. If only he was one of the Design Review judges.

"Where do you want your luggage?" Austin interrupted her musing.

She closed the refrigerator and headed toward the hall. "Down here." Heather and Kellie would share the master with the attached bathroom. She, Sarah, and Jessica would share a room, and Allie and Melissa would have the other room with the Jack-and-Jill bathroom between them.

She pulled her hang-up clothes out of her carry-on and put them in the closet. Then she walked into the Jack-and-Jill bathroom. Her macchiato was sitting on her bladder. She flushed the toilet and moved to the sink to wash her hands. The toilet didn't sound right. She lifted the lid. Water swirled and grew higher instead of going down. "Oh no!" Luckily it stopped just below the rim. But it didn't go down. Perfect, just perfect.

She washed her hands and grabbed her phone, calling the owners. Pacing out to the living room, she saw Matthew and Austin standing around. They were probably waiting on her before they left. She held up a finger and headed out to the porch. The scent of pine on the breeze and the warm sun on her face relaxed her for a moment. The owners were nice and said they'd call a plumber and get back to her. She hung up. This weekend was not getting off to a great start. She didn't want to have a plumber here when Heather arrived. The only other bathroom was in the master suite. That wasn't going to work at all.

With a sigh, she headed back inside.

Matthew studied her with raised eyebrows. "Something wrong?"

"Just waiting for a call back. Are you guys heading out?"

"Unless you need something else. The other guys aren't getting up here until this evening. We've got plenty of time." He took a step toward her. "What's wrong?"

She blew out a breath. "The toilet's clogged. The owners are going to send a plumber out—" Her phone rang, and she answered it. But they couldn't get a plumber out on a Friday night. They would be happy to give her tonight free. Thanking them, she hung up and tossed her phone on the couch and buried her face in her hands. Heather's special weekend was not getting off to a good start.

A gentle touch landed on her shoulder. Matthew's scent, like spice and leather, wafted around her. She wanted nothing more than to lean back into his strong chest.

But no, she couldn't.

"What's wrong? Talk to me, Kim."

She turned and took a step back. "Oh, nothing. They can't get a plumber up here until tomorrow. The only working bathroom is in the master, so that means if anyone wants to use the facilities, they'll have to tromp through Heather and Kellie's room. I'm sure they'll love that. Seven girls and one working bathroom? It's not going to be a relaxing weekend."

Matthew thought for a minute. "Switch cabins with us. We're guys. We don't care about the bathroom."

She appreciated the thought, but there were so many problems. "How are the girls going to know where we are? I guess I could update them with the new address. But is yours one of those 'rustic'"—she made air quotes—"cabins that only guys could appreciate?"

He crooked his finger at her. "I'll show you, and you can decide for yourself."

That was fair. She started out the front door, snagging her purse off the counter, and waited for them to exit so she could lock up.

Matthew didn't head for the minivan.

"Where are you going?"

He grinned. "Our cabin is next door."

She wanted to fume. But he was bailing her out, so she bit her tongue. "How did you know where we were staying?"

"I sweet-talked Allie into giving me the info."

She couldn't even be exasperated with him. On the other side of a copse of trees stood a cabin identical to theirs.

He punched in the code, and they went inside. Same layout. Slightly different decor. She checked the bedrooms. This would work. She walked out on the deck. From one edge she could see the deck of her cabin.

Matthew couldn't have planned this more perfectly. She could either be in his debt or deal with the weird bathroom situation. It was no contest.

But this was not the weekend she had planned. Not by a long shot.

And she knew the longer she was around that heart-breaking smile of his, the bigger chance she had of getting exactly that. Her heart broken again.

Matthew and Austin lugged everything over to the new cabin while Kim updated the owners on the switch. Since they owned both cabins, they were more than happy to sign off on the solution. He figured they would be.

He wasn't thrilled that this weekend was getting off to a rocky start for Kim, but he had to admit the set up was perfect. He couldn't have asked for a better way to help her. He knew she was wary and that he'd have to do some convincing.

More importantly, and something he'd spent a lot of time thinking about, was that if his plan worked to get her back, things would have to be different between them. He'd messed up a couple of months ago, and the distance between them hadn't made it easy for him to repair the damage. But he'd have to support her full range of emotions, not just the happy ones. Something he wished he'd done after she'd been nearly kidnapped.

And he'd have to be vulnerable himself. Over the past two months he realized beyond having fun with her, there was something more there, something worth digging deep for and pursuing. Even if it made him uncomfortable. So now it was do or die time. Was he going to be all in with Kim, no matter what it cost?

Yes, yes he was.

Austin was handing Kim items from the ice chest as she stored them in the fridge. She laughed at something he said.

Huh. Austin didn't strike him as a particularly funny guy. He was usually pretty serious, either about his programming or his video games. It never occurred to him that Austin could be interested in Kim.

Or Kim in Austin. Was there more competition than her secret admirer?

Matthew made a final trip to the other cabin. Austin had settled in to help Kim unload things. What was that all about?

At least he'd grabbed the ice chest. That was the one thing Matthew couldn't carry with his sprained wrist.

Kim was setting out appetizers and drinks on the kitchen counter. Austin was bringing her things she requested. In all the time Matthew had thought about getting Kim back, it had never occurred to him that other men would be interested in her. Which was dumb. Of course other men would be. Maybe they already were. He shot Austin a narrowed look and thought about the balloon-and-roses-delivering secret admirer. Assuming they were from the same person. Kyle hadn't said if he'd talked to Nick. And Matthew doubted he'd bring it up this weekend. But what if it was someone else? Had she gotten any more gifts and hadn't told him?

If he didn't seal the deal, then he could lose her. And that was a future he couldn't bear thinking about.

"Kim, that's the last of it. Anything else you need?" He tried to swipe a baby carrot off the tray, but she smacked his hand.

"Did you happen to bring any flashlights or candles? I got a notice about possible power interruptions due to the wind and fire danger. I have a few."

He shook his head. "No, I didn't even think about it. Though Kyle and Collins probably have flashlights. We all have our phones."

"You won't be able to recharge them, though."

This time he did get a baby carrot and popped it in his mouth. "We'll just come join you and your candlelight." He grinned.

She rolled her eyes. "The girls will be here any minute." Her face softened. "Thanks for all your help, Matthew." She turned to Austin. "And yours."

Was it his imagination or was her smile a bit brighter when she aimed it at Austin?

Her phone buzzed, and she picked it up. Her face paled a bit, and her hand shook before she nearly dropped the phone to the counter.

Not more bad news. She'd had a full plate of it today. "What's wrong? Are they shutting the power off now?"

She shook her head. "Just someone I don't need to talk to."

But her reaction was too big for that. "Is someone bothering you?" Was it Nick again? Or someone else?

"It's fine." She glanced away and fiddled with the appetizers.

He could tell this wasn't where she wanted to go with this conversation. It wasn't really his business; he half expected her to tell him to butt out. But if something was bothering her—or someone—he wanted to help. And if it was Nick, he wanted to know.

"Nick? Or your secret admirer?"

She shrugged then lifted her chin, clearly uncomfortable with the turn of events. "Like before, I had blocked him. It looks like he's texting me from another number."

She started to turn away, but Matthew took a step around the counter. He took another and was right in front of her. She had to tilt her head up to look at him.

"Any more presents?"

She shook her head, apparently giving into the turn of the conversation for the moment.

"Any guy with a legitimate interest in you would reveal himself at some point, not hide behind anonymous texts and presents. And you've made your intentions clear. I know you can do that." He grinned, trying to lighten the moment. He hated seeing Kim shaken. It reminded him too much of last March and Willie Dumas. "Maybe you should talk to Kyle."

"Not this weekend. This guy will probably lose interest and go away after a while. I can't imagine that he wouldn't."

He didn't say *liar, liar, pants on fire,* but he sure thought it. And as hard as his brain worked, he couldn't come up with a single thing to say.

He didn't have to. Kim smiled. "Thanks for all your help, guys." Her glance included Austin. "I couldn't have done it without both of you. Now get out of here." She laughed.

"Yes, ma'am. One more thing. How do you want us to surprise Melissa with Scott?"

She thought for a moment. "Do you want to send him over here like he needed to borrow something? I can send Melissa to the door."

"I like it. Then the rest of us can wander over and see if you all want to go to dinner together. What did you have planned?"

"We're not going to be able to pry Scott and Melissa apart, so plan on dinner. There's an Italian place in town, Belle Sorgenti, that has great reviews. Collins recommended it. I'll call them and change our reservation to thirteen people. I'd better do that right now." She picked up her phone, and he took that as a sign to leave.

But he didn't miss that her hand still shook a bit.

And that Austin glanced over his shoulder at her as they headed out the door.

Chapter Eleven

Kim didn't have time to dwell on Nick's text. At least she assumed it was Nick. She deleted it and scanned the room. Drinks and snacks were out. Little gift bags for each of the girls sat on their pillows filled with tiny bottles of hand lotion, their own reusable drink cup with straw, and small boxes of Godiva truffles. Oh, and ear plugs. Just in case.

Another text caused her to jump again. This was ridiculous. She couldn't spend the whole weekend startling whenever her phone buzzed. It was Allie. She and Jessica were on their way up.

The front door opened. "We're here!" Kellie's voice echoed through the vaulted living room with other female voices oohing and aahing behind her.

Kim headed down the hallway to greet Kellie, Heather, Melissa, and Sarah. "Hey, girls. Isn't this place great?" She gave hugs to each of them. "Heather, you and Kellie are in the master suite straight at the end of the hall. Melissa, you and Allie are in the second room on the left. Sarah, you and Jessica and me are in the bunk room, the first room on the left. I'll let you all get your things in your rooms, and then you can help yourself to appetizers and drinks in the kitchen. Allie and Jessica should get here just in time for dinner."

While the girls got settled, Kim checked out the cabin next door through the window. Were the guys here yet? It didn't look like it. Matthew's minivan was still the only one in the driveway.

Kellie met Kim in the kitchen and made a plate of appetizers and grabbed a sparkling water. "This place is really cute."

"Allie's boyfriend, Collins, worked up here for a bit earlier this year, and he recommended it."

Kellie wandered out to the back deck. "This is perfect. Look, there's even a fire pit. Did you bring supplies to make s'mores with?"

Pine and rich earth scented the air as Kim followed her. "No, but we can get those in town if everyone wants."

The other girls came out and mingled around the kitchen, great room, and deck. Everyone seemed pleased with the choice, especially Heather. And her vote was the one that counted. Kim snapped pictures of the cabin and the girls interacting.

When Kim thought she could get away with it, she looked out the front windows to the other cabin. Finally, she saw Collins's truck parked over there. She glanced over at Melissa. This was going to be fun. Even though it messed up her plans, she was happy for Melissa and thrilled that she was able to be in on the surprise. Heather would be happy for Melissa, too, and Kim didn't think she'd be upset by the change in plans.

A knock sounded at the door. Kim sought Melissa's gaze. "Hey, Melissa, could you get the door?" She casually slipped her phone out.

Melissa frowned because three other girls were closer, but she rose from the deep leather couch and opened the door.

She stilled, then shrieked, "Scott!" Her arms flew around him. "What are you doing here?"

He kissed her then glanced around the room with a look that said he wished they were alone so he could kiss her properly.

Would anyone ever feel that way about her? Matthew's face —and their kisses—flashed through her mind. She shoved the memories away as she captured everything with her phone camera.

"I came down to surprise you."

She tugged him inside then glanced out the door. Her eyes went wide. "You all are here?"

Joe, Collins, Kyle, Matthew, and Austin followed Scott inside.

Kim turned to watch Heather's reaction.

Heather laughed. "How long have you all been planning this?"

Ha! Kim wanted to see how Matthew got out of explaining this.

Matthew moved between Scott and Kyle and put a hand on each of their shoulders. Apparently the wrist splint wasn't slowing him down. "When I heard about your girls' weekend, I convinced these two that a guys' weekend would be a great idea. Scott needed to help Kyle say goodbye to his bachelor days. And I figured Melissa might appreciate the surprise."

She hadn't left Scott's side, her fingers entwined with his.

"That was thoughtful of you, Matthew." Heather moved to hug Kyle and give him a kiss. Then she frowned. "Matthew, what happened to your hand?"

"Training accident."

Kim shook her head.

He pointed to Scott. "Isn't that what you guys in the military say when you don't want to say what really happened?"

"I can neither confirm nor deny that," Scott said. "So what really happened?"

Matthew gave a hilarious retelling of their team-building exercise. Austin shook his head a few times but in general supported Matthew's version of the events.

Heather patted him on the shoulder. "We're glad you're okay.

You guys want to come to dinner with us? We're just waiting on Allie and Jessica."

Kim exchanged a glance with Matthew. He grinned at her. He'd won, and he knew it.

Kellie jumped in. "I think that's a great idea. Kim, did you make us a reservation at that Italian place? Do you think you can change it?"

"Already done." She smiled.

Kellie frowned. "You were in on this?"

"I just found out on the way up here. I rode with Matthew and Austin."

"Well, I haven't met all the guys yet," Kellie piped up. "I know Kyle, Collins, and Joe, but I haven't met Scott before or Matthew or Austin. I'm Kellie McAlistair, Heather's younger sister."

Melissa looked up at Scott. "How long are you here?"

"We're spending the weekend up here. Thought we'd do some kayaking and hiking, maybe some fishing."

She bit her lip, a sign Kim had learned meant she was thinking. "Where are you staying?"

Scott grinned. "Right next door."

Melissa raised her eyebrows. "Really? That's convenient."

"Thank Matthew for pulling it off."

Kim crossed her arms. So now Matthew was getting the praise for horning in on her weekend plans. Nice. But she wouldn't say anything. It was Heather's weekend. Well, Heather's and Kyle's. And Melissa's and Scott's, too, apparently.

"That's really sweet," said Kellie.

Kim gestured toward the kitchen. "Help yourself to snacks and drinks." She was certain Matthew hadn't done anything like that for the guys.

Everyone dispersed except Kellie who sidled up to Kim. "Did you get the ribbon samples back to the florist? I'm sorry I forgot. I was having such a good time with Heather. I just don't get to see her enough."

"Yes. Matthew took me by there before we came up the hill. Everything's all set. I have our spa appointments booked for tomorrow as well. Then we have the afternoon free to do whatever we'd like."

"I'm sure the girls will want to hang out with the guys."

"We'll see how it shakes out. This is supposed to be a girls' weekend away."

Kellie's gaze drifted over to where Matthew stood talking to Austin and Joe. "It might be even more fun with the guys."

Kim's stomach twisted. Was Kellie attracted to Matthew? Well, why wouldn't she be? He was tall, good looking, and charming as all get out. The thought did not sit well with her. She retreated to the kitchen, making sure the food trays stayed full and the drinks were cold. She hadn't counted on the guys being here when she bought groceries, so they were running through most of her supplies faster than she had planned.

Irritation at Matthew threaded through her. He got all the praise for thinking of bringing Scott, but he didn't do any of the other planning, figuring it would work out. It did because she'd planned. She'd need to make another trip to the grocery store. Maybe Allie could take her either tonight after dinner or tomorrow morning.

And then there was Kellie, who was currently hanging on Matthew's every word. She had done very little to help plan this weekend or any of the wedding details, for that matter. Still, Kim didn't want to rock the boat. And Kellie likely knew her sister better. Heather probably would want to spend time with the guys. It was important that Heather was happy, even if it meant Kim would have to spend more time with Matthew. Hopefully Kellie would finally chip in for everything like she'd promised, or Kim's bank account would be painfully skinny.

Heather put a hand on her shoulder. "Thanks for doing all this, Kim. It's really fabulous. I know you didn't plan on the guys coming. And thanks for getting the ribbon samples to the florist. You've handled a ton of the details, and I'm really grateful."

"I just want you to have a great wedding and be able to relax and enjoy it."

Kyle moved behind Heather and put his hands on her shoulders. "Enjoy what?"

"Your weekend, your wedding. All of it." Kim swept her hand around the room, her previous irritation melting away. All that mattered was that Heather was happy. And Kyle, too, but he'd be happy as long as Heather was.

Kim surveyed the room. Everyone seemed to be having a good time. She'd try to relax and go with it. Taking pictures helped, as usual.

Kyle started to say something, but Kellie climbed on the coffee table. "Hey, everyone. Can I have your attention?"

The room quieted.

"I just wanted to give my best wishes to my beautiful sister Heather, and her handsome husband-to-be, Kyle. May you have a wonderful future together." She raised a can of grapefruit LaCroix.

Cheers and clapping broke out around the room. But Kellie didn't get down. "I also wanted to say, let's go eat!"

Kim looked at her phone. Their reservation wasn't for another half hour, and the restaurant wasn't even ten minutes away. Plus Allie and Jessica would be here any time. But with all the agreement Kellie was getting, there was no point in going against the tide.

Matthew raised his hand. "Anyone that wants to ride in the coolest minivan ever, come with me."

Laughter followed that.

"I've got the soon-to-be newlyweds!" Kellie raised her keys.

So Kim could ride with them. Or in Collins's truck. Definitely not the minivan.

Heather grabbed her hand. "Come ride with us. It'll be all my family in one car."

Kim didn't resist. She texted Jessica to let Allie know to come to the restaurant first instead of the cabin.

As the cabin emptied out, Kim spotted the cups and plates that had been left everywhere. She put the remaining food in the refrigerator. She'd clean up when they got back. But she couldn't help but feel like her weekend plans looked as trashed as the cabin did.

Matthew pulled up in front of Belle Sorgenti on the main drag of Holcomb Springs. It was a quaint place that played up its gold rush roots. Austin, Sarah, and Joe piled out behind him. The wind had picked up, and pine needles skidded across the ground in front of him.

Kellie had led the way and was already heading inside. He caught Kim's eye as she entered the door. A tightness had formed around her mouth. He knew how much this weekend meant to her, but it seemed to him that Heather and Kyle were happy. And that was the important part.

Collins's truck pulled in next to him, and they all gathered inside the small waiting area. Kim stepped over. "They're just getting our table set up now. They didn't expect us quite this early. And they had to make some arrangements because of our increase in party size."

Kellie moved next to him. "So tell me about your work. Heather said you're moving here?"

"Yeah, me and Austin." He felt the need to include Austin in this conversation. Maybe because Kellie's attention seemed a tad too bright. Or maybe she was always like this. He explained about the DataCorp expansion and Allie, who walked in shortly after he mentioned her name.

The hostess announced that their table was ready. Matthew gave Allie a quick squeeze around the shoulder. He was glad she made it. She'd been stressed about the DataCorp account, and she deserved to have a good weekend.

Jessica followed Allie in, her gaze searching the room and landing on Scott. But he was following the hostess.

Austin's eyes were glued to Jessica, but he didn't say anything. Matthew nudged him. Everyone else was heading toward the table. They wound their way to a back room.

Collins and Allie deviated off and headed toward one of the tables in the restaurant occupied by a couple. He introduced Allie to them. Must be someone he knew from his time up here. Maybe Brett and Cassie? Matthew thought those were the names Collins had mentioned before.

Kellie smiled brightly and waved. "There's seats over here."

Correction. One seat. He glanced at Austin staring at Jessica as if she had two heads. What was wrong with that boy? Figuring Austin wouldn't know he was gone, and not wanting to be rude to Kellie, he took the seat she had saved for him.

But he didn't miss how Kim quickly looked away when he caught her gaze. She sat next to Heather at the opposite end of the table. Austin and Jessica found seats near Scott and Melissa.

Allie and Collins joined them just as the servers began taking drink and appetizer orders. Matthew scanned the menu. Everything looked delicious, and lunch was a long time ago. The veggies Kim had set out had barely made a dent in his appetite.

Kellie chattered away at his elbow about the menu, the mountains, and everything else.

He made a few noncommittal noises, but his attention strayed too often to the other end of the table. Was Kim irritated with him? He couldn't help but notice she deliberately ignored him and scowled at Kellie.

What was that about? Those two were supposed to be planning this weekend together.

The thought dawned on him just as the server took his order. He got the chicken parmesan, but his attention was on Kim. Could she be jealous?

A rush of warmth lit through him. Maybe. Could he use

that to his advantage? Would his giving Kellie attention make Kim want him more?

He thought about it a moment as Kellie placed her order and the server moved on. Kellie's gaze snapped back to him. "Do you like Italian? I love it. It's one of my favorite kinds of foods."

"Yeah, it's great." No, he couldn't do it. It wouldn't be fair to Kellie, for one thing. She'd take any encouragement from him and run with it. Which would make for an awkward weekend. Besides, he wanted Kim back, not madder at him.

He moved the conversation over to include Kyle and Heather and around to weekend plans. "So, you two are the stars of the show. What do you want to do?"

Heather glanced down at Kim. "Kim booked us spa appointments in the morning. Then I think we were going to take some kayaks around the lake in the afternoon."

Kellie wrinkled her nose. "It doesn't make sense to go to the spa then get in a kayak and get all sweaty. We should do it the other way around. Or just skip the kayaks all together and go shopping. I heard Holcomb Springs has these adorable boutiques."

Wasn't Kellie supposed to be helping Kim plan this weekend, not undermining her?

Matthew shot a look down the table at Kim. She was in an animated discussion with Jessica and Austin. She was great at making people feel comfortable and part of the group.

He had worried for a moment that Austin would feel weird hanging with people he didn't know for a full weekend, even though Matthew had talked him into coming. Austin had grudgingly agreed. And since he'd met a lot of them Sunday at church and lunch afterward, it wouldn't be as strange.

But getting back in the good graces of Kim was proving harder than he expected. And he only had this weekend to do it. Starting Monday, his new job would take most of his attention while he got his footing and launched their newest office. He wanted them to be thrilled they'd hired him, not regret it.

The server set a plate of steaming breaded chicken smothered in marinara sauce. His mouth watered.

Kim tapped on her water glass. "Before we dig in, let's ask the blessing. Joe, would you do the honors?"

"Sure." Joe pushed to his feet from his spot in the middle of the table. "Lord, thank you for your provision and care for us. Thank you for the food and fellowship around the table. Keep us safe this weekend and refreshed to start a new week. In your Son's name, amen."

Amens echoed around the table. Matthew dug into the tasty food, but he couldn't keep Kim out of his line of sight. The memories of their talks around the campfire and in his truck on the Great American Road Trip made him miss her all the more.

How had he gotten himself in this situation? In envisioning this weekend, it'd never occurred to him that he'd be sitting next to Kellie and Kim would be at the other end of the table. This was not part of the plan. Tomorrow had to be better.

Kim deliberately kept her attention away from Matthew and Kellie, which was difficult because she and Matthew were both at the ends of the table, so she had to keep her gaze to Allie to her right or Jessica to her left. She just had to make it through this weekend and ensure Heather and Kyle had a good time. She concentrated on her pasta primavera, which wasn't hard to do since it was fantastic.

She turned to Allie and tilted her head back toward the dining room. "Who was that you and Collins were talking to?"

"He was introducing me to Brett and Cassie. Brett was the injured deputy Collins covered for and Cassie is his girlfriend. She runs the Jitter Bug Too coffee shop down the street. I'd actually met them over FaceTime at one point when Collins was up here. It was good to see them in person."

Kim nodded. "Nice."

A lull in the conversation showed how much everyone was enjoying their food.

Kellie set down her fork. "So we were talking down on this end about either going shopping or kayaking in the morning and rescheduling the spa for the afternoon. Maybe the guys can find something else to do then. I just don't want to get all pampered and then get all sweaty kayaking."

Joe wiped his mouth with his napkin. "There's a red-flag warning for tomorrow. High winds and low humidity. I noticed the wind was already picking up. Might be hard to paddle a kayak around the lake if the wind is pushing back. Not to mention the lake will get choppy."

He was a firefighter; he would know. She hadn't thought about the winds messing with their kayaking plans. It was a point for Kim's plan for the spa. Though her afternoon plan would have to be adjusted.

"Then we should definitely go shopping." Kellie continued, undeterred. She laid a hand on Matthew's arm.

That didn't go unnoticed by Kim, but she ignored it. And the shopping didn't surprise her. Heather's sisters were famous for dragging her on shopping sprees, though Heather wasn't much of a shopper. Still, she would probably appreciate boutiques that carried artisan-made items. But Kim wished Kellie would have discussed this with her on one of their calls. Kellie hadn't done anything to prepare for this weekend other than agreeing to the plans Kim suggested. Plans she was now hijacking.

But that was Kellie. Spontaneous, looking for fun, not committed to a career that consumed her every waking moment. Everything Kim felt she wasn't, especially this weekend. Maybe Kellie was more of what Matthew wanted.

Matthew hadn't moved his arm away, but his gaze wasn't on Kellie. He was studying everyone around the table. He was taking the temperature of the room, trying to figure out what folks wanted to do. She'd seen him do it before. She thought of it as his superpower.

But the table was noncommittal, looking to Kyle and Heather for direction.

Matthew reached for his glass, dislodging Kellie's hand.

Kim hid a smile just as her gaze collided with Matthew's.

He grinned back at her before she broke eye contact. "I saw on a map of the area that the Pacific Crest Trail runs south of town. We could hike part of it."

He'd looked at a map of the area? She didn't think he'd done much planning—the lack of food being the prime example—but clearly he had.

She turned her attention to Heather, whose opinion really mattered. "What do you want to do, Heather?"

Heather gazed up at Kyle. "What do you think? I know you guys won't be into the spa thing, but you could go hiking or something else then."

Kyle shot glances to Joe, Scott, and Collins then shrugged. "Why don't we see what the weather looks like in the morning? We can make our decision then."

Heather nodded. "Sounds good."

Kellie was unfazed by it all. "Did you all see the fire pit on the back deck? And those cute carnival lights they have strung up? We could make s'mores under the stars when we get back. We just have to run to the store for the supplies, because Kim didn't bring any."

Kim clenched her teeth and pasted on a smile. Good thing the wedding was in three weeks. Then she wouldn't have to spend more time with Kellie. Oh wait. They'd be related, in a way. Kellie would be Kyle's sister-in-law, and there would be family events. Which would be fine. Kellie wasn't a bad person. She just wasn't the person you wanted to plan anything with. She was a lot like Matthew, now that Kim thought about it. Spur of the moment and spontaneous. Though Matthew did seem to take others' feelings into account. Something either Kellie didn't do or was unaware of.

No, that was unfair. She did take Heather's feelings into consideration. And maybe right now, that was all that mattered.

Joe shook his head. "No fires tonight. It's too dangerous with the winds, and the trees and forest floor are tinder dry. It would only take a flying ember to set this whole mountain on fire."

Kellie deflated just a bit.

Collins spoke up. "This place has great desserts. The tiramisu gets good reviews. The gelato is also popular." He was the only one who had eaten here before and had recommended it to Kim.

She met Kellie's gaze and gave her a smile. She really didn't want hard feelings between them. That would be bad for Heather.

Kellie's smile was forced at first and then turned genuine. As long as Kim didn't expect too much help from her, maybe they did have a chance at having a great weekend.

Then Kellie reached for Matthew's arm again.

Or maybe not.

Chapter Twelve

Kim was up early the next morning before everyone else. She needed to heat the baked pancake and breakfast casserole she'd brought up. While they were warming in the oven, she started the coffee and poured herself a cup. The trees outside the window were swaying in the wind, and the breeze swirling through their branches sounded like a rushing creek. It was peaceful, and she savored this moment alone.

Playing hostess meant she didn't get much relaxation. When they got home last night, the guys hung out for a while, and she picked up cups and plates, filling one garbage bag, which Matthew was kind enough to take out to the trash for her.

Gusts of wind had shaken the windows throughout the night. She was used to the Santa Ana winds in Orange County. They could be nasty and often knocked over big rigs on the freeway, not to mention blowing down power lines and trees. But this morning was calmer with just a bit of a breeze. Today she wasn't sure if that was a curse or a blessing. If it was too windy to kayak, then that meant they could keep their spa appointment. But she did have kayaking on the agenda for this afternoon. Unless Kellie's shopping trip won out.

Her phone buzzed. Maybe it was Matthew saying they were heading over. If so, she needed to warn the girls.

But it was an Instagram message. From someone she didn't know. They had an odd profile picture. It looked like it was from another piece of her dress that she had showcased on social media a few weeks ago. Almost like each of the profile pics, if put together, would form a completed puzzle of her dress. Or maybe she was just imagining it since she was obsessing over Design Review.

She clicked on the message.

Why are you ignoring me?

She plunked on the nearest barstool, uncertain her legs would hold her. Who was this person? And was it connected to the text messages she had been getting? Was it the same person or someone different?

A text came through. She swiped to delete the Instagram message and opened the text. It was from Matthew.

On r way in a few. Be decent. Or not :P

She rolled her eyes. Putting the other message out of her mind, she knocked on the bedroom doors and relayed the message about their soon-to-be visitors.

And they'd be hungry too. Matthew had confessed last night that he hadn't figured on meals, thinking they'd just grab something. She offered to feed them. She had just enough food, more than the girls needed, and hopefully enough for all of them.

A quick rap on the front door sent Kim calling down the hall. "They're here!" She pulled the door open.

Matthew stood there bearing a donut box and a carton of orange juice. "I didn't want to come empty handed." He grinned.

She shook her head and smiled. "Come on in. Coffee's ready."

The rest of the guys trailed in, bringing with them the smell of soap and shampoo. It was amazing they all had gotten up and showered before the girls had barely rolled out of bed.

Then again, they might have been motivated by their stomachs.

Kim moved to the kitchen and pulled the baked pancake and egg casserole out of the oven and set them on the counter. She had barely cut them into squares before there was a line in front of the kitchen island. She stepped back and watched. Mostly in yoga pants and hair in messy buns, the girls joined the guys. Except for Kellie. Kim had heard the shower running when she had awoken and thought Kellie was up early to help with breakfast. She entered the kitchen with hair freshly straightened and a full face of makeup on.

Kim started another pot of coffee and made sure everyone had what they needed before she snagged the last section of egg casserole. Good thing Matthew had brought the donuts. There were only crumbs left in each of the dishes. She set them to soak in the kitchen sink, and forked down her breakfast, leaning against the island.

Matthew joined her. "Great breakfast. Thanks for bailing us out." He bumped his shoulder into hers.

She smiled. "We had enough food. What are your plans for the day?"

"Joe said if we wanted to go kayaking, this morning would be better. The winds have died down a bit but are supposed to pick up later today. We could call the marina and find out. You guys want to go with us if we get the green light?"

She looked out over the great room. The couches and chairs were filled with friends eating and chatting. The group clearly enjoyed being together, and even Austin and Jessica seemed to hit it off, which she hadn't seen coming. They were so different. But maybe they were united in feeling like outsiders. Though after this weekend, no one would be able to claim that status.

"Yeah, we can put it to a vote. Or better yet, I'll get Kyle and Heather alone and see what they want to do." She glanced at his wrist. "Are you going to be able to kayak with that sprain?"

"I'm a man of many talents. You'll be amazed."

"Hmm. I'll believe it when I see it."

She wasn't sure if the spa would be able to accommodate them this afternoon, but she'd wait and discover Heather's preference.

"I'll make the call." Matthew pulled out his phone, and Kim began cleaning up. She had trail mix and granola bars and water bottles for any outdoor activities but no appetizers for this afternoon before dinner. She'd have to stop by the store after whatever they ended up doing.

Matthew joined her. "Talked to the owner of the marina, Captain John."

"Really?" She laughed.

"Yeah." He chuckled. "Hey, it's good for marketing. Don't know if he's really a captain. Anyhow, he says come on down soon. The water's pretty calm within the bay, but he expects it to get windy and choppy in a few hours."

She pushed away from the counter. "Let's go talk to Heather and Kyle." She moved to the great room and perched on the arm of the deep couch where Heather and Kyle were sitting.

Matthew gave his report.

"So, it's up to you guys. Well, mostly you, Heather." Kim grinned.

"Joe, Collins, and Scott want to try out this fishing spot one of the guys at work was talking about. But I'll do whatever you want." Kyle hugged Heather close to him.

"Good response, Kyle." Matthew cuffed him on the shoulder.

Heather exchanged glances with Kyle. "I was looking forward to getting some kayaking in. If the morning's the only time we can do it, will that create a problem?"

"Nope. We'll figure it out." Kim patted Heather's arm and stood. "Hey everyone. We have a plan. We'll go kayaking this morning before the winds pick back up, for those who want to go. I'll move the spa appointments to the afternoon."

Kellie also stood. "Those who want to go shopping can come with me."

"Okay, let's get a head count. Joe, Scott, and Collins want to go fishing. So your activity options for the morning are kayaking, shopping, or fishing." Kim put on her best activity director voice and made it sound like having a lot of choices had been the plan all along. She counted the kayakers: Matthew, Austin, Jessica, Heather, Kyle, and her.

Joe glanced pointedly at Matthew's wrist. "Sure you don't want to go fishing with us? We have plenty of gear."

"I'll be fine. Thanks, though."

Kellie was taking Sarah, Melissa, and Allie with her to go shopping. With Heather out of the way, they were whispering about wedding gifts.

That left Joe, Scott, and Collins to go fishing.

"Let's meet back here for lunch around noon," Kim suggested. If they kayaked for two hours, that would still give her time to get to the store and get groceries. The group dispersed.

"I'll drive," Matthew said.

Good thing, because Kim hadn't even thought about that. Matthew's minivan was the only thing that would fit all six of them. He continued to come in handy.

He touched her arm. "This is going to be fun."

She let out a deep breath. Yes, it would be.

Matthew pulled the minivan into the Treasure Island park next to the marina. It was a cute place off the bay with a big lawn, picnic tables, grills, and a playground that looked like a pirate's ship. There was a sandy, protected beach that would be perfect for swimming when the water wasn't sixty degrees, like the whiteboard with the current conditions had informed him. The sun was warm, so the cool water would feel good after they'd been paddling for a while.

They all got out and headed for the marina office. Captain John met them. "You must be Matthew."

"I am." Matthew shook his hand. "I brought a couple of soon-to-be newlyweds and some friends to spend a little time on the water this morning."

"Ah, so which of you are getting ready to tie the knot?"

Everyone pointed to Heather and Kyle.

"Well congratulations. I have the first test of your relationship for you. I'll put you in a double kayak. If you can make that work, then marriage will be a breeze."

Everyone laughed, but Matthew had heard the stories. He knew what Kyle and Heather had been through. He didn't think the kayak would be much of a challenge for them.

"Anybody else up to the challenge and want a double kayak?" Captain John surveyed the group, hands on hips.

"A challenge?" Matthew met Kim's gaze. If they were in a double kayak, she'd have to spend time with him. He nudged her. "What do you say, Kim? Think we can do a better job than these two lovebirds?"

She grinned.

Yes! That was the Kim from the Great American Road Trip.

"Yeah, that way you can paddle, and I can take pictures."

Captain John studied Matthew's wrist. "I'll give you a straight-bladed paddle instead of an offset one. You won't have to turn your wrist as much."

"I'll take it." Maybe he had a real chance of turning things around with Kim. This morning it seemed like they'd found their groove again, working as a team to plan today. He only wished they'd been able to plan the whole weekend together.

Next time they would.

And there would be a next time.

"These are sea kayaks." Captain John spoke as he handed out life jackets and paddles. "They handle the chop we get on the lake in the afternoon. Though today it'll be sooner than that. You'll do fine in the bay, but if you get confident and want to go out on open water, the wind comes up from the west, so start paddling that direction. Then when you're tired, the wind will be at your back on your way in. There are a lot of places along the shoreline to pull out, so if you get tired and can't make it back for some reason, give us a call, and we'll come get you."

He got them situated in their kayaks and showed them the compartments where they could stow their backpacks and the small ice chest Kim had brought filled with water bottles. He even gave Kim a dry bag for her camera.

Matthew couldn't help as much as he was used to. A fact that annoyed him.

It annoyed him even more when he forgot about his wrist and tried to help, automatically reaching with his injured arm and feeling the sharp burn of pain before the restraints of the splint kicked in. After the third time he did that, he was content to let Kyle, Austin, and Captain John deal with the gear.

"Just remember, you're at seven thousand feet. You'll feel it." He waved and pushed them off from the dock.

Heather and Kyle led the way, finding their rhythm together quickly. Matthew let Jessica and Austin go ahead of them in their individual kayaks. Austin took to it better than Matthew expected. That guy continually surprised him. Which would make for more fun as roommates than he had anticipated.

Kim sat in front, giving Matthew a great view of her bare arms and neck and occasionally her profile as she looked around. She'd pulled her blonde hair into a ponytail, and it cascaded out of the ball cap she'd pulled on. He followed her stroke pattern, and soon they found a comfortable rhythm.

The bay was protected by piled-up boulders topped by pine trees sprouting out of whatever soil they could find. It was a perfect spot for kayaks, canoes, and stand-up paddleboards. But they were the only ones out today. That was good, right? It meant they had the place to themselves.

Kim turned around. "Pretty, huh? I'm glad we did this. I'm surprised no one else is out here. It's already getting warm." She laid her paddle across the kayak and grabbed her camera, shooting pictures of their surroundings and fellow kayakers. "This is a lot of fun. I think Scott was right. Remember on the Great American Road Trip how he kept pointing out the rafting outfitters and saying we should come back and see everything from the water? I think he's on to something. I'm surprised he didn't want to come with us."

"I think he's hoping to sneak off with Melissa for some alone time. I don't think he'll even go fishing."

"That makes sense. I wonder when they'll get married. I would think being apart would be hard."

Yeah, he'd thought that being away from Kim had been hard for two months. He couldn't imagine what Scott and Melissa went through.

Kyle and Heather led their little pack around the bay. They reached the mouth, and Kyle turned back. "Everyone comfortable with paddling out into the main lake?"

Matthew had done okay paddling in the bay. He felt each stroke in his wrist, but the pain wasn't much worse. The splint definitely helped. The wind had picked up, and small whitecaps were forming on the lake. But they might as well try it. If it got too bad, they could turn back. He certainly wasn't going to be the one to hold them back because of his wrist.

Jessica and Austin nodded.

As they came out around the peninsula of boulders, the wind hit them head on and the paddling got a little more difficult, but they were still gliding over the water. The mountains rose all around them, the air scented with fresh pine that no artificial scent could compete with. He definitely wanted to do this more often. And with Kim.

"So this is more fun than fishing?" Kim asked over her shoulder.

"Oh yeah. Sitting around holding a pole isn't my idea of fun.

I'd rather be hiking, skipping rocks across the water, or anything else that doesn't endear me to fishermen. This is great."

They skimmed close to the shoreline, spotting water fowl in the reedy areas. In other places, beautiful cabins with walls of windows rose off the shore. Densely packed forest filled in the rest of the shoreline. Occasionally a fish jumped out of the water near them. This was getting into nature, without the hassle of camping, which he didn't really mind. But for a quick weekend trip, this was awesome.

The lake curved around and exposed them to the full force of the wind. The choppy water splashed over the kayak, and they had to dig deeper in the water to make progress. His wrist began to complain.

Kyle stopped, and they all pulled up next to him. "We've been out about an hour, but the wind is getting bad. Do you guys want to head back? We can paddle around the bay a bit if we want."

Kim reached into the cooler to grab water bottles for everyone. Matthew helped maneuver them around to make her job easier. Holding on to each other's kayaks, they made a floating pod. The wind was slowly pushing them toward the center of the lake.

"If we only had a sail, we could rest on the way in." Matthew uncapped his water and downed half of it, glad for the break. "Yeah, we should probably head back. Plus, someone's barbecuing something. Smells good. I must have worked up an appetite."

Kim dug around in her backpack. "I have trail mix. Your favorite, with M&Ms." She handed him a bag then passed them out to the rest of the flotilla.

"I haven't had any in two months. I'm finally not sick of it." He and Kim had eaten a lot of trail mix when they'd gotten stranded when a guy who was after Allie had siphoned the gas out of Matthew's truck last March.

They rested for a bit. The wind seemed to be getting

stronger. He studied the mountains around them. A large plume of smoke rose from the west, making its own cloud formation in the sky. "Look at that." He pointed.

Kyle dug out his phone. "No reception right here. I wonder how far away that fire is. Looks pretty close, and the wind is pushing it this direction. Let's head back to the marina."

Nobody argued.

Chapter Thirteen

Kim fought the rising panic in her chest, digging deep in the water to hurry them back to the marina. They'd need to find the others, get to the cabin, get their stuff, and evacuate. Forest fires could move fast and were nothing to mess around with. And what about Matthew's wrist? He hadn't said anything, and he seemed to be doing more than his share of paddling. Then again, it could be broken and he'd find a way to make a joke about it.

Heather's special weekend was literally going up in flames. Kim wanted to cry.

She fought the urge to pull out her phone and figure out what was going on. Though she probably wouldn't have any reception until the marina. Matthew needed her help to get them back. The wind was definitely picking up now, but it seemed like they were hardly making any progress.

But the fire was making a lot of it. The plume of smoke looked like a particularly nasty weather system moving across the horizon. With the mountain tops and forest, it was hard to get perspective on how far away it was.

The only sound was the dip-splash of their synchronized paddles and the roar of the wind. The scent of smoke grew heavier, and her lungs burned with the effort at the high elevation, not to mention the smoke making her want to cough.

What was everyone else doing? The fire looked like it was closer to where the guys had gone to fish but was farther away from the town of Holcomb Springs where the girls had gone to shop. When they got to the bay, she'd be able to look at her phone.

Could they even get back to the cabin? Her chest tightened at the thought. She coughed to clear it. And coughed again. The smoke. It was irritating her lungs. And triggering her mild asthma. The exertion of paddling was exacerbating it. And the altitude wasn't helping. She'd grab her inhaler out of her pack when they got to the bay. If she stopped paddling now to get it, they'd lose their momentum. It wasn't a big deal. She just made a conscious effort to breathe through her nose.

She began making a mental list of what they'd need to do. Contact everyone first, then get back to the cabin. Throw everything in cars and get down the hill. They could meet up in Highland at the base of the mountain and get organized and regroup.

This morning her biggest concern had been running out of food at breakfast. Now she was worried about getting everyone home safely.

The pile of boulders appeared that marked the entrance to the bay. She dug in harder, strength renewed by the end being in sight. The smoke had billowed over most of the sky and slid in front of the sun, making it look more like twilight. Shivers danced up her arms. The fire was a lot closer than it had seemed an hour ago.

Something stung the back of her neck, and she swatted at it. Wasn't smoke supposed to keep the mosquitos away? One landed on her arm. Then she noticed the front of the kayak. Gray and black flakes dusted the crevices where the wind hadn't blown them off. Those stings weren't mosquitos. They were hot ashes.

As they rounded the boulders into the bay, she glanced back at Matthew. "I've got to grab my inhaler."

He nodded and kept paddling. Even when they had been stranded in Shafer canyon, she hadn't seen that look of furrowed concentration on him. Was his wrist bothering him, or was he concerned about the fire? Or both? She dug around for her inhaler and took a few puffs.

The others had eased up as well. Kyle had pulled out his phone. The safety of the bay was an illusion. It was more wind protected, but they needed to get out of here, and fast.

"Get ahold of anyone?" Matthew shouted across the water.

Kyle shook his head. "There's a text from Joe saying they're at the cabin packing everything up. Collins is staying to help the local LEOs since he's worked with them before. And there was an emergency alert for evacuating the area. But I can't get a call out. The towers are likely impacted by emergency personnel and people calling friends and family."

"Let's get these boats back and head out." Matthew nodded at the marina. "Probably should just head down the hill instead of trying to go back to the cabins."

"I agree." Kyle stowed his phone and dug into paddling.

As they neared the marina office, it appeared to be deserted. The earlier whiteboard listing today's conditions was nowhere in sight. And neither was Captain John.

Kyle and Heather reached the dock first. He grabbed the edge to hold the kayak against it. "Heather, jump out and see if you can see anything."

She tossed her paddle on the deck and scrambled out. When she reached the office, she peered in the windows and then came back holding a piece of paper. "He left us a note. It says that the whole area has been evacuated. He assumes we got off the lake somewhere safe, but if we managed to return here, just leave the kayaks and get out."

"Let's at least pull the kayaks up on the dock so they don't get blown to the middle of the lake." Matthew held their kayak to the dock so Kim could get out. Then she did the same for him.

Of course if the fire came through here, it wouldn't matter what they did with the kayaks. But she didn't say that. She stripped off her life vest and tucked it in the kayak then grabbed her backpack and the cooler. She pulled her camera out of the dry bag and stowed it in her backpack. Her stomach growled. It would be awhile before they got food, but she did have the trail mix and granola bars. As soon as they got in the minivan, she'd get them out.

Matthew jogged to the minivan and clicked open the locks. "I'll turn on the radio and see if we can catch the local news."

Everyone else piled in. With the doors shut, the sound of the wind was reduced to wails, though gusts rocked the car. The smoke, wind, and dark skies made it seem like a storm was going to douse them any minute. Wishful thinking.

The radio reported a fire in the San Bernardino National Forest heading toward Holcomb Lake and that evacuations had been ordered. But they already knew that. Kim scrolled through her Twitter feed to find any info. She had one bar.

"Let me see if I can get through now." Kyle pulled out his phone. "I don't want us driving into trouble."

That was putting it mildly.

After a couple of attempts, Kyle got ahold of the ranger station. He put it on speaker. "We're at Holcomb Lake and want to know the best way to proceed."

"You're at the lake right now?" A woman with an uncertain voice responded.

"Yes, at Treasure Island park."

"That area has been evacuated. Units are on structure protection only, and we can't spare anyone."

"We don't need rescuing; we just need to know which is the safest way out."

"I—I don't know. Let me ask someone."

Kyle shook his head. This was clearly someone who was

called in for the emergency and wasn't an actual dispatcher. Probably someone from public information who normally wrote press releases.

"It's a simple question. Look at a map and see which way is farther from the fire." Matthew's voice was laced with irritation. He started the minivan and backed out of the parking spot.

"It's not that simple. Fires don't burn in a straight line. And she might not know where the fire line is. Or have a map. Or know how to read it." Kyle's tone didn't sound any more patient than Matthew's.

She came back on the line. "Sir?"

"Yes."

"That road is behind the fire line in both directions. I've relayed your location to units in the area, but there simply aren't any resources available." Her voice cracked, and Kim's heart softened. The poor woman obviously wasn't used to dealing with emergencies.

"Okay, okay. Just take a deep breath." Clearly Kyle *was* used to dealing with emergencies. "Let me give you our names and contact information. You have some way to write this down?"

Kyle coached her through it and gave her all of their info.

Kim wanted to throw up. Because there was only one scenario she could think of where rescue personnel would need all of their names and addresses.

And that was if it was a recovery instead of a rescue.

MATTHEW FLIPPED ON THE AC. THE SMOKE WAS SEEPING through the car. The sky darkened ominously.

Kyle hung up.

They sat in silence for a moment.

"Let's just drive out of here." Matthew hated sitting still. "The fire came from the west, so if we head east, it makes sense that we might find a way out. Anyone got a map of the area?"

He was used to his sisters, Melissa and Allie, always being prepared and planning for contingencies.

Kim pulled one up on her phone. With one bar, it was slow to load. "I don't know if it'll keep up with us while we're driving."

"Let me call Joe." Kyle swiped his phone, but they could all hear the fast busy tone that said the call didn't go through. After trying multiple times, he gave up. "The towers are overloaded. I'll see if a text will get through to him or Collins."

"Sitting here just lets the fire get closer. East is our best guess." It also was where the sliver of blue sky beckoned Matthew.

Kyle nodded. "I keep getting a delivery failure on the text. Anyone else able to get through? Everyone try." He rattled off Joe's and Collins's numbers to those who didn't have it. "Matthew, you're right. Head east, and we'll see where we can get."

Matthew's grip on the steering wheel eased as he edged out of the parking lot and turned left. At least they were making progress now. He craned his neck in every direction, watching for potential danger, but the smoke made it hard to see. The headlights switched on, the smoke and ash swirling in their beams.

A flash out of the corner of his eye.

"Matthew!" Kim's voice cut through the car just as he spotted the deer springing out of the underbrush and in front of the car.

He hit the brakes and rocketed them all forward. But missed the deer.

Letting out a breath, he tried to slow the adrenaline pumping through him. That was close. "A bunch of wildlife are going to be running away from the fire."

He moved the minivan forward again, battling between the desire to floor it and run from the fire as fast as possible and to go slow and watch for potential danger. He wasn't thrilled with hitting the rabbits and squirrels darting across the road seeking the same safety they were.

The smoke was as thick and obscure as the future Matthew tried to foresee. It was always easier to look toward the future to get out of a painful present. But he'd never been in such imminent danger before, from the fire or other threats. And he was responsible for these people, to get them to safety. For a moment, he understood the burden his sisters had borne for the family. And he'd never been more grateful for Kyle's presence.

A glance back in the rearview mirror showed everyone looking out the windows in all directions trying to spot the next threat before it was too late. They were all in this together. It wasn't just on him.

Matthew was settling into feeling he had made the right decision.

Until he saw the boulder in the middle of the road.

Kim spotted the boulder rising out of the smoke like a giant stop sign, preventing them from going any farther.

This time Matthew didn't have to slam on the brakes. He eased up to it.

Kyle slid the side door open and jumped out. He scoped out the boulder all the way around it then hopped back in. "There's not enough room to go around it on either side. The shoulder drops off steeply on one side and rises straight up on the other. And there's no way we can move it. Not even if we used the minivan."

"Pretty sure the insurance doesn't cover ramming boulders anyway," Matthew joked.

It would be a good thing if the rental company ever saw their minivan again, the way things were going. Kim pushed that thought out of her mind and glanced at her phone, willing the map app to give her any info. "I think this is a residential area, maybe some cabins. I remember looking at different areas when I was renting the cabin. And if I'm picturing the map correctly, Fawnskin is just over that way. Maybe we could find a road or a place to hike down." She turned to look at the rest of the group.

Kyle seemed to be considering her words. "Even if Fawnskin is evacuated, there will at least be structure protection. If we could find a street here that firefighters are protecting, that would be good."

Matthew backed up. "Look for a street off to the side."

Sure enough, one appeared out of the smoke. Kim almost missed it. "There!"

Matthew shifted into drive and eased uphill.

She strained her eyes trying to see through the smoke, hoping she saw danger in time. Hoping she wasn't leading them to a dead end, like many of these mountain roads.

Slowly they reached the summit. The road flattened out a bit then began its descent.

And ended. Just ended. A forest stretched out before them.

Matthew peered through the windshield and then leaned over to look at Kim's map. "It seems like Fawnskin should just be down that hill." He looked back at Kyle. "You know this area better than anyone here. What do you think?"

"It should be. But with a fire lurking out there, it's no time to wander around." Kyle frowned, deep in thought.

Kim was glad that as a detective he was used to making critical decisions in a short period of time.

"Let's hop out and see if we can see anything."

He and Matthew climbed out and immediately pulled their shirts up over their nose and mouth. Before long, they had disappeared into the smoke.

Heaviness dropped into Kim's stomach and settled there. She hoped she wasn't watching them disappear for good. No, she couldn't think like that. *Pray!*

"Hey, let's pray. I know I need to." Kim didn't know

anything about Austin's spiritual journey, but if he was friends with Matthew, he had to at least be okay being around Christians. He'd gone to church with them Sunday and had participated in the service. "I'll start, and anyone who wants can join in." She started praying for protection, guidance, and safety.

Heather prayed for the first responders and those working the direct fire lines, for their safety and protection.

Jessica's voice surprised Kim. "God, thanks for everything you've brought me through. Thanks that I've had a great weekend with these people. I don't think it's supposed to end this way. So keep lighting the path for us, like you've been doing for me."

"God, you know the beginning from the end." Austin's voice was stronger and more assured than Kim had ever heard from him. "You know our future, and we are safe in your care and protection. You will provide everything we need. Help us to rest in that. Amen."

Amens echoed through the minivan followed by a silence that was heavy with peace. A moment later, Matthew and Kyle appeared out of the smoke and climbed in, their eyes red and streaming.

"No go." Kyle slammed the side door shut against a blast of smoke. "Matthew and I were lucky we found our way back."

Heather touched his arm. "We were praying."

He nodded. "Thanks."

Matthew slowly turned the minivan around. "Even if Allie were here with her uncanny sense of direction, I wouldn't want to risk it. Been there done that. And this time, I don't think we'd live to tell the tale, not with a fire chasing us."

"Any idea if the fire is getting closer?" Kim asked.

Kyle shook his head. "The wind is swirling around. The fire makes its own weather. The wind can blow embers up to a mile in front of the main fire, starting other fires. It could easily entrap us. Our best bet is to head back to the marina. Hopefully one of the water-dropping helicopters will see us when they dip in the lake."

And if not, they'd have the ability to get into the lake if the fire got close. That was the part Kyle didn't say. He didn't have to.

Matthew nosed the minivan back the way they came, toward the marina. The ash and smoke made it hard to see. He didn't want to hit something and wreck their main option for getting out of this disaster. Water seemed the most logical destination. If they couldn't drive or walk out, then they could float out on the water until someone rescued them. It wouldn't be comfortable, but they'd survive.

A pine tree branch blew out of the smoke, scratching its way across the minivan's front before crunching under the tires.

He cut his eyes toward Kim. Her head was propped against the headrest, eyes closed. "You gonna make it?"

That brought a small smile, but she didn't open her eyes. "Oh, yeah."

No one spoke. The only sound was the rushing wind. Matthew's eyes scanned front and sides for the next threat.

The road seemed to glow up ahead, getting brighter. Then flames appeared alongside the road. He gripped the wheel tighter, fighting every instinct to turn around. But there was nothing to go back to. They'd be trapped. He sought Kyle's gaze in the rearview mirror.

Kyle's mouth pulled in a tight line. "Just keep going."

He pushed the accelerator a little harder, fighting the instinct to run from the fire as the flames grew on either side of the road, gusting across the road in parts. *Lord, keep us safe.*

The car was completely quiet, just the howling sound of wind and fire raging outside. Was it his imagination or was it heating up?

"Ouch!" Kim yanked her hand back from the window and glanced at him.

The windows were getting hot. He'd heard of glass breaking from the heat, tires melting. He pushed the gas pedal farther, praying nothing was in front of them as flames and smoke gusted across the road, intermittently blocking his vision.

And then it seemed to lessen, the flames burning along the side of the road but not towering columns like before. He eased his grip a fraction as the flames seemed to slip behind them. *Thank you, Lord.* They were clear and just back into the dense smoke. He slowed. He could only imagine what would have happened if they had decided to get out of the car earlier and try to hike out.

A deer bolted in front of him, coming out of the smoke like a mirage. His lights reflected off the deer's eyes. He tapped the brake, but his foot had barely been resting on the accelerator. A deep thump made him jump.

A scream came from the back.

The wheel jerked under his hands. The minivan moved sideways like it was pushed by a giant hand. "What—" He swung around, looking for the source.

The back part of the roof by Jessica's head crumpled inward. Smoke and ash spilled inside. He gunned the engine, but it just whined.

"A deer hit us." Jessica ran a hand over her head, her face pale.

Matthew was confused. "I saw it run off."

"There was a second one." Jessica pointed to the window, where part of a deer's body protruded.

Kim swung toward the backseat. "Are you okay?"

"I think so. I had just bent over to get something from my backpack. Good thing."

Matthew threw the car into park. "Something's stuck. Let's see if we can move it." If the fire gusted back this way, they were in trouble. He and Kyle climbed out, hot, ashy air choking him.

A broken deer lay like a discarded stuffed animal over the back of the minivan. Jessica was lucky—they all were—that he hadn't been one second earlier driving through that stretch or it could have come through a side window.

He didn't relish tugging on a dead animal, parts of which were embedded deeply in the minivan's rear fender, quarter panel, and back window. Another gust tossed debris in the air, and he turned, squinting. Even if he got the deer out of the way, the van's back end was crumpled under, dragging on the tire.

"We're not going anywhere." Kyle bent down. "We'd better start walking." He glanced back toward the way they'd come.

Was the glow getting brighter? He moved back to the driver's door and opened it. He couldn't even get the minivan to the side of the road, so if anyone came by, they'd have to maneuver around it. "The car's not drivable. We need to head back to the marina. Kim, do you have anything we can leave a note with?"

"I do." Heather pulled a notepad out of her backpack. "Just tell whoever finds the minivan that we've gone to the marina?"

Kyle nodded from the open side door. "Put all our names on there too. And our cell numbers." He glanced at Matthew. "Might as well leave the keys in the ignition to help the tow truck driver."

Matthew wasn't sure that the minivan would even see a tow truck. Or if it did, it wouldn't be until after it was consumed by fire. And in that case, the keys wouldn't make any difference.

They all grabbed their backpacks and the cooler. Since this was a rental, there weren't even any blankets or anything that might be useful. They started off at a rapid clip down the road toward the marina.

And not destruction, Matthew hoped.

Chapter Fourteen

Kim pulled her shirt up over her nose and mouth. The others did too. She wished they had bandanas or towels or anything. It was hard to keep her shirt up. Her eyes watered. She coughed. The sky was a lowering blanket of smoke, the sun obliterated. Gusting winds blew ash and dust in their faces, with the occasional ember stinging bare skin. It kept their talking to a minimum. She tried to stifle another cough but didn't succeed.

It wasn't long before her lungs were spasming, and she was suppressing the urge to cough. Something grabbed in her throat, and choking coughs seized her until her throat was raw.

Matthew was carrying the cooler in his good hand. She grabbed his arm and pointed to the cooler. He popped open the lid, and she grabbed a water bottle. Uncapping it, she took a big swig, loosening some of the mucus that suffocated her. She dug around in her backpack until she found her inhaler and took two puffs. It was probably sooner than she should have taken another dose, but then again, what choice did she have? The unseen hand of the fire chasing them pushed her faster than she would have liked.

Matthew watched her. "You okay?"

The others disappeared in the smoke. If they didn't stay together, they'd get lost like someone in a blizzard.

She nodded. Speaking less was better.

Matthew grabbed her backpack. "I'll take this."

He already had his backpack and the cooler. He slung both backpacks over one shoulder and picked up the cooler. His gaze studied her a moment longer.

She gave him a wry grin and lifted her chin indicating she was ready to go. This was more adventure than she had bargained for. Not exactly a relaxing weekend away, and certainly not what Heather and Kyle deserved. She couldn't control the fire, but it still felt like somehow it was her responsibility to give them a good weekend. If Allie or Melissa had planned it, they might have taken a fire into consideration somehow.

Then again, with all of Melissa's planning, they'd still ended up being attacked by Willie Dumas. Kim's nightmares had subsided to only occasionally. Every once in a while, she'd see someone that looked like him, and her heart would pound uncontrollably. Even though she knew he was dead.

They caught up with the others. Kyle herded them to the side of the road. "In case some emergency vehicles come through here, if we were so fortunate. They won't be expecting to see people in the road." He reached for the cooler Matthew carried.

Kim stepped off the asphalt and onto the decomposed granite and pine needles on the side of the road. It dropped off steeply, so they walked single file on the slippery ground.

Surely they were in some literary equivalent of hell, like a cross between Dante's *Inferno* and *Groundhog Day*. Because Kim was sure they had walked this way ten times before, and in fact probably had been walking it for all of their lives. Or for at least as long as she could remember.

Maybe it just felt like it.

She was tired, shaky from too much albuterol from her inhaler, and concentrating on breathing. So it was possible she wasn't paying the closest attention to the path they were taking. In fact, she was mostly content to stare at Matthew's nicely broad back and shoulders. The backpacks didn't block too much. It was keeping her mind off her breathing and helping her to focus. Yeah, that was it.

The ash was falling like a snowstorm and more frequently included hot embers. It felt like they were walking into the fire, not away from it. They were going to end up fried like those stupid people that didn't evacuate brush fires because they wanted to save their homes with a garden hose.

But what choice did they have?

She stepped on a rock she hadn't seen, and it teeter-tottered under her foot. Her other foot could find no extra purchase on the pine needles. Her ankle wrenched sideways and took all her weight as she lost her balance. "Ahh!"

Matthew swung around and grabbed her arm. "Are you okay?"

She bit down on a bad word and let the tears stream out her eyes. She could blame it on the smoke. They couldn't stay here. They had to get to the marina. She eased her weight on the ankle. It hurt, but it was manageable.

She said each sentence on an exhale, reserving her oxygen. "I will be. Keep moving."

"Kyle!" Matthew shouted and slipped his arm around Kim's waist.

Kyle and the others reappeared, stopping and waiting.

With the heavy smoke, it was almost impossible to get their bearings, but it seemed like they should have reached the marina by now. She had no idea how much farther she needed to walk on her ankle. But she didn't have a choice.

Kyle bent down and examined her ankle. "Is it okay to put weight on it?"

She nodded.

He looked up at Matthew. "Can you help her walk?"

"I'll carry her if I need to."

Kim vigorously shook her head. Though for a moment, the idea sounded wonderful.

Austin stepped over. "Give me those backpacks."

Matthew shrugged out of his and Kim's. Austin took one, and Jessica snagged the other.

"Any idea how much farther?" Matthew's arm around her waist was comforting, and for a moment, Kim leaned into his side.

Kyle shook his head. "With all this smoke, it's hard to tell where we are."

Kim could feel Matthew's breathing, his chest moving up and down under her head. Just a moment here was all she needed to regain her equilibrium. But it might be a moment they couldn't afford.

Over the wind it almost sounded like helicopters flew up above them.

"Hear that?" Kyle asked.

Matthew nodded. "Can't see them, but the sooner we get to the marina, the sooner someone will find us." He glanced down at her. "Ready to head out?"

She nodded.

He moved so she could walk on the edge of the asphalt, and he would walk in the dirt. With his help, she concentrated on breathing and walking. In. Step. Out. Step. In. Step. Out. Step. She didn't look too far ahead because there was nothing to see but Jessica's back. The albuterol had kicked in. She was okay. *Just keep telling yourself that.*

But at one point, she thought maybe she was dreaming while she was awake. Or maybe hallucinating. Because it looked like a pirate ship was coming out of the smoke like a chimera. But it wasn't a dream, it was real. Tears bubbled up in her eyes, either from the smoke or the joy at seeing Treasure Island park. Which seemed silly, so it must have been the smoke.

Matthew got Kim seated on the edge of the dock, her tennis shoe and sock off and her foot in the cool water. Kyle was attempting to get into the marina office to find a landline to call out. Or even a radio. Austin was helping him.

The kayaks sat where they had left them. At least Kim wouldn't have to walk any more. But the smoke was a problem for her asthma. And Matthew wasn't looking forward to paddling again.

"How's it feel?" Matthew squatted next to Kim. Heather and Jessica plopped down farther on the dock.

"Better now that I'm off it." She held his gaze. A flicker of hope fluttered to life in his chest. He didn't want to break this moment. He slid his hand across her shoulder. She didn't pull away.

He'd missed touching her. How could so much sass and talent reside in such a small package? His hand slipped up the back of her neck.

"Thanks. For everything you've done to help me this weekend. I know I haven't been the easiest person to get along with lately."

"Kim, I'd—" The rest got left unsaid as Kyle strode up, shaking his head. Matthew got to his feet, regretting the loss of contact with Kim.

"We got in, but the landline was dead. The lines have probably burned. No radio either. I grabbed some rope, but there wasn't much there in way of supplies. We left another note."

Matthew looked out over the water. "We'd better get in the kayaks. The safest place is staying within the bay. The wind is less, and the chop not as significant. But the smoke is still pretty bad."

Kyle nodded. "We'd be better off in the middle of the lake. One of the water-dropping helos would have to see us. Plus the smoke would be less."

"But the wind will be rougher and the water choppier. Once out there, we'll expend a lot of energy fighting the wind. And we don't know how long we'll have to manage before being rescued." Or how long he could paddle with his sprained wrist.

Kyle considered for a moment. "We could let the wind push us and not fight it unless we needed to. If we're all lashed together, we can wait it out."

Heather stood and joined them. "It's the best plan we've got. Let's get in the water." She glanced sharply at Kim, her brow furrowed. Her concern for Kim's injury mirrored Matthew's own.

The rest of them moved to the kayaks and equipment.

Matthew returned to Kim and knelt beside her. He put his hand on her back, eager to reconnect, and she didn't pull away from his touch.

She snagged her shoe and sock. "I don't know if I should bother putting them on or not."

"It'll be easier up here than in a kayak."

"True. And maybe it'll help keep the swelling down."

She slipped them back on, grimacing as she tugged on her Nike.

Matthew grabbed her hand and helped her to her feet, but he didn't let go of her until she stepped into their kayak. He was the last one to get in. His gaze landed over their small group. They were heading out under quite different circumstances than they had earlier today. Who knew that things would veer so far off course? Not being able to get them out of here to someplace safe didn't sit well with him. The training exercise accident could end up escalating to consequences far bigger than a sprained wrist.

"I think we should pray again before we take off." He reached down for Kim's hand and asked God to keep them safe, healthy, and visible to rescuers. As the *amens* echoed around him, he climbed in the kayak as he pushed off the dock. Same motions as before but under a far different sky.

He and Kim found their rhythm again, and he concentrated on not paying attention to his wrist. As they neared the mouth of the bay, he hoped that maybe they could hang out here, a bit protected from the wind and far away enough from the smoke.

Kyle stopped and turned around, waiting for Kim and Matthew to pull up alongside. Matthew was just going to put his theory out there when Kyle pointed behind them.

Looking back toward Treasure Island park and across the road, the fire had crested the ridge and was chewing up the forest in front of it. The crown of the trees blazed. The road wasn't enough of a break to stop it, and the ember cast pushed ahead by the wind rained down, sizzling as they hit the water, lighting fires where they hit land.

His stomach dropped. If they'd been a little later, the fire would have overtaken them. No way they'd be able to outrun it.

No, hanging out in the bay wasn't going to be an option. Without a word, he dug his paddle in, ignoring the pain, and their little band headed out to the choppy waves.

The lake looked a lot bigger, and the waves crested over their bows. Between the wind and the waves, it was a challenge to keep control of the kayak. But they had to stay together. It reminded him of the story of Jesus asleep on the boat with the disciples while the wind and waves threatened to drown them. Even the wind and the waves obeyed him. That was still true now. God was still in control, even though their world looked very out of control.

The smoke had eased a bit even as the wind was stronger. The biggest danger now was one of them getting blown away from the rest. Jessica and Austin were farther off than he liked. Were they strong enough to get back to the group? He didn't think any of them were expert kayakers. "Kyle!" He hoped his voice carried over the wind.

Kyle turned.

"Let's tie off before we get blown away from each other."

Kyle's gaze traveled up behind him.

Matthew turned and looked. The fire was nearly to the road, and spot fires burned all around the marina and in the trees.

When he turned back, Kyle was shouting to Austin, who was the farthest out.

Austin made a valiant effort to turn his kayak toward Kyle, into the wind. He was making some progress. He neared Jessica and said something to her which was lost on the wind. She nodded, but he pulled farther away, his stronger arms better able to battle the water.

"Toss me the rope!" Austin yelled to Kyle, letting his kayak lose ground but drift closer to Jessica.

Kyle threw it, but it fell short.

Austin grabbed for it, dislodging his paddle into the lake. He lunged for it, nearly tipping over. His fingers curled around the paddle as he righted himself.

Kyle waited until Austin was settled, then he tossed the rope again. This time it hit the bow before sliding off.

Austin had drifted past Jessica, so he paddled vigorously to get closer while Kyle hauled in the rope and readied it to toss again.

This time, the rope landed right in front of Austin, and he grabbed it. He looped it through the cording in front of him on the deck of his kayak, then paddled over to Jessica, grabbing her kayak.

Kyle started hauling them in. Jessica held on to Austin's kayak, and he paddled to help Kyle. Heather was paddling their kayak in the same direction.

Matthew leaned forward. "Let's dig in and get as close to Kyle and Heather as we can."

Kim nodded but didn't turn around. She dipped her paddle in the water, and he matched her rhythm. They threatened to slide past Kyle and were headed for Jessica's kayak, which would no doubt knock her loose from her grip on Austin's.

Matthew back-paddled to swing the end around and head them into the wind. For a moment, it didn't feel like they were making any progress, but Kim must have sensed the urgency, and they closed the gap. He wedged them in between Heather and Jessica. Kim grabbed the back of Heather's boat, and he grabbed Jessica's.

Austin fed the rope through his webbing and passed it on to Jessica, who copied him and sent it on to Kim. In short order, they were tied together in a floating pod, with the wind pushing them further into the center of the lake.

Where it soon became obvious they were surrounded by fire.

Chapter Fifteen

Kim's heart tripped a bit as she spotted the inferno barreling toward them, ringing nearly the whole shoreline. Surely they'd be safe on the lake. Their little pod bobbed in the rough water as the wind created by the fire rushed over the surface of the lake. No one spoke. *Okay, Lord. So we just keep floating?* No answer but peace wedged itself a little more firmly in her heart. Things could be worse. Her asthma was under control for the most part, and she wasn't in this alone. In fact, she was with some very competent people. This might not be her idea of fun, but they would be okay.

However, this was probably the last way Heather and Kyle expected to spend their time. Here she was supposed to be giving them a great weekend to remember—well, at least Heather—and nothing had gone as planned. Though, up until this fire disaster, it had all turned out to be a pretty good event. Thanks to Matthew.

She glanced back over her shoulder. He was studying her with that intense stare of his, a small curve at the corners of his lips. Lips she had hoped would kiss hers back on the marina. Longing washed over her. She had missed him. Those ten days on the road with him had shown her all facets of his personality. Seeing him interact with Melissa and Allie had been fascinating, since she'd only grown up with Kyle, no sisters. Though Heather had become as sweet to her as one.

They floated out from under the smoke cover blocking the sun, and it scorched Kim's arms. The fire-heated air was hot enough without the addition of the sun's rays. The drone of an airplane, and possibly the *thwap thwap thwap* of a helicopter, floated over them, but nothing was visible. Everyone's head tipped up, scanning the sky. The sound faded before they could even determine what or where it was.

Despair landed on her like a heavy blanket. She didn't realize how much she'd expected them to get spotted quickly. The fact that they passed in and out of the smoke kept them from viewing their potential rescue. Would they ever be spotted? What if they weren't? How long could they survive out here? They had some trail mix and granola bars, a few bottles of water each. She didn't want to think about drinking the lake water, but if they got desperate, she guessed it was possible.

Her arms ached from paddling, but she stretched as she could and tried to think about other things. Letting her mind run away with worst case scenarios wouldn't help at all.

"Anybody ever think being trapped on a lake, chased by a wildfire would be part of God's plan for them?" Matthew's tone was light, and Austin chuckled.

But she wondered. Given the problems with this weekend, the weirdos on social media, and now the fire today, what was God trying to tell her, if anything?

Heather gave a rueful smile and shared a look with Kyle. "No, but I never thought I'd witness a murder as part of a gang initiation gone wrong either. Still, God used it to bring good in my life. It's hard to think about the good when everything seems to be crashing down around you."

Matthew's voice came from behind Kim. "It's easy to think

God's trying to tell us something based on our circumstances. I know I've felt he opened doors for me to get this job with Data-Corp in OC. What with Allie working with them and Austin coming along, it all seemed perfect. But did I stop to think if it was really his plan for me? Or did I just plow ahead because I knew what I wanted?"

Kim didn't turn around, but she felt his gaze hot on her neck. She was what he wanted. He'd made that abundantly clear. But had she prayed about it at all? Or had she just tucked into her feelings and burrowed down, shutting him out?

Heather turned toward Kyle. "Remember that Bible study we did in our small group? I don't even remember what study it was, but I do remember the topic of circumstances coming up."

Kyle nodded. "Yeah, last fall. I remember because you had just been allowed to go back to your quote-unquote normal life."

"I probably remember it most because the illustration in the book was really dorky. I was thinking I could do a much better job." Heather laughed. "Basically, it was two pictures. One of a car on a rough road, and one of a car on a smooth road. The point was that whether the road of life was smooth or rough wasn't much of an indication of if you were in God's will or not."

"If I remember correctly," Kyle said, "you did do a better drawing. That was a good discussion. The Pharisees thought if you were born with a defect that you or your parents had sinned. But the point Jesus made was that God allows things to happen to us to bring him glory."

"So." Jessica drew the word out. Kim was surprised she was joining the discussion. She had been so quiet, which was not the Jessica Kim had grown up with. "How does that apply in real life? A lot of my pain has been self-inflicted. But you all haven't held that against me. You have been kind enough to welcome me when you could have easily shunned me. You are good people. So why is God allowing you to suffer through this mess?

Does it glorify him in some way? And how do I know if I should finish up cosmetology school? Or should I do something else?"

Kim wished she could reach out and hug Jessica.

Kyle spoke up. "You're on the right track. You're getting rid of the bad things in your life that hurt you and other people. You are using your God-given desire for beauty and to help others. All any of us can do is to pray and seek God's guidance in everything, the good times and the bad."

"And know that his plan for us is always the best." Heather smiled at her.

Jessica nodded. "Yeah, I can look back and see all the ways God has protected me." She gave a soft smile. "I have a lot to be thankful for."

"We all do," Kim added.

The smoke drifted back over them again. They grew silent.

"I'm hungry." Matthew rustled around in his backpack a moment before his hand landed on her shoulder. "Can you hand me a bottle of water?"

"Sure." Kim turned around. He was munching on a granola bar. "Anyone else want water? I've got the cooler here."

Yeses went up around their little pod, so she began handing the bottles to Jessica who could pass them to Austin, then to Kyle and Heather. "Too bad we don't have the Ungame with us." Matthew opened his water. "We've got a prime get-to-know-you opportunity right here. We used to play it in the car as kids, and Melissa brought it with her on our Great American Road Trip."

"What's the Ungame?" Kyle took a swig of water.

"It's a deck of cards with thought-provoking questions. Things you don't normally think about."

"Since you're in a contemplative mood..." Jessica pulled out her phone. "My sponsor put me on to this app of daily inspirational quotes. I thought it was kind of cheesy at first, but it's given me a positive direction to focus my thoughts on, and some things to ponder. So what do you make of this? Yesterday's quote: 'The pessimist sees difficulty in every opportunity. The optimist sees opportunity in every difficulty.' And today's quote, wait for it, 'There is no security in this life. There is only opportunity.' Anyone want to chime in on the opportunity in this particular difficulty?"

They bobbed in the water, silent but for the wind and the slap of water on the kayaks.

"I think opportunity comes after the difficulty." Austin spoke up. "You need faith to believe that it will come, that there is purpose in the difficulty because you can't see it while you're in it."

Kim raised her eyebrows. She hadn't heard Austin say that much at one time before. He exemplified the old saying, "Still waters run deep." He would be good for Matthew as a roommate and friend.

Heather nodded. "There's a lot of truth in that. I can see it in my own life, how it's come true, but only after the fact. So whatever opportunity comes out of today, we won't recognize it until we're down the road a bit."

Smoke blanketed the shoreline back where they'd come from. Kim had no idea if the marina still stood. The wind was pushing them toward the far side of the lake, the only side that hadn't burned. But the way the fire was moving, it would reach that area before they did.

Then what? Fire made its own weather, and it didn't seem like the current wind would push them into the flames. But where would it take them? She kept a tight grip on her emotions to keep from spiraling. It would be so easy to let herself drown in all the what ifs, none of which looked good. But opportunity? She was having a hard time seeing it. Perhaps that's why it was called faith.

The drone of an airplane could be heard behind the smoke but wasn't visible yet.

Matthew shifted behind her, rocking the kayak. "If we could get out of this smoke, we might be visible to those water-dropping planes I hear. They're probably getting water from the lake."

"If the visibility is good, they could use either super scoopers or helos." Kyle drained his water bottle.

What if the plane trying to scoop up water by skimming over the surface of the lake didn't see them until it was too late? Was that another danger they had to watch out for?

Get a grip. Another thought hit her. Exhaustion was making her silly, and she giggled. She turned to Matthew. He'd appreciate it. "Ever wonder if they suck up fish when they get the water? Do the fish swim out of the path? Or do they get dropped on the fire? Fish fry!"

The comment broke the tension that had enveloped them, and they all laughed, probably harder than they would have under any other circumstance.

Kyle shook his head. "I'll have to ask Joe if they ever find any fish when they're checking for hotspots after a fire."

Silence fell over them once again, the sounds of the water, wind, and fire wrapping them in an uneasy tension.

"Hear that?" Matthew leaned forward, his hand on Kim's shoulder, sending heat unrelated to the fire rushing through her.

She had to concentrate to process his words. "I don't hear anything." She turned to look at him.

"Wait." He listened again. "It's a plane." He swiveled around looking for the source. They could see a bigger chunk of blue sky now. All of them scanned the sky looking for the source of the sound.

"There." Kyle pointed.

It took a minute, but Kim saw it too. Looked like a private plane, but as it got closer she could see the red and white markings. It had to be some sort of firefighting plane. It seemed to be flying in a pattern, not dipping down to the lake to get water. At least not the part of the lake they could see.

"Wave the paddles." Matthew lifted his in the air. "The blades are white and more visible."

Kim whipped her paddle overhead and waved it, along with everyone else. Her arm was tired before the plane flew off, a white puff in its wake, with no indication that the pilot had seen them.

But right behind the first plane came a deeper, more rumbling roar. A bigger plane barely skimming above the trees. It seemed impossible something so large could hang in the sky like that.

"That must have been a lead plane," Kyle said. "Bet we'll get to watch a Phos-Chek drop."

Kim fumbled for her phone. Why hadn't she been chronicling their journey? That was what she did. She had her phone out, camera open, and aimed just as a heavy pink swath dropped from the belly of the plane onto the forest on the far side of the lake. She snapped away until the plane disappeared.

"That was cool to watch." Matthew's voice came from behind her. "At least we have a view of this no one else does."

"I suppose that's something." Kim smiled. Matthew could be like a little boy, finding joy in big toys. Or opportunity in difficulty. She rummaged in the dry bag for her good camera. He was right. She might as well get some good pictures while she was here. For a while, she busied herself getting shots of everything around them, the smoke, the fire line, their floating pod. Her photography did what only sketching and drawing could do: take her mind away from her circumstances.

She'd never taken pictures in a place like this before, floating in a pod as if they were the only people left in the world, hoping they'd get rescued. Photography had to work harder than ever before to pull her out of a pit of emotion that could swamp her and drag her under if she gave it any leeway.

Another, different sound grew. Soon she could make out a helicopter with a giant bucket hanging below it. It didn't come much closer, certainly not close enough to spot them, especially since the smoke tumbled in drifts across the lake. The helo hovered over the lake surface, the sound of its rotors carrying unevenly on the wind. The water rippled from the downdraft, and the bucket slid into the waves before being lifted, dripping.

From this distance, the helicopter and the bucket both looked like child's toys in a wading pool.

Her camera whirled and clicked away, the zoom lens bringing the helo close as she snapped shots, wishing she were as close to the pilot as her camera made it seem. Maybe then they would be spotted and finally rescued.

Chapter Sixteen

Matthew studied Kim's back as she leaned forward, stowing away her camera. After that first action, the smoke had moved over them, obstructing their view. They could hear the helos but not see them.

Kim leaned over the edge of the kayak, cupping water and letting it trickle down her neck and arms.

That looked refreshing. Sweat soaked his shirt, sticking it to the kayak seat. It seemed cruel to have all this water around and not be able to get in it to cool off. But there was no good way to get either out or in the kayak without risking tipping it.

Matthew flicked his paddle and managed to get a few drops on Kim. She brushed at her arm but didn't turn around. He adjusted the angle and tried again. A small wave bounced off the oar blade and drenched Kim's shoulder.

"What—?" She twisted around.

He grinned.

She gave him a surprised look and then laughed. "Do it again. It felt good."

He obliged her. He couldn't get a good enough angle to get more than her arm and part of her shoulder wet.

"Here." Kim snatched the paddle from where she'd tucked it

under the shock cords and contorted until she could return the favor. Splashing Jessica in the process.

"Hey!" Jessica flung water in an arc over both him and Kim.

Then Austin angled a perfect splash over Jessica, drenching her.

Her eyes went wide as her jaw dropped.

Horror crossed Austin's face, and he opened his mouth just as Jessica started laughing. His shoulders dropped, and he laughed too.

"Good one, Austin. Somehow you figured out the ideal slant."

Matthew thought Austin might try to explain the physics of it, but he just shrugged and grinned.

Nice. He was fitting in.

Jessica tried to get him back, and they continued to attempt to spray themselves with water, but no one could replicate Austin's success. The brief splashes meant the hot air sucked the water off their skin almost immediately, leaving them cooler, if only briefly.

Sounds of helicopter blades beating the air grew stronger, making them fall silent again as the helo made another dip into the lake. It was still too far away to see them, and Matthew had no idea if the plane that passed a bit closer could spot them.

It disappeared, along with another flicker of hope.

Jessica spoke up. "Kim, remember that time our families went camping at the beach? We were, what, in elementary school?"

Kim nodded. "Yeah, like ten I think. Which would make Kyle and Scott fifteen."

Jessica laughed. "They did not want their bratty little sisters following them around while they tried to pick up girls and look cool."

Kim giggled. "That's right. We followed them all over that one afternoon."

"But they got us back." Jessica's face was lit by a mischievous smile that transformed her features.

Matthew glanced at Austin, who leaned toward Jessica, focused on her.

Kyle shook his head. "Are you sure you want to tell this story?"

"Ha!" Jessica tossed her head. "Just because you guys don't come out looking like the heroes."

"How were we supposed to know?"

Heather swung her gaze between Kyle and Jessica. "What happened?"

Kim leaned back. "You want to tell it or should I?"

"I will." Jessica's gaze took in the group. "After dinner, when it was dark, the guys said we should all go down to the beach. I can't remember what excuse they gave us. But they had the flashlight. So we followed them. They spent some time flashing their light at a boat that was offshore. It flashed something back."

Kyle shook his head. "The only Morse code any of us knew was SOS. We thought it was funny. Save us from our sisters."

"I'm sure the people on the boat thought you were morons," Kim put in.

Kyle shrugged.

Jessica cleared her throat. "Anyway, that wasn't the point of the story. It just illustrated the state of mind the boys were in for what happened next."

"Our state of mind was that our little sisters followed us everywhere. Any normal person would be annoyed by that. If Scott were here, he'd take my side."

Matthew chuckled. This was almost as fun as watching his family dynamics.

"Of course he would." Jessica shot Kyle a glare. "As I was saying, the boys had the flashlight, and they kept walking on ahead of us. The beach was dark, and the tide was coming in. Cliffs were to the side of us, making the beach narrow, so we thought one big wave would get us wet. And who knew what was in the ocean at night."

"Water," Kyle muttered.

"My story. Anyhow, there was this giant thing washed up on shore, a huge mound. We couldn't tell what it was, but it moved anytime a wave came in. It looked like a beached whale. And the last thing Kim and I wanted was to run into a dead whale in the dark. So we stopped walking."

Kim laughed. "We thought for sure the boys would see we weren't behind them and would simply turn around and come back. We didn't want to walk by the dead whale without a light."

"It wasn't a dead whale," Kyle muttered again.

Heather shushed him. "Let Jessica tell it."

"Thank you. But guess what? They never came back for us."

Heather's jaw dropped, and she pinned Kyle with a glare. "You left them out there with a dead whale in the dark?"

Kyle smirked and shook his head but didn't say anything. He gestured to Jessica to finish.

"Eventually, Kim and I got up the courage to walk around the whale, since it was clear the boys were going to be useless."

Matthew leaned forward. "Was it a dead whale?"

"No. It was a pile of seaweed," Jessica said matter-of-factly.

The whole group broke out in laughter.

She raised her voice. "But that wasn't the point! It could have been a dead whale. The point is they left us alone out there. So we climbed up the stairs to the top of the cliffs and headed back to camp."

Matthew laughed. "That's it?"

"No!" Jessica was indignant. "Before we got back to camp, the boys were waiting on the periphery for us to show up. They knew they'd get into trouble if they came back to camp without us." She pointed at Kyle. "Why don't you tell everyone why you guys left us on the beach?"

"We thought you'd snuck off to run around and scare us."

Now Jessica rolled her eyes. "Raise your hand if you think that was a reasonable thought."

Kyle lifted his hand. Austin did too. Matthew eased his up, hopefully out of Kim's view. She was close enough to turn around and smack him.

Jessica shook her head. "Now raise your hand if you think the reasonable thing for the boys to do was to turn around and come back to get us once they realized we weren't following them." She kept her hand up. Kim's and Heather's shot up too.

Kim turned and glanced at Matthew. "The biggest lesson of the day? Guys and girls think totally differently."

"You got that right," Kyle said. "But you missed another big point. We knew we were responsible for you two. As much as you annoyed us, we would never have let anything happen to you." His voice softened toward the end.

Tears welled in Jessica's eyes. She dashed them away. "I know. That's why Scott wanted me to come this weekend."

Austin reached over and touched her shoulder. "I'm glad you came."

She gave him a watery smile. "Me too."

Matthew couldn't process what he was seeing. Austin always seemed reserved and quiet, except when he was playing video games, but Jessica seemed to bring out a different side of him.

"Last of the water bottles. Who wants one?" Kim held one up.

Everyone did. Kim passed them around again.

Matthew didn't want to think about what would happen when they next were thirsty. They'd be rescued by then for sure.

Kim's shoulders contracted as she clearly struggled with the bottle cap.

He touched her water-dampened shoulder. "Let me."

She turned, her eyes traveling up until they met his. He didn't move his hand. She handed him the bottle without breaking their gaze.

Was he really seeing interest in her eyes? Or was it wishful thinking? When they got out of here, they were going to have that date they had never gotten but had talked about when they were on the Great American Road Trip. He wasn't going to come out of all this "adventure" without Kim by his side.

He unscrewed the cap, using the splint as a brace, and handed the bottle back to her.

Her soft "Thanks" spoke volumes.

If it weren't for the circumstances, Matthew would have enjoyed today. Watching Kim's back and shoulders as she moved the paddle wasn't hard work. He wished they had found time alone at some point. Because life would get crazy once they got back home. DataCorp would demand all his time as they got the OC office off the ground. It was just his luck that he was stuck in a kayak with Kim—something that seemed like a dream— and yet he couldn't really talk to her. But he would take being with her on this kayak than knowing she was out here without him any day. All he could do was try to keep her safe. Whatever that meant.

Matthew just hoped he was strong enough.

Jessica twisted the cap back on her water bottle. "It's a good thing Scott and Joe aren't here. Trouble seems to follow you guys around."

Matthew appreciated that he hadn't seen this side of Jessica, trying to buoy everyone's spirits. That was usually his job. Whistling in the graveyard.

Kyle glanced at Heather. "No offense, honey, but it's the women in our lives that cause the problems. We're just along to keep them safe."

Heather let out a laugh at that and then nodded. "Okay, there's a little bit of truth in that. But you all have your own set of troubles too."

The banter flowed among them, but Matthew let his mind drift. He knew they would be rescued. It wasn't like they were on a deserted island somewhere.

The problem was that it could take awhile, and once the sun

went down, the planes and helos were grounded. And as hot as they were now, it would get cold sitting on the water. The best they could do was to push on and hope that God really was watching out for them and wouldn't let anything happen to them that they couldn't overcome.

Of course his mind flashed to dozens of missionaries martyred for sharing the gospel—not to mention a good chunk of the Old Testament heroes—so clearly doing God's will wasn't protection from harm. He didn't want to dwell there too long. That would just remind him of all the things that were out of his control. He had to rest in God's wisdom, that God knew what He was doing, and all of this was somehow part of His plan to work it all out for good.

Whatever happened.

Kim finished off her water bottle. "Hang on. I'm going to lean over the side." She slowly shifted her weight to the side. The kayak rocked a bit while Matthew adjusted his weight to counterbalance her.

She dipped the bottle in the water. "The coolness feels good on my hand. I wish it could cover my whole body." The water glugged into the bottle. When it was full, she pulled it out, removed her ball cap, and dumped the liquid over her head.

A little splashed on Matthew, but he was entranced watching the water run down her neck. He couldn't help but picture his lips tasting those drops.

She turned and smiled at him. "The next best thing to going for a swim."

His mouth was dry. He could think of better things than swimming, but cool water sounded good. "Let me try that." He drained the last of his water bottle, letting the last drops roll around his mouth and throat. Leaning over, he made sure she adjusted her weight to keep them from tipping. He poured the water over his head, washing away some of the sweat and temporarily relieving the burn of the sun on his skin.

The wind was pushing them closer and closer to the far shore and out from the smoke cover. It was the only place not burned. If they got close enough to it, they could decide then what to do. Fight the wind to keep on the water or let it push them ashore and risk the fire closing in on them.

The sound of another helo overhead grew louder. This one circled a bit then came back and hovered over their position. They waved their paddles and shouted, though he was certain they couldn't be heard.

But had they been spotted?

Kim dropped her paddle and scrambled for her camera. After adjusting the lens, she shouted. "Yes! I can see the pilot. He's giving me a thumbs up. He sees us!" Her voice broke on the last word.

The helo moved off a ways, dipped its bucket, and flew away, the bucket streaming behind him, dripping water.

"Okay, let's think about this," Kyle said. "How are they going to rescue us? They could drop a line down and pull each of us up individually. Or we could try to make it to that beach over there. Looks like there might be room for them to land." He pointed to the far shore. "Or they might even send in a team by ground."

Matthew voted for the shore. Anything was better than sitting here floating, even if it meant working through the pain in his wrist. He and Kyle started untying their flotilla. They just had to get the timing right. Get to the beach in time for the helo to grab them, but not so soon that the fire might get them.

God, we could use your help here.

Chapter Seventeen

Kim double checked that her camera was stowed in the dry bag but kept her phone on her lap. It was waterproof. The only problem would be if it went overboard and she lost it. She hoped to capture the moments of their rescue. And there would be a rescue. She held on to that hope.

Gripping her paddle, she watched as Austin and Jessica moved out of the pod toward the far shore, then she dug in. Her arms had appreciated the break, but the soreness returned after a few strokes. She'd be really achy tomorrow.

She'd gotten into a rhythm, knowing that Matthew matched her. She could feel the extra surge of power with his strokes. That had been missing before. The wind helped push them too.

"Looks like Kyle called it!" Matthew shouted over the wind.

She couldn't turn back to answer without losing their momentum, so she raised her gaze.

A helo was hovering over the landing spot on shore.

A sob welled up inside her chest. Hope—something she'd clung to but wasn't sure if it would blossom into reality. It gave her an added burst of adrenaline, and she ignored the burning in her shoulders and paddled faster. They had to reach the shore before the fire did, and their only chance of rescue would be forced to abandon them.

She fixed her gaze on the helo as it landed. A man in a flight suit got out and waved them in. And someone else, a man in jeans. Collins? Knowing he was waiting for them helped somehow. He wouldn't let them get left behind.

Each stroke hurt and cramped, but it couldn't be helped. One more. One more. One more. Chanting to herself was the game she played with her aching arm muscles. It seemed like they'd been paddling forever, and the shore didn't seem much closer. How much time did they have before the helo would need to leave due to the approaching fire? Collins would keep the helo there as long as possible, but she didn't want them to be at risk as well.

Heather and Kyle's kayak was several lengths ahead of them. Austin and Jessica must be behind, but she couldn't take the time to turn and look. As long as Kyle got to shore, he'd get them to wait as long as they could.

As Kyle's kayak neared the edge of the lake, Collins and the man in the flight suit ran over and helped pull it up. Heather gathered their backpacks, and Collins helped her into the helo.

Kyle waded to them as Kim and Matthew approached. He grabbed the front of the kayak and hauled it to the shoreline.

Kim tried to let go of the paddle, but her hands had cramped around it. She had to make a concerted effort to relax them. She fumbled up her phone and took a few shots then grabbed the dry bag and her backpack. Kyle proffered a hand to help her out of the kayak. The first step splashed icy water on her leg and shocked her. She swung her other leg over and took a step. Pain shot up, and she crumpled into the wet sand.

Strong arms scooped her up. "I've got her. You get the others."

Matthew.

For a moment, she allowed herself to be pulled against his chest, the smell of him—his lingering spicy leather, sweat, and lake water—surrounding her, reminding her of all the time they'd spent together in his truck on the road trip.

She peeked over his shoulder. Jessica was still in the water, struggling. Austin was ahead of her, shouting encouragement. Kim snapped a few more shots then Matthew was setting her on the deck of the helo.

The man inside pointed to a seat. She scooted over and strapped in next to Heather.

Matthew stood in the doorway, looking back at the lake. He shot her a look then darted off to help Kyle and Collins.

Kim glanced at Heather who reached for her hand. "We made it."

Heather nodded.

Well, almost. They still had to get the rest of them in here, and the smell of smoke was overpowering. The aircraft crew checked out the windows and gauges frequently, though Kim couldn't hear anything they said over the sound of the rotors.

After what felt like an eternity, Matthew appeared, helping Jessica inside, followed by Austin, Kyle, Collins, and the final crew member. They barely got strapped in before they were lifting up.

Kim had never been in a helicopter before, but nothing seemed so wonderful right this moment as to rise up off the ground. The higher they got, the more she could see fire was everywhere below them, a roiling inferno eating up everything in its path. How did it get so big so fast?

As soon as they got above the smoke and headed out of the mountains, she could see blue sky. Below them, a highway snaked out of the mountains, the line of cars headed all in one direction resembling a funeral procession.

She leaned her head back on the headrest, a wave of exhaustion and appreciation washing over her. She hadn't quite believed it would happen.

They were safe.

Matthew helped Kim out of the helo once it touched down at San Bernardino International Airport. Paramedics rushed over and got her on a gurney. The flight crew must have called ahead. He walked beside them as they moved her away and toward the ambulance.

Exhausted as she was, she gave him a small smile and squeezed his hand. "This really is a lot of fuss over a sprained ankle."

"You've been through a lot," one of the paramedics said. "We just want to make sure you're not hurt anywhere else."

One of them asked Matthew if he had any injuries. He said no, and the woman went to check out the others.

Matthew stood next to Kyle and Collins. "Where's the rest of the group?"

Collins checked his phone quickly. "Joe and I are working the fire. I caught a ride with these guys when the call came in about kayakers spotted on the lake. I knew it was you all. I had to make sure you were okay. Kellie drove the other girls and Scott down to the Walmart parking lot in Highland at the base of the mountains." He glanced back. "I've got to head back with the crew, but I have to say, I've never been so happy to see a group of kayakers." He pulled Kyle into a quick man hug and did the same to Matthew. He hugged the rest of the group then jogged back to the helicopter, sending them a wave before climbing in.

Kyle looked up from his phone. "They're on their way here, but we're going to need to rent a minivan to get home. I'll make arrangements." He stepped away.

That reminded Matthew that he'd have to call the rental company about his minivan. He'd need a replacement car too. His gaze drifted to Kim, where a paramedic was wrapping her ankle. He rubbed his hand over his face. He was grimy and in need of a shower and clean clothes. The rental car was going to be filled with smoky, sweaty people.

But they were safe.

The paramedic put a chemical ice pack on Kim's ankle. "It wouldn't hurt to get it x-rayed. Definitely check in with your own doctor on Monday."

It was still Saturday. The thought hit him. It'd felt a lot longer than twenty-four hours that they'd been up the mountain. And Monday, work would start in earnest. But he had tomorrow. With Kim. He hoped.

Someone found a wheelchair from the terminal for Kim, and she transferred into it. The paramedics packed up.

Kyle came back from making his calls and led the discussion as they gave their statements to the fire officials interested in their experience. No one could tell them for certain if the cabins had made it or not, but it didn't look good. Luckily they were just staying for the weekend, and the rest of their group had packed up everything. They hadn't lost anything, unlike the folks who lived up there.

When the fire officials had gotten all the information they needed, and their band had given their thanks to everyone for the rescue, they headed out through the terminal. Matthew pushed Kim in the wheelchair.

It finally hit him that they were safe. Earlier today their lives were in imminent danger, and yet by Monday everything would go on as if it hadn't happened. Reconciling the two realities made his head hurt.

"I can't wait to get home and get a shower." Kim looked up at him.

"Me too. I'm starving though. There's an In-N-Out not too far from here." He wouldn't make it to Orange County on an empty stomach.

A group of people stood inside the terminal, some with cameras and microphones. Were they going to try to catch one of the fire officials? This was not the main operations base. And it wasn't even a much-used airport. It was where the flight crews were stationed and refilled with Phos-Chek. He was missing something, but his brain was too fried from hunger and exhaustion to make out what it was.

"Tell us about your rescue."

"How did you get stranded?"

"Did you ignore evacuation orders?"

A camera focused on Kim. A microphone followed. "How did you get hurt?"

He didn't have the energy for this. And he didn't want to subject Kim to it.

Kyle stepped in front of them. Let him deal with them. It was part of his job. "Thanks for asking. We're happy to be rescued by the brave men and women of the unified command structure that involves many agencies. We had planned a day kayaking on Holcomb Lake, and never got any evacuation orders because there wasn't cell service on the lake." He summed up their journey succinctly and was gracious with the reporters.

Kyle had a lot more patience with them than Matthew would have.

"Anybody get any pictures?"

Kyle turned to look at Kim.

And Matthew groaned.

Chapter Eighteen

Kim laid on her couch with her foot propped up, a pair of crutches borrowed from Sarah leaning against the arm of the couch, air cast around her ankle. Her foot didn't feel that bad as long as she wasn't on it too much. It didn't seem broken, just sprained. But being on the second floor created a problem. It was too much of a hassle to make it to church today. Her arms hurt from paddling, and the pain worsened when she had to use the crutches. Plus, she was worn out and really didn't want to see or talk to anyone.

The TV played in the background, but the LA stations only gave general periodic updates. She got better information on the fire off Twitter. When they'd driven home last night, the fire had zero percent containment, and CalFire was focused on structure protection. The situation was so fluid, no one knew if any homes or businesses had been lost. This morning had little more information, but there would be an update later from incident command.

Were Collins and Joe safe? They were like big brothers to her. Seeing Collins yesterday had been a bigger relief than she would have imagined. It was like his presence meant they were truly rescued. She knew he would make sure they were safe.

She'd talk to Kyle later and see what he knew. Allie and Sarah were probably concerned about Collins and Joe too.

Skimming through social media, it was a little gratifying to see her photos of the fire and their rescue all over the news with her social media handles attached. She had an exclusive on that story, the kind of up-close-and-personal reporting most news media would kill for. She had some new followers, though she doubted they were into fashion. Still, maybe there was some way it would give her an edge during Design Review. Though she really couldn't see how. Unless the top designers noticed, and it brought her to their attention. Maybe it wouldn't hurt.

She clicked through the number of new messages she had from various media asking to be contacted for an interview. Maybe Kyle or Matthew would deal with them. She'd have to think about how to best respond.

She wasn't as thrilled with the photos of them all sweaty and grimy from their rescue being played over and over. Her hair limp underneath a grimy ball cap, her sweaty T-shirt plastered to her. It was the opposite of the curated image of up-and-coming fashion designer that she put out on social media. She could only imagine the teasing she'd get at work over her "look." But something else would catch the media's attention, and their rescue would be pushed down in the news cycle.

She hoped.

On the other hand, Kyle and Heather would have a weekend to remember, though not the relaxing one Kim had planned. And there wasn't time to schedule another, though perhaps a spa day? She'd ask Allie about the one she and Melissa had been to.

But Design Review was at the end of this week and the wedding the week after that. She didn't want to make Heather's schedule—or her own—more hectic. While she knew the fire wasn't her fault, if she'd picked a place at the beach, like Kellie had suggested, this wouldn't have happened. But Kim wanted to do something different, unexpected. They lived near the beach and could—and did—visit it at any time. The mountains were farther away. Something out of the everyday.

Well, they'd gotten different all right. And Heather hadn't gotten her weekend away at all.

For as momentous and potentially life changing as yesterday had been, today felt incredibly ordinary. Perhaps it was the result of burning all the adrenaline yesterday, but it seemed like something should mark the occasion of looking death in the face and surviving. How did people like her brother, Joe, Collins, and Scott do it? Did you ever get used to it?

A knock sounded at her door. Wary, she dropped her phone on the coffee table and grabbed her crutches. She should get a doorbell camera one of these days. At least she'd know if it was worth getting up for. Though solicitors didn't usually make the effort to climb the stairs.

She peered through the peephole.

Matthew.

Pulling the door open, she smiled and hopped back.

"I brought breakfast." He held up a bag. "Go sit down."

"Yes, sir." She crutched back to the couch. "Plates are in the cupboard to the right of the sink."

"I'll find them."

He rustled around the kitchen then brought over a plate with a breakfast sandwich and hash browns on it. He took the chair next to the couch. "Crutches make everything more difficult."

"Yep." Including taking a shower last night when she got home. But it had felt like the best shower she'd ever had. "You got a new rental car okay? They didn't hold the minivan against you?"

"Nah, they were pretty nice about the whole thing and were glad we made it out okay. How's the ankle?"

"It's not too bad. I'm sure it's not broken, and it'll probably be better soon. I can put weight on it, just not for very long. I'm planning on going into work on Monday."

He raised his eyebrows. "After all you've been through?"

"Design Review is this week."

"Do you feel ready?"

"I think so. Monique will have my completed design sewn up by tomorrow, but there is still work to be done. I keep second guessing myself. I hope I've made good selections."

"I'm sure you did. You have a gift."

Her heart softened. It was nice to have someone reassure her and appreciate her creativity. It didn't happen much outside of Heather. She didn't want to second guess his motives so she changed the subject. "Kyle texted me this morning. He and Heather were headed to church and they wanted to see if I wanted a ride. I passed, as you can tell. Kellie left all our stuff that they packed up from the cabins at Kyle's."

"I didn't think you'd be going to church. But I figured breakfast would be welcome." He gave her that winning grin. "And I could use my bag since it had all my casual clothes in it. Everything at the hotel is business wear." He was wearing khakis and a button-down shirt, sleeves rolled up.

Her phone dinged with a new message, and she picked it up out of habit. Most of the press had reached out to her via Twitter or Instagram, so this was likely someone she knew.

I've been worried about you, babe, ever since I saw the news. Call me so I can hear your voice and know you're okay.

Her hand shook as she tossed the phone down. Nick. It had to be.

Matthew looked up. "What's wrong? More media?"

She shook her head. He'd been supportive when she'd gotten the balloon and she'd told him about Nick, but she just wanted it all to go away. She wasn't quite sure where she stood with Matthew. Yes, she'd thought about their almost-kiss and their past kisses. And he'd been amazing through their whole ordeal, but could he really stick with her through the long haul? Or was she just responding to something familiar due to what they'd been through together?

She wasn't in the frame of mind to analyze all of that. "Just someone I don't want to talk to." Time to change the subject. "Have you talked to anyone else? How's Austin doing?" She picked up the sandwich and took a bite. It was still hot. Yum.

"He's fine. Kyle dropped us off at the rental car place last night, and Austin and I crashed when we got back to our hotel, after taking showers. Jessica invited him along to hang out with Scott and Melissa. They were going to church then get something to eat before Scott's flight left."

"I feel bad for how Heather's weekend ended. It never even really started. I keep trying to think of ways to make it up to her, but the wedding isn't far off. I don't want to try to cram something into an already packed schedule."

Matthew set his sandwich down. "Why is this so important to you? It's not your fault there was a forest fire. You couldn't have predicted that. I'm a guy, so I fully admit I don't get the whole wedding hoopla, but what am I missing here?"

She laid her head back on the sofa. It would sound weird putting it into words. And he probably wouldn't understand. "It's just... Kyle and my dad have always looked at me as this flaky artist type. And when Heather started dating Kyle and stayed with us for a while, she saw me differently. She asked my opinion on fashion and style, and she listened to me. She's been the big sister I never had. And when Kellie clearly wasn't pulling her weight as maid of honor, I just wanted to give Heather a special weekend and show Kyle and my dad that her faith in me wasn't misplaced." She shook her head. "I don't know. Maybe they're right."

Matthew leaned forward and put his hand on her knee. "I don't know anything about fashion, but I've spent a lot of time with you. You're not a flake. You're creative, and you have fantastic ideas. You did have a great weekend planned for Heather. And I'd be surprised if they really thought you were a flake. Kyle didn't give me that impression at all this weekend.

Yes, he definitely has the big brother vibe going on, but he wasn't dismissive of you."

"Maybe." Tears pricked her eyes, and she blinked. She didn't want to cry. Granted, she was emotionally exhausted from everything, and that stupid message from Nick didn't help. Matthew's kindness would put her over the edge if she wasn't careful. She slipped out from his touch, immediately missing the warmth. "So you don't think I need to make it up to her?"

He laughed and sat back. "Um, no. You don't." Giving her an appraising look, he was silent for a moment. "How can I help, Kim? I have all day free. Want to meet up with everyone for lunch? Get out of the house? We can't make up for the fun we missed, but it might shake everything off."

She really wanted to be alone. And yet, she didn't. Because then she'd have to think about what to do about Nick. And the puppy-dog look on Matthew's face… As usual, he was hard to resist. But it just proved how different they were. She wanted to stay home and—admit it—wallow. Surely she deserved a bit of wallowing time after what she'd been through. And his solution was to go hang out with friends.

"I'm just not up to going out."

His face fell for a second, but he nodded. "What will make your week easier?"

"Well, the fridge is empty. I hadn't gotten far enough into the day to figure out how to solve that one." She hated being reliant on other people, but given her ankle, she was going to need some help. And Matthew was willing.

"Yeah, I figured you were stranded here and stubborn enough not to call anyone for help."

She laughed. "Look what happened last time I did."

His gaze softened. "Yeah. You got me."

She stopped laughing and met his gaze. "Yeah." What would she have done without him this weekend?

Matthew knew there was something more to the message she got on her phone that she wasn't telling him. He wanted to give her space to process what she needed to. But he also wished she would trust him.

"We've got to get over to Kyle's at some point to get our bags. I know you don't feel up to socializing, but it's your brother. Maybe you could raid his fridge for anything you might need." He grinned at her.

She laughed. "Yeah, have you seen what he keeps in his fridge? Once Heather moves in, things will improve. But I have a few things to bounce off him anyway."

Okay. Progress. Even if she wouldn't talk to him, talking to Kyle or Heather would help her.

"I'll text Heather." A minute later. "They're at Kyle's. They just got back from church."

"Great. What do you need to go? Purse? Keys?"

"They're both on that table by the door. I can get them." She reached for her crutches, and he handed them to her. She levered herself up and hobbled to the door, snatching up her purse and keys.

Matthew opened the door. A package sat in front of it. He picked it up and handed it to her. "Looks like you've got a delivery."

She flipped over the package. "I don't remember ordering anything. Though it's certainly possible."

"Odd. There's no label, just your name hand printed." That was weird.

A basic package, a little bigger than a shoebox, wrapped in brown paper. Seemed normal enough except it was addressed to: THE LOVE OF MY LIFE, KIMBERLY ELLIS. No return address, but a photo of Kim either entering or exiting her car downstairs was taped to the top.

Was this the same secret admirer who'd sent the balloon and flowers? Or was there someone else in her life she hadn't told him about?

She dropped the box on the coffee table, sank to the couch, and wrapped her arms around her middle.

"Do you know who it's from? The balloon-slash-flowers guy or the old boyfriend?"

She shook her head. "I—I don't know. Maybe. But this was taken Friday, because I was wearing that sleeveless dress."

He remembered. "Want me to open it?"

She hesitated then nodded.

He ripped the tape open. The box was from a pair of Timberland boots. Did that mean anything? Lots of guys who didn't hike wore boots.

Matthew lifted the lid. He tilted it toward Kim. Papers filled it nearly to the top.

She frowned and reached for it, touching the papers gingerly at first, then flipping through them more quickly, and finally picking up the whole stack. "This is ridiculous. These are all screenshots of my social media posts. What an idiot!" She started to toss the whole pile back in the box then halted in mid arc.

They weren't all screenshots. The last quarter of the stack were printouts of photos. All of Kim. At lunch with Allie and Jessica, at work, at Lynnae's shop.

Someone was watching her.

Matthew jumped up and opened the door, scanning below for any signs of who might have left the package. They were likely long gone. But a small black car was exiting the far side of the parking lot. Was it a Honda? It was a common car. And it was far enough away that he wasn't even sure what he had seen.

He came back inside and locked the door. "We need to tell Kyle."

"Don't! It's nothing. I don't want him to worry. And there's no crime in texting someone to see how they are doing or sending them a box of their own posts. We don't even know who it is. It could be someone playing a mean prank. I don't want Kyle to freak out. This weekend was stressful enough. I've already told him about the balloon and the flowers." Her gaze slid away from his.

He sank into the chair. The idea of someone putting Kim in danger twisted his gut. They'd been through enough already. "So what do you want to do?"

"Throw it all in the trash and forget about it."

"How about this: I'll put it in a trash bag, and we can take it to Kyle's. If this guy escalates, it'll be evidence, and it won't be here upsetting you."

Kim let out a sigh. "Trash bags are under the sink."

He retrieved one then disposed of the box. "Let me take this to the car, then I'll come back to help you."

"I'm perfectly capable of getting myself down the stairs." She regained her crutches, stood, and hobbled out the door before pulling it shut and locking it.

He went down the stairs in front of her, glancing back frequently. If she fell, hopefully he'd block her fall. But they didn't need any more accidents. They'd had their fill.

At the bottom, he helped her into his new rental. A sedan this time. He had laughed when he got it. They apologized for only having the minivan last time, but he knew that was God's plan. If they hadn't had the minivan, things would have looked differently for sure.

Kyle was in the yard when they pulled up.

Kim giggled. "Sometimes Kyle acts like an old man, obsessing over his lawn. Every weekend he's out here." She sighed. "Or maybe he's just being a responsible grownup. But I can't imagine doing lawn work. Nothing seems more like torture to me."

"He never made you mow the lawn when you lived here?" Matthew tilted his head at her, teasing in his voice.

"Of course not. Was that your chore growing up?"

"Yep. Me and Daniel traded off. But I found if I put my headphones on and played good music, it was kinda nice. No one bothered me. And with a little work, you could see a good result. When you work in an office, you don't always see results from your efforts."

"Maybe that's why Kyle likes it too."

"Probably."

Kyle came over and opened Kim's door. "You guys come to get your bags?"

"Among other things. But before we go inside, I want to ask you something because I know you'll give me an honest answer."

"Okay. Shoot."

"Do you want me to hire a wedding planner?"

Matthew jerked his gaze over to Kim and Kyle. He had no idea where that had come from.

"What are you talking about?" Kyle leaned against the door.

She let out a growl of frustration. "Okay, look, I wanted everything to be perfect for Heather. But between Kellie not doing her part and messing up with the restaurant and the fire for the girls' weekend away, I just don't even know if I should continue helping with the wedding. I'd hate if something happened on your big day. Maybe I can bring in a wedding planner who can make sure everything goes perfectly."

Kyle leaned forward. "Kim, I don't know what you're talking about. You couldn't control the fire. Heather knows that. What happened at the restaurant?"

She explained about Kellie not confirming the reservation and her scrambling to make everything work out.

He frowned. "I don't understand. It all worked out."

"Yes, but it almost didn't. I already have two strikes. I don't want the third one to be on your wedding day."

He touched her shoulder. "Where is this all coming from? Wait. Why don't we continue this conversation inside? Unless there's something you don't want Heather to hear."

Kim shook her head. "I just didn't want her to know her sister hasn't been much of a help. I think she knows some of it. But I also know that she would be too nice to tell me she'd rather have a wedding planner." She gave a half-hearted grin. "But I didn't think you would."

"If I thought you might mess up our wedding, don't you think I would have insisted Heather hire a wedding planner? I wouldn't let anything ruin the day for her, even if it meant making my little sister upset with me."

"Oh."

"Now can we not stand in the street and have this conversation?" Kyle opened Kim's door wider.

She adjusted her crutches, eased out of the car, and headed for the house.

Kyle's gaze swung to Matthew.

"I didn't know she was upset about all of that. Well, I knew a little." Matthew reached behind the seat and pulled out the bag. "I've got something to show you." He got out of the car and opened the bag on the hood so Kyle could see inside. "This was at Kim's door today. Someone put it there between the time I got there and when we left to come here. So maybe a two-hour time frame."

Kyle peered inside, using the trash bag as a glove to pull the box out. He studied it. "Someone dropped this off. It didn't go through the mail or UPS."

"Right. If I hadn't come over, no telling when Kim would have seen it. Probably not until tomorrow morning when she left for work."

"Did you see anybody or anything that would give you a clue as to who left it?"

Matthew shook his head. "No. When Kim saw that picture, she said it was taken Friday. When I ran out to see if there was anyone hanging around outside, I saw a small black car pulling out of the far end of the parking lot. Could have been a Honda or could have been something else."

Kyle looked through the papers. "These are hers?"

"Yeah. Screenshots of her social media posts. But the photos in the back are a mixed bag. Some are from her social media, but a few are of Kim outside her home, work, with friends. Whoever this is, he knows where she lives."

Kyle's mouth tightened into a thin line. "She needs to move back here."

"There's a problem with that. She doesn't want you to know."

"That's ridiculous." Kyle pulled the bag up around the box. "Let's head inside and talk to Kim."

Matthew knew telling Kyle was the right thing to do. He wanted to keep Kim safe. But would she see it that way? Or would he lose all the ground he'd gained with her?

Chapter Nineteen

K im eased herself down on the couch in Kyle's den that she'd sat on a million times. It was weird for Heather to be waiting on her in what used to be her own house. After next week, it would never be the same. This would be Heather's house too. And while she didn't think Heather would mind, Kim wouldn't want to pop in whenever and invade their privacy.

She was secretly glad Kyle didn't want her to hire a wedding planner. But she truly did want their day to be special. She didn't want to get in the way of that.

Heather brought her a Diet Coke and an ice pack. "How's the ankle?"

"It's fine. I think I'll be off the crutches in a few days. I can put a little weight on it, but it hurts if I do that too much. The air cast helps give it support."

"I'm just glad none of us was hurt worse."

"Me too. How was church?" Kim asked. "I can't believe you felt up to going."

"I needed it. The sermon was on how Jesus is the same yesterday, today, and forever. After this weekend, it really came to life."

"I love how the Bible does that. Sometimes the words seem to jump off the page, being just what you need at the right time."

"Yeah." Heather was quiet for a minute. "After everything I went through last year, I thought I'd really learned to trust God through everything. But this weekend brought it back up. I knew God was in control when we were out on the lake, I just didn't know where he'd take us. And I had to be okay with whatever his decision was."

Kim nodded but didn't break the silence for a long while. "I've been struggling with feeling overwhelmed by life ever since Willie Dumas grabbed me in Bryce Canyon. I'm not sure I can even put it in words, but it's like my creativity blinds me to reality in some way. I get to the edge, and I can't see the way forward. Every time, someone has yanked me back, but what happens when no one shows up?"

Heather reached for her hand and squeezed it but didn't say anything.

"Before we left for the Great American Road Trip, I had this tiny idea that maybe if I got inspired and came up with enough designs that were good enough, I could go out on my own."

Emotion rose heavy in her chest. She had barely thought these things, let alone voiced them to anyone. "But now, I can't even plan a bachelorette weekend. I can't possibly make all the right decisions that are necessary to run a company. I really wanted you to have a great weekend, and you didn't get much of one. I feel terrible about that."

Heather waved her hand. "It was fine. Kim, you did such a fantastic job. The cabin was great, the little gifts, dinner at Belle Sorgenti. Even the guys surprising us." She smiled.

"That last part was all Matthew." Kim grinned.

"It still was very thoughtful of you. You did a lot of work."

Kim let Heather's words wash over her, not realizing until she heard them how much she needed them. Both Heather and her brother had been supportive. She'd take some time to think about it later, but for now, she was ready to change the subject. "Any word from Joe or Collins on the fire?"

"Sarah texted me that Joe had called and said they'd been assigned to the fire so she was taking care of his dog, Shadow. Kyle said Collins was staying to help the Holcomb Springs Sheriff's Department as long as they needed him with evacuations and traffic control. He'll bunk with Brett, the guy he covered for before. They've become friends." Heather shook her head. "After living through what we did yesterday, it's hard to imagine our friends still up there in that. Makes it far more real than just seeing it on the news."

Kim nodded. "It won't feel like this ordeal is really over until they're back. Did Kellie go home this morning?"

"Yes, she left from church. I love having her around, though my little loft isn't quite big enough for two people. I think she was ready to get back to her own bed instead of my couch." She met Kim's gaze. "I know how Kellie is. She's fun and always up for shopping or whatever plans she's cooked up. But follow-through is not her strong suit. I know how much effort you have put in—not only for the weekend, but the shower and the wedding—without a lot of help from her." She patted Kim's knee. "You don't give yourself enough credit. You are completely capable of anything you set your mind to. Your creativity just gives it all your own distinct flair."

Heather was a creative professional herself. A former magazine editor, she freelanced doing forensic artist work for LVPD and others. So her words carried more weight than anyone else's would have. Heather was the first person to believe in and respect her talents as a designer. She'd also managed to talk Kyle into painting the walls of this house colors other than beige. That memory brought a smile.

Kim rubbed the moisture from her eyes. Heather wasn't upset with her. And she just might pull this whole thing off. It was funny how the right words from the right person could make all the difference. Earlier she felt exhausted, overwhelmed, and like a failure. But Heather's words put it all in perspective, making Kim think maybe her own emotions were blinding her. As usual.

Matthew and Kyle entered through the kitchen, coming in from the garage. Kyle was carrying the trash bag. He set it on the coffee table then sat in his chair.

Matthew sat next to Kim on the couch.

"Is Nick still stalking you?" Kyle asked.

She sat up and glanced at Matthew. "Nothing other than the balloon and flowers, which I already told you about."

Kyle pointed to the box. "What else has he done?"

Leaning back, she sighed and shot Matthew a glance. "Maybe some texts. I didn't want to worry you, especially after this weekend and with your wedding coming up." He hadn't wasted any time telling Kyle. He was trying to protect her. Still… she wasn't sure how she felt about the whole thing.

Kyle was silent for a moment. "Tell me everything that he has done."

She told him everything, even what she just suspected with her social media accounts. "Even though he's been kinda creepy, he hasn't done anything illegal. Then this morning—" She unlocked her phone and pushed it over to him to show him the message that she hadn't told Matthew about. She was glad, sort of, that she hadn't deleted it yet.

He read the message, his jaw tightening. "Did you call him?" He handed back her phone.

"No! I don't want anything to do with him. I guess the rescue being on the news brought me to his mind."

"The photos in the box were taken before the rescue. Did this start after the road trip?"

"Yes. Wait. Actually, a few years ago, he showed up when I was on a date with Jared."

"I remember Jared. Nice guy, but he never had a chance." Kyle shot a look a Matthew.

Kim didn't even want to know what Matthew must think of

this discussion. "Nick played it off like it was a coincidence, but I thought at the time that he had followed us there. The next day he called and apologized, but he was clearly trying to feel out how serious Jared and I were. I guess Nick thought we still had something. I had no idea. We went to senior prom together and dated the rest of that year. But when I went to FIDM, I told him I was too busy to date, that I was concentrating on my career. I assumed that was that, and we remained friends and texted occasionally, commented on each other's social media, stuff like I do with all my friends. But apparently he thought we would be getting back together at some point. I told him I didn't see that happening."

"But he didn't stalk you before, other than showing up that one time?"

"Not that I noticed."

He pointed to the trash bag that contained the box. "Okay. Let's assume this was some sort of innocent-though-misguided attempt at getting your attention." Kyle tapped the box and slipped on a pair of latex gloves. "Size eleven shoe. Tall guy, likely." He laid out the papers. "Tell me about these."

She went through the photos, the ones taken of her the morning of the bridal shower, lunch with Allie and Jessica, leaving work, at Lynnae's shop, and leaving for the mountains last Friday. Then they went through the social media post screenshots. She pulled up the actual posts. She wasn't sure what he was getting at. She'd done all of this and hadn't come up with anything.

He sat back and met her gaze. "I had a talk with Nick last week."

When? And why? She wasn't sure if she was relieved or upset. She'd wait to determine that based on what he said. "And?"

"He said he hasn't talked to you or seen you on social media since around the beginning of the year. He figured you must have blocked him, so his conclusion was you didn't want to see him."

"Good. He understands then."

"Maybe. But he doesn't drive a black Honda. And he's not that tall, about five-nine. Probably wears a size nine shoe."

Relief, then… if it wasn't Nick?

"Don't jump to any conclusions. The box could have come from anywhere. He could borrow someone else's car. And I could be wrong, but I got the impression Nick was out of your life. He was real surprised to see me, but he answered my questions without hesitation. I did leave him with a stern warning to leave you alone." He rubbed his hand over his mouth. He picked up the pages again and studied them a minute longer. "Nick wasn't ever into photography, was he?"

"No, he was more into motorcycles and tats."

"Pretty sure these were taken with a telephoto lens."

She looked at them again. "I think you're right. Given the angle and what is in this photo, where I'm with Lynnae, he'd had to have been standing across the street."

Heather leaned forward. "Kim, why don't you stay here for a while? Until we figure out what's really going on? It would make your brother and me feel better knowing you're safe."

She didn't know what to think. "I have Design Review coming up with all that stuff spread over my condo. Plus your wedding is in less than two weeks." She picked up the pages with the photos. "These were taken other places too. Not just at my house. Nothing has really happened. I haven't been threatened. Just a weird secret admirer." She dropped them on the coffee table.

Kyle leaned forward. "I'd like you to consider staying here. I don't like any of this."

"Won't I be in the way of you and Heather?"

"No," from Heather, but at the same time Kyle said, "Not until after we're married." He grinned.

She reached across and smacked his knee. "How about this? I'll sleep here, but I'll still need to go by my apartment every day and probably work there in the evenings."

Matthew squeezed her shoulder. "I'll keep you company as much as possible."

"And I'll follow you over to your place as often as I can." Kyle grinned.

She grinned back. "Deal. But I have another question for you. What about the Kim Fund?"

He blinked. "You do know how to switch subjects. Seriously? I wasn't going to take rent money from you. It's expensive to live in this area. But I knew you wanted to prove that you could take care of yourself and pay your own way. I saved it so you would have a down payment on a place of your own." He winked at her. "And it meant you had a bigger incentive to live here where I could keep an eye on your boyfriends."

She had known all that. And yet, she hadn't really seen it as protective. Maybe her feelings that her family didn't take her seriously were more rooted in her own insecurities about her own abilities. It was something she needed to think about further, to pray about.

Still, if the stalker really was escalating, was it fair to bring it to Kyle's doorstep—and basically Heather's too—right before their wedding? She wanted to give them one more chance to back out. Heather too.

She looked at her hands, her voice quiet. "Here's the thing, Kyle. This just goes to what I said earlier. I think you and Heather need to consider bringing a wedding planner in. Even if you think I've been doing a good job, what if this person"—she gestured to the items on the coffee table— "does something to mess up your wedding? You and Dad have always thought I was this flighty artist who couldn't do anything practical. What if—"

"Wait. What?" Kyle interrupted. "How did you get that idea?"

Well this was embarrassing in front of Matthew. But a lot about her life recently had been embarrassing. He either was in it with her—mess and all—or he could leave. At least his eyes would be open about what life with her was like. "Remember that time I tried to make dinner for Mom and Dad's anniversary? I didn't understand about how to plan out when to cook what foods, so some was overcooked and some was cold. Then when I carried the big platter to the table, I nearly dropped it and knocked over the lit candle, catching the tablecloth on fire. Dad threw his water on it. You and Dad have never let me forget that moment." Tears stung her eyes at the memory. Gah, not what she wanted. She hadn't planned on telling him any of that. But she so didn't want her problems to spill over to his and Heather's wedding.

"You were twelve."

She sniffed.

"Dad and I probably shouldn't tease you so much. I didn't know it bothered you. And I don't think you're flaky. I'm proud of how creative you are." He leaned over and grabbed her hands. "I mean it, Kim."

Heather spoke up. "He really is proud of you, Kim. And you know he can't lie to save his life."

They both giggled. "True." Kim let out a long sigh. She was silent a moment. Her heart softened. It seems like she'd misread her brother, and probably her parents too. She was afraid to look at Matthew, to see what she might read in his eyes. "I guess I'm just stressed."

Kyle leaned back. "All the more reason to stay here. After what we all went through yesterday, I'm not in the mood to take any unnecessary chances. That was too close of a call."

He had a point. She felt closer to her brother and Heather, and even Jessica and Austin, than she had Friday. "And what if we don't discover who this is before your wedding? I can't stay here indefinitely."

"We can cross that bridge if and when we get to it." Kyle's gaze turned to Matthew.

Kim reluctantly shifted to see his reaction.

Concern crossed his face, his fingers rubbing her shoulder.

"Listen to your brother. Between the two of us, we want to keep you safe."

"Why don't you take your stuff home from the cabins?" Kyle suggested. "And then you can follow Kim back here tonight. Kim, if you can go to work from here in the morning, I can follow you there on my way in."

"It's not remotely on your way to work."

He shrugged.

She recognized when her brother had dug in his heels.

Heather stood. "I'll make sure the guest room is ready for you. It'll be good having you around again."

Kim laughed. "Okay, but this time I'm the one in trouble, not you."

"Hopefully your brother will change that really soon." Heather left the room.

Kim got to her feet and took a hobble step toward Kyle, wrapping him in a hug. "Thanks, big brother. I appreciate every-thing, especially your confidence in me."

"If I'd known you'd been carrying that around, I would have made it clear a long time ago." He gave her a squeeze and then set her back, turning to Matthew. "Don't let her out of your sight."

"Not planning on it."

She wasn't sure how she felt about the two of them deciding things for her. But she was too tired to argue. And it kinda felt good to be cared for.

Chapter Twenty

Kim shifted in her chair at work. She was achy and tired and wished that she'd been able to stay home. If it was anything but the week of Design Review, she would have. Her foot throbbed, so she'd found another chair to prop it up on. But everything was just so difficult with crutches. The guest bed at Kyle's house was pretty comfy, but it wasn't her home anymore.

Matthew had sent her a sweet text with a funny GIF this morning. And he'd been a huge help yesterday, taking her rescued bags upstairs. He seemed extremely pleased that someone had grabbed his super soakers. He'd spent the rest of the day with her, watching a movie on Netflix and getting her packed and back over to Kyle's.

People had been stopping by her workstation all day, commenting on the fire and the news reports, asking how she was. It seemed kind, but most of it was a thinly disguised quest for gossip. She'd gotten a few more requests from the news media. She just wanted to work to take her mind off things.

But Joe and Collins were never far from her thoughts. There was a group text where Sarah, Allie, and Kyle reported any latest news. They had gotten the fire twenty percent contained, so they were making progress. But there had been no word on how many houses had been lost. Or lives.

Surprisingly, both Juan and Eliza stopped by. She didn't think Eliza even knew where the junior designers worked. Except maybe Henry.

"So you have a lot of media talking to you," Eliza commented. "Make sure you're mentioning House of Elan every time. Include our hashtags too."

Yeah, that would be a real natural segue from the fire to design. But she merely smiled and nodded. Eliza moved off.

Juan was more concerned. "Are you sure you're okay? It's unfortunate that we can't give you any extra time for Design Review. Maybe you should just take this year's competition off, save all your work for next year."

"No, I'm fine. I won't need any extra time." No way was she taking this year off. They had just sent out a memo saying the winning designs would be featured in the fall look book. A huge boost to getting her designs in front of industry decision makers.

He frowned but patted her arm and moved off.

Henry's aim wasn't disguised at all as he sidled up. "So I see you were sporting a new look for the press this weekend. Dystopian chic, was it? I'm sure the senior designers were watching. Was that why you missed the roundtable on Friday?"

Henry knew right where to hit her. And considering his connections with the senior designers, particularly Eliza, he might well know what they were thinking. Still, it never paid to let him see it. She smiled sweetly. "Thanks so much for your concern for my well-being. Yes, it was scary escaping a raging inferno, but we survived and are thankful to be alive." It was nearly verbatim what she'd said to the press.

He huffed and moved on.

Maybe she should always have a canned response for Henry.

Matthew stood outside the last condo on their list with Austin and Allie. His phone was buzzing with texts from work that needed his attention. Everyone wanted details about the fire. He'd been copying and pasting pretty much the same text to everyone, and he was over it. There was too much work to do.

At this point, any of the places Allie had shown them would do. He just needed an address for the moving company to bring his stuff to. Luckily DataCorp was paying for the relocation, and Allie was coordinating with the moving company. He didn't have to do much.

Which was good because his mind was on Kim and what Kyle had said. He was glad she was staying with Kyle, but it wasn't a permanent solution. He just hoped Kyle could figure out who this guy was before Kim got hurt. He turned back into the conversation about the condo.

Austin, surprisingly, had been the picky one. He was concerned about the light—and the ability to block it out—as well as noise from their surroundings. It was going to be interesting having him as a roommate. Matthew hadn't planned on having one, but when he had convinced Austin to take the job with DataCorp, Austin had asked if they could share an apartment. His father was suffering from early dementia. He had planned to stay in Phoenix to be close to them to help but realized that if he conserved money by having a roommate, he could pay for care they couldn't afford.

Matthew would never have guessed that about Austin and respected him for wanting to take care of his family. How difficult could sharing an apartment be?

"What do you think, Austin? Will this do?" Matthew studied him, resisting the urge to force him to make a decision. Austin was methodical and took his time analyzing a situation from all angles. Pretty different from his own tendencies to jump right in.

Allie looked like she had all the time in the world. She was clearly used to dealing with many types of people.

Austin nodded. "This will do. And I can even ride my bike to work once we move into the new office building."

"Great! Let's head back to my office and fill out the paperwork, and we'll see how soon I can get you both a signed lease and a set of keys."

"How about I grab lunch and bring it over?" Matthew normally wasn't a big multitasker, but filling out paperwork was a special kind of torture for him. Lunch would be a good distraction.

Allie laughed. "I'll get the paperwork started so you have to spend as little time as possible on something you hate."

And that was the advantage of working with your sister. She knew him well. Once he and Austin were in the car, he entered their order on the restaurant's app. With any luck, he'd just have to swing by and grab it.

He took a moment to check his texts before pulling out. Nothing terribly urgent. He also shot Kim a quick GIF to follow the one he'd sent this morning. Now that they'd found a place to live, maybe he could see Kim tonight, even if she was at Kyle's. Provided Edward didn't come up with something else the core team in residence needed to do. He seemed to think since they were all staying in the hotel, they would want to work all hours of the day. Balance wasn't part of his life plan, apparently. Matthew just hoped it passed.

Austin nodded at Matthew's phone. "How's Kim doing with her ankle?"

"It's not too bad. She was able to go to work today." As he came to a stoplight, he slid a glance at Austin. "Talked to Jessica at all?"

He shrugged. "We've texted a bit. She's chatty." He grinned.

"She and Kim have been friends for a long time. It's good to see you two getting along. I wouldn't have thought she was your type."

"She's not. I mean, I have no plans to get serious with anyone." He nudged Matthew. "We just got here. Shouldn't we check out all our options? No need to get tied down. Seems only logical."

"I don't know that there's anything logical about the matters of the heart, my friend." Yes, what Austin said made sense on the surface. But his heart only wanted Kim. And his biggest fear was that she didn't want him.

He picked up the food. They were right by Kim's office. He looked around the rental car. "Is there any paper in here? Something I can write on?"

Austin pulled a notepad out of his backpack. "Will this work?"

"Perfect." Matthew jotted out a quick note. He pulled into the parking lot at House of Elan and searched for Kim's Bug. There it was. He hopped out and tucked the note under her windshield wiper. He didn't know if she'd see it soon or not until she left work for the day, but he hoped it made her smile.

They headed back to Allie's office and ate while going over the forms and answering Allie's questions. Matthew finished his food and began scrolling through his phone. He didn't want to head back to the hotel, but he did have an afternoon meeting and needed to take care of a few things. They had several of the conference rooms at the hotel for their use. One served as a more quiet workspace, while the others were for meetings. Next week they would begin transitioning to their permanent office space. If Edward okayed the final improvements.

Chris Sandoval texted him.

Can you get back to the hotel ASAP? Anne says Edward has told the CEO to cut the sales department out of this branch. We need to talk him out of it.

He groaned. This is what they'd been afraid of, but he and Chris thought they'd made real progress with their trip to Seattle.

"I've got to get back to the hotel to deal with a crisis."

Austin stopped gathering his trash and looked up. "What's going on?" He'd heard the rumors, too, and had asked Matthew what he knew. There was no going back to their old jobs since their previous employer wasn't too thrilled with their decision to leave. He was a guy to whom loyalty was everything. So that bridge was pretty well toasted. And he hadn't been shy about letting everyone know that.

"So far, it looks like it's just the sales department in danger. Allie, do you have everything you need from us?"

"Sure. I'll get back to you with all the final approvals from the owner."

"Thanks." He stood and motioned to Austin. "If you want to ride with me, we've got to go now."

He nodded and got to his feet. "Thanks, Allie."

"Happy to help, guys."

They left her office and hopped in the car. Luckily the hotel was close, and they got there in a few minutes.

"How bad is it really?" Austin asked.

Matthew shrugged. "You'll be fine. And I will too. One way or another, we'll get this all worked out." He didn't want Austin to worry. And since Matthew had convinced him to go on this adventure, he had to make sure everything worked out for him.

Chris met him in the lobby. "Anne got a copy of the proposed budget. There's nothing there for us other than travel allowances from Seattle."

"Are you kidding me?" Matthew had just upended his life, not to mention the other people like Austin who had too. Edward was already responsible for one current pain point of his, the sprained wrist from the ill-conceived team-building exercise. He didn't need Edward to give him another. "Let's go speak to him. Surely he can be talked out of it. Sales is what we do best, even if it means selling our own COO on the necessity of a local sales department." He headed toward the conference room Edward was using as an office.

Marisa—Matthew couldn't remember her last name—sat

outside the room at a folding table, working on a laptop. She'd gotten roped into serving as Edward's admin. Poor soul. She looked up.

"Is he in?" he asked.

"Yes, but—"

He didn't listen to the rest of it but moved around the table and pushed the door open, Chris on his heels. A part of his brain said that maybe he should let his boss take the lead.

Edward was on the phone. He glanced up and raised his index finger, scowling.

Matthew shot a look at Chris, who gave a small shrug. Matthew stood there, trying not to do anything to cue his impatience. But his wrist was throbbing, and he had forgotten to take ibuprofen with his lunch. Probably because of Chris's text.

"What's going on? Isn't Marisa outside?" Edward got to his feet as if he was going to check on her, but slumped back in his seat.

Chris took a step forward. "We wanted to talk with you about the proposed budget. I think there's been a mistake."

Edward didn't answer. He looked a little pale, maybe even gray, and was loosening his collar.

"Are you all right?" Matthew frowned. Was he sick?

Edward didn't answer, just rummaged through his briefcase.

"Edward? Are you sick?"

He pulled out a bottle and struggled to get the top off.

Matthew took it from him. It was a bottle of aspirin. He popped the top off and shook out two into Edward's hand.

Edward chewed them and slugged down some water from a bottle.

Matthew grimaced. Chewing aspirin? He couldn't think of anything more bitter. And why do that for a headache— "Are you having a heart attack?"

He nodded as Matthew nearly vaulted the table. "Chris, call 911." He tried to get the man's tie off. Hard to do with one hand in a splint. "Here, lay down on the floor before you fall." He eased Edward down, took off the tie, and undid the top buttons on the shirt.

Chris was on the phone with the dispatcher, giving information and their location.

"It's probably just indigestion, and then I'll be embarrassed by all the fuss." Edward's voice was weak. Sweat pilled up on his forehead and upper lip.

"They're on their way." Chris pocketed his phone. "I'll let Marisa know what's going on and to head to the lobby to show them where we are. I'll see if I can get hotel security too." He disappeared out the door.

Matthew wasn't sure what to do. He shot up a quick prayer for wisdom. Edward had closed his eyes, but his chest was still moving up and down. Matthew felt for a pulse and found it. So no need for CPR. Which was good because Matthew wasn't sure he knew how to do it right. Or with one hand.

He scanned the room looking for anything that could be helpful. Spotting Edward's suit jacket on the back of the chair, he grabbed it and laid it over the COO. Should he elevate his feet? That was for shock. But would it help or hurt for a heart attack? Matthew didn't know, so he didn't do anything. Helplessness washed over him like a bad breaking wave. He sat next to Edward and watched his breathing, his hand on Edward's wrist.

Hotel security burst in with an AED device. "He's having a heart attack?"

"I think so, but he still has a pulse. And he's still conscious."

The security officer opened Edward's shirt and began placing sticky pads from the AED device. "Just checking the heart's rhythm. If he still has a pulse, likely he won't need to be shocked unless it's erratic. Everyone stand back, and don't touch him so we can get an accurate reading." He studied the machine's display. "Okay, no shock. We just wait for the paramedics to get here."

Paramedics jangled up the hall with their equipment and into the room. Matthew pushed to his feet and moved toward the back wall. He watched and answered the questions they asked him as best he could about Edward's name, age, state of health, and medications. And then they were gathering up Edward and taking him out of the room, leaving silence behind as real as a physical presence.

Matthew didn't know what to do. Which was almost as unsettling to him as Edward having a heart attack. He picked up Edward's jacket off the floor and hung it over the chair back.

Moments ago it seemed so important to convince Edward he was wrong. And now… Now Matthew didn't know. Didn't know what would happen to Edward. Or Matthew's department. Or any of them.

He tapped the desk and looked around one last time.

There was one thing he could do. He prayed.

Kim checked the time. Close enough, especially considering how long it took her to hobble around. She shut down her computer and slung her purse across her body before grabbing her crutches. Nodding to Ashley, she said, "I'm heading off to lunch."

Ashley stood and grabbed the door for her. "I can bring you back something, if it'd be easier. I'm heading out soon. Or you could have something delivered."

"Thanks, I just need to get some fresh air."

"Okay. Well, let me know if you need anything when you get back."

"I will." Kim headed down the hallway.

The sun was out as Kim pushed her way out the door to the parking lot. No June gloom today. Hard to believe that a massive fire still raged only two hours away. As she neared her Bug, a piece of paper under the wiper blade caught her eye. Another gift from her secret admirer? Hesitantly, she reached for it, grabbing it only by the corner. She snapped it open. And smiled. Matthew.

She slid inside her car. Relief. Stowing her purse and crutches, she leaned her head back for a minute. Kyle had told her not to go anywhere alone. So she wasn't.

And Matthew's note had been the perfect thing after her morning. He didn't say much, just that he was thinking of her as he drove by and decided to leave her a note. It wasn't much different than anything he'd texted her, but this was permanent. She could keep it and re-read it, and it was in his handwriting. It was an unexpectedly thoughtful gesture. She tucked the note in her purse.

When she had pulled in this morning, she'd taken a turn around the parking lot, after waving goodbye to Kyle who'd followed her in. It was ridiculous, she knew. Her eyes had been practically glued to her rearview mirror, searching for a black Honda. Which made her surprise even greater when she spotted one in the parking lot at work. She slotted her car near it. Now to wait and see if the owner came out for lunch.

The good news about everyone stopping by her desk was she was able to ask them what car they drove. And she was even somewhat sly about it. She mentioned that her car had died last week—true—and she was looking for a new one—theoretically, she was always looking to see what was out there. What did they drive? Did they like it? As she should have expected, in a group of creative people, no one admitted to driving anything as pedestrian as a black Honda. Classic cars, sports cars, electric cars, yes. Henry even drove a Tesla with personalized plates.

So it made the Honda in front of her all the more curious.

She knew it was a long shot that the person would come out for lunch. Or that this was even the black Honda she was looking for. They might have brought their lunch, walked some place close—there were a few restaurants nearby—or ridden with a coworker.

Why would someone at work stalk her? Yes, the fashion

industry could be cutthroat, but most were like Henry—open about their desire to see you fail.

But since she wasn't that hungry herself and wanted some space, it seemed worth a shot. She had a power bar in her purse if she really needed it. But mostly she just wanted away from the prying eyes. She hadn't gotten another stalkerish text since yesterday. So maybe the person had made his point. After all, what else could he do?

Actually, that wasn't a good thought. To distract herself from that line of thinking, she checked on the fire's progress on her phone. Nothing new, but Collins had sent an update to their group text. He was patrolling the area and had apparently swung by the marina. Because there, still smoking, were the remains of a pirate ship playground, its metal structure poking out like a skeleton. Resembling a surrealist painting by Dali, instead of melting clocks, it was a melted pirate ship.

Tears filled her eyes. The poor kids who wouldn't get to play on that darling structure anymore. Would they even be able to rebuild it? Smoke shrouded the marina, so she couldn't see what had happened to it. But a cold chill washed over her. That could have been them if they hadn't gotten back in the kayaks.

It was the second time in a few months that her life had been in danger. The thought splashed over her like icy water, and for a moment, nothing at work mattered. She could have died. Would her death even create much of an absence in the world? Her family and friends would miss her, but would the world? No, she didn't think it would. It was depressing to think about. Perhaps she'd been too wrapped up in proving herself in the design world that she hadn't looked at what impact she was making in the bigger world. Did she need to make a big impact in the world for her life to have meaning? Or was it enough to support family and friends, like she was doing for Heather and Jessica? It was a weighty thought, one she wasn't prepared to wrestle with.

She wiped her eyes, glad she had read the text in the privacy of her car. The rest of Collins's text was actually good news. Only a few buildings had been lost, and so far, no lives. That was definitely something to thank God for.

Jessica sent her a text, asking how she was doing. Considering it was all too much to explain via text, she called her and gave her the update. She was enjoying having a sober Jessica in her life again, remembering how fun she was and her dry sense of humor. She hinted around a bit about Austin, but Jessica didn't bite. So maybe Kim had imagined it. But perhaps the four of them could have dinner one night. She floated the idea to Jessica.

"Sure. Just let me know when and where. And if you need anything or anyone to keep you company, let me know."

After an hour, no one had come out to the black Honda. She reluctantly headed back inside, a little more energized after her time alone and her call with Jessica. It was enough to get her through the afternoon.

Chapter Twenty-One

Kim headed back to her department from lunch. A man was in the hallway coming toward her. She hoped he stepped to the side because maneuvering on crutches was difficult enough.

Then she recognized him. Zander Jakes. His longish brown hair swept back from his forehead. The three-day growth of beard and the untucked, unbuttoned-shirt-over-tee with jeans and boots gave him a casual vibe.

He smiled at her. "Hey Kim. I was hoping I'd run into you today. I saw you on the news. Are you doing okay?" He reached out and touched her arm. "What happened?"

She shrugged and gave a half laugh. "I'm fine. It's just a sprain, and not even a bad one at that."

He frowned. "Do you have someone looking after you? You should be resting."

"It's Design Review week, so not much resting going on."

"Right. I heard you're using my photos in your portfolio. I just love your designs. When I was shooting for Lynnae and asked whose designs the models were wearing, I wasn't surprised to hear they were yours. I was just disappointed that you weren't there. I was hoping to see you. I enjoyed having you at the shoot we did last February." His brown eyes bore into hers for a touch too long.

She looked down the hall. "That's sweet. Well, I've got to get back to work."

"You're so talented. My sister's going to school for design too. Maybe you could give her some direction."

She had no room for anything else on her plate. But Zander had a lot of influence in her industry. If she helped him, perhaps he could help her. "I'd be happy to meet her for lunch sometime. After Design Review." She shifted a crutch to the side.

He took a step closer. Since he was tall, she had to look up to meet his gaze. "Let's have lunch sometime and talk about your career. I have the perfect place in mind."

"Okay, great." More than great. She couldn't believe he was offering that. And likely nothing would come of it. People made empty promises all the time. But it was nice to have her work complimented by someone who saw a lot of designs. However, her arms and leg were throbbing. She needed to sit. "I've really got to get back to work." She eased around him. "See you later."

"Bye, Kim. Yes, I will see you."

She kept going to her workstation. Who was doing a photo shoot here? Usually they were done off site. Perhaps it was just a meeting. No telling with designers. And it was Design Review week. Though Zander wasn't cheap. She didn't think one of the junior designers could afford him. She couldn't afford him. Nor would he associate his name with someone with no reputation. Kim was lucky because of her connection with Lynnae. Must have been one of the senior designers.

Then again, Zander didn't have any camera gear with him. So maybe it was just a meeting.

She slid onto her seat and propped her crutches up. This was for the birds. As soon as her foot was up to walking, she was ditching the crutches. Her arms hurt too much, making it hard to use the mouse.

Something about Zander was niggling at her, though. She was tired and not thinking straight. She needed to work on her trade show prep. Instead, she hobbled down to check in with Monique on her sample design. It was nearly done. And it looked fantastic. It was a capstone-worthy piece. Monique hoped to finish it tonight. Kim would see the finished project when she came in in the morning. She couldn't wait.

Matthew texted her, asking if he could escort her home and eat Chinese in with her tonight. He was taking Kyle's charge seriously, but she'd rather spend time with him than her big brother. So she agreed. She texted Kyle her plans. It was weird reporting in. But she didn't want to add to his stress before his wedding. The least she could do was behave as he asked. It was a small price to pay.

At the end of the day, she texted him when she was done and headed out to her car, waiting for Matthew's rental to pull into the parking lot. Then it hit her. How had Zander known she was using his photos in her portfolio? She thought through who would know. Except something else caught her attention.

Something was missing. The black Honda was gone.

Matthew waved at Kim in her cute blue Bug and leaned back against the driver's seat as she pulled in front of him and he followed her home, the scent of the Chinese food on the seat next to him making his stomach growl. It beat returning to his hotel room. Hopefully he wouldn't be there much longer. Allie had worked her magic, and he and Austin would get the keys to their new condo on Saturday. Five days away. Plus, it would require a trip back to Arizona to grab what he didn't want the movers packing and to get his truck. He grabbed his phone to make some notes. That would require leaving Kim, which he didn't like. But it couldn't be helped.

He wanted to spend time with her, to assist her as much as

he could. She had a lot on her plate with Design Review and Heather and Kyle's wedding. Not to mention her sprained ankle. There wasn't much he could do to help her with most of that, especially since his schedule was so crazy and would likely get worse in the wake of Edward's heart attack.

Edward had gotten into the hospital in time and had gotten into surgery right away to open his blockage. His prognosis was good. Chris and Anne planned to get together tomorrow to create a revised budget to present to the CEO, Alan Martin, that included keeping the sales department in Orange County.

Matthew couldn't help but think that Edward's heart attack had been good timing for them, though he felt horrible even thinking that. He'd like to think that he and Chris would have been able to convince Edward of the need to keep it, or that the budget had been a mistake. Now they'd never know. Unless Edward brought it up on his return to work.

It had been a strange day. He was finally having dinner with Kim alone. Kyle trusted him enough to protect her. And he'd saved his COO's life. Since he'd come to OC, life seemed to be rocketing changes at him faster than he'd ever imagined. Normally, he embraced change. But this might all be a bit too fast even for him.

For tonight, all his focus was on Kim. Yes, they'd almost kissed on the marina dock while the fire was chasing them. He'd felt that closeness. And she wanted it too. Didn't she?

Yesterday had been an emotional day for her. But it was good to see that side of her. She was so creative and accomplished, that it never occurred to him that she had doubts. And that she'd said all those things to Kyle in front of him spoke volumes. He wasn't going to take that lightly. He didn't want this to be a result of the emotional fallout of the fire or stalker danger. He wanted to know that they had something strong enough to stand on its own, that they wouldn't go back to texting just funny GIFs and surface-level things.

Because if they didn't have a future together, he had no business pursuing her. It wasn't fair to either of them, and right now neither could afford the distraction.

But the thought of Kim as merely a distraction made his stomach sick. No, she was much more than that to him. Never in his past had he pursued a woman for so long. They usually pursued him, and he lost interest fast. But Kim was different.

She was worth fighting for. And until she told him flat out that she didn't want to see him, that they didn't have a future together, he was going to work to get her back.

Kim looked around her condo as she opened the door, not that it had changed much since last night. She hadn't realized how messy she'd left it. When she was stressed, she tended to let things get out of order.

A savory aroma that made her stomach growl had accompanied Matthew as he had followed her up the stairs.

"Yeah, I see how it is. Most women want me for my looks. You just want my food." He stepped inside.

"Priorities." She locked the door behind him.

He glanced at the coffee table. "I'll put this on the counter since you're working in the living room."

She hadn't thought about where they'd eat. She didn't have a kitchen table. The coffee table was strewn with sketches and fabric samples, and Heather's wedding box sat in the corner. But she'd lose her place if she picked all that up. So it remained. If Matthew truly wanted a relationship with her, then he'd need to see her in all of her messy glory. No point in pretending to be someone she wasn't. "How about we eat at the counter?" She did have two barstools.

He unpacked the Chinese food. He'd remembered her favorites: beef and broccoli and orange chicken. Her mouth watered. That power bar at lunch was long forgotten. She perched next to him.

He took her hand and prayed, and then they dug in.

"How's the ankle feel?"

"It's sore. But the crutches are a pain. They make my arms hurt. I hope it heals soon so I can ditch them. How was work today?"

"Austin finally settled on a condo, so Allie's finalizing that for us. And Edward had a heart attack."

"What?"

He told her about the proposed budget, what happened to Edward, and the latest update on him from their CEO.

"Wow, so you've had a full day."

"Yeah. It's good to be here with you. Any more weird texts?" Matthew pushed a carton toward her.

She shook her head. "No. Not since yesterday. Likely it was Nick, and he lost interest when I didn't take the bait. Or when Kyle talked to him. Which just shows what a sicko he is."

"I'm glad for your sake that he's stopped." He emptied the remains of the carton onto his plate. "I don't think I ever asked you. How did you get into design?"

Kim pushed away the last of the box. "Are you done?"

He nodded.

She hobbled to the sink and loaded the few dishes into the dishwasher, throwing empty food containers in the trash. She scooped up the fortune cookies. "Want some coffee to go with these?"

"Are you stalling?" He reached for her hand and wrapped his around hers, sending a buzz through her whole body.

"Just want to get comfy before I tell you a lengthy story."

He held her gaze for a long moment. "Okay. But you go sit on the couch. I'll make the coffee." He slowly released his hold on her hand.

She moved to the living area.

"Okay, spill." He clattered around the kitchen, adding water to the Keurig and pulling down mugs.

She watched him over the back of the couch. "When I was little, like early elementary school, I was sick a lot. I had scarlet fever and ended up getting my tonsils out. Mom was a stay-at-home mom, but she had Kyle to take care of, too, though he was older. Still, I was on my own a lot. Mom subscribed to all the ladies' magazines. I had some fashion paper dolls, and I didn't like all the clothes that came with them. So I cut out pictures from the magazines to dress my dolls with. Then I started drawing my own designs for them."

Matthew scooted the things on the coffee table a bit to make room for the two mugs. He sat on the couch and pulled her legs up on his lap. "You need to keep this elevated." But the humor in his eyes said he had ulterior motives.

Still, it was nice to be taken care of. She sipped from her coffee. "Grandma taught me to sew, and I started making outfits for my Barbies and then simple things for myself, like a wrap skirt." She took another sip, stalling.

Matthew's voice was low. "Sounds like you used the situation to be creative. Was your mom supportive of your interests?"

"To a point. I think she was glad I had something to keep me occupied. And then as I got older and started making my own clothes and subscribing to the high-fashion magazines, I think maybe she thought it was a phase.

"I was just beginning to understand fashion and its possibilities one time when I went shopping with Grandma at the mall. One of the upscale stores had an interesting mannequin display, and I spent some time studying it, trying to understand the thought process between the clothing combinations. And then I moved on to the handbags and scarves. My mind was just rolling with the possibilities and all the combinations. I was pulling things off the shelves and arranging them in different orders. A sales lady came over and scolded me for 'making a mess' of her displays." Kim made air quotes.

She took another sip of the coffee. She hadn't told anyone about this. "I tried to explain to her why this was a better arrangement of color and patterns. Someone in the store had design sense because the mannequin was on point. She didn't want to hear it, didn't even want to talk to me like a human being. She just called security, and they escorted me out of the store and told me not to come back." Her face flamed just at the memory.

"Grandma spent hours looking for me—I wasn't allowed to have a cell phone yet—and was furious when she finally went to security to report me missing and they informed her that I'd been kicked out of the store. She finally found me standing outside the store waiting for her. When I tried to explain, she didn't listen. She was upset that I had embarrassed her. What about me? I was pretty embarrassed. I've never gone back to that store."

Matthew reached over and took her hand. "The misunderstood artist, huh?"

"Yeah." Tears pushed against her eyelids. "Not only did I suffer as an artist, my family did too. And that was not acceptable." She gave him a wry grin. "Kyle was the perfect older brother, of course."

He moved her legs to the coffee table and scooted closer. "You know what I see?" His voice was low and husky, sending swirls into her stomach. "I see a woman who didn't give up, even when no one supported her."

Kim let out a breath. Her workday had ended with her being tired, sore, and hungry. But now she felt understood, cared for. Matthew had done that. She wasn't sure what to make of it.

She shook her head. "I wanted to prove that I was right, that I could accomplish something. That's why it's so important for this wedding to be everything Heather wants. I need my family to see I can do that."

"From what Kyle said yesterday, he already does." He ran a finger down her cheek and along her jaw, leaving heat trailing behind. "But even if no one else does, I'm always going to be on your side. Do you believe me?"

She wanted to. But her heart was too confused to give him an honest answer. Instead, she did what she'd wanted to since last Saturday at the marina.

She leaned in and kissed him.

Chapter Twenty-Two

Kim floated into work the next day, even if she was on crutches, reliving her night with Matthew. While she might have kissed him first, he responded with the kind of passion that made her think he'd been waiting a long time for it too. She reluctantly had him escort her back to Kyle's.

Mostly, she'd felt understood. Matthew had seen her side of the story, something she hadn't realized how badly she'd needed until it happened. Coming on the heels of what Kyle had said Sunday, it changed her perception of things she'd always believed. She wasn't sure what to make of any of it.

Unfortunately, he was leaving Wednesday morning with Austin to fly back to Phoenix to pack up his stuff and get his truck. He'd be back Saturday, but the idea of not having him here while she went through Design Review left a hole. And it meant she'd be confined to Kyle's house for the most part.

Once at her workstation, she booted up her computer and began finalizing everything for Design Review, in addition to her regular work for trade shows coming up in the fall. It was two days away, and she didn't want any last-minute surprises. She got a funny GIF from Matthew and sent him one in return.

Her phone buzzed again. Jessica this time.

Hey, got time for lunch today?

Kim was kinda hoping she'd be able to slip away for lunch with Matthew. But she wanted to support Jessica. If she had reached out, she might really need company. And Matthew wasn't going anywhere. She smiled at that thought.

Sure. Sounds great!

I'll swing by your office and text you when I'm there.

See you then!

She put her phone away. It would be good to see Jessica. But now, she had to focus on finishing up for Design Review. The last item was checking on the final design that Monique had sewn up. Kim was taking it home with her today, not wanting to risk anything happening to it this week. When she reached the workroom, Monique seemed surprised to see her. "Oh, I thought you'd already come and gone."

"What do you mean?"

"You came and got your design. I finished it up last night after you left, but you must have gotten it this morning. Did it meet with your approval?" Her gaze cut to the empty dress form where Kim's design had last resided.

Kim shook her head. She couldn't make sense of what Monique was saying. "I didn't get the dress. I haven't seen it since I talked to you about it yesterday."

Monique's brow furrowed. "I don't know what you mean. The dress is gone. I thought you took it."

"No, I didn't." Panic rose in her chest threatening to cut off her air. No, there was a logical explanation for this. "Did someone move it, put it away somewhere?"

"I don't know who would, but let's check all the cupboards and drawers."

The two of them searched the workroom as Kim hobbled from place to place. Nothing. This was the capstone of her presentation. The rest were drawings and computer renderings, but the competition required one finished piece. Her brain fogged with pain and outrage, and she wanted to wail. No, this was so unfair. Who would do this to her?

One name floated out of the fog. Henry. Would he be so cruel as to sabotage her like this?

She was going to find out. "Monique, keep looking any place you can possibly imagine and even places you can't. Ask the other seamstresses if they saw anything. I'll check with the other designers."

She made a quick calculation. It had to have disappeared between the time Monique left last night and before anyone got in this morning. Because creatives kept creative hours, it wasn't unusual for someone to be working very late or very early, and they all had key cards to get in the building. She stopped at the various workstations asking if anyone had seen her completed outfit and if they knew if anyone had worked late or come in early. Not that it would make them a suspect, but perhaps they'd seen something. No one had seen anything or come in early or stayed late.

Had the cleaning crew accidentally damaged it and then decided to get rid of the evidence? She didn't relish the idea of digging through trash bags. Likely that trash was long gone anyway. Plus, it wouldn't get her design back. She slumped into her chair, head in hands, trying to think. Should she go to security? Maybe the senior designers? No, not them. The rules were strict for a reason. A person could sabotage their own designs to get more time.

Assuming her design was gone for good, or at least in time for Design Review, she pulled up options on her computer. Maybe they could re-create the design in a simpler form. She clicked through her files to find the patterns. Except they weren't here. Had they been misfiled? She clicked through every possible option and was so deep into her work that she jumped at Henry's voice.

"I hear one of your designs went 'missing.'"

Kim heard the air quotes in Henry's voice. She lifted her

head. He hadn't been in the office earlier. "Did you work late last night?"

"I don't need to. My portfolio is already set for Design Review, and it's a winner. And not that my schedule is any of your concern, but I was on a date. Just getting in now." He gave her a smirk.

"Where did you go?" If she could poke at his alibi, maybe it would fall apart. Henry had the most to gain by the disappearance of her final design.

He put a hand on his hip. "None of your business. You're starting to get a bit worked up, Miss Taylor. Only divas can get away with that. And you're no diva. How do we know you didn't trash your own design because you knew you couldn't compete with mine?" He shook his head. "They'll see right through your pathetic attempts at sympathy."

Anger sluiced through her like lava. It was all Kim could do not to smack him. She was certain Henry was behind her missing design. And she was also certain that she couldn't prove it. And as much as it galled her, he was right. Any stink she made would just reflect badly on her.

She glared at Henry. Her attempt to leave with any kind of dignity was ruined by the crutches, which she cursed as she hobbled past him. She needed to take a walk to cool down and come up with a plan that would salvage her career. But that was out of the question.

Reluctantly, she emailed Juan.

<hr>

MATTHEW REALLY HATED HIS JOB TODAY. HE GLANCED around the standard hotel conference room that served as a workspace. Uninspiring.

Okay, he didn't hate his job. But after last night's kiss, all he wanted to do was think about Kim, and work kept demanding his attention. Especially since he and Austin were flying out tomorrow morning to pack up their places in Phoenix and driving back Friday night.

He wished Kim were going with him. But she had Design Review. Sometimes it really sucked being a grownup.

But that kiss last night… well, memories of it kept replaying in his mind. And not just the kiss, but the fact that Kim had trusted him with something important to her, something she hadn't told anyone else. He wasn't going to take that lightly and screw this up.

His feelings for her ran deeper than he had even acknowledged to himself. And a good portion of those feelings had fear wrapped around them, something he tried never to feel. But he was scared for Kim. Since Kyle didn't seem to think her stalker/secret admirer was Nick, that left a lot of possibilities. None of which reassured him. Especially since he was going out of town. Though he had to wonder, was he enough? Could he keep her safe even if he was in town? Could he live with himself if the worst happened?

He ran a hand over his face and stood. He did not like these kinds of feelings and physically needed to shake them off. Taking his phone, he paced out to the hallway. Maybe she'd have time for lunch. He texted her but didn't get a response. Maybe she was in a meeting. After stalling in the hall as long as he could, he headed back to his laptop.

Time dragged on and still no reply. If he didn't get ahold of her, he'd have to eat without her. He wanted the reassurance of seeing her face.

Chris tapped the lid of Matthew's laptop. "Hey, want to grab an early lunch? I have a few things to run by you." He glanced significantly around the room where a few others were working. Ah, something he didn't want other ears to hear.

He took one more glance at his phone. Still no response. Was Kim having second thoughts about last night? Or was she busy trying to finish up her work for Design Review? He shoved his phone in his pocket. "Sure. Let's go."

Edward had recovered well from his surgery and was ordered by his doctor and the CEO Alan Martin to strictly rest, so Marisa was forwarding anything that needed his input to either Anne or Alan. That had taken the pressure off Chris, and he and Matthew had time to work on their team game plan.

They were eating fish tacos at Baja Fresh when Chris revealed what he wanted privacy for. "I really liked what you did in Seattle. You have a good knack for reading people. You handled the disaster of a team-building exercise well, and you jumped in when Edward was having a heart attack. It surprised me, frankly, because you originally struck me as the happy, pretty face who was great for sales but not much of a team player. But since the fire, you seem more mature, more of a team leader."

Matthew let Chris's words sink in, choosing not to respond until he knew where he was going with this.

Chris took a sip of his drink. "As the rest of the team comes in over the next two weeks, I'd like you to think about what their strengths and weaknesses might be, what roles they'd be best suited for. To match clients with sales staff. I'd also like you to be the hub of team morale. Building a new team is always a challenge, but I think you can get it off to a good start. And we won't have a reenactment of the team-building challenge Edward designed."

They both laughed. "Yeah, no. I can come up with something way better than that."

Chris picked up his taco. "I wouldn't have you do this if I didn't think you were capable. But I do think it's going to stretch you. Your tendency is toward the upbeat. Not a bad thing. But if you're going to take on a leadership role, you'll have to deal with the ugly side of people and hard things." He grinned. "I think you're up to it."

"Yeah, I'm up for the challenge." Matthew let Chris's words soak into him. There was a lot of truth and wisdom in them. Funny, an hour ago he was irritated at his job because he wanted to spend time with Kim. Now he'd been handed a compliment and a challenge. Was he up to it?

Of course he was drawn to the fun of the team-building event. His mind started spinning with ideas. This would be a fun thing to noodle on during the trip to and from Arizona. In between thinking about Kim and her secret admirer. And Chris's words about challenging people.

Chapter Twenty-Three

Kim found Ashley at her desk. Ashley eyed her crutches. "How much longer do you have on those?"

Kim shrugged, as much as the crutches let her. "My ankle feels better every day. I see the doctor tomorrow, so hopefully I can ditch these soon and just use the air cast. I don't know if you heard, but my capstone design went missing."

Ashley's eyes darted around and something unreadable flashed across her face before she gasped and put her hand over her mouth. "No. What happened?"

"I don't know. Monique finished it last night after I left, and it was gone when she got in this morning. There's not enough fabric to recreate it. Or time. But even if there was, the patterns were also deleted off the hard drive. I think that's really weird. Do you think IT could look into that?"

"Um, sure. I guess they could. Are you sure you didn't save them somewhere else by accident?"

"I just finished looking. I've got an appointment with Juan in a few minutes. Then I'm heading home to figure out what to do." She'd meet Jessica for lunch first—Kim didn't want to bail on her, and an hour wasn't going to change her reality—but Ashley didn't need to know that. "I'm taking tomorrow off. I sent a note around to the team. I'll be in Thursday morning to turn in my portfolio before nine."

"Oh, okay. Sure. I hope you work it out." She gave Kim a soft smile. "It was such a pretty design."

"Thanks. I thought so too." She glanced around. She didn't want to head back to her workstation just to turn around and go to Juan's office. The ladies' room was on the way. She'd stop there.

Ashley had picked up her phone, probably to add to the rumor mill. Nothing Kim could do about that. Maybe it would even turn up something.

When she got to the ladies' room, Kim saw all of Matthew's texts. Luckily, the bathroom had a couch and a lighted mirror area, a touch of old Hollywood glam, so she collapsed there and texted him back so he wouldn't worry, telling him she was headed home soon and she'd give him all the details when they talked. She ran through her options. None of them were great. But one thing was clear. She needed time.

She came up with a rudimentary plan with options to run by Juan. At least he could see she was bringing him a solution, not just a problem. And she was asking for his advice as to the best option. Satisfied she'd done all she could, she levered herself up and checked her makeup in the mirror. No smudges under her eyes, so she was good.

Hopping over to the door, she tugged on it. It didn't budge. She reset her balance so she could pull harder. The door moved a little in the frame but still didn't open. What the heck? The lever moved a little. Was it a stuck mechanism? She tried again, feeling stupid. What was she missing? How hard was it to open a door?

She glanced at her phone. Her meeting with Juan was in two minutes. If she couldn't get out of here, she would be late. She texted Ashley to come help her in the ladies' room. Maybe she'd think Kim had fallen. No matter what, it was going to be embarrassing.

While waiting for Ashley to text her back, or even just show up, she found the company directory on her phone. She should call maintenance and have someone check out this door. Something was clearly wrong with it.

She wasn't going to make her meeting with Juan. She typed up a quick message that she was going to be late. But she hesitated sending it. If she didn't give him a good reason, she'd look like a flake. If she told him what was happening, she'd look like an idiot. She couldn't win. She mentioned that she was stuck in the middle of something and would come by as soon as she was free. It was the truth.

Where was Ashley? Had she gone to lunch early? She found the number for maintenance and called it, explaining her situation, feeling her cheeks heat. The person who answered said she'd send somebody over to check it out.

Nothing left to do but wait. Kim flopped on the couch and scrolled through her phone, but her mind was on what to tell Juan. Between her missing design and being stuck in the bathroom, he was going to believe that she was either the unluckiest person in the world or she was creating her own drama. If it were anyone else, she'd find it hard to believe too.

A scratching sound came from the door then a quick knock. "Anyone in here?" a voice called from outside.

"Yes!" Kim scrambled up and crutched over to the door that was cracking open. She pulled it the rest of the way. "Oh thank goodness."

A man in a maintenance uniform looked at her. "You okay?"

"Yes, thank you. What was wrong with the door?"

He shook his head. "Nothing. It opened right up."

"Can you check the lever from the inside? I couldn't get it to turn all the way."

He shrugged and flipped the inside lever. It moved completely.

"I swear it didn't do that before." Maybe she was just too weak to get the lever to work. Were her wrists really that bad?

No, she'd tried. But nothing would be accomplished by standing here arguing. She needed to get to Juan's office on the off chance he hadn't left yet for lunch.

She moved into the hallway. "Thanks for rescuing me." Heading around the corner toward Juan's office, she spotted a broom leaning up against the wall. Which was odd since this whole area was carpeted. Why would a broom be up here? She stopped. Its handle could have been shoved through the lever of the bathroom door, trapping her inside. But who could have done it? It wasn't like she could sneak the broom home and have Kyle run prints on it.

She shook her head and kept moving. Juan was gone of course. Sigh. Her phone buzzed with a text. Jessica was here. Kim crutched toward the front doors. Maybe some fresh air and sun would help clear her head.

Jessica waited out front in her car and drove them to a close-by place with a shaded patio. As they ate salads, Kim got Jessica up to speed on the morning's events. It was good to unload it all on someone who believed her completely.

Jessica wiped her hands on her napkin. "So do you think Henry's behind it all?"

Kim let out a long sigh. "I don't know. He's the most obvious subject. If it's not him, I have no idea who it could be. No one else benefits from me being eliminated." She pushed her food away. "After what we went through with the fire, a real life-and-death situation, this just seems so petty. Anyway, that's enough about me. How are things going for you?"

Jessica pursed her lips before answering. "I hear what you're saying about the fire being a defining moment. It made me think about how stupid some of my past decisions had been. Flirting with death, really. So dumb. But my sponsor recommended I start journaling to process my thoughts. It's really helped. I guess some things I didn't realize I had been holding on to, like feeling the weight of expectations from my family to replace my brother Christopher. He died before I was even born, yet I've always felt like I had to be what he should have been: an athlete, a star student. When I couldn't meet those expectations, I tried numbing myself with alcohol. Totally bad move. My consequences could have been so much worse. At the beginning of my recovery, I needed to stay busy, distract myself. But since the fire, I find myself wanting some alone time, some peace and quiet to process things. That's not usually me."

Kim leaned her arms on the table. "It's funny, we grew up together, but I never saw that happening in your family. I guess being a kid and all. I wish I'd known."

"I didn't even know. Not enough to put it into words at the time. And it's hard to say how much was just my folks not wanting to lose another child and how much was my own interpretation of what they said and did. Anyhow, the fire put some clarity on a lot of things. Forgiveness has come much easier when I realized I might not have as much time as I thought I did."

Kim was quiet for a moment. "Did you think we might die out there on the lake?"

Jessica looked away for a moment. "Maybe. I thought it could be a real possibility. Though with brothers like ours, always the heroes, it's hard to believe that they won't come through for us."

"Yeah. I figured Kyle would have a solution. He always does. But it did seem so much bigger than him."

They sat for a moment, the noise of the restaurant patio surrounding them. Kim checked her phone. "I was going to head home after lunch, but I need to touch base with Juan."

Jessica drove her back to House of Elan. "Has anyone checked Henry's office?"

"I doubt it. I don't think anyone suspects him other than me. Nobody but me even thinks anything is going on."

"Well, maybe you could give me a tour of the place, and we could happen by his office. If he's not around, we can peek in. If anyone suspects anything, you can say you were showing me around and I'm nosy." She laughed.

Kim thought for a minute. There wasn't anything to lose. "Why not? Let's go in." It was early. Everyone would likely still be at lunch. But if she could catch Juan, that would help.

They headed back toward her work area, taking the long way to detour close to Henry's workstation. He wasn't there. Jessica stepped closer to his desk, examining things. She even tugged on a drawer, but it was locked.

Kim didn't dare get close to his desk. She couldn't move away quickly if someone came by. She tapped nervously on her crutch grips. There was nothing here; they needed to go. "Jessica!" she stage whispered.

Jessica took a leisurely look around and then stepped close to Kim. "You're right. There's nothing there. But I don't suppose he'd advertise his guilt."

Kim giggled and showed Jessica the rest of the workplace. She was impressed, and it was encouraging to see things through her eyes. They passed by Juan's office, but he still wasn't in. She'd have to send him an email. She texted Kyle she was ready to leave and followed Jessica out and climbed in her own car. They hadn't run into anyone—everyone was still at lunch. A good thing, because it would be awkward to explain why she had said she was taking the afternoon off to work on her presentation and yet was showing her friend around.

Jessica waited with her until Kyle showed up, which didn't take long. On the drive home, she considered her actions. Jessica had talked her into some crazy things as kids. But snooping in Henry's office left her feeling icky. How was she any different than he was?

Did she want to succeed at Design Review and even her job too much? Had it become too important to her? If she couldn't do this job in an upright manner, then maybe she should walk away. The thought turned her stomach. She'd spent a lot of money going to FIDM. She didn't think her dad would be too thrilled if she quit, considering he thought it was too expensive for an iffy career at best. She'd hate to prove him right.

But if God had given her these talents to use, then she needed to use them for his glory. She had to trust him. Even when it didn't make sense.

MATTHEW AND CHRIS WERE JUST ENTERING THE HOTEL lobby after lunch. Kim's text had been weighing on him. He wanted to talk to her and find out what was going on. "I'll catch up with you in a minute," he told Chris. "I have a call to return." He headed into a small alcove in the lobby for privacy. "Hey, what's up?"

Kim poured out the story of her missing design and her suspicions. "It doesn't matter anyway. It's too late to fix it. Monique doesn't have enough of the material to remake it. I could find a substitute, but the patterns are gone too. There's no way this is an accident, but any attempt to point that out to the designers will make me look bad." The frustration in her voice was loud and clear.

"What can I do?" He wanted to do something. He'd felt a step behind everything today.

"I don't know. Nothing. I'm home now to pack everything up and take it to Kyle's place to work. I'll be up all night trying to figure out what design I can create a pattern for and get sewn up quickly. Monique is willing to work late for me, bless her, but I've got to give her something to do. And there's only today and tomorrow left." Her voice broke at the end.

"I don't have anything else pressing today. Why don't I come over so you can stay there and work? I can work on my laptop. We can order dinner in and can brainstorm a list of what needs to be done. A plan makes everything better."

Now she really laughed. "Said Matthew never. Are you channeling your sisters?"

"They might have rubbed off on me. I'll see you in a few minutes."

Now he had something to look forward to. He really did want to help lighten Kim's load. She'd been dealt a raw deal lately, and he wanted to make it better any way he could. Plus, he'd had a restless night dreaming about the fire. Maybe time with Kim would replace those memories and make his sleep easier tonight.

He sent Chris a text and hopped in his car. But his mind ping-ponged between Kim and what Chris had told him. He hoped his efforts would pay off somewhere.

Chapter Twenty-Four

Kim knew she should probably care more about her appearance, but when she'd gotten home, she'd changed into yoga pants and put her hair up in a messy bun. She had work to do and wanted to be comfortable. Besides, Matthew had seen her at her worst. He sat at the kitchen counter working.

She limped around the condo. Her ankle was sore but tolerable. She was sick of the crutches, and she could hobble around okay with just the air cast. On her computer. she scrolled through all her designs. Which could be made up most quickly, and yet would still have the wow factor to impress the judges? Then again, maybe she should just go with anything that was complete. Making something new meant there was a chance it wouldn't get finished in time. And she'd get disqualified.

And she did have a few complete items. She called Lynnae and explained the problem. "I need one of those samples back as insurance, in case I can't get something done. Which do you think would be best?"

They compared and contrasted different outfits, trying to read the mind of the judges.

"Kim, this job has just gotten more and more stressful for you. I know you want the designers to see and appreciate your talent, but perhaps you don't need their approval to be successful. You know you always have a place here with me. Not only designing for my customers, but I can get you in front of other buyers. It would be a whole shift in direction, so don't worry about it now. Just know that you have options."

Her eyes teared up. Lynnae had always been so supportive of her. And Kim would consider her words, when she had some time to spare. Perhaps there was something to that. Hadn't she just been wondering if her focus on Design Week had veered into obsession?

She got off the phone with Lynnae and stared at Matthew. Their dinner had been delivered while she was on the phone.

He opened his arms. "Come here."

She flung herself into them and let the tears fall. Anger, frustration, the unfairness of it all... she let it pour out down the front of Matthew's shirt. At the end of one of the worst days of work, she came home to someone who wanted to listen to her troubles, to walk through them with her. Such a contrast to work where someone deliberately sabotaged her, was going to great lengths to ruin her. And yet, she had to look at her own heart too. How much did she want this job?

And he didn't say anything. He just held her and rubbed her back. Her head rested on his broad chest, the smell of laundry soap and his spicy aftershave surrounding her.

Her stomach rumbled, and she pushed back, laughing. "I guess I'm hungry."

"Did you eat lunch?"

"I had lunch with Jessica. But something else happened before that."

He set out their food on the counter. "Eat and you can tell me what's going on."

She picked up a street taco and took a bite. Savory meat with the bite of onions and the coolness of cilantro filled her tongue. She told him about getting locked in the bathroom.

His brow furrowed. "I don't like that at all. First your design goes missing, then someone locks you in the bathroom. Did you tell Kyle?"

She shook her head. "No, it just sounds so stupid. I don't even know if I was locked in or just couldn't work the lever."

"I still think you need to tell Kyle."

"I will. But I'm not going to be at work until Thursday, so there's no rush. After we eat, we need to swing by Lynnae's shop to pick up my designs. One of them will be a backup if I can't create a new one fast enough that's as good."

"So you can't just use something you've already created? You have to make up something else?" He had demolished one taco already. He pushed the chips and guacamole toward her.

"Usually the created piece is the capstone of all the other work, highlighting the designer's talent with creations that can actually be sewn up. You can draw anything you want, but making something that is wearable is another skill set. One I'm quite good at." She shook her head, sick over the loss of her dress. "That dress was fabulous. Now it'll just be shown in the portfolio as one of the drawings."

"You don't have time to re-create it?"

She shook her head. "I thought about that, making it slightly simpler. Monique said she'd work all hours with whatever I came up with. But strangely enough, the patterns are missing too. They were deleted off the hard drive. I asked Ashley our admin to have IT look into it."

"So this wasn't an accident."

"Nope." She shoved another taco in her mouth.

"Do you think it's related to your stalker? I know it doesn't seem like it, but it is an escalation. First texts, then the balloon, the flowers, the package with pictures of you, then your missing outfit. And then you get locked in the bathroom. It's getting closer to you physically."

Kim stopped chewing. "I don't know. I hadn't thought about that. It would mean that my stalker is someone at work. And not Nick. He'd have no access to my designs. But we don't know if the stalker stuff is related to work. It would be just my luck that I've managed to tick off two different people at the same time." She swallowed, but the food sat heavy in her stomach.

"You said it could be a cutthroat business."

"Theoretically, it could be anyone. Henry's the most obvious choice, but he was on a date last night. Plus—" she realized too late that she was about to confess to snooping in his office with Jessica.

He raised his eyebrows. "Plus what?"

"Um, Jessica wanted to see the office after work, particularly Henry's. She snooped a bit but didn't find anything."

Matthew shook his head. "Not the smartest thing you've done. What if someone had caught you?"

"I know. It was stupid. I guess it was a combination of falling back into old patterns with Jessica and wanting to support her. I regret it. But, bottom line, there was nothing obvious in his office. Like my dress lying across his desk chair or something."

"He could have an accomplice."

"True. That makes everyone I work with a suspect. I don't like that feeling at all." She put the last taco on Matthew's plate and threw the container away. "It doesn't change anything. I still have to figure out how best to replace the missing outfit."

He slid off the barstool. "Let's go to Lynnae's. I'm eager to meet her. Anyone that's a fan of your work gets high marks in my book."

She gave a half laugh, grabbed her purse, and they headed out the door, leaving her crutches behind.

Matthew followed Kim into an upscale boutique nestled in a strip of similar stores, none of which looked like anything he'd ever step foot in. This was a whole other world, Kim's world, one he knew very little about. But he was holding her hand, taking some of the weight off her ankle, since she didn't want to use her crutches.

A woman about his mom's age, but with far more expensive clothes, met them at the door and let them in. "You must be Matthew. I'm Lynnae."

"It's great to meet you. I hope you can help Kim with this problem."

She locked the door behind them. "We've discussed it. Come on back to my office." A clothing rack stood to the side in a room that was part luxurious office, part workstation.

He recognized one of the outfits from Kim's Instagram photos of her drawings.

Lynnae handed out sparkling water from a small fridge.

He opened his and took a drink, studying Kim's designs. He'd only seen the one outfit of hers up close. The rest had been drawings or concepts. "Hey, where's that one that you wore up to the mountains, with the embroidered top thing." He didn't know the words, but it had looked amazing on her.

Lynnae frowned. "You have another part of this collection?"

Kim shrugged. "I've worn it, testing it out. I also had jewelry made to compliment any of the pieces in the Southwest collection and some sandals. But it's too casual."

Lynnae tapped her chin. "Do you have a picture of it?"

Kim shook her head, but Matthew whipped out his phone. "Yep." He'd snapped it of her that first night when she wasn't looking. He pulled it up and passed it to Lynnae. "Glad Kellie was able to get our stuff out of the cabins and down the mountain."

"Maybe we're going about this all the wrong way. Did you design the embroidery pattern yourself?"

Kim nodded. "And the jewelry, though Veronica Still made it. See how they match?" She pointed to parts of the images.

Lynnae nodded. "Yes." She turned to Kim. "Look, I know this is a bold idea, but the fashion industry is about boldness. What if you highlight your Southwest collection with your drawings and sketches? You've got the fabulous images from the photo shoot. And then show this as your final design. It's casual, but it is unique. And that is your brand. It's who you are. Maybe if you stop trying to force yourself into their mold, you'll be happier."

Kim paled a bit, and Matthew winced. Lynnae's words were hard, but she'd known Kim a lot longer than he had. Maybe it was what she needed to hear.

She sank on a reddish velvet couch. He joined her. What was she thinking? He had no clue what to do here. So he didn't do anything. Which was hard for him. But he didn't want to make light of the situation.

Finally she nodded. "I think you're right. I've been going about this the wrong way. The Southwest collection was my first set of designs where I was truly myself, did what I wanted. I only had you in mind as a customer." She glanced up at Lynnae. "My other work was trying to impress the designers at Elan. But I don't need to be like them. I need to be like me. And if I don't fit in there, well..." She swallowed.

He covered her hand with his. He wanted to tell her to jump out there and be her own woman, that everything would work out. But he had no idea if that was true. He was way over his head here. All he could do was support her. And maybe that was just what she needed.

Lynnae tilted her head. "I think you know the answer in your heart. Why don't you take all of these? Just bring them back. I'll need them for my fashion show in a few weeks. And I know I'll have a ton of orders for them."

Kim gathered up the clothing, zipping it back into the garment bag, which Matthew took from her. Lynnae walked them to the boutique's door to let them out. "Good meeting you, Matthew. Kim, let me know how it goes."

Kim nodded and gave Lynnae a final hug before taking Matthew's hand again and slowly heading back to her baby-blue Bug. It was perfectly her. Not so much for him. He squeezed himself in the passenger side, draping the bag across the back seat.

The ride back home in the dark was a silent one for a long time. He worked hard at letting Kim take the lead and keeping his mouth shut. It was hard, but he'd do it for her.

"What time is your flight tomorrow?" She glanced over at him at a stoplight.

"Nine." The hotel was close to the airport, and he wasn't checking anything. "I wish I could hang out with you tomorrow, bring you food and snacks while you work."

She laughed. "Yeah, you bring me a lot of food. What's up with that?"

"I think about food a lot."

She flicked a gaze up and down him. "And yet you manage to keep your girlish figure."

"I try."

She let the silence draw out again. Then finally said, "What do you think about what Lynnae said?"

"About you embracing your own style?" At her nod, he continued. "I don't know anything about fashion, but I do know you need to do what makes you happy. Seeing you now compared to how you were on the road trip with your photos and drawings… you seem less happy and more stressed. I know some of that is just the nature of the difference between work and vacation, but you really seemed to love the creative part of the trip. And if you can make a living out of it, seems like you should."

She didn't say anything for a long moment. Had he said the wrong thing? He didn't know. Just when he was ready to take everything back, her voice came through the darkness.

"Yeah. You're right. I just worked so hard to get a position with the prestigious House of Elan that I've done everything to prove that I was the right choice, that I would be an asset to them, hoping one of the top designers would notice my work. But what if I hate it?" Her hands draped over the steering wheel, and her shoulders slumped.

He reached a hand to her knee and patted it. "It's going to be okay. You don't have to decide right now."

She put her hand over his and squeezed. "You're right."

When they reached her condo, Matthew brought in the garments, and she settled in at the couch. "Thanks for going with me. You didn't have to. But I'm glad you met Lynnae."

"Me too. Where do you want these?"

She brought a garment rack and dress form out of her second bedroom.

"Let me hang them up, and you get to work." He unzipped the bag and unloaded it. Not hearing anything, he turned around.

Kim stared at him.

"What?"

"I've just never had anyone help with this before. I've always done this alone."

He closed the gap between them and pulled her close. "You're not alone." His lips found hers, and pulled her even tighter, heat and possession rushing through him. She was never going to be alone if he had anything to say about it. Her hands threaded through the hair at the back of his neck, and he suppressed a groan. Reluctantly, he set her away from him. But her rosy lips and glossy eyes tested his willpower.

"You need to get to work." He guided her to the couch. "I'll make coffee and bring you anything you need."

She stared at him a moment longer. "Okay." She settled back and opened her laptop, flicking him another glance. "Don't you have work to do?"

"I can do it tomorrow on the plane." He made a shooing

motion. "Go on. Pretend I'm not here except for when you need something."

She shook her head and laughed. "Like that could ever happen." She stared at her laptop a moment. "This could go late. Kyle won't sleep until I'm over there. We should probably pack everything up and work at his place. You up for that?"

"Absolutely." And it would definitely make sure things didn't get out of control.

Chapter Twenty-Five

Kim couldn't figure out what was poking her in the throat. And why was it so bright? She opened her eyes. She was on Kyle's couch, where she'd fallen asleep last night working on her portfolio. Her sketchbook lay across her chest, its edges tucked under her chin. The source of the poking. Based on the light coming through Kyle's sliding glass door, it was morning. What time? She reached for her phone on the coffee table but stopped.

Matthew. He was asleep on the other end of the couch, sitting up, her legs draped over his lap. Why was he still here?

She remembered finally getting the pieces of the portfolio arranged in the way she thought best. But she had been so tired, she couldn't trust her judgment. He had suggested she close her eyes for a bit then she could look at everything with fresh eyes. He'd said he wouldn't leave without letting her know.

And he hadn't. Poor guy.

She was stiff from lying on the couch. He must feel worse from sleeping sitting up, with his head crooked back. Or he would when he woke up. She eased her legs off his lap. He didn't stir. She grabbed her phone. Eight thirty. It was later than she thought. She didn't have to be in the office since she'd taken the day off to work on her portfolio and missing design.

Wait.

Oh no.

"Matthew!" She shook his shoulder.

His eyes popped open, confusion crossed his face, and then a smile. "Morning, sunshine. I have to admit it's nice waking up to your beautiful face."

She rolled her eyes as he stretched. "Um, it's eight thirty. No way can you make your flight. I'm sorry. I never should have let you stay to help me. I didn't know I'd fall asleep." She was surprised Kyle hadn't come and kicked him out. Given the time, Kyle had already left for work. She'd somehow slept through that.

He reached for his phone. "Ah, I see Austin gave up all hope on me and took an Uber to the airport." He texted a message then put his phone down. "I'll catch a later flight. It's not a problem. Why don't we grab breakfast and then you can review your portfolio, see if you need anything else?"

The idea of sitting across from him having breakfast sounded wonderful. He made popcorn for her last night at some point—she knew where Kyle kept the stash—but the tacos from dinner were a long time ago.

She pushed off the couch and hustled to the bathroom. Ugh. Her face was lined and her hair half out of its bun, flopping all over the place. And Matthew saw her like this. Well, he hadn't run screaming, so that was something. And he had seen her camping on the Great American Road Trip. She quickly brushed her teeth, splashed water on her face, and redid her hair. "Bathroom's free," she called as she scooted into the guest room for a quick change.

It wasn't long before she was sitting across the table from him with a mug of steaming coffee and a stack of pancakes on its way. Her stomach rumbled. She reached for his hand. "I'm sorry you missed your flight. Thanks for keeping me company last night and making sure I stayed hydrated and had snacks." She giggled at the end.

He brought her hand to his lips. "Anytime, Kim. When I get back from Arizona, we're going to have a real date. Okay?"

She smiled. "Okay."

After breakfast, Kim said goodbye to Matthew at the door to Kyle's house. Since they'd brought everything over last night, she might as well finish working there.

Matthew pulled her in for another kiss. "I'll text you when I land. And I'll probably call you as I'm driving back here Friday night. It's going to be lonely in my truck taking a road trip without you."

"I'd go with you if I could. But I'll tell you all about Design Review."

"I'm counting on it. You'll do great." He kissed her forehead, got in his rental car, and drove off, waving.

An odd sense of loneliness settled over her as she locked the door behind her. Which was weird because she'd been alone a lot. And often preferred it. But she'd never gotten sick of Matthew's company. Usually because he could make her laugh. He hadn't done that yesterday or last night. He'd listened, asked good questions, but he hadn't tried to make light of her dilemma.

Huh.

So had the Matthew that had tried to cajole her into a better attitude after Willie Dumas had grabbed her been the real Matthew? Or was this the real Matthew? She liked this one better, but she couldn't risk the old one showing up. Her heart couldn't handle it. And right now, she had too much to do to analyze any of it. Maybe his being gone a few days would be a good thing.

Matthew sat in the boarding area. He fired off a quick, funny GIF to Kim. It seemed to have become their thing, communicating through GIFs. Funny how much you could say in a repeating picture with a bit of text. Or not say.

He couldn't get to Phoenix fast enough, because then he could get packed up and head back home. Two days seemed like an eternity, which was odd because he'd been apart from Kim for two months before.

But they'd become close. It had been a sneak peek into her life when he'd gone with her to Lynnae's. He was admittedly ignorant of all things fashionable, but Lynnae definitely wasn't. And her respect and encouragement of Kim was something to see. He had a feeling Kim didn't let too many people into the protected artist part of herself. Even on their road trip, she hadn't let anyone see her sketches, flipping the page when someone walked over.

But she had let him.

Last night had been amazing. He hadn't done much, mostly watched her, been a sounding board while she thought out loud, and kept her filled with drinks and snacks. She pointed him in the direction of where Kyle kept things. Kyle had wandered out a few times but turned in early, leaving them alone. When she'd closed her eyes on the couch, he watched her sleep. Feelings he couldn't identify filled him. He just knew he could watch her sleep for the rest of his life.

At some point, he'd fallen asleep too. While he was still trying to work out the kink in his neck from that, he wouldn't have traded their morning for anything. It had spoiled him for all lazy mornings to come.

For her to share her past with him, to open up and let him know what really made her tick, what she loved about design… it was something special. She was the first woman that made him want to dig deep, to be more than the good-time guy most people knew him as. To be vulnerable, to share the tender places in his heart with her. He didn't like thinking about difficult or sad things, but he knew it was important to share deeply with another person to build true intimacy. And Kim was someone who would treasure his words, who wouldn't use them as weapons against him.

It was finally his turn to board. He filed onto the plane and found his seat, stowing his carry-on above.

Kim sent him another funny GIF just before he put his phone in airplane mode. He'd call his mom when he landed. She'd pick him up and take him to his place. Then, he'd be free to call Kim from the privacy of his own place. He wanted to know how she felt about her portfolio. It had been fascinating watching her work last night, sticking pencils in her messy bun and pulling them out again to chew on the end. Comparing photos and fabric swatches, talking to herself.

He could see himself spending many evenings doing just that. He'd tried to do a little work but ended up closing his laptop and just watching her. The flight was so short that it wasn't worth pulling it out now. But after he'd culled out the items he didn't want the movers to pack tomorrow, he'd be free to get some work done.

He'd likely be home too late Friday, but by Saturday she'd have Design Review behind her. They could actually relax and do something fun. Yeah, he'd start thinking about where he could take her for a date Saturday night. Might have to get Allie's help again. He grinned.

Kim had sent Monique an email saying not to worry about sewing up another sample, she had taken care of it. She hoped it didn't hurt Monique's feelings, but until she knew who was behind her missing design and the deleted pattern files, she wasn't giving details to anyone.

Sitting on Kyle's couch, she reviewed her portfolio one more time. Each drawing, photo, computer rendering, and fabric sample. Late last night, she had decided to do what Lynnae had suggested. Be bold, be herself. And that meant going with her Southwest line. Zander Jakes's beautiful photos didn't hurt at all. Those should set her apart by far. But it was a big shift from the more expected line she had planned.

She had no idea what the other designers were doing. Perhaps if she'd gone to Juan's roundtable she would have gotten a glimpse of what some of them were thinking, to see how far outside the box she really was. She was sure that was why most of them had shown up.

But it didn't matter. She'd listened to Lynnae; she'd prayed about it. Whatever would happen, this was the portfolio she was supposed to turn in. Wasn't that why she'd become a designer? To share her thoughts and ideas with the world the way she saw them? Strange how that changed once becoming recognized and successful meant fitting into someone else's ideal.

She'd gotten a quick text from Matthew when he landed, saying he'd talk to her tonight. She was looking forward to that. He'd been a far bigger support to her than she had imagined. Not once had he tried to talk her out of her feelings. He'd listened as she'd poured out her story about the department store and then again at Kyle's when she'd brought up what she'd believed Kyle and her dad thought about her. There was real substance under that gorgeous grin. And she couldn't wait for him to get back so they could spend more time together, and she could get to know him more, see what life looked like for them on a day-to-day basis.

She texted Kyle a reminder about her doctor appointment. She thought it was a bit ridiculous for him to follow her everywhere, but he insisted. If it made him feel better, she'd go along with it.

He showed up at the house in time for her to get to her appointment. "Did Matthew get on his flight okay?"

"He missed the first one but caught a later one." Would Kyle say anything about Matthew staying over?

He gave her a long look and then a short nod. "Okay, let's head out."

By the time she got into see the doctor, her stomach was growling. Her big breakfast had made her skip lunch, but she was regretting that. Maybe Kyle would be up for an early dinner. As she sat in the exam room, her phone dinged. A text from Ashley.

Hope you're having a good day off. Make sure you get out and get some fresh air.

She'd added a smiley face emoji.

I got a lot done. Hoping to reward myself soon with a Hawaiian hamburger and chocolate lava dessert.

Kim's stomach rumbled more just thinking about it.

Ooh. Islands? Love that place. Enjoy.

I will.

The doctor walked in. He examined her ankle and told her she could walk on it as long as she was comfortable. He gave her a brace to wear that was more comfortable than the air cast. He was a little more concerned about her wrists. He said she had repetitive motion injury and should rest and use ice on them. He gave her a pamphlet on it with advice on how to adjust her desk and a prescription for anti-inflammatories. She had a return visit in a month, and he told her if things weren't better, he'd prescribe physical therapy.

She wasn't sure how she'd be able to do her job and rest her wrists more. But that was a problem to worry about after Design Review this week.

Kyle sat in the waiting room, and she walked over to him. "Want to get an early dinner at Islands? I'm craving their chocolate lava."

"Sure. Everything okay with the doctor?"

"Yeah. I'll tell you about it on the way." As he drove, she gave him a summary of what the doctor had told her.

They pulled into the parking lot just as Kyle's phone rang.

He motioned for her to go in, and he followed her, phone to his ear. They entered the tropical-themed foyer.

"Two?" the hostess asked.

Kim nodded.

"I've got to take this. I'll meet you at our table." Kyle moved to the side.

With Collins still up the hill working on the fire, Kyle had been on his own again. Though both Collins and Joe were supposed to come home this weekend if they continued to increase the fire's containment. Residents were being allowed back in some areas.

She followed the hostess to a booth and slid in, perusing the menu, even though she knew what she wanted.

Someone stood in the aisle next to her table. "Hi, Kim."

She looked up. "Oh, hi, Zander."

"It's good to see you without crutches. You must be doing well." He slid into the booth across from her.

That felt a little too… familiar. But Kyle would join her soon.

"So Design Review is tomorrow, right?"

She nodded. "Yep. I'm celebrating being done with my portfolio. Whatever will be, will be." She gave an overly cheerful smile.

"I know you'll knock them out with your designs." He smiled at her.

Something about that turn of phrase…

"How was it running for your life from a fire? I can't even imagine."

"It's not anything I want to do ever again. I don't know how the firefighters do it. It's terrifying."

"So you used kayaks to get to the middle of the lake? That was smart thinking. How did the helicopters know where you were to rescue you?"

She really didn't want to talk about this. Why was he so curious? But how could she change the subject without being rude?

But Kyle showed up, standing next to the table and frowning.

Zander glared at him. "Who's this?"

"This is my brother, Kyle. Kyle, this is Zander Jakes, a well-known fashion photographer. I think I've told you about him."

Kyle stuck out his hand. "Good to meet you."

Zander's face relaxed. "So you two are having dinner together. How nice for a brother to celebrate his sister's success. I'll let you get to it." He slid out from the booth. "Good luck, Kim. Knock 'em out." He made a small punching motion.

She gave a little laugh, and he headed toward the foyer.

Kyle followed him with his gaze as he eased in across from her. "He's got a crush on you."

"What? No. He's a big-name photographer. I'm just lucky he seems to like my designs. He could be very influential."

"I know what I saw. Does he know about Matthew? Or where you live?"

"I don't see how. I mean, he had a lot of questions about the fire, so if he followed the stories at all, he'd have seen Matthew pushing my wheelchair. But there's no way he'd know where I live."

The server came and took their orders. When she left, Kyle leaned over the table. "He knows where you work. He could have followed you home one time. It's just one more reason I'm glad you're under my roof."

Their food came, but Kim didn't find it as appetizing as she had anticipated.

Chapter Twenty-Six

K im walked into her department early the next day, portfolio clutched to her chest. She'd left the crutches home and concentrated on not limping. She could do it if she went slow. The brace helped. She hadn't felt this nervous coming into work since her first week here.

She'd left Kyle's house at eight, giving herself plenty of time to get to work in case there was traffic or something happened to her car. Kyle was more than happy to leave early to follow her. Now she was here and ready to turn her portfolio in. But the room where they'd check in their portfolios wouldn't be open until nine sharp.

She wasn't letting her portfolio out of her sight until then, so she dropped her purse off at her workstation and headed to the break room to grab a cup of coffee, portfolio tucked under her arm. Not that she needed the extra caffeine, but she needed something to do.

She was a little sore. Last night Kyle had insisted on running through some self-defense moves with her again. She couldn't argue with him. They had helped her last March when Willie Dumas had grabbed her. And if it made Kyle feel better, she'd play along. Plus, she wanted to try out a move on him she'd heard about. He grabbed her, and she went completely limp, pulling him off balance.

"What was that?" he'd asked.

"My new technique to get an opening."

He shook his head then hauled her up and tossed her over his shoulder. "Not that great of a technique."

She'd started laughing, and that had been the end of that. But she felt the effect today of using muscles she hadn't in a while.

On her way back, she had to pass Henry's workstation. Ashley was there, leaning over him while he was seated in front of his computer. So he was here early too. She had wondered if he actually had any nerves. Guess he was like the rest of them.

Ashley glanced her way then back at Henry. He waved a hand, seeming unconcerned about whatever she was telling him. Huh. She'd never thought Ashley and Henry were that close. But as a design student, it would make sense that Ashley would want to make connections anywhere she could.

Kim headed to her workstation, chin lifted as she passed Henry's desk, which had gone suspiciously quiet as she neared. Who cared? She was tired of being gossiped about. Tired of gossip in general. Maybe Lynnae was right. Maybe Kim should consider working directly with buyers like her and other shop owners she knew. It would get her out of this crazy, competitive space.

Still, the chance to work with a senior designer wasn't something she was going to throw away. She'd think about what Lynnae said after Design Review.

Then again, if she got to work with a senior designer, she wouldn't want to leave. And if she didn't, then wouldn't her leaving look like sour grapes? She sighed. Why did life have to be so complicated? It didn't matter. She didn't need to make a decision today.

While she waited, she pulled out the pamphlet the doctor had given her and adjusted her workstation to be more ergonomically correct. And she set some timers on her phone to take breaks and stretch.

Deciding she'd waited long enough, she headed to the room to turn in her work. Maybe they'd open early. But when she arrived, she saw that three other designers had the same idea. They gave each other nervous smiles and waited silently until the door opened and Juan's admin took their portfolios and checked their names off a list.

Today the senior designers would review all the portfolios. Tomorrow the junior designers would present them and answer questions. Then the winners would be announced next week. Unfortunately, they went in alphabetical order. And since Taylor came after Smythe, she would be going right after Henry.

She could only hope the differences in their styles would be refreshing, not jarring.

Ashley came up to her after she'd returned to her workstation. "Have you heard the news?"

She remembered Ashley's and Henry's heads together this morning. "I don't want to hear any gossip."

"Oh, it's not gossip. It just hasn't been officially announced yet. There's going to be a round of layoffs soon. I saw the memo when I was doing filing for the department head. Design Review will play a part in who stays and who gets let go." Ashley twisted her fingers together. "I just thought you should know. In case you wanted to make plans."

Kim had only felt like eating a granola bar this morning. Now it and her coffee threatened to come back up. "Um, thanks for that." She gave Ashley a tight smile and turned back to her computer, not seeing the screen but waiting for Ashley to leave. She did, after a moment.

Great. If she'd known that, she might not have decided to take the risk with her Southwest portfolio. Too late now. If she didn't do well in the competition, would she lose her job? Despite what Kyle had said, she was certain her dad would want to say, "I told you so." He hadn't wanted her to spend her money on design school. He'd thought it was foolish of her to buy a condo on such a "flimsy" job. He had a standing offer that he hauled out any time she mentioned a frustration or discouragement. She could go work at his accounting firm. It made her want to poke her eyes out. But if she lost this job, she'd have to consider it since she had a mortgage payment to make.

Ugh. She was borrowing trouble, as Grandma used to say. There wasn't any evidence that Ashley was even telling the truth. And until she knew for sure, there was nothing to do.

She rubbed her wrists. She didn't want to ice them at work and draw attention to herself, but she'd now take what the doctor said more seriously. If she lost her job, she'd lose her medical insurance too.

***

Matthew scanned his nearly empty apartment. The movers had arrived early this morning and had made quick work of the place. He was ready for them. There wasn't much he was taking with him in his truck other than some more clothes and his bike. And he could handle all of that even with his sprained wrist, which didn't bother him too much until he forgot about it and tried to do something he shouldn't.

He didn't have a lot, but he was glad DataCorp was paying for movers. He hated packing and moving stuff. He'd still have to unpack on the other side, but he bet he could get Kim to help him. And that would be fun.

And of course Allie and Melissa would make sure everything got put away in an organized fashion if he asked for their help. Getting closer to his sisters was going to be fun. Until their road trip, he hadn't realized how much he missed their grounding influence on him.

He was having dinner with Mom; her boyfriend, Larry; his younger brother, Daniel; and Daniel's fiancée, Nikki; and Brittany. He'd crash at Daniel's tonight then head back to OC

Friday. But as he packed the last of his clothes in a box, he thought about Kim and how her Design Review was going. Hopefully smoothly. She didn't need any more complications in her life. She'd texted him when she'd turned in her portfolio. Tomorrow would be her presentation, toward the end of the day. He'd look forward to hearing about it on his drive home.

All he had to do was come up with a great date. And it would let her have some fun and take a break from all the pressure she'd been under. It would show her just how much she'd come to mean to him.

His phone rang. Austin. Why was he calling? Hoping it didn't mean bad news, Matthew answered.

Austin got right to the point. "Before I let the movers drive away with my stuff, I need to make sure you think this Data-Corp thing is going to fly." His voice softened, as if he didn't want anyone to overhear. "My parents are more upset about this move than I thought. They'd prefer I stay here and help them. But I know the bigger income from DataCorp will provide things for them I otherwise wouldn't be able to afford. But all of that is a moot point if the OC branch never gets off the ground."

"Anne and Chris are taking care of it. Alan hasn't said anything about Edward's budget, so we're safe. But I know you've got to be worried about your folks. You've taken on a lot of responsibility." He'd never had someone else's future at stake before. His stomach turned a bit. He'd always been confident of his ability to find another job.

But Austin had worked for their old employer his whole career. It had taken weeks to convince him to apply for the DataCorp position. Matthew had thought he was dragging his feet because he didn't like change. Now he saw the level of responsibility weighing on Austin's shoulders. Had Matthew inadvertently put Austin's future at risk?

No, even if DataCorp shut down the OC branch, they'd keep someone like Austin on. He was gold.

"So have you. I see how Chris and Anne have included you. Which is why I'm trusting you on this. I've gotta go, but I'll see you Saturday."

"Drive safe."

But the unease didn't leave him. He'd do whatever he needed to do to make sure Austin and his family had a secure future.

After the movers had taken the final load, closed up the truck, and left, he put the last few boxes in his truck bed. He came back to his apartment and looked around the final time. Time to close the book on this chapter of his life and open a new one. One that included being close to his sisters, a roommate, and new responsibilities. And one that included Kim.

Chapter Twenty-Seven

Kim smoothed down her skirt before stepping into the room full of designers. It had been a long, torturous day, but now it was her turn. She moved smoothly through her presentation the way she'd rehearsed it. She hit the points Lynnae had specifically told her to mention, showed the detail work on the embroidery and the matching jewelry. Zander Jakes's photos showed her work off to its best light.

She had found her rhythm and the presentation was going as well as she could have expected. She relaxed and let her breath out a bit.

But as she flipped to the next design, she heard a noise from Jane Martelle, a gasp.

Kim glanced in her direction and saw a scowl. What had triggered that? Did she not like the design? Kim let her gaze slide to the other designers while she tried to find her place and keep going.

What was going on? There were scowls, frowns. Several were sitting back with their arms crossed.

Kim had no idea what she had done wrong. This had taken a bad turn, a very bad turn. She flipped through that design and hurried on to the next. But the looks remained.

She wanted to cry. She had made the wrong choice. Being bold was not what she should have done. She pushed down the voices in her head. She needed to remain a professional. She finished out her presentation, closed up her portfolio, and turned to leave.

She headed to her workstation, grabbed her purse, and headed for her car where she finally let herself burst into tears.

It was too early to call Lynnae. The shop was still open. She texted Kyle that she was ready to head home. But she wanted to stop by her house first to change out of this suit and hang it up.

Be there in 15. I want to hear how your presentation went.

That was something she didn't want to tell him about. She just hoped no one from Elan spotted her sitting crying in her car. She picked up her phone and called Matthew.

IN HIS TRUCK, THE BED PACKED WITH BOXES AND HIS mountain bike, Matthew left Phoenix proper behind him on the I-10 as he headed west toward California, his new home, and Kim. He'd talked to her last night after dinner with his family. She didn't seem to mind staying at Kyle's house, especially with Matthew gone. But how long would Kyle insist on the protection? They hadn't heard from the stalker since Sunday. Not even any social media messages. But Kim had too much on her plate with Design Review to have to deal with a creeper.

His phone rang. Kim. He smiled.

"Hey, are you on the road?"

"Yep. About half way. Should be there in about three hours, depending on how much traffic I hit in Orange County."

"Are you and Austin caravanning?"

"No, he left first thing this morning. Even after the supposed goodbye dinner last night, I got roped into breakfast again with

Daniel and Nikki. Since I'm not planning on coming back until Thanksgiving, I figured I could give them a few hours."

"Good thought. Family is important." Her voice sounded funny.

"Kim, what's going on? How did your presentation go?"

Sniffling came through the line. "Kim? What happened?"

"I don't really know." She told him about the reaction of the designers. "It was like they were disgusted with me. I really don't get it. My designs might have been different, but they weren't horrible. It seemed like a huge overreaction. I could understand that coming from one or two of them. There is a lot of drama in design, after all. But all of them? I just don't know." She let out a long breath.

"When will you hear?"

"Monday or Tuesday. They like to give themselves plenty of time to make a decision. The senior designers announce who they have chosen to work with them. Not all designers choose someone. And then the rest of us get a paragraph or so from each of the designers, anonymously, on our designs. Since I doubt I'm going to be chosen, I'll have to wait on the feedback to see what I did wrong."

He didn't know what to say. He hated that she was hurting, and all he wanted to do was make her feel better. But that had backfired before. What could he do? "I'm so sorry, Kim. I wish I could make you feel better. It sounds like they were unprofessional at the very least. And maybe there's more to the story than you know."

"Actually, there might be." She told him about the rumor of layoffs. Those kinds of things could trigger all sorts of infighting, whether they were true or not.

"I have a question for you, but I want to make sure you've said everything you want to. I don't want you to think I'm making light of anything. But I do hope I have a plan to get your mind off things." It sounded better in his head. But he didn't want her to think he was rushing her past the bad parts.

And maybe the timing of the date wasn't good. Should he make it another time?

"I think we can safely change the subject. You know everything I do at this point. There's nothing left to do but wait. So what's the plan to get my mind off things?"

"Do you think you'll be up to going on a date tomorrow with me? You can say no if you don't think you'll be up to it."

Her smile came through the phone. "Yeah, I think that could be arranged."

Whew. Okay, he'd done the right thing. "Good. I was talking to Allie earlier, getting ideas and making some arrangements. When we lived in Southern California before, it was in the Inland Empire, sixty miles away. So I feel a bit like an out-of-towner here. And while I know you probably know all the best places to go, I wanted to surprise you. Thus, Allie's help." And he'd already created a plan.

She laughed, which warmed his heart. "I was just wondering yesterday if it will be weird for you to come back to SoCal but only be around your older sisters."

"It's funny. I moved to Phoenix to take my previous job before anyone else moved there. I teased them that they all followed me. Mom, I think, did, and Brittany followed her. Mom's never stayed put in one place too long. We moved a lot as kids once my dad left us when I was eleven. And Brittany had just gotten out of college and didn't know what she wanted to do. Daniel came about six months later because the housing was cheaper.

"So then Melissa and Allie were the outliers. But they've always known exactly what they wanted to do and haven't relied much on the family at all. If anything, we rely on them. Allie was good about coming out for holidays. Melissa not so much. I don't know what this year is going to look like."

"Seems like Melissa and Scott will at least be engaged by then. Collins and Allie seem headed in that direction too."

"This will be a year of a lot of change, that's for sure. But good change." Kim had definitely been a benefit he hadn't expected when he'd first scoped out this job months ago.

"I can't really imagine Kyle without Heather anymore. And yet, I've been realizing more and more that once they're married, it'll be different. It'll be Heather's house, not my old house. So my staying there feels like a last hurrah. Although, it's been a little weird being in the guest room. My old room is still empty. Heather's going to turn it into an office, since she works from home."

She paused before continuing. "Part of that conversation with Kyle Sunday made me think. I thought for sure my family all considered me this head-in-the-clouds artist who couldn't do anything practical. Kyle and my dad teased me about it enough. But then what Kyle said about not entrusting the wedding planning to me if he thought I'd mess it up made me think." She gave a rueful laugh. "Granted, he cared more about Heather having a great day than his little sister's ego. But I just had never thought of it that way. For a long time, I thought they'd perceived me a certain way, and maybe that just wasn't true."

She sighed. "It's been interesting to think about. I've been wondering if I let my own insecurities about my art be projected on to their normal family teasing. On the other hand, if I do lose my job at Elan, then I may get stuck working at my dad's accounting firm, a fate worse than death, if you ask me."

He chuckled. At least she was trying to find some humor in the situation. "I think we take on roles in our families. It always felt like my job was to keep everyone happy, especially Mom. She's bipolar, so her mood swings can be pretty dramatic. She's a lot of fun when she's happy until she gets to the manic phase. But the depression is worse." This was harder to talk about than he thought. But over the phone, not seeing the pity on her face, made it easier. And knowing that it was helping to get her mind off her troubles… well, he could do it for her.

"One time, we walked home from school to find the power off. I think I was in first grade, so Melissa was in sixth. I didn't really know what was going on, but I could hear Mom crying in her bedroom. Brittney and Daniel were just playing on the floor. Melissa and Allie did what they always did and figured out food, got out the lanterns, and lit candles. They made it seem like a campout that night.

"I noticed that the lanterns made fun shadows on the wall, so I started doing goofy things, seeing what I could make. Brittany and Daniel became entranced and started laughing, even though Daniel was two years older than me. I just got sillier and sillier. Mom came out and found us all laughing, and she smiled and joined us. I thought I'd really worked some magic. So when I could make them laugh, Mom wasn't so sad. It seemed like it was my job after that."

"That must have been so much on your young shoulders."

He shrugged, though she couldn't see it. "Melissa and Allie did a lot more, probably even more than I knew. It just seemed normal to me."

"Was your mom upset that you're leaving Phoenix?"

"I don't know. She says she's proud of me. And she's happy with Larry, her boyfriend. She's been staying on her meds. So I think she's okay with it."

"Whatever happened to your dad?" Her voice was quiet.

"When I was a junior and demanded some answers from someone, Melissa told me he couldn't handle my mom's bipolar disorder. He'd been having a long-term affair with another woman and had gotten her pregnant. He went on to have a family with this other woman. He completely forgot about all of us."

"I can't even imagine."

"We did okay. I was only two when he left, so I don't even really remember him. I think it was harder on Melissa and Allie who do have memories. Melissa tracked him down one time. She really laid into him, told him that life had been hard, and he never should have left them. His wife came out and said that they were his family now and that we should never come around again. And she didn't. None of us did."

"Wow."

"Yeah. We were probably better off without him." It's what he always said. He wasn't sure he believed it entirely, but it didn't matter. They couldn't go back and change things.

But he would never be that kind of person. He wouldn't abandon someone he loved. As the highway spooled out in front of him, he had Kim's voice for company in his lonely truck cab while he shared things with her he'd never talked about with anyone, not even his sisters. He was hanging in there with uncomfortable emotions as he headed toward a new life.

KIM FINISHED HER CALL WITH MATTHEW AS SHE PULLED into her condo parking spot, Kyle slotting in next to her. She hopped out and headed for the stairs, using the railing to help with her sore ankle. She didn't want to talk to him about her presentation here. She just wanted to change out of these clothes, grab a few more things, and head to his house. Then, properly fortified with mint-chip ice cream, she'd tell him what happened.

"Kim, wait for me."

She didn't slow. After her day, if anyone was waiting for her, they should watch out. She unlocked the door and pushed it open, taking a few steps inside before she realized what she was looking at. Her house was trashed.

Kyle's arm snaked around her waist. He pulled her back to the doorway. "Stay here." He slipped his gun out of its holster and moved into her condo, toward her bedroom.

She wrapped her arms around herself and leaned against the doorframe. From what she could see, everything had been pulled out of her kitchen cupboards, her fridge stood open. Heather's wedding box was upended. It was like they were looking for something. But what? She didn't own anything of value. Gratitude that she'd taken her clothing samples to Kyle's crashed over her.

He came out of the hall, holstering his weapon. "It's clear. I want to show you something." He stepped into her bedroom doorway.

She crossed the room, watching her step on the debris-scattered floor, and stood next to him. Her room was as much of a disaster as the rest of the house. Clothing strewn everywhere. Bedding ripped off.

Kyle walked over to her bed and pointed to the one pillow that remained, slipping on a glove. One on her knives pierced it, trapping a piece of paper. He pulled the knife out and lifted the paper where she could see it.

It was a photo printed out of their group at the terminal of San Bernardino International Airport after being rescued Saturday. Except that Matthew's face had been crossed out. And at the bottom a note had been printed: "You're mine. He's dead."

She ran into her attached bathroom and threw up. Who would do this? She scanned the bathroom. Crushed cosmetics, creams, and lotions smeared everywhere. It would cost a fortune to replace everything. She couldn't even think about it. She levered herself up, trying not to touch anything.

Kyle stood in the doorway. "You okay?"

She shrugged.

He slipped his arm around her shoulders and pulled her close. "It'll be okay. I've got a team coming, and I'll get you back to my place."

"Okay." Her head was whirling. She couldn't grab onto one thought long enough for any of it to make sense.

Kyle guided her to a barstool, and she sat. He studied her. "If this is the same guy who delivered the box, the balloon, and the flowers, this is an escalation. While the others were more admiring, this is someone who sees you as belonging to him and Matthew as a threat. I don't like either of those things."

"I have no idea who it could be. Henry wouldn't see Matthew as a threat. And you already talked to Nick." She rubbed her arms, chilled by all of it. She just wanted to go to Kyle's and take a hot shower. Guess she'd have to make do with the clothes she had there since everything here was evidence.

Footsteps sounded on the stairs, and Kyle went to meet the officers. Kim was grateful for his presence as he explained what they'd found and what he suspected.

"I already have her fingerprints on record for elimination. That won't be a problem. I'll bring the box in, but it only had her prints and Matthew's. I'm sure the guy used gloves this time too."

She frowned. How did her brother have her fingerprints? She didn't want to know. When Kyle had brought everyone up to speed and she had answered all their questions, she was free to go.

"You okay to drive home?" Concern shadowed her brother's eyes. "I can get someone to bring your car to my house."

"I'm fine. It's not far." She wanted some space and privacy.

Kyle followed her as she drove to his house. Had the person who'd done this expected her to come home later? Or earlier? What if she hadn't had to wait for Kyle and had come straight home? Could she have walked in on him? It was one thing for someone to leave "presents" outside her house. It was another to break into it. She felt so violated. How would her cozy little condo ever feel safe again?

***

MATTHEW PUSHED THE ACCELERATOR DOWN, GLANCING AT the speedometer. Then he backed off. It wouldn't do to get a speeding ticket. And nothing would get him home faster. Kim was with Kyle; she was safe. That's what he kept telling himself while she told him about the break-in and the photo of their group with him crossed out.

He didn't care that he was in some wacko's crosshairs. He was much more concerned about her. "Oh, Kim. I'm so sorry you've had to go through all of that. I'm glad you're at Kyle's."

"Yeah. He might end up having me under armed guard at this rate." She gave a wry laugh.

"I'm glad he's protective." Fear for Kim washed over him in waves. What if that person had come in while Kim was home? The thought of losing her slammed into him and stole his breath. After her encounter with Willie on the road trip, he'd assumed danger was behind them. He hadn't even really entertained the idea that she would refuse to let him back in her life. The idea of life without her made him sick, and he thought for a moment he might have to pull over.

He let out a deep breath and just listened.

"Be careful when you get home tonight, okay?"

The worry in her voice touched him. "I'm staying at a hotel with security, and I'm always surrounded by people. It's you I'm worried about. I'll text you when I'm in my hotel room, okay? And if you don't feel like going on our date tomorrow, I'll understand."

"No, that's something I'm looking forward to. Not sure what I'll be able to wear, but maybe Kyle will get some of my clothes released from the crime scene." Her sigh came over the phone.

"You're beautiful no matter what you wear." The need to pull her into his arms and never let her go was almost overwhelming.

After he hung up with her, he spent the rest of the trip trying to figure out who was after Kim. Because until they found this guy, she wasn't going to be safe.

Chapter Twenty-Eight

Kim was glad she had the date to look forward to today. Otherwise, she'd be tempted to lay around and mope. She did let herself sleep in. Kyle had returned with a box of donuts for breakfast. He was actually a pretty good brother most of the time. After giving herself a sugar rush, she stared across the table at him. "When can I get back to my condo?"

"Probably later today. I'll talk to Patino and see if they need any more time. I know they're rushing things as a favor."

She nodded. "I left a message with my insurance agent last night. I don't want to do anything until I talk to him. But I don't have any date-worthy clothes here."

He frowned. "Looks to me like there are a lot of clothes in the guest room."

She rolled her eyes. "Work clothes, casual clothes, but not date clothes."

"There's a difference?" Then he grinned.

She whacked his arm. "Heather's got her work cut out for her."

"She knows what she's getting into. I'll find out if we can go over there and grab a few things."

She spent the rest of the morning doing laundry and cleaning Kyle's house. She needed to keep busy. The weekend threatened to be a long one, sandwiched between her failed presentation and the repercussions on Monday. Throw in a trashed condo, and there was absolutely zero she could do about any of it. Second guessing herself wouldn't help, so she refused to do that.

Instead, she focused on her upcoming date with Matthew. The advantage of having someone like him in her life meant that on days like today, he was guaranteed to help her do something fun and look at the world from a new perspective, something she was mature enough to realize she needed from time to time.

Heather showed up mid-morning and helped her. The companionship was comforting. "Why don't you borrow some of my clothes for your date tonight? I can return the favor you did for me last year."

Kim smiled at the memory. "Good plan."

Kyle came in from the yard and overheard their conversation. "I'll drive you, and we can get lunch on the way back. We can bring some things back here from your loft anyway." He and Heather exchanged one of those looks that people in love do. Their wedding was a week away. What would she do if they hadn't caught her stalker by then? She wasn't going to worry about it today. It wouldn't help.

"I see you've got your priorities in order, big brother." Kim smiled.

"Absolutely." He dropped a kiss on Heather's forehead.

On the way, she told them about her presentation.

"It doesn't sound like you did anything wrong." Heather turned from the truck's front seat to look at Kim in the back seat.

"I don't think I did. Anyhow, I'm trying not to think about it until Monday." Adding to the list of things she wasn't going to think about.

"Good plan."

Heather unlocked her condo. "The boxes that are ready to go to your place are in the garage, Kyle."

"Got it."

Heather started up the spiral staircase to her lofted bedroom. "Do you know what you're doing tonight?"

Kim followed her. "It's a surprise."

"So something that could be dressy enough if you go to a nice restaurant but casual enough to be comfortable."

"Right."

Heather pulled a few outfits out of her closet, and the day became fun for a few moments while they talked about clothes and shoes.

They were still chatting on her bed when Kyle called up. "You ladies ready to go? I've got the truck packed."

Kim scooped up the clothes. "Yep." She looked around the loft. "This sure is a cute place. If I didn't have my own, I'd buy this from you."

Heather started down the stairs but looked back. "There's been a lot of good memories here. But more are to be made with Kyle."

They exited Heather's home and piled into Kyle's full truck. After stopping on the way to grab sandwiches, they arrived at Kyle's and unloaded the boxes. After lunch, Heather began unpacking boxes, and Kim helped until fatigue fell on her like a blanket. "Not to bail on you, but I think I'm going to lay down for a bit. Otherwise, I won't be very good company for Matthew tonight."

Heather shooed her away. "You've been through a lot. Let your body process it the way it needs to."

Kim nodded and collapsed on the guest bed. She turned on some soft music, closed her eyes, and fell asleep. But visions of an unseen person chasing her woke her. She glanced at her phone. She'd been asleep about twenty minutes. Staring at the ceiling, she decided sleep wasn't going to be her friend this afternoon. Maybe caffeine would. She scrolled mindlessly through her phone then padded out to the kitchen to snag a Diet Coke.

Heather came in from the garage. There were fewer boxes in the kitchen. "How was your nap?"

"Fine until the nightmares started. Looks like you've made some progress." She sipped her soda.

Kyle stepped into the kitchen behind Heather. "Be careful tonight. Watch your surroundings."

"I will."

"And I'll wait up until you get home."

She punched him lightly in the arm. "I don't remember you doing that before when I was living there."

"You didn't have a stalker after you before."

Good point. She helped Heather and Kyle with the rest of the boxes until it was time to get ready. She spent a little extra time with her hair and makeup, appreciating the distraction it provided.

And it was all worth it when Matthew knocked at Kyle's door. She let him in, and his eyes widened. "Wow. You look fantastic." He kissed her cheek and handed her a bouquet of flowers.

"Aw, that's so sweet!" She brought them inside and actually found a vase. It must have been Heather's.

He looked pretty fabulous, too, in his button-down shirt and dark jeans. He held her hand as they went out to his car.

"Is the stuff you brought back at Allie's?" she asked as he helped her into his truck.

"In her garage. I didn't bring much. Austin parked his boxes there too. We'll be in our place on Monday."

It was good to have him back.

Delight shot thorough Kim as Matthew found a parking spot and pulled his truck next to the curb at Laguna Beach's Crescent Bay Park. The sun hovered over the watery horizon. She loved watching the sunset over the ocean. She stepped out of the truck, and Matthew grabbed a cooler and a blanket from the back then reached for her hand.

They walked toward the sun along the sidewalk to the park area. The park ended at a bluff top overlooking the ocean and rocky cliffs far below. A soft breeze lifted her hair from her face, and the scent of salt water brought relaxation to her bones.

Matthew spread the blanket on a concrete step that ran in a semi-circle facing the spectacular view in front of them.

She sat, and he put the cooler down, sitting next to her but leaving a space between them.

He began pulling things out of the cooler. Blood-orange flavored San Pellegrino, two small containers, two forks, a small loaf of French bread with a cutting board and knife. "Our first course."

She popped the lid on her container to find a small Caesar salad. She took a bite of the tangy, salty salad with a bit of parmesan and the crunch of the crouton. It all tasted better out here.

He handed her a piece of bread. "Allie said she thought you liked Caesar salads. I know it can be a bold choice. Not everyone likes anchovies."

"I like them in this. It's wonderful." She swept her arm around them. "All of this is amazing. Thank you for thinking of it."

He leaned toward her. "I know you think I don't always take your feelings seriously enough. And I know I'd prefer to look at the sunny side of things. But I want to lighten your load, to share adventures with you."

She gave him a soft smile. "This is a good start."

He laughed. "There's more. Stuffed pasta shells in marinara sauce and a decadent chocolate torte for dessert."

"You did think of everything."

He grinned at her. "I tried. Including the timing of the sunset, hopefully just after we finish eating. I considered a fancy dinner, but I thought nature put on a better show than anything I could find."

"You thought right."

"Plus, it reminded me of all our meals around the campfire on the Great American Road Trip."

She smiled. Good memories.

They finished their meals with soft conversation. A few people wandered by to check out the view, but mostly they had the place to themselves.

After dessert, Matthew placed everything back in the cooler. "Just in time to watch the day end." He slipped his arm around her shoulders as the sun slipped below the horizon, turning the water to a fiery streak before disappearing. Twilight was long this time of year, and the wind settled down, making for a peaceful evening.

"Good timing." Kim turned her face to his just inches away.

"I planned it that way." He lowered his mouth to hers slowly at first, but then with more passion.

He tasted of chocolate. Kim wound her hands up the base of his neck, pulling him closer, forgetting everything of the past week except this moment and being with him.

He pulled back, resting his forehead on hers, tracing her lip with his thumb. "We have one more thing to do."

"What's that?" She could hardly form words.

"Make a wish on the first star tonight."

She giggled. "Matthew, you continually surprise me."

"That's the plan." He snuggled her against his chest while they looked out over the sea, watching the sky gradually darken, looking for the first star of the night.

"There it is." He pointed.

She squinted. "I think that's a plane."

He laughed. "Nope, it's the first star."

"Are you sure? It's not twinkling, and it seems to be moving."

"Well maybe my wish involves travel."

She laughed. "You really can see the bright side to everything, can't you?"

His voice lowered to just above a whisper. "I try." He leaned his chin on her head. "What did you think about what Lynnae said? If you could do anything you want, work with anyone, who would you choose?"

"There's this designer I follow. Maurice Worthington. He's fantastic. Classical lines with a twist. Creative yet wearable. I would learn so much if I could work with him. I saw him once, from a distance, at a fashion show in LA last year. I follow his Instagram."

"Would you ever want to work with Lynnae?"

She was silent for a long time. "I've been thinking about that. On the surface, I'd love to. She's offered before. I could meet a lot of people from the other side of the business, the buyers' side. Which could be a good thing. Ultimately, you want people to buy your designs. I'm not sure I'm ready."

"She seemed to think you were."

"Yeah."

They sat in silence, just the peace of the evening settling over them as the waves crashed below. The beach had always been a place signifying fun and relaxation to her. And now she could add romance to that list. There was no better place for her to be right now than here.

For now, everything was perfect, and she wasn't going to think about designs or work or stalkers or anything but being here with Matthew in this moment.

Chapter Twenty-Nine

Kim walked into work Monday with an equal mixture of nervousness, excitement, and anticipation. She'd had a great date with Matthew Saturday and had spent Sunday at church and lunch afterward with him and their friends. She was able to put Design Review and her condo out of her mind—mostly—and concentrate on Heather and Kyle's wedding this Saturday. As long as the rehearsal went off without a hitch, everything was planned and ready to go.

The police had released her condo, and the insurance adjustor was coming over. She'd given Heather a key to let him in. Then Kim could begin the cleanup at some point this week. She didn't want to think about it.

She hoped they'd hear the results of the Design Review today and who would be working with which designers. Maybe she'd figure out what their reaction to her presentation was all about. Or perhaps it had been exaggerated in her head. After all, she was nearly the last person to present. They had to be fatigued.

The department was mostly subdued, nobody wanting to pretend to be too eager for the results of Design Review, but no one actually doing much work because they were too busy waiting for the results.

Kim pushed it all out of her mind and set to work on her trade show projects. If she did get to work with a senior designer, that job would be given to someone else. But in the meantime, she was responsible for it.

Ashley came up to her. "How was your weekend?"

She thought about her date with Matthew. She wasn't going to mention the break-in to anyone at work. They already thought she was a drama magnet. "Really great." But that was just a pretext. Ashley wanted something. "How was yours?"

"Fine. I didn't really do anything. Have you heard anything about the results?"

Kim wanted to roll her eyes. Ashley should just spit it out. "No. I'm waiting like everyone else."

"Well, I heard that some of the top designers are going to take their juniors with them and leave and form their own company. So if they leave, will Elan need to make cuts or will that make things worse?" She pinched her skirt.

More rumors. She didn't have time for this. "I don't know. I guess we'll just have to wait and see what happens." Why did Ashley find it necessary to tell her this gossip? "You know, it might all just be a rumor."

Ashley shrugged. "Maybe. I just thought you should be prepared. Make plans if you need to." She moved off, probably to gossip with someone else.

Kim shook her head. Sometimes she wondered if people ever really left middle school.

Just before lunch, Juan sent her a message to meet him in the conference room. She didn't know what to make of that. Usually the list of designers and their chosen junior designers came out via email. She headed toward the conference room, uncertainty flowing through her.

Juan motioned her in. "Close the door, please."

She did as he asked and took a seat.

"Someone from HR will be joining us in a moment, but I asked to have a word with you first."

HR? That made no sense. What did HR have to do with anything? Was Ashley right about them laying off people?

"You've always done good work, been responsible and creative. So I wanted to ask you why you did it. Why did you feel you had to steal Henry's designs and pass them off as your own? You're being fired, of course, there's no doubt about that. But I really want to know why." Juan folded his hands on the table between them.

"What?" Heat rushed through her. She didn't know what to say or where to start. "I didn't steal Henry's designs. I don't know what you're talking about."

"Kim, there's no point in denying it. We all saw it. You presented right after he did, so there wasn't even any time for us to forget what we just saw or to possibly be confused. I know the fire experience must have been stressful for you. But if you'd just come to me, I could have helped you. You're better than this."

"Juan, I don't know what you are talking about, but I can assure you, I did not steal any of Henry's designs."

He brought out both of their portfolios and flipped open Henry's first.

She gasped. Her designs had been redrawn, but they were her designs from her Southwest collection. He had drawings and computer renderings. His finished sample wasn't the same as hers; he had chosen one of the other designs. But her finished sample showed up in one of his drawings.

If she wasn't seeing it with her own eyes, she wouldn't believe it. She was stunned. Why would he do this? It would be so obvious that he had copied her.

She sat back in the chair. No, it wouldn't be. She might never have known. She hadn't planned on going with her Southwest collection originally. Based on her sample piece, she was going in a different direction. She would have included a few pieces from the Southwest collection, but it wouldn't have been her whole portfolio. And a few pieces might be explained away.

He'd made a few stylistic changes, though the basic styles were the same.

"These are my designs. Henry copied me."

Juan sat back and crossed his arms. "Why would he do that? He's a decent enough designer."

"I don't know. Why would I copy him?" Anger tinged her words, and she worked to keep her emotions in check. Getting upset wouldn't accomplish anything and might just reinforce Juan's idea that she had panicked and copied Henry because she couldn't cope.

"I can prove to you how I got my ideas and when I got them." She told him about the trip through the Southwest with her friends. "I have my sketchbook at home, but I can show you my Instagram." She pulled out her phone and scrolled back to last March. "Here's where I was documenting my trip."

He studied the images. "All this proves is that you were inspired last March. I'd need to see some of your designs with dates on them. Then I can ask Henry the same questions."

Her heart plummeted. "I don't generally date my sketches. I have so many of them." Even if she did, that didn't prove anything. She could have written any date down. "But the computer-generated ones would have creation dates and version histories." She pulled her portfolio to her and opened it to the photo shoot Zander Jakes had done. "Look at all these created samples. That takes time. And Lynnae MacKenzie will confirm when she first saw these samples and scheduled the photo shoot. Oh and the embroidery on this one—" She pointed to the photograph of her sample. "See how the jewelry matches? I had Veronica Stills design the jewelry to match. She can tell you when I contacted her and gave her the design."

Juan studied everything for a moment. "You make a good argument, a compelling case. But it's all circumstantial. I'll talk to Henry as well, see what he says. Unless one of you can produce hard evidence of when you created your designs—like a dated computer file—it'll be your word against his."

He met her gaze. "I have to tell you, Kim—"

There was a knock at the door.

He raised his voice. "Just a minute." He lowered it again. "That's HR. I'll tell them what I've discovered. You're not going to be fired until I get to the bottom of this."

Fired. The word fell like lead into her stomach.

Juan stood and moved past her, opening the door. He said something to the person outside and then turned to her, waiting.

Oh, she was supposed to leave. She stood on shaky legs and walked past him, having no idea what to say. Best to say nothing. She returned to her workstation in a daze, feeling like everyone she passed by could see the stigma of Juan's accusations floating above her head. How could she prove her work was actually hers? It wasn't something she'd ever considered.

At her computer, she pulled up the information on her designs and took screenshots of the creation and modification dates. Then she printed it out. Given what happened to her patterns, she wasn't taking any chances. The hard copies went into her purse.

She picked up her desk phone and called the IT department. "Hi, this is Kim Taylor in design. Our admin, Ashley Jacovich, was supposed to ask someone in your department to find out about a missing file. I'm calling to see what you discovered." She gave him the details of the file and the location where it was supposed to be.

"I don't see any request from anyone in your department."

"It would have been last Tuesday or Wednesday." Ashley had told Kim she would get on it.

"We don't have it. But I can look into it for you."

"I'd appreciate that, thanks." Kim hung up, thinking. Why hadn't Ashley made the request? Had she forgotten? Or was something else going on here?

She headed to Ashley's desk, but she wasn't there. A flash of memory, of Ashley and Henry talking at Henry's station when

Kim walked by, looking like they were talking about her. It could be nothing.

Or Henry could have had help.

She walked over to Henry's workstation. She didn't want to see him or talk to him. Who knew how that would get misconstrued. But she did want to see if Ashley was there. She eased around the corner, trying to not look suspicious. No one was paying any attention to her.

And Henry sat at his workstation. Alone.

***

Matthew sat in the hotel conference room with Chris and a few others from their team on a conference call with Edward, Anne, and the remaining few who hadn't relocated here yet. While Edward's doctor hadn't cleared him to come back to work, he still insisted on being in on the weekly update conference calls. Which made them much longer because he insisted on details and information that everyone else already knew and had moved on from.

Matthew hated meetings. And he really hated redundant ones.

He checked the time. Allie should be at his new place right now waiting for all the utilities to be turned on and the internet hooked up. The movers were coming Wednesday, and they had their hotel rooms until then. But he was eager to see his new place and get the boxes out of Allie's garage where he'd stashed them when he'd gotten into town Friday night.

But if he didn't get out of this meeting soon, he wouldn't have time to get his real work done, and that would put a crimp in tonight's plans. He was going to show Kim his new place, empty though it was, and then they'd grab something to eat before she went back to her brother's house. He hoped she would have good news to share about Design Review. She deserved some good news.

They finally ended the conference call. Matthew rose and headed out the door. He needed to stretch his legs and get some fresh air. It was almost time for lunch.

A hand touched his arm. "Do you have a few minutes?" Emma Rojas stood there. She and her husband were relocating from Northern California, and she was visibly pregnant. He couldn't imagine how challenging that made everything.

"Sure. What do you need?"

"Could we talk in private?"

"Yeah." He glanced around. There was a small alcove in the lobby with a few chairs. He'd gotten some work done there before. It was quiet. He led her in that direction, and she eased into an upholstered club chair.

She made some small talk, and he let her take the lead. He had no idea where this was going.

But when she started crying, he froze. What did you do with a crying woman? Melissa and Allie never cried, or they never came to him if they did. And Brittany always went to Melissa or Allie. If he couldn't joke her out of it.

But Kim… She'd cried on his shoulder. He hated how helpless it made him feel. But he'd learned that it wasn't about what he wanted or felt.

He didn't think Emma wanted to soak his shirt. What would she want? He spied a box of tissues and handed them to her. And just listened.

She'd heard the rumors about the OC branch potentially not happening. She wanted to know what he thought, since he seemed to have access to Chris and Anne. The whole thought of uprooting her family's life and coming down here, just to have it not happen… She couldn't get through a sentence without bursting into tears.

First Austin and now Emma. The company was rife with rumors before it even had a physical location. He rotated his previously injured wrist now free of its brace. He stopped fidgeting and paid attention. He realized that she mostly wanted a listening ear and some reassurance. He told her what he knew, and stated his confidence that the branch would open, that it was Chris and Anne's intent too.

At the end, she took a shaky breath, gave him a hug and thanks, before heading out to lunch.

Huh. He felt kinda good, in a strange way. He'd helped her by really doing nothing but listening. Maybe that's what Kim was trying to tell him. Earlier today he would never have thought that listening to a pregnant woman cry would make him feel like he'd helped. But it had, and now he had a bit more confidence moving forward that he could handle his team, even when it wasn't all fun and games.

Which gave him another idea. Kim was busy awaiting the Design Review results at work, but he could still encourage her.

***

Kim couldn't get her mind back on work. In fact, unless she cleared her name, she wouldn't have a job. So working on anything else was pointless. She headed out to her car. What she wanted to do was have a good cry and drown herself in a pint of fudge brownie ice cream. But that would not solve this problem.

Maybe she should just quit design. Her dad would be right, and she could go work for his firm and be miserable. But then she'd be safe. Who got themselves into these situations anyway? She did. What was it about her that brought them to her?

A piece of paper sat under her windshield wiper. Last time it was a note from Matthew. Was it him or her stalker? Not wanting to take any chances, she snapped a photo of it, then used a tissue from her purse to remove it and unfold it.

Then she laughed. It *was* a note from Matthew. Relief that it wasn't more contact from her stalker flooded her, along with the joy of the surprise.

Thought I'd leave you a note instead of a text. Kind of like a little present. You'll be happy to know I let a woman cry today without doing anything but listening. And she thanked me for it. While I don't think I'll ever understand how women are wired, I'm willing to keep learning. Thanks for being willing to keep teaching me. Looking forward to tonight.

Love, Matthew

She smiled as she tucked the note into her pocket. She loved these peeks at his handwriting. Or printing, rather. And he was right. A note was a nice little present, something she could keep rather than a text that scrolled up and away.

She started to climb in her car, but something was missing. It took her a minute to figure out what. The black Honda. She had been parking near it every day since she'd first spotted it to see if she could determine who the owner was. She'd never found out. And since she hadn't seen the car again after the wedding shower, it didn't seem as important as it once was. It was likely just a coincidence. Still, parking near it made her feel like she was at least doing something.

She pulled out her phone. She really wanted to call Matthew and thank him for the note and pour out her story. But he was at work. It was a busy week for him with his team getting into town and having three days of intense meetings. She would see him tonight. And Matthew wouldn't help clear her name, other than to vouch for her inspiration during the Great American Road Trip.

She tapped Lynnae's name. Hopefully, she'd be available to talk. And she was. Kim gave her the rundown of what had happened. She left out the part about her condo, though. One problem at a time.

Lynnae was as mad as Kim, a comforting thought that made her feel supported. And not like she was losing her mind. It was what she needed. "I'll completely vouch for you, Kim. What they are doing is so unprofessional. I'll be happy to tell them what I think of your talent, more importantly, what my clients think of your talent. There's no way you copied anyone's designs. You have zero need to do so."

"Thank you. That means so much to me. I really appreciate that you believe in me."

"Honey, I think you should kick the dust of that place off your feet and come work with me. They don't deserve you if they are treating you this way."

Kim smiled through the tears that pooled in her eyes. "You're the best, you know that?"

"Then come work for me." Her voice had become more teasing.

"I just might do that. I can't even think that far down the road. Right now I have to clear my name. I don't want any lingering doubt or rumors following me around that I was a cheater or not original enough to create my own designs. If I just leave after the accusations, doesn't that give credence to them?"

"I know. You have to defend your honor."

"Yeah, where's my knight on a white horse?"

"Well, he might not have a white horse, but that handsome man that you brought with you the other night sure seemed willing to defend your honor."

Kim let out a sigh. "Yeah. We're having dinner tonight."

"He's a good man. And he adores you."

"I don't know about that."

"I do. Believe me. I've seen a few things in my life, and how he looks at you… it's what every woman wants."

"He is pretty special. Okay, before I go down that road, I need Zander Jakes's number from you. I thought with his repu-tation, he could vouch for when he shot my designs. He was here at Elan last week, so someone here must think highly enough of him to hire him for a shoot." She didn't mention running into him at dinner last week.

"Sure. Let me find it." The sound changed as Lynnae

switched to speaker phone. "You know that it's not his real name, right?"

"It's not?"

"No, it's something Russian or Polish. Hard to pronounce. So he just goes by Jakes. Oh, here it is." She rattled off the number as Kim entered it into her phone.

"Thanks, Lynnae. I'll keep you posted."

"You do that, hon. Let me know if I need to come down there and kick some butt."

Kim was laughing as she hung up. What would she do without Lynnae? Life had handed her some hard knocks lately, but she had some good people on her side. Wasn't that what she really needed anyway? *Thank you, Lord, for letting me see what is really important. No matter what happens.*

THAT EVENING, KIM OPENED THE DOOR AT KYLE'S HOUSE, and Matthew couldn't wait to wrap her in his arms. He stepped inside first, closed the door, and pulled her to him. He held her close, breathing in her smell, feeling her softness pressed against him.

Kyle cleared his throat.

Matthew set Kim back but didn't let go as he raised his gaze. "Hey, Kyle."

"Hey. Did you get everything from Phoenix?"

"Yep, I have some boxes stashed at Allie's, and the movers are coming Wednesday."

"If you need anything, let me know."

"I appreciate it."

Kyle looked like he wanted to say more, but he simply said, "Have a good time. Be careful."

"I will." He met Kyle's gaze, hoping that it conveyed how much Kim meant to him and that he wouldn't risk her life for anything.

Kyle looked at Kim. "Let me know when you get in. I'll be up."

She stepped forward and gave him a kiss on the cheek. "Thanks, big brother."

He nodded.

Matthew followed her out the door and into his truck. "Food first or a trip to see my new place?"

"Let's check out your place before it gets too dark. You won't have any lamps in there."

"Good point."

A short while later, they turned into a well-maintained complex. He parked the truck in an empty spot and pulled out the keys Allie had dropped off and let them in. It smelled like carpet shampoo and fresh paint. The layout was similar to Kim's place with an open kitchen and living area. But it had two master suites. He and Austin wouldn't have to share a bathroom. There was a small fenced-in patio in the back. He could see putting a grill back there.

Kim looked into every room and closet before nodding at him. "This will work. You've got some good storage. Austin was right about the light since his room faces east. How does it feel to put down roots here?"

He pulled her to him. "Good. Very good." He kissed her to seal the deal. "I like that it's close to your place, close to work. Now that it has your approval, are you ready to go eat?"

"I'm starving." She grinned at him.

And they were on their way to California Fish Grill for dinner. He'd never thought about putting down roots before, didn't really think he was doing it now until Kim had mentioned it. But the words coming out of her mouth sounded good. Real good. He let the idea roll around in his head. Yeah, putting down roots, planning a future with Kim, making a real contribution at DataCorp, even being close to his sisters… Life had morphed in ways he'd never imagined. And it was good.

They placed their orders at the counter then grabbed their

drinks and an outside table. The casual restaurant with great seafood would give them lots of time to talk with no pressure to give up their table.

"So I got your note today. That was very sweet. And you're right, it's like getting a little present. It couldn't have come at a better time too. But I'll tell you more about that later. Tell me about the crying woman." She grinned.

He gave her the summary about Emma's concerns and his response.

She nodded. "People often just need you to sit with them and support their feelings. I don't think most people expect you to fix their lives. They just want to know they have a safe place to be honest." She met his gaze and reached for his hand. "I always want you to be honest with me about your feelings. Even if it might make me upset."

He squeezed her hand. He wouldn't want to make her upset, but he supposed that was an inevitable part of relationships. The idea terrified him, however.

Their pager went off, and Matthew grabbed their food.

As they ate, the story came out. Matthew found himself growing angrier on Kim's behalf.

Her phone buzzed with an incoming call. She looked at it, indecision on her face. Then she sent it to voicemail. "That was Zander Jakes. I called him earlier and left a message about seeing if he'd vouch for me about when he did the photo shoot of my sample designs. I'll call him back tomorrow."

Matthew nodded. "Kim, you don't deserve any of this. I'm happy to show them my phone and the photos I took of your designs and you working on them during the road trip. I don't know if it would help or not, but it could add to the evidence."

"That's sweet of you." Then, "Wait, you have pictures of me and my designs?"

"Sure." He'd been surreptitious when he'd taken them back in March, intrigued by her but not sure how she felt about him. He opened his photo app and scrolled back then handed her the phone. Those were good memories, back when they were just getting to know each other without the pressure of work. It had been a fun trip. Until the end when an escaped rapist, Willie Dumas, had grabbed Kim to use her as leverage. She was able to use some self-defense moves Kyle had taught her to break free, but it had shaken her deeply, and Matthew's response hadn't helped. It was good to go back to the time before that.

A soft smile crossed her face as she swiped through the photos. "I had no idea you'd taken so many of me."

"My favorite view that whole trip was of you."

She glanced up at him; he was sure she expected him to be joking. But he wasn't. He let his gaze linger on hers until she looked away.

She pushed the phone back to him. "If I need these, I'll let you know. Lynnae has already volunteered. But I just don't know if I even want to be there anymore. That Henry could do this to me, and that they could blame me… It's just been disheartening to see that with people I've worked with."

He reached for her hand. "Whatever you decide to do, I'm behind you. And if you need me to squirt some people with my super soaker, I can do that too."

She laughed.

Ah, good. So this time his humor was welcome. "It's going to be crazy for me the rest of the week. I'm meeting with Chris and Marisa tomorrow to make sure everything is set for the Seattle group, and then we've got two days of meetings setting up new territories, brainstorming and goal setting, vision casting, and all that other fun corporate speak stuff that has to be done whenever you start something new. Friday should be more fun with a final team event. The timing stinks. I wish I could be more of a support for you this week. I know it's going to be rough."

She squeezed his hand. "I appreciate it. Kyle said they released my condo. He obviously doesn't want me staying there, but I've got to at least get the food cleaned up. I'm not looking forward to it, but I just keep focusing on Friday. That's the rehearsal dinner for Kyle and Heather. Then the wedding Saturday. And I absolutely won't be thinking about work on those two days."

"And all the out-of-town folks are leaving Friday afternoon and evening, so I'll be done with them. Will you need my help with anything for the rehearsal?"

"I could use your moral support. We'll be at the gazebo in front of Las Brisas to run through the wedding. It's pretty simple since it's on a public part of the beach. I just have to make sure everyone is in the right place at the right time. But since there's not room for a huge bridal party or even a lot of guests, it shouldn't be too complicated. We're headed to an Italian place after to eat. But I'm going to check in with Las Brisas to make sure all the reception details are in place." She grinned. "I'm excited for Kyle and Heather, and it's something to look forward to after this week."

He couldn't agree more. And he was looking forward to spending some time on the dance floor with her, holding her close. And dreaming about the future.

Chapter Thirty

Kim hadn't seen Juan all day today. The results of Design Week hadn't come out yet, and people were whispering about it. What was the reason for the delay? Unfortunately, she could make a good guess. She just hoped the delay meant her defense was being taken seriously. But she was lining up other folks on her behalf as well. Which reminded her, she needed to call Zander Jakes back, but she didn't want to do it where anyone could overhear.

She headed for one of the conference rooms. She could find an empty one and have some privacy. She came upon the one where she'd met Juan. She heard voices, so it was occupied. As she walked past, she could see through the small window that Juan and Henry were in there.

Her stomach plummeted, and her feet slowed as if they were weighed down by cement. She shouldn't eavesdrop, but she was dying to know what excuse Henry had for stealing her designs. She forced her feet to keep going and ducked into the next conference room, which was empty.

But Henry's raised voice carried through the walls. "I can't believe you're falling for her crazy delusions. Here's a designer who made it look like her own sample went missing just to gain sympathy. So she'd have an excuse when her designs weren't up to par. And then, she went a step further and stole my designs. She's crazy and jealous of me and my talent. That's why she copied me. Her own designs aren't any good. Just look at this so-called proof you've presented. Who actually has proof lined up? Only someone who thinks they'll be accused of stealing. Because they actually stole. I can't believe you all are falling for it. There's a lot of creative geniuses in this business, but she's flat-out neurotic. I wouldn't be surprised if she started that forest fire to gain sympathy and attention."

Kim couldn't stand to hear any more. Hot tears pooled in her eyes. Henry was turning her proof against her. She pushed out of the conference room and into the women's bathroom, locking herself in a stall and dabbing her eyes. She hadn't heard Juan's response, so she didn't know if he was buying what Henry was saying or not.

Oh, she was so angry! Why should she even have to defend herself against someone who had it in for her, who had stolen from her?

Life definitely wasn't fair.

But she had more than just her word. She had Lynnae and Zander, respected industry professionals, backing her up. Or she hopefully had Zander. She needed to call him. Since the confer-ence room was out, she could go to her car.

Stepping out of the stall, she wet a paper towel and patted under her eyes. Satisfied that she looked more in control, she headed to her workstation to grab her purse and head outside. She could grab a sandwich and cookie at the lunch place that was on the other side of the greenbelt. A walk through what passed for nature in the city might be just what she needed.

As she started down the path in the greenbelt, her phone buzzed. A text from Heather.

Available for a quick FaceTime?

Sure.

Her phone rang, and she swiped it on. Heather's face filled

the screen. "Hey there. Hope it's okay, but I let a few people into your condo." The image on the phone moved, and Sarah's face, then Jessica's, joined Heather's.

"Of course it's fine. But why?"

Heather turned the phone and let it sweep across Kim's clean, put-to-rights condo.

Tears filled her eyes. "You guys! You didn't have to do that. I can't believe it."

"We wanted to. We all pitched in when Sarah's condo was broken into. Jessica played some up-beat music, and we got it all done in record time. The good news is, nothing other than the food that spoiled was really destroyed."

Kim was glad this part of the trail was deserted so no one could see her tears. "You guys are the best. I don't know what to say."

"You don't have to say anything. It's what friends do for each other."

Kim thanked them again and hung up as she arrived at the sandwich shop. She ordered her food to go. She was too emotional, and all she wanted was the seclusion of her own car. Holding her bag and drink, she headed back. The wind whipped through the trees providing a soundtrack. Occasionally she thought someone else was on the path, but when she turned to look, she was still alone. It was early for lunch, which was what she was counting on. She wanted the privacy.

The weight of having to clean up her condo was lifted. She couldn't believe it. She had great friends. It didn't resolve all the problems in her life, but it took care of one big one. And more importantly, it reminded her that she wasn't alone, that she had other people to rely on.

As she neared the office building, she definitely heard footsteps. She turned and caught a glimpse of someone dashing behind the landscaping. A chill washed over her. She was alone, though there were plenty of office buildings nearby in the business park. It was likely her overactive imagination. It had gotten her in trouble before. But Kyle would not be pleased that she was out here. The whole Design Review fiasco was muddling her thinking. She quick-walked the rest of the way to her car and slid in.

The car's interior warmth enveloped her like a soft blanket, and she leaned back into the seat. A few people exited the building, heading to their cars, likely on their way to lunch. She ate hers, listening to worship music. She needed something to focus her whirling thoughts on.

She also needed to call Zander back, the original task that had resulted in her ending up here. With a sigh, she lifted her phone just as she spotted him walking across the parking lot. Oh, convenient. He must be here to meet a designer. Perhaps he'd put in a good word for her with whoever he was meeting with.

She opened the door and hopped out. "Zander!"

His gaze snapped up, and he smiled and headed her way.

"Hey, Kim. I'm glad I ran into you. I was hoping I would. I was surprised when you didn't call me back last night. Everything okay?"

"Well, there's a bit of a situation here at work."

"Oh, I heard about that. I meant last night. Why didn't you call me back?"

She was caught off guard. How had he heard about what was going on at work? Had the rumors started in the industry? Was her reputation already being damaged? And, what did he mean about last night? She gathered her things out of her car and locked it, walking toward the building with him.

"Um, yeah, everything was fine last night. Just dinner with a… friend." What was Matthew anyway? Definitely more than a friend. But it seemed weird talking about her boyfriend in a professional environment.

"I thought maybe you had a hot date." His tone had taken on a distinctly gossipy vibe, and he gave her a sly grin.

She suppressed a sigh, tired of being the subject of rumors

and innuendo. "Something like that. Anyhow, what I really wanted to talk to you about was my samples that you shot earlier this month. There's been some discussion around Elan that those weren't my designs. Another designer is taking credit for them, and I wondered if you might vouch for when Lynnae hired you for the shoot and what she told you about the designs."

"I'd be happy to, Kim. You're a fabulous designer."

She breathed out a breath of relief. "Oh, thank you. I know your opinion is respected around here. Who were you shooting for the other day when I saw you here?"

They reached the office doors, and he pulled one open for her.

"Thanks." If it was Eliza, then she might even have a chance to convince everyone of her innocence.

"Oh, I know all the designers here. So many shoots, I can't even remember them all. But I have an even better idea. Why don't I do a shoot just for you of all your designs, even the ones Lynnae didn't use? It'll be like your own private show."

"Wow, that would be fantastic." If a big-name photographer wanted to shoot her designs, he must believe in her, right? It would go a long way toward establishing her credibility as a designer. He wasn't asking Henry. At least, she hoped he wasn't. Why was he here? He hadn't said.

"Perfect. I know just the spot."

"That place where you did Lynnae's photo shoot?"

"Actually I was thinking of Laguna Beach, near Recreation Park. There are a lot of public sculptures that will work as good back drops. The sun doesn't set until after eight, and we'll have a nice, long golden hour."

Kim pulled up her calendar app on her phone. "Sounds great. When were you thinking?"

"This Friday."

"Oh, I have another commitment. My brother's getting married Saturday, and the rehearsal dinner is Friday. But it's also in Laguna, at the gazebo not too far south of Recreation Park."

She chewed her lip, thinking of how to make this work. "They'll be working with the photographer around seven, scouting locations for wedding photos, so they won't need me until seven thirty. It's within walking distance. And you won't need me for the whole shoot. Or any of it, really."

"Oh, I definitely need you there." His voice had turned low and husky.

She wasn't sure what to make of that. But before she could say anything, he continued.

"Then it's settled. I'll make all the arrangements. You just bring yourself."

"And the designs."

"And the designs."

They had arrived at the T in the hallway. To the left was her work area, to the right, the senior designers. Zander stood there with his hands in his pockets, not making a move.

"Well, thanks again. I'll see you Friday." She gave a small wave and headed back to her workstation, hoping this would be the project that would turn things around for her at Elan. Between a Zander Jakes photo shoot and Lynnae MacKenzie's vouching for her, Henry didn't stand a chance.

As she rounded the corner, she glanced back. He still stood there, watching her.

Chapter Thirty-One

Matthew headed for the coffee carafe at the back of the conference room when they took a break. The movers arrived today, and Allie was there to tell them where to put things. He didn't much care. He figured whatever she did would be fine. He just wanted to sleep in his own bed tonight, though being in the hotel would be more convenient. He sent Allie a text asking how it was going.

He poured himself a cup of coffee, needing the caffeine. This was only the first day of their meetings, and it was a long one.

Chris met him back there. "It's going well, I think."

"Me too. Better than I anticipated."

"We've got dinner reservations tonight for the whole team at the Royal Hawaiian Fire Grill in Laguna. We can't bring these folks to Southern California and not show them the beach."

"True."

"Do you have your team-building challenge together for Friday?"

Matthew grinned. "I do. I think it'll be a lot more fun than what we did with Edward. I'll hand out rules and teams on Thursday. They'll want some strategy time. I've been watching and thinking about who to put on what teams."

And not just for Friday. Today and tomorrow they were looking at new product lines and territories, game planning how to approach new business. Chris had asked for his opinion on who would be best suited for what roles. With everything being new, it was all up for grabs, and Chris was looking forward to making some changes he thought had been long overdue. If their branch did a good job, it could be an opportunity to recreate their methods at other DataCorp branches. And prove the necessity of the OC branch.

Chris clapped him on the shoulder. "Let's talk tonight after dinner." He paused and turned back. "Emma told me that she had a good conversation with you."

"We talked. Or she did. I mostly listened."

Chris smiled. "That may be the best skill a leader can have. Glad to see you're learning it early on." He grabbed his cup and walked off.

Huh. A leader. He hadn't necessarily thought of himself that way. His sisters, yes. But him? He was the guy that kept everyone smiling. His vision shifted slightly as he saw himself reflected in Chris's words. This job was turning out to be different than he expected in more ways than one.

No, he wouldn't be sleeping in his own bed tonight. But he would find some time to talk to Kim, to find out what was going on with her. They'd exchanged text messages and their daily GIFs, but he hadn't seen her since dinner two nights ago. His job was keeping him occupied just when she could most use his support. But she'd told him last night about what Heather, Sarah, and Jessica had done in cleaning her condo. He wasn't her only support. Which was good, right? They'd get past this week, enjoy themselves celebrating Kyle and Heather's wedding, and find their own rhythm. They had to find a way to make this work.

THE SCUTTLEBUTT OVER THE TARDY DESIGN REVIEW LIST had speculated everything from the designers couldn't decide because everyone was so good to they were fighting over who got to work with certain junior designers to they hated all of the designs. It only fueled the existing rumors of layoffs and designers leaving.

Kim knew the truth—at least about Design Review—but kept it to herself, staying occupied as best as she could. It was too bad that Matthew was so busy with his meetings with all the out-of-town colleagues. She could have used his humor to keep her mind off things. But she didn't want to disturb or distract him while he was being put into a leadership role. She'd have to wait until after the rehearsal dinner Friday to hear how it all went. By then, she'd know the status of her job too.

Finally, Juan called Kim into the conference room on Wednesday.

She entered and closed the door behind her, trying to read what the outcome was based on his body language. But she couldn't get anything.

"I've talked to Henry and heard what he had to say. I've talked with the other senior designers."

She really wanted to know what he thought of Henry's defense, but she doubted he'd share and asking didn't seem professional or very confident, so she waited for him to continue, hoping she was keeping her features neutral as well.

He let out a long sigh. "Personally, I believe you. The problem is not all the designers do. Eliza is particularly enchanted with Henry and wants him to work with her. The other designers have more mixed feelings. I'd say on the whole, most believe you. But Henry has spent a lot of time ingratiating himself with Eliza, Jane, and others. And he has connections with them. It's just easier for them to believe him because they know him more than they know you."

She didn't know what to say. She hung on to his *I believe*

you, but it was disheartening that others didn't. "Even with all the proof I have?"

He gave her a rueful smile. "I know. Lynnae Mackenzie has been chewing off my ear and anyone else she can get ahold of. But here's the thing. Some of the designers already have a bad impression of you. No amount of proof is going to sway them. They've already decided they like Henry, and if it comes down to choosing between you and him, they choose him." He rubbed his hand over his face. "You won't get fired. But your reputation here is ruined. Kim, I believe you. I'll work with you. The Design Review results are going out in an hour. Henry is with Eliza, and you are with me."

A little relief at being on the list at least leaked through. But then… "He's not going to be able to use my designs, is he?"

"No, that was one of the agreements we came to. Eliza brushed it off, said he was good enough to come up with something new anyway."

At least there was that. She let out a breath.

"But, you can't use them either."

What? She'd worked hard on them, created a whole line based on her Southwest trip and had ideas for more. She clenched her jaw and then relaxed it. Lynnae would buy them; they couldn't keep her from doing that.

"Fine. But what about Zander Jakes? He wants to do a photo shoot of just my designs on Friday. Doesn't that carry any weight?"

Juan raised his eyebrows. "Really? It doesn't hurt you, but it doesn't prove that you created those designs. Just that Zander Jakes likes them." He paused, studying her. "Or he likes you."

"What does that mean?"

"Just that he's been known to take women under his wing, his proteges, and do what he can to boost their careers as long as they give him credit for their success."

That sounded creepy. Something about what Juan said triggered loose a thought in Kim's brain, but she didn't have time to follow that path. "So what happens then?"

He shrugged. "People forget about them. They move on; he moves on. Though there were rumors one model had to get a restraining order against him. Then again, you know how this business is. It's possible someone is trying to smear him. Just… be careful. I like you, Kim. I'd hate to see you—or your reputation—get hurt."

This whole conversation had made her stomach turn. The only good thing was that she wouldn't be publicly humiliated. Her name would be on the Design Review finalists list. That was something, she supposed. Whether it would protect her from the supposed layoffs was another issue. One she didn't think she'd get an answer about today.

"I'm serious about wanting to work with you, Kim. I believe you, and I think what's happened to you isn't right. But unfortunately, it happens in this business. How you recover from it will determine how you make your way in this industry. I think you can do it, and your designs—and I believe they are your designs—show real promise. But it's your choice. I realize it could be hard to stay here after all that's happened."

She nodded, appreciating his candor and his sense of what her feelings might be. "Can I think about it? My brother's getting married this weekend, and there's a ton of stuff going on. I won't even be able to really think things through until it's over. Can I get back to you on Monday?"

"Sure. And just take the rest of the week off. Anything you'd be working on would get handed over to another designer if you decided to come work with me. And if you decide to leave, well, same thing. Your brother's wedding is a good excuse to miss a few days." He stood and reached out a hand.

She shook it. "Thanks, Juan. I appreciate all you did. I know some people wouldn't have tried to figure out what happened."

"I know. But I have watched your work. And I see some real talent there. Whatever you do, don't waste that."

She gave him a tight smile and left the room. With a quick stop at her computer to send out a department email about her brother's wedding, she picked up her things and gave a look around her workstation. Whatever happened, she wouldn't be back here.

Chapter Thirty-Two

Kim was glad for the day off. She had planned to work half days and had gotten that approved, but after the Design Review fiasco, she was glad Juan had suggested the full days off. Now, she'd be able to focus on Heather and Kyle's wedding this week without that hanging over her head.

She and Heather spent most of the morning packing up her clothes and personal items and taking them over to Kyle's. Kim would be charged with getting Snowflake over to Kyle's house after the wedding while he and Heather were on their honeymoon. She and Snowflake would hold down the fort while they were gone. Kyle had talked over the options with her. He didn't like leaving her alone, but Hilary had agreed to stay at Kyle's house with her until they came back.

Kim looked around Heather's fairly empty loft after their last load of clothes. Only her furniture was still here and the few things she'd need until the wedding. Her dress hung off the closet door. It was so Heather. Lace straps, a lace-covered bodice to a fit-and-flare skirt. Tiffany-blue satin peep-toe sling backs were her nod to something blue and the unexpected. The color matched the bridesmaids' dresses.

"Are you nervous about marrying my brother?"

"Not a bit. Living with him, that's a different matter." She laughed. "It's funny. We have to decide what of each of our furniture to keep, what to get rid of. We both had completely furnished houses and kitchens. It's not like we're just setting up house and need everything. We actually have too much. No, it's an easy problem to fix. I'm sure Matthew and Austin will take what we don't need. But it will take some compromise on what stays and what goes."

"I suppose every relationship has to make compromises."

"Every good one."

"Are you going to miss this place?" Kim leaned over the pony wall that separated the lofted bedroom from the living area below. "It's so cute."

Heather sat on her bed and looked around. "It was a good place for me. But it's time to move onto something better. What about you? Are you going to move onto something better at work?"

Kim let out a sigh as she joined Heather on the bed. "Not sure. I'm trying not to think about it and just focus on your wedding."

"It's hard to leave a place you loved and had dreamed about succeeding in at one time. I know I didn't want to leave the magazine where I was an editor. But God has been so good at providing me something even better. Something that uses skills and gifts I had let languish." She squeezed Kim's arm. "I know he'll do that for you too."

Kim nodded. "I know. And I'm praying about what the right thing to do is." She looked at the time. "But we've got to get to the nail salon to meet the other girls for the mani-pedis. Have you heard from Kellie and Aimee?"

"Kellie texted that they checked into the hotel. Aimee is thrilled to have a weekend away before the baby is born. Daryl drove them down. Mom and Dad are coming tomorrow. Thanks for creating those cute welcome baskets for them."

"Happy to. It's nice to show off our part of the state to out-of-towners."

Snowflake meowed and hopped up on the bed. Heather petted her. "She doesn't like change. She knows something is up."

"Well I'm going to like having your cat to myself for a week. At least she's familiar with Kyle's house from when you were in protective custody." Kim scratched Snowflake's head. "I'm going to spoil you with treats and pets. And you can sleep on my bed."

Heather stood, laughing. "She won't miss me at all."

As they met up with Sarah, Melissa, Kellie, and Aimee at the salon, they spent the rest of the afternoon relaxing and getting pampered. Heather was enjoying herself, and all the girls would head out to dinner tonight for one final time. Everything was coming together as Kim had planned, and she put work and her designs out of her head.

It was difficult to believe how quickly life could change. She never thought she'd voluntarily leave House of Elan or that she'd be accused of stealing. How could she ever face Henry again knowing that he'd lied about her and stolen her work? Or stand up under the accusing gazes of the designers who didn't believe her? None of those were decisions she'd have to make now. Tomorrow when she met Zander Jakes would be soon enough to think about her next steps.

But for now, it looked like she'd actually pulled off the wedding planning duties. She'd enjoy her girl time with her friends and soon-to-be sister-in-law and look forward to the wedding.

Matthew swiped Kim's number as he sat in his hotel room. It was late, but not too late. Other than a quick stop at his new place to see how Allie had arranged things, he hadn't spent any time there. He hadn't been able to shake this place yet. It was too convenient with as late as they were staying up meeting with the out-of-towners. Dinner would segue into sitting around the lobby volleying ideas back and forth. It had been productive and good for getting to know each other, but exhausting. He was glad they were all leaving tomorrow.

Kim picked up, sounding a bit out of breath. "Hey, I'm glad you called. Hang on a sec. I just got to Kyle's." Her voice was fainter as she said something, probably to Kyle. "Okay, we just got back from dinner with the girls. And I have pretty nails." She laughed.

"Wow, you sound in a better mood than I've seen since Design Review started."

"Yeah. It's behind me, and I don't have to make any decisions until after the wedding." She told him about her day with Heather and tomorrow's shoot with Zander. It was good to hear her relaxed.

"So what does Kyle think? Is he going with you to the shoot?"

"I don't think it's necessary. It's a public place, and how much of a professional would I appear if I let my brother tag along? But he insisted. So hopefully that won't be awkward. At least it will put him down there early for the wedding rehearsal. He'll have to leave by seven to walk down and meet Heather and the photographer. I should be there, too, so it shouldn't be a problem. It's not like I'm going to be in the shoot. That's what the models are for. I don't even really have to be there, but Zander insisted."

Matthew had no idea how these things worked and didn't care. He was glad Kyle would be there. "Once everyone heads to the airport, I'll be free. I should be there in time to watch the shoot with you. Or Kyle and I can hang back, and Zander will never know we're there."

She laughed. "Yeah, right. I can only imagine the two of you shooting daggers at him. But it would be great if you could make it so we could head to the rehearsal together."

"Shouldn't be a problem." He heard what sounded like Kim smothering a yawn. He grinned at the image. "I'll let you get your beauty rest. Tomorrow's a big day for you and your pretty nails."

"So you're done with all your meetings tomorrow?"

"Yeah. We have a morning meeting, then we'll blow off some steam in the afternoon. Got my super soakers already in the car. I'll be done in plenty of time to meet you."

She laughed. "A water fight? Sounds like important work stuff."

He could almost imagine her rolling her eyes at him.

The smile was still in her voice when she said, "I'll see you tomorrow."

"I can't wait. Sweet dreams."

He stared at her picture on his phone for a moment. It had been a long week. But tomorrow, work would be off his plate, at least for the weekend. And the wedding festivities would get started, and he'd get to spend time with Kim. Sounded like the perfect way to end the week.

He'd get out of this hotel room and into his own place. He never thought he'd acclimate so quickly to Orange County, but he had a job, an apartment, and friends. He was already well rooted in this new area. Only good things lay ahead. Right?

Chapter Thirty-Three

After lunch, Matthew and Chris gathered their teams together. But Edward made a surprise visit. He wore a sports shirt and slacks instead of a suit and tie and looked a bit paler than normal. But he left no doubt as to who was in charge when he co-opted their schedule and gave an impromptu speech about the importance of their team and the future of DataCorp. Matthew checked the time on his phone. This was going to put them behind schedule. He really wanted to make Kim's photo shoot. Mostly because he didn't trust Zander. But Kyle would be there. Still, he couldn't wait for Edward to finish up.

Finally, they were able to leave the hotel and head to the park. There were two teams: one led by him, one led by Chris. Yesterday at dinner, he'd assigned the teams and explained the rules. They would head to Mason Park where each team would have a base with a flag. The goal was simply to capture the other team's flag. With a twist. They'd all be armed with super soakers. If you got hit in a non-vital area, like an arm or a leg, you'd sit with the referee for three minutes. The referee was the rather-pregnant Emma who didn't need to be running around a park. If you got hit in the head or chest, you had to sit out six minutes.

However, two team members with linked arms could stage a jailbreak.

They'd all had time last night after dinner to look at maps of the park to see where each of the team's bases were and to plan strategy. He and Chris headed up the teams because he wanted to see how they thought and worked together. He planned on having these groups work together permanently, and nothing like good old competition brought out the best—or worst—in people. It would be a good demonstration of what they were made of and how they worked together under pressure.

If he was being honest with himself, he was a little nervous about how this was going to come off. He had thought about talking it over with Kim last night, but she was in a good mood, and he didn't want her worried about him. Plus, he could think on his feet. No matter what happened, he'd find a way to salvage it. As long as no one ended up in the ER. And he'd planned to take everyone for ice cream after. It couldn't be too bad if it ended with ice cream.

They piled into the rental cars and headed to the park. He made a last-minute decision to drive separately, so he could head straight for the rehearsal. Matthew gave Chris a heads up, and he agreed to make sure everyone got to the airport on time.

Figuring he was a likely target and would spend a good amount of time wet, he left his phone in the truck glovebox. A text from Kim caught his eye. Kyle wasn't going with her to the photo shoot because he had to wrap something up with work before he was off for two weeks. She had promised Kyle that Matthew would be there, so she was just checking to make sure that would still work.

He paused. It should, if everything went as planned. But he couldn't leave the park early. This was a challenge Chris set up for him, and it had a lot of ramifications.

Besides, if Kyle wasn't going with her, he must not be too concerned, right? He thought of Kyle's remark about Kim's overactive imagination. Matthew hadn't told Kim how important today really was. She likely thought he was free.

And he should be able to do both. As long as nothing else unexpected happened and the traffic wasn't too bad. He shot her a quick text then closed the phone in the glovebox.

Once at the park, the teams split up and headed to their bases at opposite ends. The park was big with a lot of dips and hills and a lake in the center. Each of the bases could be covertly approached. He gathered his team at their base and planted the flag.

"Okay, guys. Strategy counts. Everybody remember their role?"

Nods went around. Last night they had assigned base guards, forward units, spies, replacements for wounded and had come up with a basic plan for approaching the other team's base.

Once Emma reached the hill in the middle of the park where she could see both teams' bases, she raised her arm and after a second, blew her whistle. The teams took off to execute their missions.

Matthew never thought work could be so much fun.

Kim was headed for Recreation Point when her phone rang. Kyle. Frowning, she answered it.

"Just making sure Matthew is going to be with you. I don't like leaving you like this, but it is a public place. Please be very aware of your surroundings. And keep your phone with you. Don't hesitate to call 911 if something doesn't feel right."

It was his standard speech. She'd heard it a million times. "Yep, he said he was going to make it. Kyle, you don't need to worry. It's not a big deal. I'll see you at the gazebo at seven. You'd better not be late." She tried for a mock serious tone. "Collins has to be on time too."

"We will be. I still wish you'd reschedule for when I'm back. Or even when Collins could go with you."

"I'll be fine. I can't wait that long to salvage my reputation. This is important."

His tone was begrudging as he warned her again before hanging up.

She continued driving toward the beach. Using voice commands, she called Matthew. Just to make sure. But there was no answer. That was odd. She thought he was free this afternoon. She remembered his comment about the super soakers and goofing off. He was entitled to have fun, but did it have to be today? Was he going to be dependable when she needed him? Maybe he was like her brother and father, not taking her career seriously. This was not the train of thought she wanted to have going into an event that could make or break her career.

Her mind scrolled through who might be available to come early and watch her photo shoot. Kyle was right; she should have someone with her. Just to be safe. And since she wasn't sure she could depend on Matthew… Jessica. She would probably enjoy the chance to watch a photo shoot since she was going to cosmetology school. She wasn't part of the wedding party, so she probably hadn't planned on coming to the rehearsal. But maybe she wasn't working. She dialed Jessica's number.

She answered. "Hey, Kim. What's up?"

"I'm heading to a photo shoot in Laguna Beach, and I wanted to know if you wanted to come along. Sorry for the last-minute notice."

"Oh wow. I wish I could. I'd love to be a part of something like that. I just can't today. I've… got other plans."

Her voice sounded strange. Kim instantly went alert. What was going on? Was Jessica… no, she didn't sound like she'd been drinking. Still. Kim's phone beeped. Lynnae was calling. Good grief. She had to talk to everybody today, apparently. She let it go to voice mail.

"Oh? What kind of plans?"

"Well, Melissa's with me. We were going to, um, talk. So I probably need to go. But I thought I might come to the rehearsal tonight, if that's okay."

"Yeah, that would be great. If you guys get there early, walk up to Recreation Point. That's where we're doing the photo shoot."

"Yeah, okay. That sounds great. We'll— I'll try to make it. See you then."

Kim didn't think she'd ever had a stranger conversation with Jessica. At least she'd see her in a couple of hours and could find out what was going on. She listened to Lynnae's voice mail.

"Hey, Kim. I was hoping to talk to you. I think you're on your way to the photo shoot. I just remembered something. You know how people talk, but I want you to be careful. There's been some rumors about Zander, that he's been inappropriate with some of the models. Obsessive, stalking them on social media, and one girl apparently got a restraining order. I don't know if it's true. You know how our business is. Maybe someone's just trying to make him look bad or smear his reputation. I wouldn't normally repeat any of that, but you've had a rough run of it lately. I just want you to be careful, okay? Your protective brother and your handsome friend should help. You're probably already at the shoot or on your way, but at least text me when it's done, okay?"

A chill ran down Kim's back. She hadn't even told Lynnae about her condo break-in. Taking a deep breath, she realized she was nearly to Laguna. She'd done all she could. Matthew would be here soon. They were in a public place. It would be okay. *Lord, please keep me safe and help me to know what I should do, even if it makes me look foolish or ruins my career.*

Yeah, she might have been a little too focused on her career lately. Her desire to be chosen by a top designer during Design Review had put undue pressure on her. What if none of that really mattered?

It was a beautiful summer day, which might make parking a

problem, though it was late enough in the afternoon that she should be able to find something. She was able to slot her car along the curb on Cliff Drive. She was going to enjoy the beach and her brother's wedding and not think about work until she had to.

She gathered her garment bag of samples from the back, along with another bag of jewelry and matching shoes. Hopefully, they'd fit the models. She assumed he'd be using the same ones he did for the look book he shot for Lynnae, but he hadn't said. Her designs had fit them beautifully.

Arms loaded, she locked her car and headed down the sidewalk. And halted. A black Honda was parked a few spots down from her. She shook her head and started walking again. This was ridiculous. It was a common car. But as she passed it, a flash of cerulean blue caught her eye. She stopped again. That looked an awful lot like her sample that Monique had made up. She peered in the back window, getting a better look. It sure seemed like it.

"Hey, I came to look for you." A familiar female voice came from behind.

Kim spun. Ashley. "What are you doing here?" Her mind whirled trying to put pieces together but not quite making the connections.

"I'm helping with the shoot."

Click. Lynnae had mentioned that Zander Jakes's real name was something Eastern European. Perhaps Jacovich like Ashley's? Were they related? But that didn't explain about Kim's dress in this car.

"Is this your car?" Kim pointed at the Honda.

"Yeah. How'd you know?"

"What's my dress doing in it?"

Ashley smiled. "Let me take some of those bags from you. Believe me, it'll all make sense soon."

Kim hugged the bags tighter to herself. "How about you explain first?"

Ashley sighed. "Zander Jakes is my brother. He's a big fan of yours. Remember those flowers?"

"He sent those?"

Ashley's smiled widened. "Yes, wasn't it romantic?"

"Why didn't he sign his name?"

"Because he's a secret admirer, silly. Now, let's get the shoot started." Ashley started to walk off, but Kim stopped her.

Lynnae's message played through her head. How much was true and how much was rumor? "That doesn't explain why you have my dress."

"Oh, right." Ashley unlocked the car and pulled the dress out, plopping it on top of the garment bag Kim held. "You can have it back."

"Did you take it from the workroom?"

"Yes, but you'll see it was for a good cause. Look, this will be a lot easier to explain with Zander. Let's go." She took off down the walkway, and Kim reluctantly followed. The path wound toward the cliffs looking out over the ocean and was edged by large lawns. It was a peaceful place.

She juggled her items, dug out her cell phone, and called Matthew. Voice mail again. Where was he? "Hey, I'm here at Recreation Point. Ashley's here. She's Zander Jakes's sister. And she had my stolen design. I don't know what all is up, but I wish you were here to help me figure it out. Get here as soon as you can. I need some sanity in this mess." She checked the time. Why wasn't he answering his phone? And why wasn't he here?

She slipped her phone back in her purse and followed Ashley out to the cliff top. The path ended at a sweeping circular patio with curved benches looking out over the sea. The ocean crashed against the rocks far below, separated from them by only a small metal railing.

Zander stood there, booted foot propped up on the bench, looking at the back of his camera.

Click. Boots. Timberland, if she wasn't mistaken. Had he sent her the creepy photos? And the balloon? Ashley said he was a secret admirer. That was just weird. She tried to rearrange the information that she knew. What she'd blamed Nick for, could that have been Zander? How had he known so much about her? Ashley as admin had access to their personal information, including home addresses and phone numbers. She could have given it to him. Had he broken into her condo? Was he that jealous of Matthew? Shivers ran up her arms. But how did that relate to Ashley taking her dress? She needed to get to the bottom of this so she could get Juan the facts. And salvage her reputation.

Ashley came over and pulled the items out of Kim's arms. "You know my brother, Zander."

So definitely related. "Yes. Can you explain what's going on here? Ashley, you still haven't explained about the stolen dress." She dropped her bags and purse on the concrete bench.

Zander raised his camera in her direction and began snapping pictures. He was likely just getting lighting measurements. When he'd done it at the first photo shoot she'd been at with him, it had disconcerted her, until Lynnae had explained. Where were the models?

"I didn't steal it. I just borrowed it. Look, it's better if you're not at Elan. My brother can get you better gigs. When he discovered I worked with you, he wanted to know all about you. Where you lived, what you did for fun, if you had a boyfriend. I told him what I could. But Henry was the true genius. He said that if I helped him, he could make sure that you would go away and I could have your spot."

"So you stole my dress?"

"Borrowed. And I also 'borrowed'"—she made air quotes —"your sketchbook and made copies of it for Henry."

Kim remembered the night she couldn't find her sketchbook. She'd thought she'd lost it. But it was on her desk the next day.

Ashley's face fell. "I actually didn't know he was going to use your designs. He told me he just wanted to know what you were up to. And that if your dress was missing, you'd have to pull out of Design Review." Ashley took a step forward. "Really, this was all for your good. Zander has great plans for you. He has contacts and knows people. He's got a whole plan. It's way better than Henry's. Who I'm not working with anymore. Not since he stole your designs. You've gotta draw the line somewhere."

The irony of her own words was lost on Ashley. So Kim had proof that Henry had stolen her designs. Would Ashley tell Juan the truth? Probably not, given her role in things. "Ashley, you have to tell Juan what happened. Some of the designers think I stole Henry's designs."

She shook her head. But before she could speak, Zander lowered his camera and took a step forward, touching Kim's shoulder. "I know this is a lot to take in. My sister is a little over zealous, shall we say? I had no idea all of this was going on until you called me. Then I asked her to give me an explanation. If she'd only come to me first, we would have been much more above board with everything."

"What, about your plan to get me fired?" She took a step back, out of his reach. His "gifts" hadn't been very above board.

"No." He frowned. "About giving you other options. Better options."

Ashley shot her brother a narrow-eyed look. "This is your fault anyway, Kim. If you'd taken any of my suggestions, then I would have felt I could trust you with the whole plan."

Kim had no idea what Ashley was talking about.

Her face must have conveyed that because Ashley continued. "Remember that time I made some suggestions on your designs and you blew me off?"

Kim still drew a blank.

Ashley put her hands on her hips. "Really? Zander, I don't know. Maybe she's not the right one. There are plenty of other talented and pretty designers."

A memory flashed in Kim's mind. "Oh, now I remember. You wanted me to shorten the hem line of that dress. But that wouldn't work. It would make the proportions all wrong. And I design for real women. Most aren't comfortable with a good portion of their thigh showing. You need to put hemlines at the most attractive part of a woman's leg. For most of us, it's not the thigh." She stepped toward Ashley. "It's not that I didn't value your input, but you have learning to do. If you listen and want to learn, you can pick up a lot from experienced designers that you don't learn in school."

Ashley tossed her head but didn't say anything.

Zander moved closer and whispered something in his sister's ear.

Kim was done with crazy and had no desire to do a photo shoot now. It was all too much. Had there even been a photo shoot planned? She hadn't seen any models. Disappointment burned hot once again. Henry, Ashley, and even Zander. All people she'd worked with. Conspiring to get her to lose her job. What had she done to make these people hate her so much? Well, Zander didn't hate her. But, he hadn't been honest with her either. And if Ashley didn't confess to Juan, Kim was still going to look like a crazy person.

Zander stepped into her space. "Kim, forgive me for not being upfront about my attraction to you. I shouldn't have used Ashley as a go-between. I didn't know she was helping to steal your designs. You have to believe me."

Actually, she didn't. She was out of here. Where was Matthew?

Chapter Thirty-Four

Matthew sped down toward the beach. He was sweaty and hadn't taken time to change. But he'd be able to clean up in one of the beach bathrooms and change his shirt. It was later than he wanted to be, and he didn't want Kim wondering where he was.

His team had won, and while he would have liked to hang around and have celebratory ice cream with them, a sense of unease had him begging off. He was already behind schedule, and he didn't like the idea of her being there alone, even if it was a public place. Not to mention it had been a long week of not spending time with her.

He had wished everyone a good weekend and congratulated them on a job well done. Chris said he'd make sure everyone got to the airport. Was there a little disappointment in his expression at Matthew's early departure? Possibly, but he'd given work plenty of attention this week. He wasn't going to dwell on it. He didn't even take time to dig his wallet or phone out of the glovebox. He needed to get on the road and only hoped Friday traffic didn't slow him down.

Ashley slid a sly smile to Kim. "Well, I'm out of here. Ta ta! I'll see you around." Spinning on her heeled sandal, she sashayed down the sidewalk toward the parking lot.

"Hey, wait. You have to promise to talk to Juan." Kim started after her, but Zander grabbed her arm.

Ashley snagged Kim's purse as she dashed by. "Zander will tell you where to find this. Just do what he says."

She wanted to strangle Ashley. What would her brother do? She pushed back the tears and fought for calm.

Zander kept a firm grip on her arm. "We're supposed to work together. I just know it. We could be a great team. Just give us a chance."

She wanted to tell him no, to let her go. But there was a look in his eye that was just this side of crazy. A little too desperate, unstable, and unpredictable. She glanced around. Ashley was gone, and this area was deserted. The cliffside path and the others that branched off it wound in and out of tree-shaded areas and kept only short sections of the path visible at any one time. *Lord, give me some wisdom. And safety. A way out.*

She forced a smile. "Sure. I think you might be right about that. I'm just upset by the Ashley thing. It was unexpected. Plus, it looks like your models didn't show up anyway. We should just reschedule."

He didn't release his hold, just smiled at her, a bit too much like a fox in a henhouse. "You, my dear, are the model. The perfect one. I don't need any other but you. I've known that since I first saw you on that photo shoot back in February. I have photos of you on my wall from that shoot."

She nodded, hoping she was hiding how creeped out she was. "Okay, but let's do it another time. I'm just too upset now. I wouldn't be a good model today. I'm sure I'll come to see all of this as working out perfectly at some point, but right now it's going to take some getting used to."

Zander moved to the garment bag and unzipped it, flipping

through the outfits. He pulled one out. "This. It's perfect. You were wearing it the day you went up to the mountains."

He was right. But how did he know? Oh, he *had* been the one taking pictures of her. It made perfect sense. She took a step back, easing herself away from him. No phone, no keys, no purse. But if she could run toward one of the restaurants…

He turned, eyeing her up and down. "Go change in one of the bathrooms." He pushed the outfit at her.

Now was her chance. She took it and headed down the path, but he followed right beside her, grabbing her hand.

She glanced at it then at him. "You're hurting me, Zander." She kept her voice even.

He dropped her wrist. "Sorry, just got over excited." But he moved closer, putting his arm around her shoulders, pulling her close.

She stopped. "You know, I still think we need to reconsider. My brother's expecting me. We really don't have time now for a photo shoot. If I don't show up, he and his cop friends will be here looking for me." She swallowed and stepped closer to him. She'd have one chance to sell this. "We'll have more time later if I make an appearance now. I can join you… tonight."

He drew a finger down her cheek. It was all she could do not to pull away. He leaned in and kissed her cheek where his finger had trailed.

A jogger headed toward them. As he neared, Zander turned, distracted.

Kim shoved the outfit at him and took off running. Down the path, around the corner, and then jumped into the bushes. She dashed through the ice plant and ducked behind the bougainvillea, catching her shoulder on one of its thorns. She squatted down, refusing to think about what creatures lived in the ice plant. They were preferable to Zander. He called for her. She heard his footsteps. For certain he'd be able to hear her breathing and pounding heart.

Safety was so close, and yet so far. And with no cell phone, she had no way to call for help.

———

FOR A FRIDAY, THE TRAFFIC HADN'T BEEN TOO BAD. BUT HE couldn't find a parking spot close to Recreation Point. He'd ended up farther down, closer to where the rehearsal would be. Which was probably better. After the rehearsal, they wouldn't have to walk as far back to get to his truck. He popped the glovebox to grab his phone and wallet and snagged his duffle off the seat. A message from Kim lit his phone. He listened to it as he headed down the scenic walkway.

Ashley had stolen Kim's design? And was Zander Jakes's sister? The whole thing was super weird, and he didn't want Kim to have to deal with it alone. Something felt off about it all. He passed the gazebo where Heather and Kyle's ceremony would take place. A few people—he thought they were Heather's family—were hanging around it and looking down at the beach. He kept on moving. Heather was below on the sand with the photographer. He raised a hand, but he didn't know if they saw him or not. Where was Kyle? Maybe he was already with Kim. That eased a bit of his worry.

The public bathroom came up, and he ducked inside. A quick wipe down and a clean shirt, and he was back on his way.

He was almost to Recreation Point when he spotted a dress on the sidewalk on a hanger. People sometimes lost clothes they were carrying to and from the beach, but they weren't usually on a hanger. He backtracked. It sure looked like the outfit Kim wore for the weekend in the mountains. He bent and picked it up. It was hers. No one else would have that embroidery on the front. Good thing he found it. Kim would have been devastated if she knew she dropped it. So she must be around here somewhere.

He kept walking to Recreation Point. An open garment bag

and a camera case sat on the concrete bench, but no one was around. They must be close. They wouldn't leave their stuff unattended.

But when he arrived at Recreation Point, he didn't see Kim. He didn't see anyone. It was deserted.

He scanned the pathways all around Recreation Point, behind all the bushes, lawns, and sculptures. No Kim. He headed to the edge of the cliff and leaned on the railing, looking out over the ocean, trying to decide where to go next. He'd text Kim and see where she was. He pulled out his phone.

"Ah, the infamous Matthew. Am I right?"

Matthew turned. He hadn't seen the guy before, but he knew it was Zander Jakes. "Hey, you must be Zander. How did the photo shoot go?" He didn't know what was going on, but he didn't like the vibe he was getting from this guy. He'd play it cool to see what he could discover. But if this guy had hurt Kim…

"We had to postpone it. Kim has an admirable sense of duty to her brother." Zander moved to his camera bag and unzipped a pouch.

If this guy was telling the truth, then somehow he'd missed Kim and she was with her brother. Maybe she'd been down on the beach with them and he hadn't seen her. He prayed that was the case. "Yeah, that she does. Well, I was just looking for her, so I'll head back—"

Zander pulled out a gun. "No, I don't think so. You see, you're going to be distraught when I tell you that Kim has decided to run away to Mexico with me. Tonight, in fact. After the rehearsal. No one will miss her until the wedding tomorrow, and by then we'll be long gone over the border. But you, you will be so overcome that you'll jump off the cliffs. If not to your death, then to a very painful injury."

This guy was certifiable. Matthew would play along. The more he could delay, the more it was likely someone would come looking for them or would wander by. Though, he didn't want an innocent bystander involved. But he needed to know one thing. "So Kim is safe? With her brother?" Not that he could believe anything this guy said, but he had to know.

"She is. No thanks to you."

He let out a small breath. He'd promised himself after Kim had been grabbed by a predator in Bryce Canyon that he'd never let her be in danger again. Okay, that was one thing he didn't have to worry about.

Now, he just had to figure out how to get out of this situation. Kyle and Collins were somewhere nearby. He either needed to catch their attention or hope that someone came looking for him. Though he wasn't part of the wedding party. Did anyone but Kim even know he was coming? Would she even look for him? He hadn't responded to her texts. She could easily think he was blowing her off. And even if she was worried, why would she look for him up here?

"I never thought you were much of a concern," Zander continued, the gun steady. "Her posts from the road trip just had you as one of the group for the most part. But when I saw the images of the two of you after the fire, how protective you were of her, I knew we would have a problem. It's a good thing Ashley was obsessed with taking Kim's position at Elan. It worked out perfectly." He laughed. "Well, maybe not for you."

The problem was they were around a bend in the walkway. No direct line of sight to the gazebo. The shore was far below the rocky cliffs. He was still holding his phone but couldn't think of any way to send a message to anyone while Zander still had the gun on him. He shifted his weight back, down the pathway another couple steps and closer to the cliffside.

How good of a shot was Zander? If Matthew was able to leap over the fence and cling to the cliff, maybe even work his way down, Zander would have a hard time getting off a shot. And wouldn't people notice the gunshots?

Or he might slip and fall, breaking his neck. It was more of a last-resort plan. But the sun had hit the horizon. There was a long twilight, but the shadows were lengthening and deepening. He was running out of time.

Kim crouched in the bushes. How long should she wait here? Was Zander out there watching for her? Had she told him where the wedding rehearsal was? Yes, she thought she had. Would he show up there? And do what? Say she was missing? Make up another story about her? She had no idea what his endgame was. She just hoped it didn't ruin Heather and Kyle's rehearsal. She had to get out of here.

Had Kyle arrived yet? And where was Matthew? Without her phone, she had no idea how much time had passed. Why wasn't he there when she needed him most? He was out goofing off and lost track of time. If he'd been here, Zander wouldn't have grabbed her. Now she wanted to cry. She really did. But she wouldn't. She had to think.

What if Matthew was out looking for her and ran into Zander? Who knew what Zander would do or say, considering he was likely the one that had sent her the photo with Matthew's face crossed out and a death threat. Was he serious? She hoped not. But she didn't want to take the chance.

If she were honest with herself, this was all her fault. She was so worried about getting her reputation back. She should have left the moment she'd seen Ashley with her dress. Or rescheduled, the way Kyle had wanted her to. None of that mattered now. She just wished she'd been willing to walk away from it all earlier.

She heard voices. Matthew? Her knees and ankles protested as she eased herself up from a crouch. Slowly, she peeked around the bougainvillea, hoping to avoid the thorns this time. There was no one on the sidewalk, but it quickly curved out of view in both directions. She stepped gingerly across the ice plant. Footsteps coming up the walk froze her. But they were coming from the direction of the gazebo and sounded like sandals, not Zander's heavy boots. If the person had a cell phone, she could call for help. She jumped out.

Straight in front of Jessica who bit back a yelp. "Kim. I came to see the shoot."

"Shh!" Kim grabbed her arm and spoke in a whisper. "Am I glad to see you. Zander tried to grab me. I think Matthew's here somewhere, but I don't want Zander to find me. Do you have your phone?"

"Sure." She pulled it out.

Kim heard voices this time. Definitely Matthew and Zander. She edged forward around the curve until she saw part of Matthew's back and his hands upraised.

"Call Kyle. I think Zander has a gun on Matthew." Then she turned and walked toward them.

Matthew let his mind spin out ideas. He was not going to leave Kim vulnerable to Zander's plan. He was good at talking. Maybe that would be an advantage here. He raised his voice. Maybe someone would hear.

"So, Zander, tell me how you first became infatuated with Kim. Does anyone else know?"

"She was mine long before she was yours. When I first saw her at a photo shoot in February, I knew we were destined to be together. I don't care if you think you know her because you went on a road trip with her or were caught in a forest fire together. Nothing of that matters against destiny."

Matthew nodded. "Yeah, I can see how you'd think that." Especially since he was delusional. "Does Kim feel the same way?" A few steps toward the cliff edge.

"Of course. She just can't show it at work. She's a professional. But once we go to Mexico, there will be no need to hide our relationship. We'll be a famous team in the fashion industry."

"Yeah. I can see how that'd work." Footsteps? Was that what he was hearing? Hope and terror fought for dominance inside him as he hoped for help and feared someone innocent getting caught up in this mess.

He heard a sharp intake of breath and knew without turning that it was Kim. *No.* She must have come looking for him. If he'd only been able to text her something, anything so she wouldn't have tried to find him.

"Zander! What are you doing?" Kim's voice came from behind him.

He risked a quick peek over his shoulder—was there someone else? Bushes blocked his view. He edged between her and the gun.

No, Kim. Go away.

"I'm getting rid of any impediments to our being together."

"But if you shoot him, the police will be after you."

"We'll be over the border. They won't find us. And it will look like Matthew was distraught because you ran off with your true love, and he killed himself by jumping off the cliff."

Did anyone know Kim was here? Given that the sun was about to set, shouldn't they be getting to the rehearsal part? Wouldn't Kim be missed? Did anyone know where she'd gone? He thought he'd heard a set of footsteps, but then he didn't hear any others.

"No." Kim stepped in front of Matthew. "I'll go with you. Just let him go."

He grabbed her shoulders and pushed her behind him.

But Zander closed the gap and grabbed Kim's arm. The gun had dropped, no longer sighted on Matthew, but Zander had Kim firmly in his grasp.

She collapsed to the ground.

Matthew lunged for the gun hand, throwing his full body weight behind it and taking Zander to the ground with him. He grabbed the gun and leveraged his body on top of Zander's arm so he couldn't move it, but Zander let go of Kim and rolled on top of Matthew.

Kim's foot landed on Zander's arm, her heel grinding down.

With a yelp, he let go of the gun, and Kim snapped it up. She flipped the safety on.

Running footsteps registered in Matthew's mind just before he swung at Zander's jaw, knocking him off balance and giving Matthew the break to shove the man off him and get to his feet.

Kyle and Collins were there, trailed by Jessica, Scott, and Melissa. Collins rolled Zander facedown and pulled his arm behind his back while Kyle was on the phone.

Matthew met Kim's gaze. She handed the gun to Kyle, and Matthew pulled her into his arms.

She was safe. And he wasn't going to let her go.

Chapter Thirty-Five

Kim slipped her arms in the too big sweatshirt Matthew had brought her. The police officers were still talking to Kyle and Collins, but the rest of the wedding party assembled on the concrete bench that looked out over the dark waters of the ocean. Kellie had cancelled their reservation at the Italian restaurant and changed it to an order for pizzas, which Melissa and Scott had picked up and brought back, along with the previously ordered family-style meals of lasagna, pasta, garlic bread, and salad. Collins would take them to the police station so they wouldn't go to waste.

It wasn't the rehearsal dinner Kim had planned. Instead of celebrating Kyle and Heather's wedding, reminiscing, and enjoying their last night as single people, everyone was sitting around eating pizza and giving their statements to the police.

At least Zander had been taken away, and she didn't have to look at him anymore. The police had gone to Ashley's house and found Kim's purse, phone, and keys. Ashley was being questioned, but she insisted that she hadn't done anything wrong.

But Kim and Matthew still hadn't talked. She moved down the railing overlooking the dark ocean, away from the McAlistair clan, wanting a few minutes to herself to gather her composure.

She concentrated on the waves and inhaling the salty air. It had always been a place of comfort and relaxation. It would be awhile before she could view it that way again.

Melissa joined her at the railing.

Kim turned. "Where's Scott? Didn't you pick him up at the airport today?"

She laughed. "Something like that." She tilted her head. "He's talking with Jessica." Scott and Jessica stood down the path a ways looking out over the ocean. The discussion looked serious. Then Scott walked over. "Jessica's going to take off to her AA meeting. Kyle released her so she wouldn't have to break her six-month streak. I told her we'd find a way home."

Kim frowned. "Jessica brought you? How come you didn't drive?"

Scott slipped his arms around Melissa's waist. "Jessica and I cooked up a little surprise for Melissa today." He kissed her cheek.

Melissa raised her left hand, glowing. Something glinted on her finger.

Kim took a closer look. "Is that an engagement ring? When did that happen?"

Melissa shushed her. "Today. It was a surprise. Only Jessica was in on it. But we don't want to take any attention away from Heather and Kyle, so we're keeping it quiet."

"Okay, but I've got to hear the story behind that."

"You will. Scott's not leaving until Monday." Melissa met Kim's gaze. "Have you talked to Matthew yet?"

Kim let out a sigh. "No. We've all been too busy talking to the police. But we need to talk."

"He's got a good heart, but his execution is often lousy. But I've seen some real growth in him this past year. A lot of that is because of you. Juggling the new job, the relocation, and you... it's more than he's ever had to do. For the most part, he's doing it well. But he's not going to be perfect at it right away. Give him a chance to do better. Speaking of…" Her gaze drifted over Kim's shoulder.

Kim turned as Matthew came over from where he'd been talking with Kyle. "Feel up to taking a walk? Kyle said they're done with us."

She glanced around. Despite everything, she still felt responsible for the wedding rehearsal gone bad. If she hadn't agreed to meet with Zander for the photo shoot, out of her own desire to prove something to the people at Elan, none of this would have happened. "Let me see if Heather and Kyle want to run through anything. After all, this was supposed to be about them." She went over to where Heather was talking with her family.

Heather turned. "Are you okay?"

Kim nodded. "I'm fine. I just feel bad that all this impacted your rehearsal. Do you guys want to run through anything tonight?"

Kyle came over and slid his arm around Heather's shoulders. "I don't think I need any rehearsal to make this woman my wife. We just have to stand up and say our 'I do's' in front of the pastor. That's the important part. Everything else is just fluff." He grinned.

Heather raised her eyebrows. "Okay, Mr. Romantic. But to answer your question, Kim, no, I don't think we need to go through anything tonight. I was just going to send my family to their hotel since Aimee's dead on her feet."

"Okay." Kim hugged Heather then Kyle. "I'll see you both tomorrow then. I'm safe to stay at my own place tonight, aren't I?"

"Yes, just be careful."

"I will."

She let Matthew take her hand and lead her down the path away from everyone. They found a spot overlooking the ocean, the moon lighting a streak across its surface.

"I'm so sorry I didn't get to you sooner." He turned to face her, taking both of her hands in his.

"I just don't understand what was so important that you couldn't come when I needed you. You were goofing off with your friends. I'm afraid that's always going to be in the back of my mind, will you come when I need you or will you be out chasing the fun?"

"I wasn't really goofing off. I didn't tell you the whole story because you were stressed out with everything with Henry and Design Review and the wedding. I didn't want you to worry about what was going on with me."

"What was that?"

"I told you about all the meetings we had this week. Chris was handing over a lot of responsibility to me, to make working teams and chose who should go in what positions. He was asking for my input, and we were up every night reviewing how the day had gone. He told me in confidence that he was up for a VP job in Seattle and if he got it, he was putting my name in as his replacement, director of sales for the OC branch. It would be a huge move, one I'm not even sure I'm ready for yet."

"Matthew, that's great news. And I'm sorry that all my drama made it difficult for you to share what was going on with you." She shivered.

He pulled her to him and turned her around, her back to his chest, his arms around her. "Better?"

"Yes."

"So today was the final day, and we were doing a team competition. It was a game of Capture the Flag with super soakers. So, in a sense it was goofing off. But for me, the stakes were high. The last team-building event had gone really bad. I had the sprained wrist to prove it." He grinned. "I had to make sure the teams could work together under stress but also have fun. It was the one thing Chris had left totally up to me."

"I didn't know. I'm sorry that I jumped to conclusions." She leaned her head back against his chest. "How did it go?"

"We won." A smile laced his voice. "We all went out for ice cream; everyone seemed to have had a good time. There's talk of a rematch. But because I knew water would be involved, I left my wallet and phone locked in the glovebox of my truck. So until I arrived, I hadn't even gotten your message. Then when I did, I couldn't find you. That's when Zander found me."

"My heart about stopped when I saw that gun pointed at you."

"That's how I felt when he grabbed you. But nice move. You provided a distraction."

"That's what I was hoping for. Kyle had told me that going limp wouldn't work; the guy would just pick me up and carry me off. But I knew all I had to do was get the gun pointed away from you. If he tried to pick me up, he'd have to lower the gun."

He kissed the top of her head. "I love your creative thinking. Have I told you that?"

She smiled. "A time or two." She turned in his arms and lifted her face to his, letting him kiss her in the moonlight to the sound of the crashing waves.

Chapter Thirty-Six

Kim stood under the gazebo holding her bouquet of wildflowers next to Kellie—the maid of honor—and Sarah and Aimee. All the girls wore dresses in shades of aqua but in different styles. Hers had a halter neck with a ruched bodice, wide-banded waist, and flowing chiffon skirt. Jessica had done a fabulous job on everyone's hair and makeup. Kim was thrilled to see she had real talent.

The men—Joe, Collins, Scott, and Mark Patino and Bernie —stood next to Kyle in navy sports coats and tan slacks.

But Kyle and Heather only had eyes for each other, and as the sun touched the watery horizon, the pastor pronounced them husband and wife, Kyle took Heather's face in his hands and kissed her tenderly. The crowd cheered, and Kyle and Heather exited the small gazebo, the wedding party trailing. They gave hugs and congratulations as they made their way up the walkway to the nearby Las Brisas restaurant, where they'd had their first date and where the reception was hosted. Given that the gazebo was standing room only, close friends and family were the only ones present for the ceremony. But the reception would be the big party.

Kim took Matthew's hand as they headed toward the restaurant. He'd picked her up this afternoon at her place, because she'd wanted him too, not because she'd needed him. And this time with no fear of stalkers or black Hondas.

She thought back to the first time he'd come to her rescue. A lot had changed in these few months. For the better.

After a wonderful dinner on the patio overlooking the ocean, with a fire pit and heaters to keep the chill at bay, Kyle and Heather made their rounds, thanking everyone for coming. Heather wrapped Kim in a hug. "Thank you for making our day so special. You thought of everything."

"You did good, sis." Kyle hugged her.

After everything that had happened—the fire, the shower fiasco, the attempted kidnapping—it had turned out to be the perfect day for the two of them, and she couldn't be more pleased. "I'm so happy for you both. And I'll keep an eye on Snowflake while you're gone." Perhaps she had misread her family's support of her creative efforts. Or maybe they just loved her for who she was.

They were taking their honeymoon up the central coast of California to Monterey and Big Sur after spending their first night at the Blue Lantern Bed and Breakfast in Dana Point.

The dancing started with Kyle and Heather leading the way. When others joined them on the floor, Matthew pulled Kim out with him, holding her close when the music turned slow and romantic.

She tapped Matthew's shoulder and tilted her head. "Look." Austin and Jessica were slow dancing. Austin was mostly swaying, but it was more than she would have guessed he'd do. Kyle and Heather had invited him after they'd all survived the fire together.

"An unlikely couple, but I think he finds her easy to talk to. She's been dragging him not only to church but to the singles group to meet other people. I thought for sure I'd be the one introducing him to people and helping him fit in."

"He's definitely become part of the group."

The song ended, and Matthew pulled her to a quiet corner of the patio, finding two chairs off to the side.

He took her hand. "I'm so glad you're in my life, Kim. I was miserable after the road trip when you were upset with me. I've always been rewarded for being the funny guy. Serious emotions make me uncomfortable. But that's not a bad thing. I'm learning to sit in the discomfort. All I wanted to do was to win you back. But what I want more than anything now, is for you to be happy. I hope with me, but if not, I still want that for you."

Tears filled her eyes, and she rapidly blinked them back, not wanting to smear her eye makeup. "You make me happy, Matthew. You help me find the bright spots, and you support my creativity and crazy ideas."

"I have something for you." He reached into his pocket but didn't pull anything out. "Remember how I left you those notes? At first it was an impulse, and then I thought it was a nice antidote to the creepy stuff you got from the stalker. But I discovered that the true value was that I could express my feelings a little easier when I wrote them out. So I thought we might share this." He pulled out a leather-bound book. "It's a journal." He flipped it open. "I started it. I figured we could write in it and pass it back and forth. What do you think? Too hokey?"

She took the journal from his hands, fingering the soft leather. It was too dim to read the writing. She'd rather do it in private anyway, when she could respond. "I think it's a fantastic idea."

He let out a breath. "Good. That felt like a bit of a risk, but you're worth it. I have something else for you." This time he pulled out a long, slender box. "Open it."

She lifted the lid and found a gorgeous necklace with a twisted design set with a gem in the center. "Oh, it's beautiful."

"Veronica made it for us. It's our initials intertwined there with a blue topaz in the center, to match your eyes. I think it symbolizes that together we make something beautiful."

"That we do."

"I love you, Kim."

"I love you." She put her arms around his neck and kissed him, full of promise and hope for the future. When she pulled back, she flipped open the journal and pulled a pen out of her purse. "Something else to remember tonight by." And as he watched, she sketched a couple dancing, ones that looked suspiciously like the two of them.

Chapter Thirty-Seven

Kim fanned herself in the private Mediterranean garden they had rented for the fashion show. It was a warm July day, without much of a sea breeze. And she was behind the partitions that separated the backstage area from the runway and the audience.

The models looked as cool as if they were in an air-conditioned palace. She made an adjustment to the drape of a skirt on one model before she hit the runway.

This was the first show she and Lynnae had put on together. Kim had decided to join Lynnae as a partner, to be the featured designer of her boutique and design directly for their clientele and other buyers.

Lynnae came up to her. "They're loving it. I've got people asking to place orders before the show is even over. Great work!" She gave Kim's shoulders a squeeze and disappeared back into the audience.

Jessica took Lynnae's place. "You did good."

Kim nudged her. "So did you. The models' hair and makeup look fabulous. Thanks for joining us on this."

"Are you kidding? You won't be able to get rid of me." Jessica laughed and glanced around. "This suits you."

The final model returned, and Kim took her place with all the models as they made their way down the runway to thunderous applause. She couldn't believe this was actually happening, and she focused on enjoying every minute of it.

Her eye caught Matthew giving her a thumbs-up and a huge grin from where he sat in the audience. They were going out to celebrate afterwards. And they had a lot to celebrate. Not only her new position with Lynnae, but Chris had gotten the VP position and would be moving to Seattle, leaving Matthew as the director of sales for the OC branch.

The applause died out, and the crowds eventually disbursed. But one face showed over the rest. Maurice Worthington, probably the designer she most admired. Lynnae had said she had invited him, but Kim couldn't believe he'd accepted.

"Mr. Worthington, thank you for coming." She reached out and shook his hand.

"Please, call me Maurice." He gestured to the catwalk. "Impressive show, especially for your first one. I'd love to talk with you about how we might work together." He handed her his card, tipped his deep-purple fedora, and disappeared.

She stared after him, fingering his card.

Matthew came up and slid his arm around her shoulders. "Who was that?"

"Maurice Worthington. The designer I've always admired most and would have given anything to work with." She held up his card. "But now, I love what I'm doing. It's different than what I thought. I assumed I had to be mentored by a big-name designer. But what I'm doing now is an even better fit. What I'd always wanted, really, but had been too afraid to even dream about."

Matthew kissed her forehead. "Let's go celebrate our achievements and think up some new dreams to make come true together."

"I like that plan. But I love you."

"I love you more."

She grinned at their old argument. One she hoped they kept having until they were old and gray.

Are you curious about Jessica and Austin? Will they find love, or are they destined to be friends?

And how exactly did Scott and Melissa get engaged?

This last question is answered in the short story, exclusive to members of my Insider Updates. You can get it by going to https://www.jlcrosswhite.com/Melissa&Scott

You'll also get the prequel novella to the Hometown Heroes series, *Promise Me*— Grayson and Cait's story.

My bimonthly updates include upcoming books written by me and other authors you will enjoy, information on all my latest releases, sneak peeks of yet-to-be-released chapters, and exclusive giveaways. Your email address will never be shared, and you can unsubscribe at any time.

If you enjoyed this book, please leave a review. Reviews can be as simple as "I couldn't put it down. I can't wait for the next one" and help raise the author's visibility and lets other readers find her.

Keep reading for a sneak peek of *Over Her Head: In the Shadow book 3.*

Acknowledgments

This book would not be possible without the patience and willingness to read early drafts by Diana Brandmeyer and Jennifer Lynn Cary. Jenny gets an extra dose of thanks for helping me brainstorm when I got stuck. Special thanks to Sara Benner for her expert proofreading! Many thanks to my beta readers Anita Stafford and Malia Spencer and my early reviewers!

Much thanks and love to my children, Caitlyn Elizabeth and Joshua Alexander, for supporting my dream for many years and giving me time to write.

And most of all to my Lord Jesus, who makes all things possible and directs my paths.

Author's Note

When we last left Matthew and Kim in *Off the Map*, their relationship was on the rocks. Despite Matthew's best intentions, he treated Kim the way he wanted to be treated, not the way she needed to be treated. It takes the whole book of *Out of Range* for him to learn what she needs.

Kim has to learn what is truly important to her. And that she might be putting some thoughts and feelings on her family that aren't exactly there.

I think we all act a bit like Matthew and Kim at times, especially with those closest to us. It's easy to feel taken for granted and misunderstood. But it's worth it to make the effort to communicate well with those we love. Even when it doesn't come easy.

I hope you come away from reading *Out of Range* with a little clearer understanding of how God is the author of our dreams, and they can be safely entrusted to his hands.

About the Author

My favorite thing is discovering how much there is to love about America the Beautiful and the great outdoors. I'm an Amazon bestselling author, a mom to two navigating the young adult years while battling my daughter's juvenile arthritis, exploring the delights of my son's autism, and keeping gluten free.

A California native who's spent significant time in the Midwest, I'm thrilled to be back in the Golden State. Follow me on social media to see all my adventures and how I get inspired for my books!

www.JLCrosswhite.com
    Twitter: @jenlcross
    Facebook: Author Jennifer Crosswhite

Instagram: jencrosswhite
Pinterest: Author Jennifer Crosswhite

facebook.com/authorjennifercrosswhite

twitter.com/jenlcross

instagram.com/jencrosswhite

pinterest.com/jtiszai

Sign up for my latest updates at www.JLCrosswhite.com and be the first to know when my next series is releasing.

Romantic Suspense

The Hometown Heroes Series

Promise Me

Cait can't catch a break. What she witnessed could cost her job and her beloved farmhouse. Will Greyson help her or only make things worse?

Protective Custody

She's a key witness in a crime shaking the roots of the town's power brokers. He's protecting a woman he'll risk everything for. Doing the right thing may cost her everything. Including her life.

Flash Point

She's a directionally-challenged architect who stumbled on a crime that could destroy her life's work. He's a firefighter protecting his hometown… and the woman he loves.

Special Assignment

A brain-injured Navy pilot must work with the woman in charge of the program he blames for his injury. As they both grasp to save their careers, will their growing attraction hinder them as they attempt solve the mystery of who's really at fault before someone else dies?

In the Shadow Series

Off the Map

For her, it's a road trip adventure. For him, it's his best shot to win her back. But for the stalker after her, it's revenge.

Out of Range

It's her chance to prove she's good enough. It's his chance to prove he's more than just a fun guy. Is it their time to find love, or is her secret admirer his deadly competition?

Over Her Head

On a church singles' camping trip that no one wants to be on, a weekend away to renew and refresh becomes anything but. A group of friends trying to find their footing do a good deed and get much more than they bargained for.

Writing as Jennifer Crosswhite

Contemporary Romance

The Inn at Cherry Blossom Lane

Can the summer magic of Lake Michigan bring first loves back together? Or will the secret they discover threaten everything they love?

Historical Romance

The Route Home Series

Be Mine

A woman searching for independence. A man searching for education. Can a simple thank you note turn into something more?

Coming Home

He was why she left. Now she's falling for him. Can a woman who turned her back on her hometown come home to find justice for her brother without falling in love with his best friend?

The Road Home

He is a stagecoach driver just trying to do his job. She is returning to her suitor only to find he has died. When a stack of stolen money shows up in her bag, she thinks the past she has desperately tried to hide has come back to haunt her.

Finally Home

The son of a wealthy banker poses as a lumberjack to carve out his own identity. But in a stagecoach robbery gone wrong, he meets the soon-to-be schoolteacher with a vivid imagination, a gift for making things grow, and an obsession with dime novels. As the town is threatened by a past enemy, can he help without revealing who he is? And will she love him when she learns the truth?

www.ingramcontent.com/pod-product-compliance
Lightning Source LLC
Chambersburg PA
CBHW031628200726
48288CB00019B/384